# DISCORD

## The Exiles of Ondd: Book One

### K. S. DEARSLEY

*FOR ALL THOSE WHO NEVER STOPPED BELIEVING*

# CONTENTS

# Chapter One

How much longer? Ro tucked her hands under her armpits to keep from covering her ears. Maybe if she could block out the sound of the hearers' droning song and squeeze her eyes tight shut she would be able to will the baby out of her sister's womb. She glanced towards the shuttered window. Outside, the sunshine made all the colours sparkle and put a smile on everyone's face. There was only enough breeze to give the few clouds an occasional gentle push, but the Air-hearer had insisted that even small movement was enough to disturb the harmonious vibrations between mother and baby. She had shut the day out.

Ro snorted, drawing angry glances from the hearers, and tried turning it into a cough. She had long ago given up the impossible task of gaining their approval, but her mother, the Earth-hearer, felt all their impatient glances. Ro did not want to cause her more pain. Especially now.

She concentrated on the song, trying to synchronise her rhythms to those of the hearers. Hours must have passed since Ussu had experienced the first waves of pain. Maybe this wait was normal, like those music-stories that kept promising to build towards a climax only to fall back to the original refrain. Ro wished now that she had paid more attention when there had been other births in the village. If she had watched more carefully, she would have known what to expect from her first birth-song. She had tried asking Ussu when her sister had told her she was pregnant.

"If you were normal I wouldn't need to tell you; everyone else can feel what's going on." She had folded her slender hands across her belly in an imitation of the hearers that Ro thought ridiculous on her willowy sister.

"But Ussu, you know I can't help it."

"I know no such thing. You won't concentrate, you have to question everything. How can you expect to feel anything when

you're so full of yourself? Now go away, you're causing ripples."
Ussu had waved her away, and Ro had almost choked on the urge
to tell her what she was full of.

Now all the smugness had left Ussu's face. The pale blonde
hair clung damp to her forehead and the aqua blue eyes wavered
between moments of calm concentration and shrill panic. The song
was picking up its urgency again. The most senior of the hearers,
Verron, tapped a rapid beat on the hand drum she cradled to her
chest.

Ro found her breath quickening with the beat as Ussu
strained forward, teeth clenched against a long grinding note.
Their mother, Lar, stroked a calm tempo down her arms and back.

"For Ondd's sake!" Verron's voice had lost its smooth edge.
The other hearers gasped and for an instant the unbearable drone
ceased. Even Ussu was startled out of her pain long enough to turn
outraged eyes on her sister. Ro's arms were wrapped tightly around
herself with fingers drumming on her back–off-beat as ever–
disturbing the harmonious energy the others were working so hard
to build and putting both Ussu and the baby in danger.

Lar was exasperated. "Go!"

Ro looked an appeal at her sister, but she was totally absorbed
once more in her efforts.

"Go!" Lar commanded, her voice hoarse with over-use and
anxiety.

Ro fled, stumbling from the room, not caring that her sobs
and jerky movements sent shockwaves bouncing off the walls. She
ran down the narrow road oblivious of the decorated houses lining
her path and all else save the need to escape.

The sound of the hearers' song faded and was overlaid with a
complicated weave of percussion. Of course; the men would have
gathered in the pit to wait with Raimi for news. If her
marriage-brother saw her, he would know something was wrong
and the link with Ussu would be weakened. She slowed her steps.
The waiting men would probably have heard her pell-mell descent
from the birth-house.

Passers-by were meant to pick a harmonious course over the
stones and logs of varying thicknesses which formed the roadway.
Ro had never been good at creating melodious paths, but could
usually remember someone else's route well enough not to cause
discord. In her flight she had been heedless of the noise she made.

She paused, listening. The men's percussion continued with no change that Ro could detect.

As quietly as she could, Ro retraced her steps, tiptoeing on the packed earth between the resonating surfaces, back to the junction with Water Street. She passed the rills flowing over pebbles or bouncing off cymbals into pools, which marked the affinity of those living there, and focused on an image of silent fields where she would be able to escape everything except herself.

Ro skirted the goat pens at the end of the street and kept a calm pace across the open space between the pens and the palisade. The gate stood open and would not be closed until the goatherds returned from the autumn meadows with the sunset. At this time of day it was usually deserted, but Ro dared not look up to check.

If she had been like the others, she would have been able to feel if anyone was there; as it was, the soft whistle made her start.

Ro turned. It was one of the younger girls with a basket over one arm. She had probably been looking for late berries. Ro waved and hoped the girl would leave her alone. Guilt quickened her pace so that she was among the scrubby bushes on the edge of the copse before she knew it. She released her skirt from a branch and stood under the first tall tree, taking a deep breath. No one ever came here much except her; here she would be safe. She meandered through the trees allowing the tears to come at last. As ever, she found herself drawn to the clearing where a band of grass as green and lush as if it had been tended surrounded a still pond whose surface reflected a disc of sky.

Ro threw herself on the grass. No one had ever been thrown out of a ceremony before. She bowed her head over her knees using her arms to shut out the world.

It was so unfair. Everyone thought she could be like them if only she would try, but she had tried and it was impossible. Music for her was merely a series of notes with no particular meaning or appeal to her spirit. The strains which produced joy or contentment in others offered no more than a source of irritation to her. Worse than that, she felt no other sounds either, nor the vibrations which others heard. She felt no affinities, not even for vitae, the force which pervaded every living thing. She was cut off, different–crippled.

3

Now, she had hindered a birth. Perhaps the baby would never be born, reluctant to face a world where there were discordant spirits such as hers. Perhaps Ussu and the baby would continue the struggle until Ussu was exhausted and they both died.

Ro sat up–she might have killed them both! Even now the hearers might be intoning the death song, and she would not know. She began to pace about. It was unfair of the others to blame her; they did not blame the headman's son for being born with a limp. His was an affliction he had no control over, and she had none over hers. All her life she had had to put up with jibes and impatience. They damned her for not being able to understand sounds she could not feel, yet where was their understanding for her? Borne up by indignation, Ro began to search the bushes for berries.

The weather had been unseasonably kind, and she soon had a haul of plump fruit. She popped a brambleberry into her mouth and burst it on her palate. Her taste-buds were swamped with a sensation of... of... brambleberry. Ussu would have found a musical comparison. Ro had heard other people describe sensations in colours or size, calling shapes 'loud' or sound 'fruity', but Ro's disability robbed her of the gift. For her, the fruit tasted of brambleberry, nothing more. All she could do was pretend. Years of practice had developed Ro's ability to feign comparisons she could neither see nor hear, or to merely smile and look knowing. As a child it had often worked so well that she had astounded the elders with her perception and sensibility, but by the time she reached her teens, her vibrations being so at odds with her words and demeanour gave her away.

Ro turned a berry over in her hand, as if it could solve her problem. How could she blame others for not understanding, when she had taken such pains to hide her lack, when she blamed herself?

"Ro! Ro!" Raimi's voice made her heart lurch. Her tongue felt glued to the roof of her mouth.

"Ro! Come on, answer me, I know you're here."

Twigs and dry leaves cracked nearby. He would be able to feel her presence.

"Here I am." Her voice sounded odd even to her, but no more so than Raimi's. There was a wildness in it that made Ro curse the lack which prevented her being able to tell whether it was good news or bad before he found her.

He crashed into the clearing, and immediately she saw the news was good. Her marriage-brother's features were transformed with joy. Ro's spirits hovered between relief and jealousy; who would ever look that way for her?

"It's a girl. She's perfect, Ro, you should see her. She's got big blue eyes just like Ussu. Verron says all babies have blue eyes, but hers are the bluest. Ussu's fine, too. Come on, you must come and see."

The new father could not stand still. She found herself smiling, even though the thought of returning to the tongue-lashing the hearers would give her made her stomach flutter.

"You go on ahead, Raimi. I'm pleased everything's well."

"You don't look very pleased." Raimi frowned at her. She dropped her gaze.

"I couldn't be more pleased, honestly. Especially after... It's just... well, I don't think they'll want me there."

"Are you in trouble again? Hiding away in this dismal place?" He looked amused. Her marriage-brother never took her troubles seriously. He was quite the opposite of Ussu in that. The slightest mishap made her sister sharp and accusatory, but Raimi simply took everything in his stride.

"Things'll be better tomorrow," he would tell Ussu. It made her more unreasonable than ever, but Ro always found his gentle teasing reassuring.

"What's wrong with this place? I like it, it's quiet."

Raimi shrugged, then his face filled with joy once more. "Come on, we're keeping my daughter waiting. Whatever you've done, I don't think you need worry; they're all too busy crowing over her. Anyway, it was Lar Marriage-mother who sent me to look for you. She probably just wanted to get you out from under her feet."

They ran most of the way back and arrived breathless and laughing at the birth-house door. Raimi tiptoed over to the bed while Ro hung back, still unsure of her welcome. Inside, it was as if the pain and anxiety of the hours before had not happened. The shutters were thrown back allowing the afternoon sunshine to slant into the room. Ussu cradled the baby as if she wanted to show it off and hold it close at the same time.

Lar rose from her position by the bedhead as they entered and gestured Ro forward. There were lines of weariness around her eyes and her skin had lost its usual glow.

Answering Ro's look she said: "It's all right. The little one's got a strong, healthy cry and a suck to match, and as you see, Ussu couldn't be happier."

Ro's sister looked up, her face one big smile.

"Go on, hold her," Lar urged. Ro's instinct was to draw back. She saw Ussu's hands automatically clasp the baby closer.

Ro shook her head. "I'll probably make her cry."

"Nonsense!" Lar gave her a gentle shove.

The baby woke at the change, drowsily opening unfocused sapphire eyes, then gave a small sigh and settled. The tension left Ro's arms as a feeling of real peace swept aside her willed calm. Here was a bond. Was this what the others felt? Reluctantly she gave the baby back.

The double-week between the birth and the naming was one of activity and excitement, heightened by the traces of anxiety that attended every naming ceremony. Would the baby share the parents' affinities? Would its music be that of a healer or a grower, a herder or a maker? The double-week of welcome for the baby would culminate in the evening's ceremony, and it seemed the whole village had to be remade to ensure the occasion's harmony.

Houses had been repainted and fresh colour applied to the wavy sound tracks on the walls. Horses and herd beasts were washed and groomed. Flowers decked doorways and wind chimes on each corner vied with the birdsong. The air and the ground beneath them hummed a welcome to the new life.

Ro did not feel the vibrations, but she saw the sunny looks of others and revelled in the baby's continued acceptance of her as she set about making herself presentable. Despite her disgrace at the birth, she was to be allowed a place in the naming procession, and this time she wanted to make everyone proud of her, especially the baby.

She smoothed her light brown hair behind her ears and fastened it securely. Today her eyes had a bluish tinge borrowed from the sky and the scarf draped around her shoulders. She would never be a beauty–her figure lacked the flowing elegance of water, fiery grace, earthy curves or the light quick movements of air. Unlike the vitae affinities, who seemed to combine the best of each element, Ro resembled none of them. She was sturdy and tomboyish; not ugly, but plain. If she stood next to another member of the village, the eyes of anyone looking would slide from her to her companion, barely registering her presence until her inability to harmonise with her surroundings made them uncomfortably aware of her.

No clumsiness of hers would risk the baby's welcome today. Fixing a sprig of woodstar in her scarf, Ro took one last look at herself. She had come across the fragile white blooms when she visited the copse that morning to try and calm the bubbling anxiety in her stomach. Finding these symbols of the spring so late in the year had to be an omen of good fortune. Anything seemed possible in spring when all was starting anew, fresh and alive with hope. Late it might be for woodstar and Ro both, but there was no reason why she could not flower too.

Downstairs, Ro found a place in the crowded room filled with Raimi, his aunts, sisters and mother along with Ussu and the baby. All the female relatives were there except Lar. Her mother's position as earth-hearer meant that at this moment she would be preparing for the ceremony with Verron and the others. Thought of the Vitae-hearer made Ro shrink back into the shadows.

The room was cut in half by sunshine slicing through the unshuttered window. Dust motes hung in the air despite the double-week's cleaning, and Ro watched as they whirled and danced every time someone in the room stirred. Raimi's oldest sister was in the middle of a song about the dragon, Ondd. Ro only half listened. There were many such songs about how Ondd fought the worm, Lethir, in the time of chaos, how life beats to the sound of Ondd's heart. This one was about how Ondd strode about the world surveying its domain and how water gathered in its footprints to form the lakes. The songs were sung so often that even for Ro with her lack of music they came to mind automatically.

Had it not been for the fact that each woman would be expected to sing in turn until the hearers arrived, embellishing the melody as the moment demanded, Ro would not have attended to the song at all. As it was, she tried to calculate how long it would be until it was her turn, hoping the hearers would get there first and save her the humiliation of singing what she could not feel before so many others.

7

There were still two singers to go when the swinging beat of the hearers' approach interrupted. Ro's heart responded with a throb that hurt her ears, as the rest of the room fell silent. With heads bowed and hands folded in laps, the others tuned in to the rhythm of feet and staves drawing nearer. Only the baby, with tiny fists and feet constantly on the move in her basket seemed to be unconcerned by it. The beat halted, and outside the closed door the voice of Verron rose in the song of welcome. Those of Lar and the other hearers joined it.

Raimi's mother flung open the door and the women-folk sang the response as they assembled behind Raimi and Ussu, who carried the baby in her arms. Headed by Verron and the subordinate hearers, the procession flowed down water street to the shrine with the palisade where the Water-hearer's pool stood. The new baby was sprinkled with the cool liquid, accepting the process with a thoughtful frown. Up and down the streets, the procession wound, collecting villagers as it went, coiling back and forth like Ondd's tail. At the Air-hearer's exposed shrine she was raised high for the wind to ruffle her downy hair; at the Fire-hearer's hearth a candle was lit and circled around her head. Lar placed the baby on the cold stone of her shrine, surrounded by pebbles of different shapes and colours, watching carefully the movements of fists and feet before selecting one and placing it in a pouch to be worn at all times.

Now only one shrine remained: that of Verron, the vitae-hearer, in the centre of the village. The vitae shrine was a garden hung about with plants trailing fronds to caress the hair of those who passed beneath. A path of herbs, which exhaled fragrance, snaked back and forth within the garden to its centre where an ancient tree bearded with creepers spread gnarled arms over their heads forming a living canopy.

The procession arranged itself around the outer rim of the garden while the hearers, followed by Raimi and Ussu with the baby, proceeded to the tree at the heart of the coil. The hearers formed a circle around the trunk and began a slow, whirling dance to the accompaniment of their drums and cymbals. The steps had an interrupted beat whose syncopation required great concentration and balance. They wove around each other, their movements calm and graceful as they completed the circle. Abruptly the dance ceased and all was stillness. Verron stepped up to the tree and with arms spread branch-like, rested her forehead against the trunk. Ro wondered whether the skin would be patterned when the Vitae-hearer turned away, then chided herself, caught in a lapse of concentration.

Drawing a long breath, as if waking from a sweet sleep, Verron turned once more and took the baby from Ussu's arms. She held her up to face those gathered.

"Hear now, people of Iyessa, the baby born of Raimi and Ussu has been brought to the elements—they are within her and without her, as they are within and without all of us. We are joined to them and to each other, just as the newborn one is. Know then her name and feel her presence—Lalli."

Something like a sigh passed through the waiting village, then in silence Ussu, Raimi and the rest made their way along the coiling path to bow before the baby, contentedly sucking its fist in the Vitae-hearer's arms. All trod with delicate quiet before Lalli, passing between the motionless hearers.

As Ro passed Lar she glanced towards her. Her gaze lingered a moment too long. Her foot caught and cymbals jangled as she collided with the Fire-hearer, pushing her off balance. Struggling to stay on her feet, the Fire-hearer wildly grabbed at air and dragged Ro down with her into an undignified tangle on the herb-cushioned path. In the shocked silence that followed, Ro sucked in her breath fighting off a surge of giggles—if only she could shut her eyes and make herself invisible. She dared not turn her head to look at Verron, or worse still, Lar. For all that her sound-sense was dull, Ro knew there was no peace in this silence. The faces around her were all turned towards the Vitae-hearer, waiting. Ro heard the rattle of playsticks, the children's toy incongruous, yet making the silence deeper.

Verron's voice was flat. "You had better all go home."

Ro turned and saw what the others had seen. Lalli was gazing totally unconcerned at the pattern on Verron's scarf. Ro's initial surge of relief plummeted. The sound of playsticks rattling now on this, now on the other side of her head failed to distract her. Verron's gaze slowly lifted to meet hers.

"What—what is it? What's wrong?" Ussu's shrill voice demanded. She stepped forward, but Lar intervened.

"She's deaf, my love."

Ussu looked past her shoulder at the absorbed baby. She shook her head ignoring the groans and whispers of the watching villagers.

"It's true. Look–could you keep so still with sound so close? She can't hear it."

Ussu broke free from Lar and lunged at Ro with nails clawing. "You!"

Ro made no move to evade the blows. Raimi and Lar struggled to hold Ussu back. She threw herself against their restraining hands.

"Please," Ro whispered. "Let her go."

"Please," Ussu spat. "This is your doing. You and your 'I can't help it.' See what you've done? I curse you as you've cursed her."

There were gasps from the waiting people. Verron stepped between the sisters.

"This is your baby's naming, Ussu, there will be no cursing. Take her home with you now. All of you–return to your homes–we have much to think about."

Ussu hesitated, then the baby whimpered and Ussu took her. As Verron signalled the other hearers to her, the people began to disperse. Their dipped shoulders and dragging feet displayed their emotions to Ro more clearly than any resonance could.

"Go home, Ro." It was her mother. Ro noted the lined forehead and the deep creases by her mouth. Not angry, not sad, but tired.

Ro felt a surge of resentment; Lar had expected her to ruin things. "No, mother."

"Go home."

"You'll be discussing me, won't you?"

"How can we avoid it?"

"Then I have a right to be here."

"Lar–we're waiting." Verron's voice was uncompromising.

Lar took Ro in a hug. "Don't worry." As she released her, the woodstar caught her gaze. "Where did you get this? Never mind." She took the flower from Ro's scarf. "Go, now."

Remaining there would be seen as hiding behind Lar's skirts. Ro had to show them all that she bore no guilt. When she arrived home she paused for a deep breath before opening the door. There was no sudden hush as she entered. Somehow Raimi had persuaded the gaggle of women to leave.

"It wasn't that hard," he answered Ro's surprised look. "It was a choice between staying here to see what we do, or talking about us, and that's more easily done behind our backs." He tried to smile.

Ussu was singing softly to the baby before the empty hearth. "Lalli, Lia, my Lalli."

Ro sank onto the nearest chair while Raimi set about making a fire, moving as if wading through deep water.

"Wait!" Ussu whispered eagerly, halting Raimi's preparations. "She heard you–she did, she turned her head. She did, I tell you, they're wrong."

"No, Ussu." Raimi clapped his hands by the baby's head. Lalli never flinched. "We have to accept it. Our daughter can't hear. It's hopeless." He held Ussu firmly by the shoulders.

"Who says so?" Ro blurted. "Lalli's beautiful, she's my niece, and I'm not going to give up on her, no matter what the others say."

For a moment Ussu's eyes sparked and Ro waited for a tirade of accusations. Instead, her sister fell to crooning over the contented baby once more.

Ro struggled to open her eyes. She was waiting for the procession to arrive. As the footsteps drew nearer, she felt a prickle of fear. Something was going to go wrong and she had to stop it. Casting about the room for a way to escape, she found faces crowding in upon her–silent, accusing.

Her head dropped forward, jolting her awake. Raimi stirred at his post beside the couch where he had eventually persuaded Ussu to lie down with Lalli. Ro rubbed her face, then recognised the noise at the back of her mind. Massed footsteps–not the regular pace of the procession, but ragged.

"Raimi." She reached across and shook him. "Something's happening."

He listened a moment. "You stay back with Ussu." He began barring the shutters.

"What is it?"

He hesitated.

"You know I can't feel it."

"But it's so strong, the fear."

The noise drew nearer and louder. The baby started to grizzle. Blows made the door jump against the latch. Ussu woke with a yelp and Raimi signalled her to keep quiet. The blows came again.

"What do you want? It's the middle of the night." Raimi's voice was angry, but his face was apprehensive and Ro doubted those outside would be fooled. There was a pause, filled with murmurs and the sound of shuffling feet.

"We have no quarrel with you, Raimi. It's the girl we've come for."

Ussu gasped and clasped the baby closer.

"You can have no business with any of us at this time of night." Raimi's eyes met Ussu's.

"Don't let them take our baby," she whispered.

"It's not Lalli they want." Ro sounded far calmer than her hammering heart. She put out a finger for the baby to grab, feigning nonchalance. "It's me."

"You!" Ussu sneered.

"Ro, come out here." The voice outside grew bolder.

"But why... " Ussu began, ignoring Raimi's signal for silence.

"You blamed her yourself, Ussu–in front of them all," he reminded her.

Ussu looked horrified. "But I was upset." She turned to Ro. "I didn't mean it."

Ro smiled. The moment felt right, as if all the pieces were finally in place. She ought to be worried, instead there was exhilaration.

Another voice called. "It's all right, Raimi. They won't hurt her." It was his mother.

Raimi's face set. "If no harm's meant, why so many of you? Why come when folk should be abed? I'm ashamed of you, mother: I'll open the door to no one."

Ro released her finger from the baby's grasp and stood. "It's not your decision, Marriage-brother, no matter how well meant." She began to straighten her clothes, trying to brush away the slept-in creases, repeating in her head "I am guilty of nothing". Maybe she could not control the waves of fear and anger which made her hands shake, but she would not give them the satisfaction of looking scared or ashamed.

Raimi exchanged a look with Ussu. "You can't seriously mean to go out there."

Ro waited or him to step aside. The blows began again.

Ussu clutched her arm. "They say they only want you, but once the door's open how could we stop them taking Lalli?"

Ro hesitated, then shook her head. "No, Ussu. They'd never hurt a baby."

She hugged her, but Ussu did not return the embrace.

"Then you do think they might hurt you."

Ro's mouth twisted as she pushed Raimi aside. "How could they? I don't feel anything, remember?"

She began to unbar the door, keeping her movements measured through years of practice at pretense. Well, she would not have to do that anymore; no more struggling to fit in. The banging stopped as those outside heard the bar draw back. Then the door was open, and Ro stood in the flare of torches held in uncountable hands.

# Chapter Two

There was silence. Not a blank emptiness, but one full of snatches of the day's events, and of emotions remembered rather than felt. Ro looked at the faces in the torchlight.

"Well? Here I am, what do you want?" The eyes that met hers quickly dropped.

Another voice echoed the question. "Yes, what do you want?" It was Verron.

A murmur rippled through the crowd as the Vitae-hearer strode with her fellows to stand beside Ro. There was no hint in her face of what she thought, and once more Ro cursed the lack which made her rely on unguarded looks and half-formed gestures. She snatched a glance at Lar. Her mother's lips were pressed into a line and the granite-coloured eyes glittered.

"I am waiting for an answer."

There was an edge to the Vitae-hearer's voice, which Ro knew betokened a scolding.

"The girl's cursed." The woman's voice came from somewhere behind the torches. Verron searched for its owner.

"Stand forward–if you have the courage to speak, have the courage to be seen."

Now even Ro could hear it, Verron was angry. People parted to let Raimi's mother through.

"We've always known she was cursed, but we hoped... especially with a hearer as mother..." She gave Lar a slight bow. The hearer stood as cold and still as the bones of the earth. The spokeswoman shrugged. "She is as she is, but now she's spreading her contamination and she's got to go."

Murmurs echoed her. The Vitae-hearer waited.

"It's my family she's hurt, Verron."

A gesture from the hearer stifled Ro's protest. Still she said nothing. The other woman's hands began to knot themselves.

"I warned Raimi, but no, he would go ahead with the marriage. Look what's come of it–our baby tainted, like her!"

"I'm not deaf," Ro blurted.

"You might as well be. You're not one of us–I wish you no ill, girl, but you must go."

Ro looked an appeal at her mother, but the Earth-hearer stood fixed like a stone pillar.

"And what of you others?" Verron challenged the crowd. There were more murmurs. She gestured silence. "Know then, that we the hearers of the Iyessi have given this matter much thought, and not only tonight. Ro, daughter of Lar is neither cursed nor blessed. You will hear our decision tomorrow. Now go home, and listen to your hearts. All here is not as it seems."

There were disappointed grumbles, but the Vitae-hearer ignored them and entered the house. Ussu and Raimi stood as if struck dumb, while the hearers arranged themselves about the room. Ussu absentmindedly rocked the grizzling baby.

"Sit, sit all of you." Verron sat heavily in the nearest chair. Ro was inclined to disobey. "Sit," she repeated more softly, patting Ro's hand as she complied.

"All is not as it seems, you said."

"Yes. Perhaps you would rather explain this, Lar?"

The Earth-hearer gave one shake of her head.

"You found this today?" Ro's confusion grew as Verron drew the woodstar from her healing bag. "It's beautiful, fragile, innocent–yet it's out of place. No woodstars should flower in this season–it doesn't belong. Ro, nothing can survive where it doesn't belong."

"Mother? She's saying I must go too, isn't she?"

Lar nodded, then covered her face with her hands.

"All right. Why should I want to stay?" Ro could not keep the tears from her voice. "But you said I wasn't cursed."

"No more is this flower, but it's unnatural and like finds like. Wherever you go things that shouldn't happen, happen, and now there's Lalli. If you sway things from their normal path, what will happen now there are two of you? No, you must both leave."

"Both?" Ro's question was echoed by Raimi and Ussu.

"But she's a baby, you can't mean it! She doesn't, does she, Mother?"

"This is all nonsense." Raimi brought his fist down on the table. There was no hint of gentle teasing in his face now.

"Lalli and Ro must leave," Verron repeated.

"Surely it's enough if she goes." Ussu jerked her chin at Ro. "Say something, Mother. Not even a Vitae-hearer can force a mother to give up her child." Ussu looked wildly from one face to another.

"No power on earth can make a mother do that. Although only the two afflicted must leave, we know you will wish to accompany them."

Ussu's eyes widened. "This is a joke! Raimi, tell her she has no right. Mother... "

Lar took her hands from her face and Ro almost cried out at the weariness and sorrow on it. "They do have the right. I've told them I won't stay where those I love are spurned. We'll leave together as soon as all we need is packed."

"You can't!" The wild excitement Ro had begun to feel at the thought of leaving the village was choked. This was all her fault.

"There's no more to be said." Lar's voice was rough. "Now, if you don't mind, sisters, I'm going to bed."

Verron rose.

When they had left Ussu burst out. "Why didn't you speak up for us?"

"Because I think we should go, not because I think you're cursed," Lar added to Ro. "But because this isn't a place for those who can't hear. Perhaps there's a cure for Lalli elsewhere, and you, Ro, you may find a place where you do belong. Now, I'm tired. Tomorrow we'll think about what to take with us."

Ro expected Ussu to turn on her once the door closed behind their mother. Instead, a startled Raimi suddenly found himself under attack.

"So, your mother warned you against marrying me, did she?"

"Mm... and she was right, your tongue is sharper than a skinning knife."

"I suppose you wish you'd taken her advice now."

"Never!" He held Ussu by both shoulders. "I'd sooner give up breathing than give up you and Lalli."

Embarrassed at witnessing this sudden intimacy, Ro slipped out of the room.

Two days later, Ro said 'good-bye' to the familiar rooms and streets for the last time. She knew the others were looking on them with eyes eager to retain every detail, but she found it difficult to match their subdued mood. While Ussu, Raimi and Lar secured the house, settled their belongings on the horses and tucked Lalli into the carrier on Ussu's back, Ro imagined jumping over the road in any old fashion creating as much discordant noise as she could.

The villagers had kept their distance once Verron had explained the hearers' decision. Even those who could not resist watching their departure did so through the corners of windows, dodging out of sight if Ro happened to glance in their direction, as if a mere look from her could strike them dumb. They would head for Najarind, the capital of the Ortanian empire, two double-weeks' ride to the east. People were drawn to the city from the empire's most far-flung reaches to worship at the great temple of Ondd–where better to find a cure?

When they reached the village gates the four remaining hearers were waiting with Raimi's family.

Verron stepped forward. "Won't you reconsider, Lar? You know there's no one whose earth affinity matches yours. The Iyessi need all their hearers."

"You know my answer: either we all stay or we all go."

Verron bowed her head, then took Lar in an embrace, speaking softly. "We've listened to the land beyond the gates. Our reach is less than it was once, but we found no definite ills, only a confusion as of many voices the further we sought. You may find your hearing of little use out there."

"You forget, Verron, 'out there' is not entirely new to me." Lar released herself from the Vitae-hearer's grasp and bowed with her fingertips touching her lips to each of the hearers. Ro hardly had time to wonder what Verron meant, before there was a commotion. Raimi's mother had thrown herself at his feet, clasping his knees.

"Don't go, there's no need. I never wanted this–you're my son."

He removed her hold. "If you thought I'd behave otherwise you little know me. I'm ashamed to call you 'mother'."

He pushed her aside and strode after Lar. Only Ussu paused for one brief last look, as the song of farewell rose behind them. While the keening voices could still be heard drifting on the breeze they travelled in silence. Despite her longing to be gone, Ro took care to tread carefully, not wanting to remind them that she was the cause of it all.

At length, she began to look about her. The road they followed appeared never to have been more than a narrow track trampled into hard-packed earth. Whenever boulders or tangles of brambles stood in its way, the path skirted around them, and in places it disappeared altogether. No one knew how far it extended like that. Unless... Ro remembered Lar's words to Verron: "'out there' is not entirely new to me."

The Iyessi kept to themselves, so that. Najarind and other distant places might as well have been legends. If Lar had travelled to the capital of Ortann, it must have been the biggest event in her life, yet unlike the old hunters, who never tired of recounting past kills, her mother had never mentioned it. She burned to ask Lar what she had meant, but the sombre silence stopped her.

They continued with only the drumbeat of the horses' hooves and their scuffing footsteps as bass line for Lalli's intermittent gurgles and coos. When the latter turned to hungry yells, they found a flattish space with nothing more uncooperative than field grasses to beat down, and paused for a meal.

"It's just as well we packed all those provisions, if the land is all like this it'll give us nothing," Raimi said as he stowed their gear away again.

"Further on we should come to a stream, the earth around that's more generous. Still, we'd do well to be careful," Lar said.

Ro asked: "How far do you think we've come?"

Raimi squinted, calculating. "About twelve miles, not far."

"Twelve miles? My feet feel as if I'd walked twice the distance. Can't we rest a while this afternoon?" Ussu loosened the straps on her boots.

"Rest?" Lar snapped. "We've hardly started out. We have at least two double-weeks' walking still ahead of us, so you'd better get used to it."

"What's wrong?" Ro asked.

Ussu snorted, as if their exile was answer enough.

"We have a lot of ground to cover, that's all, and listening to check the path is wearing."

As they shouldered their packs again, her neck cracked and her heels felt hot where the boots rubbed, but she said nothing. If she could, she would willingly have taken on their burdens too. Ussu had no such scruples. Her complaints grew more intense throughout the day and did not abate over the next one. Ro stayed out of her sight whenever possible.

The third day was no easier. They walked in file with Lar in the lead checking their path, Raimi with the horses, then Ussu carrying Lalli, and Ro bringing up the rear, trying to distract the baby whenever she looked inclined to grizzle, which was every time Ussu tried to hitch her sling into a more comfortable spot. The grunts and mutters, which accompanied the action, gradually became louder.

"Would you like me to take Lalli for a while?" Ro offered.

"No, I would not!" Ussu swung round so fast she almost knocked the sling into the horse in front. She muttered something in which the only word Ro caught was 'freak'. She felt the defiance which had buoyed her up when the villagers had surrounded her beginning to burn again.

"I was just trying to help."

"Well, don't. Your help's nothing but trouble."

"Ussu... " Raimi warned.

"I won't be shushed. It's her fault we're here, and if we had any sense we'd go in the opposite direction to anywhere she was heading. We could join our Sud-Iyessi cousins at the Singing Lake."

Ro flared up. "Go if you want! I never asked you to come with me."

Lalli added her screams to the argument.

"Now look what you've done!" Ussu shouted.

Raimi tried to separate them. "Shut up the pair of you. Save your energy for walking. We've already discussed it, Ussu–the lake's too far away."

"How dare you speak to me like that, and in front of our daughter too!"

Lar's softly spoken "Quiet!" cut through the argument. "Don't you think finding our way is hard enough without all this discord? If anyone is at fault, Ussu, it's me–now hush until we make camp. Raimi, I want your opinion."

They headed back up the path leaving the sisters open-mouthed behind them. Even Lalli's screams seemed shocked into a whimper. The consultation between Lar and Raimi took quite a while.

Ro felt uncomfortable. "I never wanted to cause trouble."

"I know. I didn't mean what I said."

"Yes, you did."

"All right, I did, but I was wrong. Forget it."

"Okay."

"Okay."

There was a pause.

Ro's uneasiness increased. "What do you suppose is taking so long?"

"Perhaps they're thinking about where to camp."

"Perhaps we're lost."

Ussu snorted. "Not everyone is as insensitive as you. Mother will feel the path."

Ro was not so sure. Her mother and marriage-brother looked troubled and kept gazing ahead as if they expected something to materialise out of the air.

As Raimi took the horses' halters once more, Ro asked: "Everything all right?"

He smiled, but Ro thought that had Ussu not been so preoccupied with her sore feet she would have scolded him for creating ripples of insincerity. They trudged on until the early autumn evening began to lose its glow. That night they ate in exhausted silence. Lar pushed her empty plate away.

"I didn't wish to alarm you earlier, but now I must tell you. The path I once followed has changed. I feel the same energy in the earth, but I recognise nothing. I'm no longer sure I can find the road to the city."

"So you have been there before!"

"You mean we're lost?"

Ro and Ussu spoke together.

"Yes, and maybe. It was a long time ago, Ro, before your birth." She held up a hand to stop Ro's flood of questions. "Such a long story deserves to be told when I have the voice for it. The point is, we can't go further until we're sure we're heading in the right direction. Tomorrow, Ussu, Raimi and I will search for the watercourse I spoke of. It runs under earth some miles before becoming a stream. Once we find that we'll know we're on the right path. I'm sorry, Ro, but you must stay here to look after Lalli and our things." Lar tried to make it sound like an important job, but Ro knew it was only to prevent her feeling useless. Seeing Ro about to interrupt, Lar continued. "We should all rest now. There are many nights ahead for the telling of old stories."

Lar started rolling out her makeshift bed, giving Ro no choice other than to follow suit. Thoughts buzzed around her head and would not let her sleep. She had to find a way to help. There must be more ways of finding a watercourse than listening for its vibrations.

The following morning Ro paid close attention to the list of things Lar said she remembered close to the stream. It was not much: the energy of the rock through which it ran was so strong she had not needed to memorise her route.

"The pull of the stone was enormous. I spent the night in the shelter of an old wall. It must have belonged once to a livestock pen or some such, it was so tumbled it hardly looked a thing made by men–the pull of rock to rock–earth to earth. As I sat there with my back against the wall, the stone filled me with its music, blotting out the echoes of the hills beyond. I still feel the pull of the stone, but I can't feel the water–that's what we must find. Ussu, you have such a strong affinity with it–you take the likeliest route."

The plan was simple, Ussu would follow the path ahead, while Lar and Raimi branched off to either side. They would aim to be back at the camp by noon. Ussu issued so many dos and don'ts to Ro about the baby, that Ro began to think they would not set out before then, let alone be back.

"Honestly, Ussu–what harm can she possibly come to? I'm not a complete fool."

Her sister looked doubtful.

Ro watched until they were all out of sight, hidden by undergrowth and twists in their path. She checked that Lalli was still asleep, then that the horses were still tethered properly, then looked about for something else. Each shake of a horse's head or rustle of dry stalks had her jumping. Before long she almost envied Lalli's deafness. The baby slept on oblivious to everything.

"This is no good, Lalli–I've got to concentrate on something or I shall go mad."

Water–how could she find water? Ro had an image of the lush, intensely green grass around 'her' pool. She tried going over Lar's description of the land again. Her thoughts strayed back to Lar's previous journey and her own particular problem. Lalli woke, and Ro picked her up.

"What was Mother doing here before, eh, and has it got something to do with me?" She stopped rocking the baby. "They said I didn't belong, not just Verron, but Lar too. Lalli, what if I'm not Lar's daughter, after all? What if she just found me out here?" Ro looked at the wilderness about her. "Well, not out here maybe, but in the city." She began rocking the baby again. "But why would she have gone to Najarind in the first place?" With such thoughts for company it seemed a long time until noon.

Raimi was first to return. He was dusty and one of his sleeves was torn.

"You'll catch it when Ussu sees that." Ro poured him some water. His scowl deepened. "You didn't find it then."

"All I found was thorns and this." He slapped his tunic and a cloud of dust flew out.

"If you like, I could sew that sleeve up. With a bit of luck I'll be finished before Ussu gets back."

Some of the tension left Raimi's shoulders. "Thanks." He watched as Ro threaded a needle. "You know, Ussu isn't as bad as she seems," he said. "She does the most shouting when she's worried, she doesn't really mean any of it."

"Oh no? She's my sister. I've had to put up with it for as long as I can remember."

"But whenever you've been in trouble, she's always stuck up for you, right?"

Ro let the tunic fall in her lap. "That doesn't mean she doesn't agree with what everyone else says, she just doesn't want me to dishonour the family, that is–her."

"Believe me, she's harder on herself than she is on you, especially with Lalli being, well... she thinks maybe it's something in the blood that she passed on."

Ro snorted. "If you say so, Raimi, then I'll believe it, even if my own eyes and ears tell me differently."

"When it really matters, you'll see, Ussu will always stick by you." He looked into the distance. "Where is she anyway?"

Ussu and Lar returned in no better humour and no more successful than Raimi.

Ussu flung herself down on a pack for a seat. "My feet are one big blister! I can't possibly walk further today."

Raimi began patiently rearranging their baggage so that she and Lalli could ride one of the horses.

Ussu sulked. "But which way shall we go?"

"We'll carry on our original path and hope," Lar said.

"I don't see why we can't go back to the village. We never tried reasoning with them properly. They wouldn't let us starve out here, surely?"

Lar took hold of Ussu's shoulders. "Listen to me, Ussu–all of you. We can't go back, and I wouldn't if I could. Don't you want a full life for Lalli? We'll continue and we'll find out the cause of... " Lar hesitated. "When we reach the city, we'll see."

They set off again. There was little change in the terrain until the following afternoon. The thick air added to their burdens. It did not need a water affinity to know a storm was waiting to fall on them. In the distance they saw a darker blur on the horizon which could only mean hills against the gloomy sky. As they marched wearily on, it became clear the range crossed their route.

Lar turned. "Now we know we've come the wrong way." Dust and sweat had gathered in the creases on her forehead.

Ro felt she had swallowed a stone. "Why?"

"Because water doesn't flow uphill, stupid!"

"Stupid yourself, darling sister, it might flow down from the hills."

"Mother would remember."

They looked at Lar, whose expression was uncertain.

Ro persisted. "But there were hills when you journeyed before–you said you saw them in the distance when you rested, and you would have been facing homewards, so you would have been on the other side of them."

"What do you think, Raimi?" The question proved Lar's weariness. Ro had never known her defer to a non-hearer's judgement before.

"I think we've got nothing to lose by going on."

Ussu looked as if she could strangle him with the reins, but it was decided: they carried on. As they slogged upwards the first big splatters of rain began to fall. Before long the horses' coats were dripping and the grass was slick and treacherous. There was no hope of hearing the watercourse with such a downpour all around.

Raimi called ahead. "Lar, we should camp–it's useless going on in this."

Ro struggled through the long undergrowth, which whipped unpleasantly wet against her legs. "Maybe not. On the other side of the hills we can look to see if the rain forms run-offs. They might join the stream."

Lar shook her head. "I know you want to help, but Raimi's right."

By the time they had found a place to rig their rough canvas shelter even Lalli was grizzly and bad-tempered.

Ussu took it out on Raimi. "Don't hang that wet jerkin there! Honestly! It's dripping all over Lalli's things."

He pulled a face. Ro stared out at the rain listening to their bickering and the rhythm of water dripping from the canvas. The constant patter was like gnats buzzing around her. She stood up and immediately attracted Ussu's peevishness.

"Where are you going?"

"I need a walk."

"I would've thought you'd had enough of traipsing around in this wilderness. Why don't you try helping?"

"Let her go," Lar said.

She could still hear Ussu complaining as she struggled up the slope. The ground rose steadily, and Ro made for the crest. The downpour obscured the distant view and the parched ground seemed to suck the rain in. Maybe the earth had sucked away the stream as well in the unseasonable warmth. She tramped on, encouraged by the increasingly frequent patches of porridgey ground and the thinning of the rain. If it stopped the ground would dry out again. No wonder Lar felt lost here. There were no streams, no trees worth the name, merely straggling bushes and occasional jumbles of rock, which almost looked as if they had been placed there deliberately.

A stone turned under Ro's foot and she found herself on all fours–jarred, bruised and splattered with mud. She stood and surveyed the damage. The wrench on her foot had put a strain on the boot's stitching. Ro picked up the offending stone and threw it hard. She had the satisfaction of seeing it bounce off a larger boulder ahead. There was no choice now, she would have to go back and do what she could to repair the boot unless she wanted to arrive in Najarind barefoot. She turned, took a few steps and stopped.

A wall that hardly looked man-built–that was what Lar had said. Ro turned and ran to the boulder. It was one of a pile similar to others she had already passed. She squatted to get a closer look. In places they fitted together so tightly they could have been slotted in place. Working a smaller piece loose with her fingers, Ro found her breath coming in gasps. If it had been worked Lar would know, and if it was, then she must be near the water course. The light was already fading and finding the wall would do her little good if she lost the others. She hurried back.

The camp looked calm when Ro returned, but Ussu scowled at her. Ro's waves of excitement must have been deafening, long before her clumsy movements became audible. She handed Lar the chunk of stone, trying to keep her thoughts as neutral as her face. The older woman turned it over in her hands while Ro helped herself to some supper.

"I don't think those who shirk the chores have a right to eat," Ussu said, "especially if they haven't even the courtesy to clean themselves up first."

"And I don't think those who do nothing but complain are worth listening to." The way Lar kept turning the stone over told Ro she was right. It had been part of a wall, and all Ussu's bleating counted for nothing.

Finally, Lar asked: "Where did you find it?"

"Where the hills finish–I've marked the way–too close to them to be your wall, I think, but still within sight maybe when the skies clear."

Raimi put his arm about his wife's shoulders. "Well, Ussu my dear, I would say your little sister has earned her bread tonight, after all."

They started out the following morning with Ro in the lead. She found it hard to keep her pace to a reasonable walk. The rain had stopped, but the ground was still slick in places. She retraced her route without hesitation.

Lar placed her palms flat upon the pile of stones. "Yes, this is the same type of wall."

"But still no watercourse," Ussu pointed out. "That's what we needed to find."

Ro was already moving on. "Follow the ruins on this line and we should come to it.

Raimi caught up with her. "It's off to the right–over there! Feel it?"

Ro looked where he pointed. She felt nothing, but saw the dark green spiky leaves of reeds.

"Not exactly enough to splash around and celebrate," Raimi said as they reached the bank of what had evidently once been a fast-flowing stream. Now it was a trickle choked by weeds and attractive only to midges and beetles.

Lar frowned but said nothing.

Ro walked on a cloud of elation that blocked out Ussu's expressions of disappointment. "Who cares what it looks like? We've found it!"

They kept to the path Lar remembered, but her frown of the morning had deepened by the time they camped. As the days passed they began to come across signs of habitation, baked mud houses with straw roofs gradually wisping off on the wind. They were home now only to nesting birds and small animals that skittered away from them on the straw strewn floor. Unglazed and unshuttered, the windows gazed mournfully at them as they passed. Lar would quickly avert her eyes and hum a low chant.

"Why aren't there any people, Mother?" Ro asked.

"There was sickness here once–and the city draws people to it." Lar shivered.

Gradually the terrain changed. The dry grasses vied with furze and heathers until the land was completely carpetted in moors. Here it was autumn in earnest. The wind whooped over the land, stinging their faces. Around midday they neared a turf hut.

Ro relaxed at the prospect of shelter and a hot drink. "You'll be able to feed Lalli inside, Ussu."

But as they approached, the man who had been struggling against the wind to repair the roof, shooed his livestock into a ramshackle corral and disappeared inside the hut.

"What's the matter with him?" Ro almost choked on her disbelief. So much for the laws of hospitality. Maybe they did not apply outside Iyessa. She remembered the mob that had gathered after Lalli's naming.

Ussu grumbled. "I don't see what he's so scared of."

Lar shrugged. "Some people are scared of anything different, and I doubt he's seen any of our people for many a year."

After a particularly gloomy supper when Ussu's tongue lashed out in all directions and Raimi's teasing had been peppered with spite, Lar was more silent than ever. Even the bickering brought no response.

Ro took courage to speak. "You can all feel something, can't you? What aren't you telling me?"

Ussu and Raimi glanced at Lar then became studiously engrossed in their tasks.

"Tell me."

Lar continued to stare into the fire.

"Mother!"

"Leave her alone, can't you?" Ussu ignored Raimi's warning look. "The earth's playing different music. Nothing's where it should be–why do you think we got lost before?"

"But we're not lost now." Ro waited, watching the firelight flicker in Lar's eyes.

The Earth-hearer spoke as if waking up. "No, we're not lost, but we might as well be. It's time to tell you, I suppose."

# Chapter Three

"Tomorrow we should reach the city." Lar paused as if seeing memories in their camp fire. "The man we saw today is unlikely to be the only one who's wary of us. The city people aren't harmonious. They create noise, so much conflicting sound that the beat of the elements is almost lost. We may all be deafened there!"

The enormity of what the banishment meant to her family took some of the glow from Ro's image of a city with pristine walls warmed to gold in hazy sunlight.

Lar sighed. "Perhaps it's this which makes them so hard. My memories of the city aren't good ones."

Ussu burst out. "Then why are we going there?"

"Because it's where this trouble began. I was warned not to go to Najarind. Your father didn't want me to, but he had to go, so I chose to accompany him. You were only small." Lar smiled across the fire at Ussu. "At least I had the sense to leave you with the hearers. But you..." She patted Ro's hand. "You I was carrying, although I didn't know it then, so you had to come too."

"But why did any of us go?" Ro asked.

"The king wanted music for the great temple of Ondd. I know I said they aren't a harmonious people, but they enjoy superficial tunes. Anyway, they sent to Iyessa for help, and your father said he'd go. He was to create... " Lar hesitated "... an instrument. Fever broke out in Najarind and he wanted me to leave–by this time I was growing big with you–but the king's adviser, Lord Torslin, thought he wouldn't finish the task if I left and forced me to stay."

Ro interrupted. "But he'd volunteered to help! They had no right to hold you hostage."

"Maybe not, but Torslin had other work for your father, work that he knew was against our beliefs. There was no choice, your father did what they asked and when he'd finished they let us go. Only your father had already caught the fever. The night we were supposed to leave he died." The simplicity of her words somehow made the pain behind them stronger. "You see, Ro, you heard only discord and death at your birth, so if there is any guilt, it belongs to me."

Ro sniffed hard and tried to sound brisk. "No, Mother, it belongs to the people who summoned Father and kept you there. I think we should go somewhere else." She looked at Ussu and Raimi for support.

Lar shook her head. "Najarind was the beginning of our trouble, and Najarind's where we must look for an end to it. I have hope."

Ro tried to persuade her to reconsider, but Lar shook her head.

"It's the one hope for Lalli too."

They looked at the sleeping baby's face and fell silent.

There was little anticipation in any of their faces when they set out the next day. Instead, they trudged on, each occupied with their own thoughts. When the first turrets and roofs became visible in the distance, Ro tasted bile. She straightened her shoulders and quickened her pace to draw level with Lar.

"Don't be angry, Ro."

She swung round, surprised for a moment, before she remembered what ripples she must be causing. No wonder Lalli had not wanted Ro to carry her that morning. She made an effort to melt the hard lump of bitterness in her throat. As they approached the walls, which emerged from the hillside like outcroppings of exposed bone, Ro's anger began to be replaced by doubt.

They joined the other travellers who passed to and fro on the road to the main gate. Most went on foot or tried to squeeze top-heavy carts past the ramshackle stalls, which clustered about the towered gates. Shouts from competing stallholders either encouraged people to loiter or to pull their headgear further down over their faces determined not to be caught by the sales talk. Most wore drab clothing, except for the occasional lord or grand lady attired in rich velvets and brocades with gauzy veils trapped in the elaborate coils and plaits of their hair. Their servants were tall and comely to match their mistresses' splendour. They elbowed the commoners aside to make way for them.

The activity intensified inside the gate. People barged past each other, too intent on their own business to take care where they trod. The quiet, careful dignity of the Iyessi set them apart as much as their clothes. Those Najarindians who found themselves close to them, shrank as if from contact with rotten meat. Ro spotted one holding a handkerchief in front of her nose and others made the thumb and finger sign to ward off evil.

They turned into a side street and immediately the noise was cut to a background rumble.

Ro risked a question. "Where are we going?"

Her companions hissed her quiet. The tension was making her teeth ache. She looked up at the houses lining the street. They loomed taller than any others she had seen–five or six floors high. The stonework was well-crafted but old and pocked with repairs like the scars of childhood fever. She caught Lar's shudder from the corner of her eye. Here and there a new building shouldered the ancient stonework aside, erupting mushroom-like in the narrow streets. The gutters were full of rubbish and rank-smelling water. Ro began to feel she was in a nightmare where she would walk on and on forever. Lalli's peevish grizzle echoed her mood.

"We need to make for the temple," Lar said as they paused at a corner. Her face wore a tight look.

Najarind was a jumble. There were chimes and fountains at the junctions as there were in Iyessa, but these merely served to provide space for yet more pedlars and idlers. The cacophony was made more discordant by children chasing cats and each other between the legs of people going about their business, provoking snarls and threats. Ussu began jogging Lalli until the baby's grizzle was on the verge of becoming a full-blown wail. Raimi was fidgety too, adjusting and readjusting the horses' gear. Yet now Ro was becoming accustomed to the jostling and noise, she almost felt like laughing. Najarindians moved and spoke with a freedom she had never known existed. Here she could walk where and how she wanted, whistle out of tune and no one would notice, let alone care. She could be herself and be valued for what she could do rather than censured for what she could not. The question was, what could she do?

Ro glanced at Lar again, and some of her elation evaporated. "Are you all right, Mother?"

Ussu swung round. "Of course she isn't. How did you stand living here for all those months?"

Lar gave her a tense smile. "Not far now." She moved into the stream of people and pointed past the rooftops to a dully glowing golden egg-shape suspended there. "That's the dome of the temple of Ondd. Should we get separated, just head towards it."

Ussu and Raimi exclaimed together.

"Separated?"

"Ondd? But surely... "

Lar sighed. "I know. The power from such a holy place should make the ground tremble beneath us. Perhaps there are too many people too intent on other things. Once we get past the next corner we should find ourselves in a great square."

Ro moved closer to her, realising it was not simply the noise that her mother found painful, but the resurrection of sad memories. On top of this, her companions could no more feel the elements than she could in the crush. Brushing away the guilty thought that they might be more sympathetic in future, she pushed through the mannerless throng. Progress was difficult until she noticed how people stood aside to allow a mailed soldier or golden-robed priest to pass. Ro fell into the wake of one of the latter, who appeared to be heading in the right direction. They reached the corner. The crush of people eased little, although the buildings retreated before the grand pile of stonework that was Ondd's temple. Layer upon layer rose above the city and stretched fingers out into the square. Surmounting all was the massive ovoid dome. They left the horses in what the proprietor claimed was a pilgrims' compound and entered.

The temple's grandeur was equally impressive inside. Glass and metal tesserae gleamed on the walls. The cavernous space under the dome swallowed those who entered. After the chaos of the streets, the temple was as still and quiet as the depths of a lake. Ro felt drawn to the central altar where the light from crystal lamps reflected from the burnished dome, casting a hazy nimbus around the officiating priests. A touch on her arm made her look around. Lar gestured to one of the long stone benches shaded by a carved pillar. They sat.

"Now we wait," Lar said. Ro opened her mouth to ask, but Lar forestalled her. "You'll see why."

So they waited. A priest gave praise to the dragon, Ondd, whose victory against the worm, Lethir, had forced the evil one into retreat and given rise to centuries of peace. Mighty Ondd had earned its rest, sung to sleep by its followers. The priest's voice would have done the same for Ro, had the cold not begun to seep through the stone bench and soak into her bones. Beside her, Ussu shifted position trying to ease the arm that held Lalli. Ro took the baby from her and propped her securely in the corner between the back of the bench and the pillar. The little one seemed happy enough with her new vantage point, but as soon as Ro tucked her cold hands under her armpits, Lalli set up a thin grizzle. The worshippers on a bench nearby clicked their tongues and tutted. Ro began tickling Lalli and pulling faces to keep her occupied, but nothing worked for long. She was about to pick her up again when a deep booming note halted her. The light began to flicker and flash different colours.

As the first note died away, the roar and rush of a great storm followed, and a gleaming dragon swooped above the heads of the priests. There was a collective gasp from the Iyessi. It was a machine, a representation of Ondd in all its glory driven by a concoction of cogs, springs and bellows. As it flew it sang. So this was the musical instrument her father had made. Ro could not make out words, and could only guess the emotions it was meant to evoke, but she felt held to the spot. Beside her the others were transfixed. Raimi sat forward on the bench, his knuckles white where he gripped the back of the seat in front of him. Ussu clamped her hands over her ears, and Lar's head was bowed.

Ro became aware of a small wandering voice and noticed frowns from people on the benches nearby. Lalli was singing. But she could not be. Ro stared open-mouthed at the baby, who had slipped sideways so that her ear and cheek rested against the pillar. There was no mistaking the contented scribble noise she was making, which rose and fell with the sound from the dragon, now perched on a crystal branch above the priest, turning its jewelled head this way and that to address its congregation. It extended its wings and with a flick of its tail soared back to its eyrie in the heights of the dome. Its song died away and there was a moment of complete silence before the central priest began to intone the remainder of the service. Lalli's singing ceased with that of the mechanical dragon, but her head still rested against the pillar as if listening to the dying vibrations. Ro shook Lar's arm.

"Mother! Lalli heard it. She's not deaf any more. Ussu, Lalli's cured!"

Lar shook her head. There were tears on her cheeks.

"But she did hear it, truly," Ro repeated, looking to Ussu for a more positive response.

Lar clapped her hands behind Lalli's head. The baby neither flinched nor started. There was a rustle of cloth behind them and a commanding voice.

"Either remain quiet or leave. You Iyessi savages have no respect and no manners."

Ro blushed. "I'm sorry, but... " Her stammering explanation died as the insults sank in. Ussu found that moment to come out of her shock.

"Abomination." It was only a mutter, but the priest heard it. "What?"

"Abomination!" Louder this time. "Abomination!" Now she had started, Ussu did not seem able to stop.

"How dare you!" The priest signalled two of his colleagues. "Fetch the soldiers—we have defilers here!"

A group began to gather around them. Ro's heart beat faster remembering the mob of villagers outside their door.

"Oh no, no. We're on a pilgrimage, that's all. To find a cure for my sister." Ro gave Ussu a warning look. "She's a little troubled here." Ro tapped her forehead. "You know."

Ussu opened her mouth, but thankfully nothing came out of it. There were one or two murmurs of sympathy from the congregation. Ro plunged on, grateful that the Najarindians did not have the sensitivity to pick up the vibrations of a lie. "Where better to find healing than in the famous temple of Ondd?"

A breathless priest pushed through the rapidly growing group, followed by a trio of soldiers.

"These the troublemakers?" The leader was sturdy and unremarkable. His manner was brusque.

"Captain Pachand, these savages now pretend to be devout followers of Ondd, but they've behaved as if Ondd's temple is a puppet show and they've spoken heresies. Of course, since the proclamation warning us all to be wary of Amrad spies I... "

"Yes, very commendable." Captain Pachand signalled his men. They began manhandling the Iyessi out.

The priest looked about to protest at his abrupt dismissal, thought better of it and began a tirade against the congregation's easy distraction from their prayers. Flanked by soldiers, the Iyessi had no choice but to follow the captain.

"Where are you taking us?" Ro tried to sound grateful, as if he was their saviour rather than their captor.

"To the citadel for questioning," was the blunt reply.

"But we intended no disrespect, truly."

"Save it for the commander. Orders are that all suspected insurrectionists and spies are to be taken in. Personally, I've got nothing against you provincials that a proper education and a good wash wouldn't fix, but I do what I'm told."

They walked in weary silence heading ever upwards towards the centre of the city where the blue-grey walls and turrets of the citadel protected the royal palace. The green and yellow pennants, snapping and fluttering from its roofs, proclaimed that the king was in residence. They approached a set of towered gates ablaze with the royal emblem of harlequin scaled emerald and gold dragons. A tune akin to the mechanical dragon's played above them, making Ro's companions hunch their shoulders, and the gates swung open for a man and woman ahead of them. Ussu's indrawn breath and Lar's downcast eyes told Ro that this was the other work her father had been forced to create.

She concentrated on a couple walking ahead of them to quell the rush of heat that made her ears buzz. The figures were dwarfed by the painted dragons, but Ro judged that the woman would have looked slight wherever she went. The mailed guards on either side of the portal were massive and clumsy by comparison. Even her companion was at least a hand's breadth taller. Captain Pachand sucked his teeth disapprovingly as the pair hurried across a parade court and disappeared around the side of the palace.

The guard would have waved the soldiers through, but Captain Pachand paused. "Was that who I think it was with Prince Channan?"

"Yes, Captain. The Prince has brought the healer to offer King Berinn–er–treatment, I believe." The other guard sniggered.

Captain Pachand looked at him sharply. "I find nothing amusing in the King's sickness."

The guards straightened immediately. "No, sir, I only meant– well, Prince Channan and that healer–they say... "

"I don't wish to hear that 'they' say and neither should you. Don't let me hear you repeating such grubby gossip again." He jerked his head at the Iyessi to follow.

The exchange meant nothing to Ro except that their captor was now in an even worse humour. He led them up the broad steps and beneath the columned entrance of the palace. They were taken up stairs and along corridors until they came to a set of double doors. Beyond was an audience chamber. People decked in sombre finery stood in clusters or paced its length. A soldier sat on a bench staring moodily at his hands.

"Any change?" Captain Pachand asked him. He looked up and shook his head.

They passed on through a narrow corridor, one of several from the audience chamber, to arrive in a small sparely furnished room. A man was slouched half-reclining on the desk. He straightened as they entered.

"Prisoners, Lord Fordel. Caught spreading heresies in the temple."

"Not more of them!" the lord complained. His drawl matched his sleep-bleared blue eyes. His dark hair and beard looked as if they had been carefully groomed the day before. "Can't you deal with it, Pachand?"

"Lord Torslin's orders. While Amradoc threatens us, prisoners are to be questioned by the highest ranking officer on duty."

"Yes, yes, you don't have to look so pleased about it." The Lord waved dismissively. "You may go–oh, and fetch me a goblet of wine, will you? I have such an unquenchable thirst today."

The Captain stiffened. "I'll have a servant fetch you one."

Lord Fordel's eyes narrowed as he watched the Iyessi in silence. But silence was balm after the streets of Najarind. It lasted until a servant deposited a flagon and goblet on the desk and departed. Lord Fordel poured some wine with hands that shook, and drained it.

"Now, what have you been up to?"

Ro repeated the story she had told the priest. The Lord sighed.

"You haven't done much lying, have you?"

Ro blushed.

"I have," he added. "I do it all the time, and I can spot a fellow inventor of stories before they even open their mouths."

Lar nodded at Ro. "We are seeking healing, but for the baby, not my sister."

Ussu hissed and held Lalli closer.

"She's a pretty mite–not the fever, I hope?"

Ussu relaxed a little. "It's her hearing. What are we to do?" She turned on Lar. "How could you bring us here?"

"To the temple?" Lord Fordel interrupted with a lazy smile.

"That abomination–that pretence of Ondd's voice–and on the gates–music to trap!"

"To protect, surely. To keep out harm, and the automaton? It's a pretty toy, and I would take care not to shout too loudly about abominations–the priests are rather touchy about such things since so many people from the colonies started settling here."

Ro relaxed. He would not speak that way if he believed the charges brought against them.

At last Lar spoke. "Its music is soulless, and my husband created it."

"I'd heard Iyessi had funny ideas about music."

Raimi wound his arm around Ussu's waist to restrain her. "We try to live our lives in harmony with the beat of the elements."

"There's little enough harmony here, that's certain," Lord Fordel said. "And if the little one can't hear, she can't live a melodious life, is that it?" His tone was sceptical.

"She might not be able to hear, but she can feel music, I'm sure of it!" Ro insisted.

Ussu inhaled sharply. "Are you suggesting she's attuned to an abomination, a thing without a soul?"

"There you go again with that 'abomination' business," Fordel wagged his finger at her. "If I'm to let you go, I need your assurance that you won't start stirring up anti-religious feeling."

Ro could have slapped her. "How can you say such things, Ussu? Father couldn't create something soulless. It's his music."

Lar spoke gently. "The machine's song stays the same, it's meaningless."

"Ah, now there you're wrong," Fordel interrupted. "That's the fascination of it, you never know which of its songs it'll sing or exactly when it'll appear." His eyes gleamed. "When I was a youngster, I thought it was magic–and the gates–if it hadn't been for your husband's music I doubt my parents would ever have got me to go to prayers. I'm really rather fond of the toy."

There was a moment's silence while the Iyessi tried to come to terms with an attitude that treated the great dragon as entertainment. Raised voices could be heard beyond the door.

Lar corrected him. "Maybe, but it's a dangerous toy."

"Whatever–if I let you go, I want your sworn oath you won't go near it again." He stood and slapped the desk for emphasis, then groaned and put a hand to his head. The voices outside sounded closer. "What is all that commotion? Don't they know my head feels as if it's about to fall off?"

He flung open the door and walked unsteadily to the audience chamber. The Iyessi followed. The attendants had drawn back from an argument at the far end of the room. A bald man with smooth sallow skin made sickly by bright yellow robes was complaining shrilly.

"I am the king's physician—I, Ayif, was appointed by the king himself. If I am not now to be trusted I shall depart this cruel cold land and return to Gindul where I can at least be warm."

The man he spoke to had an air of solidity and heartiness enhanced by his stocky build and rosy complexion. He was old enough to be the father of the man behind the physician and the young woman at his side. Ro recognised the sandy hair of one and the autumnal locks of the other as belonging to the couple who had entered the citadel ahead of them.

"Ah, so our canary's nose is out of joint," Lord Fordel muttered.

Next to the older man stood a tall woman with luxuriant dark hair and a stern expression that had cut deep lines beside her mouth.

"Really, Channan. You've been told Father needs rest, yet you bring this—this charlatan to poke him about."

"Careful, Sister, Dovinna is a respected healer," the Prince warned.

The older man smiled. "I'm sure Princess Ersilla intends no insult to her, but Ayif did give instructions that the King was not to be disturbed."

"I assure you, Lord Torslin, all he needs is calm and rest to recover his strength."

The name sent a jolt through Ro, as a woman with an unassuming manner and features that were a plainer version of Channan's stepped in front of him.

"They wouldn't even let me in, Channan."

"That's ridiculous! How could Princess Anni's presence possibly disturb my father? And I don't see that getting a second opinion would do any harm. My father's condition hasn't improved."

Ayif bowed stiffly. "I'll pack my things immediately."

"Now, now." Torslin gestured for calm. "All this commotion will do the King no good at all. I appreciate the regard in which you hold Mistress Dovinna, Prince Channan, but we must give Ayif's measures time. It's what your father would want."

"And if we wait too long there'll be nothing anyone can do."

Torslin drew the Prince to one side. "It pains me to remind you, Channan, but you know how your father feels about you associating with this woman. Only think, if he should wake and find her at his bedside. He doesn't like to be disobeyed."

Channan hesitated. Ersilla gestured impatiently.

"Make a decision for once, Brother," she snapped.

Torslin grasped the healer's arm and started to propel her down the room. "Should it prove necessary, we will, of course, send for you at once. I'll have a guard escort you home and recompense you for your time." His smile chilled Ro.

Lord Fordel stepped forward. "Perhaps I can assist—it would help solve a small difficulty of my own." There was a subtle difference in his smile now. Ro thought she was beginning to understand what he had said about spotting a liar. Lord Torslin's eyes skimmed over them, full of distaste for them all including Lord Fordel. Ro felt Lar stiffen behind her. This was the man who had kept her mother hostage. If anyone was responsible for Ro's disability it was he. Yet he did not even recognise the Earth-hearer. He nodded curtly at Fordel and strode away. Ro heard him introduce them to the healer through a buzz of anger.

Fordel recounted their tale. "They need a healer, Dovinna, and somewhere to stay. I know how much you love lost causes— you seem the ideal person to take them under your wing."

"Of course I'll help," the healer said.

Lar placed her hands palms together with the fingertips touching her lips and swayed into a small bow.

The healer returned the formal salute then turned on Fordel. "And who are you, Fordel, to talk of lost causes?"

"Ah, Dovinna, don't you know you've broken my heart? If it wasn't for the fact that it was my good friend Channan who stole you away, I don't think I could bear it."

The healer looked stern. "I'm in no mood for your teasing, Fordel."

"Yes, I'm sure my heart will break, my head's splitting already."

"Then I suggest you take more fresh air and less wine."

Fordel grinned and saluted the Iyessi. "I leave you in safe hands. Good luck!"

They retraced their steps through the palace in Dovinna's wake. Once free of the citadel their stride relaxed.

The healer smiled for the first time. "You've experienced our city's hospitality–may I suggest you try to copy the direct way we walk, and–I'm sorry–speak as little as possible in public? Your accent's too musical, it gives you away."

It seemed to Ro that her nightmare was coming true, and she would never be able to stop walking the streets of Najarind. Their path wound down increasingly narrow streets. The houses grew humbler with some leaning together for support. Tucked under the shelter of the city wall was a house neater than the rest.

"Here we are." The healer ushered them inside.

By Iyessi standards the room was a dull monochrome with only a jug of wildflowers to draw the eye, but the rich smell of herbs drying in bunches from the ceiling or heaped on shelves laden with pots and jars more than made up for the drab decor. Ro was tempted to plunge her hands into a pot the size of a grain bin and feel the fragrant leaves and flowers run through her fingers.

Dovinna busied herself stirring up the stove and laying the table. "I don't have much room, but at least I can offer you something to eat and drink, and a roof to sleep under."

"We don't want to inconvenience you," Lar began.

"I'm a healer. Sometimes that means providing people with a meal and a safe haven."

Lar nodded. They were too tired to protest. Ussu crooned to Lalli and Raimi rubbed his face, leaning back on the bench and stretching his legs under the table. Ro felt equally incapable of action, but a teasing thought would not let her rest.

"Why did Lord Fordel let us go? I thought we'd broken your laws in some way."

Dovinna looked up from her cooking. "He's no fool. If you treat friends like enemies, they become enemies. What harm did you actually do?"

Ro looked at a loss.

"Exactly! Now, let's have a look at this baby." Dovinna held out her hands for Lalli. Raimi picked her up and showed her to the healer. Her methods were strange to the Iyessi. She asked them questions as she looked in the baby's ears with a magnifying glass.

"I'm sorry, I can't find anything: no blockages, no infection and no history of bumps or bruises."

Raimi put his arm around Ussu. "It's what we expected."

"Perhaps... " Dovinna hesitated. "You mustn't tell her I sent you, but my teacher, Varda, lives in Kabonn Forest. We didn't part on good terms, but I've never known her turn away those who need our help–it's against the healer's code."

"Kabonn Forest," Lar repeated. "Maybe once we've tried all possibilities here."

They ate their meal in silence, too tired to hope or despair. Despite her exhaustion and the relative comfort of sleeping indoors, Ro had a disturbed night. Tumultuous dreams where she wandered through increasingly narrow streets searching for something that was always out of reach, were interspersed with restless periods where indecision pricked and poked her awake. The following morning they were all subdued.

As they ate a basic breakfast, Lar announced: "We need to find somewhere where we can hear the elements to help us decide on a course. There is one place, even in Najarind, where that should be possible."

Ro cleared her throat. "If Dovinna doesn't mind, I'd like to stay here–after all, I won't be much use, will I?"

They got their things together and left while it was still early enough to avoid the bustle of trade.

Dovinna called after them. "Where are you going?"

Lar turned and waved.

"I hope they'll be careful. Even Fordel might not be prepared to let them go without penalty a second time." She turned to Ro. "Where are they going?"

Ro shrugged. "I'm not sure." She started clearing the breakfast things.

"Why didn't you go with them?"

Ro took a deep breath to try to explain, but an urgent knocking at the door interrupted.

"Dovinna–come quickly!" It was Fordel's voice. He almost fell through the door as she opened it.

"King Berinn?" she asked.

He nodded. "You must come straight away–and you," he added as he spotted Ro.

"But... " she protested.

"Don't argue! Are these your drums?"

"No, they're... " But he had already shoved them into his saddlebags.

Ro and Dovinna shared the horse he had brought for the healer. They rode surrounded by a mist of frozen breath in streets now uncomfortably quiet and empty. Everywhere there was the hush of those determined not to make a sound. They hurried through the halls and corridors of the palace where the tense expectation sucked the air from the rooms. Only the princesses, Lord Torslin and a couple of apprehensive servants remained in the audience chamber.

"An Iyessi! Have you gone mad, Fordel?" Princess Ersilla folded and unfolded her hands. There was an exultant edge to her voice.

Anni rose from a seat shadowed by wall hangings. "I suggested it to Channan. The music might soothe father." She looked evenly at Torslin.

The adviser bowed. "Quite right, quite right... we must try everything." He nodded Dovinna and Ro through to the bedchamber, but held up his hand to halt Fordel. "You can make sure the princesses get some rest. I'm sure their company is more to your taste than a sick-chamber."

Fordel smiled and bowed exaggeratedly.

"It might be more to the Lord's liking, but I'd rather be at my father's bedside." Again Anni challenged Torslin with her eyes.

"We'd be in the way, Sister. Torslin will send someone when something happens." Ersilla tugged her away.

The tableau around the King's bed scarcely registered their entrance. Prince Channan stood at the foot of the richly draped couch, his breathing shallow, as if he feared to disturb its occupant. King Berinn lay almost buried under the quilts. He was just past his prime with strong bones on which the flesh now hung. His sweeping brows and narrow nose gave him the look of a raven, as Princess Ersilla's would one day. His lips moved as if he was engaged in a difficult calculation, and his eyes were fixed on something behind Ro. She turned. On the wall hung a portrait of a woman whose homely appearance and placid expression reminded her of Anni. Ro doubted the King could actually see the painting. His breath came in deep shuddering gasps, dredging air from some fathomless well. His limbs were rigid and his fingernails punctured the flesh of his palms.

Dovinna moved quietly to the head of the bed where Ayif held the King's wrist in a weak grip. The physician shook his head as the pair consulted in murmurs.

Channan watched with anguished eyes. "You can save him, Dovi?"

Ayif answered. "We must prepare ourselves for the worst, I fear."

"You said it was just exhaustion."

"Alas, Highness, your father's depleted state left him prey to infection and he has no power to fight it. This is what I feared when I banished all from His Majesty's chamber. Who knows what contagion has been brought in?" He looked pointedly at Dovinna.

She ignored the implication and beckoned Ro over as she examined the patient. "What do you think, Ro? Have you seen anything like it before?"

Ro felt a surge of panic. She held one palm above his face and the other over his chest as she had once seen Lar do, trying to keep her hands from trembling. "Music might help him find a way back, but my mother's the one with the skill," she whispered.

Dovinna smiled encouragingly. "Do your best."

Ro hesitated. She could not hope to find the King's wandering spirit, but surely her playing could do no harm. She set up a soft rhythm on Lar's drums before thoughts of Lalli's deafness could intrude. She avoided eye contact with everyone, staring across the room in what she hoped they would take to be trance-like sightlessness. Dovinna searched her bags of herbs.

As they began work Ayif rolled his eyes and threw up his hands. Torslin frowned at him, and the physician retreated to the table where he had set up his phials and potions, and began packing them away.

Dovinna selected some stalks and warmed them in her hands before crushing and scattering them on the King's pillows. A pungent essence suffused the room and Ro felt her heart beat more calmly. Colour began to return to the King's cheeks and his eyelids flickered.

"King Berinn, King Berinn–it's time to come back. Your empire is waiting for you." There was no response. Dovinna straightened. "I need a goblet and hot water."

A servant was sent. Ayif answered the knock that announced his return and took the tray from him. A low mutter escaped the King, startling them all. Dovinna called his name once more. The physician held the goblet up to the light. He looked at Lord Torslin, who gave the merest nod, and handed it to Dovinna. She half-filled it with a thick syrup, then stirred in hot water. Gently raising King Berinn's head, she poured a few drops between his parted lips. He swallowed and she tipped a little more until only the dregs remained. He sighed and turned over.

"He's asleep," Dovinna announced. "He should wake in a few hours, weak but otherwise all right."

Channan's face shone as he looked at Dovinna. Ro had seen Raimi look at Ussu in the same way. Torslin clasped his shoulder.

"Thank Ondd, lad. You should get some rest now."

Channan protested.

"Mistress Dovinna and her friend will watch over the King. You'll have to deal with matters of state until he's fully recovered, and that takes a clear head."

The Prince took Dovinna's small hand in his, searching for words.

Torslin interrupted. "Come now, we have good news to take to your sisters."

Channan put Dovinna's hand to his lips then left with Torslin and Ayif. Ro sank onto the nearest chair.

"Forgive me, Mother," she murmured.

"She'd be proud of you. I couldn't have prevailed without you." Dovinna followed Ro's example and sat.

Ro's mouth twisted. "I've no skill in such things. I hear music, but I don't feel it. The pulse of life doesn't flow through me. Proud? It's because of me we left home. I'm a liability."

Dovinna watched her as she would a patient. "And you wish to be like them rather than yourself."

Ro nodded. Dovinna made no comment. Ro went to the window. It looked out over a walled rose garden and further, to stables and courtyards. Watching the ebb and flow of court life, Ro gradually tamed her confused bitterness and relief. It was the small sounds of movement that alerted her. She turned. Dovinna was sitting with her head resting against the bedpost, eyes closed. It was King Berinn. He had begun to twitch. As Ro watched, what had been small tics became jerks.

"Dovinna!"

The healer roused instantly. The shout brought Torslin barging in.

"What's happening?"

By now the jerks had grown to spasms. The King's limbs and head turned and flailed, almost knocking Dovinna from her feet as she tried to soothe him.

"Ayif?" Torslin roared for the physician.

He rushed in, pushing Dovinna aside as Berinn took a long juddering breath. Then there was stillness. The King's last exhalation seemed to have turned them all to stone. Dovinna's face wore a look of disbelief. Channan arrived with his hair and clothes still disordered from his rest. He picked up his father's lifeless hand. Torslin dropped to one knee.

"All hail King Channan."

Channan stared from one to another.

"I don't understand it," Dovinna said. "His heartbeat was steady, there was no fever."

"I've seen these symptoms before–they're caused by consuming the crushed seeds of marronia. I think I may have an explanation, Your Majesty." Ayif picked up the goblet by the stem.

Channan replaced the dead king's hand on the coverlet. "What are you implying, Ayif?"

The physician floundered, casting a sideways look at Torslin.

"Are you suggesting that King Berinn was poisoned?"

Ayif took a step back under the forced evenness of Channan's words. "Not intentionally, maybe. Medicines can become tainted. Or maybe it was one of Mistress Dovinna's ingredients." He sniffed the goblet. "Marronia can be beneficial for some conditions, in small doses."

Dovinna shook her head. "Impossible! It's not the sort of mistake a trained healer could make!"

"Condemned out of her own mouth," Torslin said. He took the goblet by its stem and sniffed it himself. "We should ask the royal materiologists to test the substance that remains." He looked expectantly at Channan. "It is for you to command, Highness."

Channan looked an apology at Dovinna. "Do it. The tests are as likely to prove innocence as guilt."

"Meanwhile Mistress Dovinna and her confederate should be placed under guard in the palace. If word gets out people may be tempted to take the law into their own hands."

Channan nodded. Torslin summoned guards to escort them. Ro tried to take comfort from the new king's parting words.

"May the right be protected and the innocent walk free."

The sound of heavy iron bolts thudding into place outside their drab cell knocked away the last traces of optimism.

# Chapter Four

Dovinna paced the cell twisting and twisting the ring on her finger. Ro stood quietly beneath the small window set high up in the wall. She had not felt before how irritating ill-considered movement could be.

"Why do you do that?" she asked. Dovinna stopped. "All that walking about going nowhere."

"It helps me think."

"In Iyessa stillness is thought to promote contemplation." Ro considered a moment. She had never known it to work for her. She joined Dovinna in her pacing.

"I don't understand what happened." Dovinna halted once more. "It wasn't the fever, he wasn't heated, he appeared to be sleeping–peaceful, didn't he?"

"You forget I'm no healer, but yes, he appeared at rest."

Dovinna shook her head. "I simply don't understand it."

"Why should you be accused of poisoning him?" Ro tried to sound casual. Lar would have been able to sense what was true here; even Ussu would have, providing she had not been overwhelmed by the injury of incarceration, but Ro had nothing except reason to work with, and reason required facts she did not have.

"Because the symptoms fit–the sudden onset of the tremors and their violence," Dovinna hesitated. "And King Berinn wanted Channan to marry a foreign princess, not some commoner with no connections or ancestry."

"Everyone has ancestry," Ro interrupted, remembering the Song of the Forebears, which was sung at the start of each spring's renewal.

"Well, no one knows mine. Varda, my teacher, took me in as an abandoned babe."

"Then that's your ancestry–surely as good as any bloodline."

45

"Not if you need to command the respect of neighbouring princes and your own aristocracy. You saw how Torslin and Princess Ersilla could barely bring themselves to be polite to me."

Torslin! After the agony he had caused her family, Ro had to count any enemy of his a friend.

"But Prince Channan knows you wouldn't have done something so evil–he'll let us go."

"As Prince Channan he would, but he's king now. He can't risk suspicion falling on him; it would jeopardise the whole country."

They paced in silence for the width of the small cell.

"I'm sorry you were involved in this."

"At least the others weren't there." Ro stopped abruptly. "They'll send guards to find them, won't they? They'll think if I'm involved, they must be too." Ro's knees gave way. She sank to the floor with her back against the wall. "What have I done? First exile and now imprisonment because of me."

"The guards will probably wait for them to return to my house. Perhaps your family will realise something's wrong and stay away."

Ro could not be so sure, remembering their confusion in Najarind's busy streets.

"They're bound to find you're innocent–then we'll all be free."

Dovinna sat on the floor beside her. "Perhaps. But even when the materiologists find my medicine was pure, King Berinn may still have been poisoned, and we were alone in the room with him."

Ro saw an image of the king's physician holding up the goblet to the light. "What about Ayif? Who had more opportunity than he?"

Dovinna shook her head. "Why would he do it? It sounds like a desperate excuse, and that's just what Ayif will claim it is."

"Maybe his loyalty wasn't really to the king." Ro told Dovinna about the look she had seen pass between the physician and the king's adviser.

Dovinna shuddered. "He has no love for me–but he was one of King Berinn's oldest friends. No one would believe it."

"We have to do something." Ro scrambled to her feet and began pacing once more. What if the guards tried to arrest the others, and Ussu protested or Raimi tried to protect them? They might be hurt, or worse.

"We just have to wait and trust to Ondd," Dovinna said.

Ro slapped the wall. At home the action would have earned her a reprimand for spreading negative ripples.

"Ondd!" she spat. "If the dragon can allow an innocent baby to be born deaf, why should it care about this?"

And so they paced and they waited, and they sat and waited. Eventually Ro's thoughts wandered to sit on the lush turf by the pool where she had so often found peace. A tune kept running through her head–something to do with Ondd's scales and the riddle of life, but she could not quite place it. Suddenly she jerked awake. Dovinna was dozing beside her. There was a strange, warm smell on the air. Then she heard it again: a long slithering sound of metal drawn against metal. She shook Dovinna's arm.

"What's happening?"

The healer woke slowly. "Blisswort! That smell, it's blisswort." She held her skirt in front of her nose and mouth.

"I heard something." Ro forced herself to go to the door and listen. The peaceful depths of her pool beckoned. She could hear deep snorting breaths, but no other movement. She peered through the cracks between frame and door.

"I can't see the bolts."

Dovinna gently pushed the door and it swung open. The guard was slumped over a table. A bottle, now empty, had rolled away from his fingers.

"I don't like this." Dovinna picked the bottle up by the rim and took a small sniff. "He must have felt the full force of the drug when he took out the stopper."

"Is it... is... ?" Ro hesitated.

"Not poison. When he wakes he'll have a headache as though he's drunk too deeply and the drug evaporates so quickly there'll be nothing in the bottle to tell him otherwise." Dovinna checked his pulse.

"Would your prince do this?"

The healer shook her head.

"The murderer then. We should go." Ro went to the far door to listen.

"It's a trap–we'll be killed."

"Maybe he only wants us out of the way." Ro pulled at Dovinna's sleeve. The healer shook off her hand.

"Everyone will think us guilty."

"Whoever set this trap's bound to check on it. We could still get killed 'escaping' if we stay here. I don't want to wait to find out." Ro listened at the door. There was no telltale creak of armour, no sigh to give away an ambush. She peeped through the crack between the door and its frame. The view was blocked by the rough cloth of a jerkin. She signalled to Dovinna.

"What do we do?"

Ro's glance lit on the bottle. "When I open the door, you throw yourself across the doorway," she whispered.

"You're crazy," Dovinna hissed. "What if there's more than one? And he's bound to have a sword at least."

Ro tried to still the trembling of her hand as she picked up the bottle and stepped back to the door. She raised her voice.

"I tell you, I'm not waiting here to be killed. Don't try to stop me!" She rattled the handle and scuffed her feet against the door as if they were struggling. She mouthed "Fall!" at Dovinna and flung open the door. Dovinna dived across the gap. The assassin with sword raised to strike, tripped. Ro stepped from behind the door and brought down the bottle, shattering it on his skull. He sagged, losing hold of his sword, then crumpled. Ro dragged Dovinna from under him. All the power drained from her legs. Dovinna shook her.

"Help me."

Somehow Ro managed to take one of the assassin's arms and drag the unconscious form to their cell. Dovinna slid the bolts home.

Ro swallowed. "Is he dead?"

Dovinna shook her head. "Come on." She took a deep breath and stepped into the corridor. Ro followed.

"Which way?" she asked.

"Not the servants' corridors, it's too obvious. Besides rumours spread faster than inkstains among the maids and cleaners. The courtiers may not know yet what's happened."

Ro followed Dovinna's lead. The healer halted as they turned into a grander corridor.

"We're near the courtiers' chambers. Let's see if we can find you some less conspicuous clothes."

Ro listened at the nearest door. She could hear nothing. She took a deep breath and tapped on the wood. There was still no sound of movement within. They entered. A few minutes later they emerged attired in the decent yet unremarkable gowns of ladies of middle rank. Ro had to curb the urge to push her hair away from her ears and dip her head, feeling more noticeable than ever in the unfamiliar garments.

"If we meet anyone, smile and bow so." Dovinna demonstrated a graceful inclination of the head. "And keep going– as if you're on an important errand. The courtiers are usually so full of themselves we might get away with it."

They kept a purposeful but unhurried pace along the main corridor of the residential wing. As they approached the exit, the square of sunlight through the open doors to freedom urged Ro to quicken her stride, but Dovinna stopped and began brushing an invisible spot from her skirt. Ro only had time to look a question before a uniformed silhouette detached itself from the shadow of the doors. To go back would be sure to alert suspicion, but they could not go on either.

A door was flung open behind them with a crack against the wall that brought the guard springing to attention.

"Really, this is so inconvenient. I have a hundred and one things to do today and now I must scour the merchants for mourning clothes!" A waft of perfume and rustle of taffeta brought two ladies alongside them. The voice was an irritated drawl. It was answered by a flat murmur of sympathy.

"Whoever decided we should wear purple when someone dies? I've never met anyone yet who didn't look like a corpse wearing it–have you?" The question was aimed directly at Ro. Her leaping heart almost choked her. "No, of course not!" The lady answered her own question as she and her companion swept past.

The guard blocked their path.

"What's the meaning of this? Stand aside, young man, we have important business to transact." She waved as if brushing away insects. Ro and Dovinna found themselves automatically included.

"I'm sorry, Lady, but we've had orders to search everyone. It seems there may be spies in the palace."

"Don't be ridiculous! You know very well who I am!" The woman rounded on the guard. Her companion sighed and walked out into the sunlight where she stood tapping her foot. Dovinna followed her, trailed by Ro, and made sympathetic tutting noises. The guard held up his hands, but the woman cut off his protests.

"I shall speak to your captain about this, and you may be sure that I shall mention your sloppy appearance, your... " she continued berating him as she swept past and gathered up the waiting women like her skirts. They flowed across the space between the palace and the citadel wall. The woman's indignation relieved Dovinna and Ro of any necessity to do more than nod and smile, and carried them past the wall guards, who were left with their ears as red as if stinging from physical slaps.

Outside the gates, the crowds were more subdued than before, talking in murmurs and shaking their heads, but trade still occupied most. The only effect the king's death had on them was that the stalls were draped in purple. Dovinna and Ro managed to drift away.

"What now? Even if this isn't a trap, someone's bound to start looking for us soon." Dovinna clasped her hands together to prevent them from shaking.

"Lar," Ro answered. "We'll find Mother. She'll know what to do."

"So you do know where they went."

Ro hated pricking the relief in Dovinna's voice. "No, not exactly, but it would be somewhere free of the clamour of the city, and there is one place I know Lar would have wanted to meditate at before leaving."

"Ro, only the dead are quiet in Najarind," Dovinna objected. Ro returned her look steadily. "I see. You realise we'll have to cross virtually the entire city to get to the Garden of the Dead?"

"You did say we must take the unexpected path."

Dovinna straightened her shoulders. "Very well."

Wherever possible the pair kept to the crowded areas where it would be hard for the soldiers to spot them and easier to slip away from trouble. Their path zigzagged, but after half an hour of unhurried progress the press of people began to thin. Behind them was the great dome of Ondd's temple, and ahead, equally impressive in its way, was a tall hedge which stretched in a wide arc. Emerging from its base and sprouting from its heights were clipped beasts and geometrical fantasies. The figure of Ondd arched across the gateway. As they walked under its belly the noise and movement of Najarind was sliced off. Yet the Garden of the Dead was as crowded as the living city. Statues of stone or living evergreen climbed over each other for space to mark the dead. The sound of chimes held in stony fingers or water tapping on metal provided them with perpetual accompaniment. All was still, yet it felt as if everything was striving and struggling in endless movement. At the centre was a tree as twisted and wrinkled as a sour old woman; a living thing, but as oppressive and grasping as the monuments surrounding it.

"Are you sure your family would have come here, let alone have stayed?" Dovinna shivered.

"My father must have been returned to the elements here." Ro looked about for flashes of colourful Iyessi cloth. "There should be music–a song of passing."

She made her way towards the tree. From the centre she should get a better view. In each direction there were only the writhing clipped forms or stone figures to be seen.

"Perhaps if you were to sing," Dovinna suggested. "It wouldn't be as obvious as calling, and they'd know it was you–if they're here."

"But they should be able to tell I'm here," Ro protested. All the elements were mixed together creating an impression of chaos rather than balance. Even if Ro knew what her father's affinity had been it would not help.

"Of course, your father was a stranger–we're looking in the wrong place." Dovinna headed for an area where the hedge had been allowed to become unkempt. Squeezing through what had once been a gateway, they entered an area bounded on three sides by hedge and a steep rocky slope which fell away on the fourth. There were no monuments or paving here, and the rank herbs grew freely underfoot. Ro approached the edge of the slope and saw the white scar of a recently trodden path leading down until it disappeared halfway. She started to scramble down it, followed less eagerly by Dovinna. As she neared the end, she could see an overhanging rock had obscured the entrance to a narrow cave from which a trickle of water emerged. Ro held out a hand to steady Dovinna as they arrived at the cave-mouth scattering loose stones.

"At last!" It was Ussu.

It was a typical welcome that put the first genuine smile on Ro's face in what seemed like days. Inside the entrance, the cave opened out with a ceiling as impressive as that of the temple hung with dripping spires of stone. As they entered, Ussu's voice repeating "last... last... last..." bounced off the walls from all sides. Raimi was seated on a stump of stone with the sleeping Lalli in his arms.

"Lar?" Ro whispered in awe of the cave's echo, which contrived to make the repeated "ah... ah... ah... " a round song. It explained why she had not heard their music.

"Beyond." Ussu showed the way.

"Ondd... Ondd... Ondd... " cried the cave.

They followed the course of the water to a low passage at the back. Down a few steps and round a corner they found themselves in another cave, narrower than the first and made treacherous to negotiate by cairns of quartzy rock. Lar stood before one of these. Ro curbed the urge to rush to her, instead moving quietly to stand at her side. Her mother's face was wet with tears as she put an arm around her.

"Good. Now we can leave." The older woman looked beyond Ro to the healer. "What's wrong?"

Ussu threw up her hands. "I knew it. I knew she couldn't stay out of trouble."

Ro explained as quickly as possible with Ussu's exclamations as punctuation.

"We'd already decided we wanted to leave," Raimi said.

Dovinna shook her head. "Perhaps if I returned they'd let you go. They'd have a culprit, there'd be no need to search for more."

"No," Lar objected. "I'll deliver no one into Torslin's clutches. Besides, whoever is behind this underestimates us."

Ro looked from one to another. "What?"

Raimi grinned. "Water, Ro. It comes from somewhere and it goes somewhere."

"We simply follow it out of the city," Ussu concluded. "We'll have to leave most of our things behind though."

"Including the horses," Raimi said.

Ussu squeezed his arm. "We'll manage."

"How can you be sure the water will lead us out? The path might grow too small." Dovinna spoke as they retrieved their packs.

"Lar is an earth-hearer. My sister and Raimi both have water affinities. If they say there's a way, you can trust them."

"It's where we should head once we're free of the city that bothers me," Ussu muttered, strapping Lalli to her back in a sling.

Armed with one of the torches, Raimi took the lead, followed by Ussu, Dovinna, Ro and Lar. The way wound deeper into the hillside. It was uneven and slippery, so that the party often had to steady themselves against the rock walls. The torchlight flickered and danced over stone glistening with moisture and flashes of crystals. The footing became increasingly treacherous as the passage began to rise again. The air grew stale and Ro feared the torch would go out. Still, their progress was steady until they came to a place where the stream divided.

Raimi hesitated. "Down or up?"

Lar and Ussu stood with heads tilted, listening.

"It gets faster down there," Ussu said.

"I believe we should go up," Lar agreed.

They continued climbing. Each time Ro paused to gather her breath she strained her ears for the sounds of mail and leather scraping on stone that would signal pursuit. Nothing. Perhaps the soldiers would be waiting where they finally emerged. The ceiling came lower until they were forced to crawl.

"Perhaps we should go back," Ro suggested. "If the ceiling comes any closer, Ussu won't be able to carry Lalli."

"It's all right, Raimi called back. "We're almost there."

Even as he spoke his torch went out. Ro could still see the faint outlines of those in front. A current of air wafted the scent of earth to her. Abruptly, the passage widened and they found themselves on the edge of a pool fed by moisture pouring down the fractured walls above it and spilling over to form the stream they followed. A shaft of daylight cast an artificial moon onto the surface of the pool. It would be a soaking climb, but one which the hatched surface of the walls made possible. They started upwards. By the time Ro emerged high on a hillside, the air had turned chill and the light was a pale golden orange, flaming off Ondd's dome far beneath them. Torchlight formed fragments of stars in the distant streets and the tinkle of the gate chimes drifted up to them.

"Will they look for us up here?" Ro asked, shivering.

Dovinna nodded. "Eventually, but they'll probably think we're hiding in the city for a while. We have a little time." She twisted her ring, head bowed. "Channan gave me this. A token of love." She made a derisive noise.

They turned away, and so did not see the torchlight glinting off the armour of two columns of soldiers riding out of the city. The columns split to follow the roads radiating from Najarind.

Fordel cursed as he mounted at the head of a column. The discomfort of a night in the saddle would be as nothing compared to the last few hours. He closed his eyes against the memory.

The glance of the guard who had brought him the news, had kept straying sideways to his unconscious fellow soldiers and the open cell door.

"Don't just stand there, man. Get these fools a healer and clear up this mess!"

The guard had burst into action like a released spring. Fordel had relieved his temper by slamming the door behind him. Curse the idiot guard! Curse that stupid chit, Dovinna, and more than all, curse Torslin for putting him in charge of the cells. His head still throbbed from saluting King Berinn's passing with a flask of Najarind's finest vintage. It really wasn't fair that an amiable chap like himself, who only craved a peaceful existence, should be burdened with such unpleasant tasks.

As he paced along the corridor he could already hear Torslin's reaction to his news. The king's adviser reminded Fordel of his father, to whom Fordel had been life's biggest disappointment. Fordel checked his pace. Perhaps he could get to Channan first. His friend would understand–might even be pleased that his ladylove was free. Vain hope! King Channan was not alone in his sitting chamber. As Fordel entered four heads turned towards him. Sitting with his chin resting in his hand, Channan gave him a sad smile; Ersilla halted her nervous pacing and turned away; Torslin, who had been leaning across the table in front of Channan emphatically gesturing at the documents spread there, frowned. Only Princess Anni looked relieved to see him. She moved her chair to make room for him.

"Well, Fordel?" Torslin snapped. "You see we're engaged in serious matters."

Fordel had to remind himself that he was at least six inches taller than the florid lord and not a schoolboy. "I have news for His Majesty." He swept Channan a bow. Formerly the gesture would have been greeted with giggles.

"Get on with it then," Torslin ordered.

Fordel explained in as soldierly a fashion as he could manage. Torslin slammed his hand down on the table.

Ersilla's breath hissed through her teeth. "You see how you've been deceived in her?" The Princess's eyes shone so that Fordel was forced to curb a shiver.

Anni took Channan's hand. "I'm so sorry, Channan."

The King's face remained immobile. He withdrew his hand.

"This confirms it, then." Torslin shook his head.

Ersilla brought her face close to Fordel's. "You incompetent. Do you realise you've let our father's murderers go free?"

Fordel stepped back. "That awaits proof, surely?" He looked at Channan for support.

"The materiologists gave us that proof minutes ago. There was poison in the glass Dovi gave my father."

Fordel cursed under his breath. "She can't have got far, after all, there are guards everywhere and that Iyessi stands out like a sow in a flowerbed."

"Delicately put," Torslin interrupted. "Although as I hear, that Iyessi has fooled you into releasing her and her companions once already."

"I hope you're not suggesting that I'm a traitor."

"Just incompetent. If you'll excuse me, Highness, I'll go and see what can be done to remedy this situation." Torslin pushed himself to his feet.

Channan nodded. "I want them alive, Torslin. I want to know why."

Torslin bowed. As he turned to leave he frowned away the exultant smile on Ersilla's face. Fordel had hesitated, trying to find words for Channan that would not sound trite. Looking at his friend's set face, none came.

Now, riding out of Najarind alongside Captain Pachand, Fordel cursed again. He had the uncomfortable feeling at the base of his neck that if he wanted to keep his head on it he had better appear to consume more and get drunk less.

Even with the exertion of clambering over the rough hillsides searching for a place that was less exposed, Ro was still shivering. Her damp clothing made her bones ache. The light was almost gone before they found a slope covered in dry bracken that promised reasonable cover. There was little food to share and no hope of a fire. They huddled together talking only when necessary and then in murmurs. Ro hugged her knees miserably; now she had even deprived her family of their music. Dovinna seemed equally morose, gazing at her ring's small white stone and swallowing tears.

Of them all, Ussu seemed the brightest. "At least we're free of the city."

Her cheerfulness made Ro scowl. "Not missing your creature comforts, then? Not scared of catching cold?"

Ussu tutted. "The air might be cold, but it's free and it's true. If I'd had to stay any longer in that place of discord and contradiction I'd have gone mad."

Ro shook her head at her sister's sanctimonious tone. "You're priceless, Ussu. We're fugitives."

"Fugitives, exiles... " Ussu shrugged.

Dovinna broke free from her ring-held trance. "We have to prove our innocence."

"Each verse in its order," Lar answered mildly. "When the moon rises we'll go on. We'll need better cover than this come the day."

"But go where?"

"To find Lalli's cure," Ussu said. "You said your teacher would help, and now we have you to guide us there." There was a hard edge behind her smile.

"I'll help all I can, of course. But you'd be better off going there without me. My recommendation will do you no good at all." Dovinna returned to twisting her ring. "I'm not even sure Varda will let me find the way."

"Between us we'll manage," Lar told her.

Something of the others' confidence and determination passed its way to Ro, so that when the ghostly moon silhouetted the bracken, she found the strength to clamber to her feet without complaint.

Finding the forest would be no problem. The vast tracts of trees would be haloed in vitae, which would act like a lodestone to the Iyessi. Crossing the intervening land would be more difficult. The bracken scratched and snatched at them as they passed, and hid the unevenness of the ground. Ro lost count of the number of times her ankles turned on unseen roots and bumps. The Najarindian gown she had purloined hampered her further, tripping her so that she almost fell into Dovinna's back more than once. At last the occasional wind-tortured trees began to gather together into whispering huddles and the black outline of the untidy vanguard of Kabonn could be made out against the moon-washed sky. Pausing to take a last look behind them Ro's heart sank. The trail of broken plants cut a black line across the terrain, as clear as if they were hoping to be caught.

Dovinna came alongside her. "Don't worry. Any search party won't find it so easy to track us in Kabonn."

They had set out for Najarind with such bright hopes, fleeing from prejudice and persecution, seeking freedom and an end to their troubles. Now they were fleeing the city where they had received prejudice and persecution in even greater measure, ostensibly to find a cure and a place where they would be welcome, but Ro never had truly belonged anywhere or found any reason why she should be afflicted. As she followed the others under the black canopy of branches, all Ro had heart to hope for was a warm meal and an uninterrupted night's sleep.

# Chapter Five

The forest was a warm stuffy black, like the inside of a velvet sack. It was comforting and strange. The deep layer of pine needles and old leaves absorbed the sound of their footsteps. Gradually their eyes adjusted to their surroundings and they became aware of curious trees standing in huddles or leaning over each other as if to get a better look at them. There was nothing as definite as a path to follow, only a less tangled route through the grasping brambles and ivy. The place had a smell of earthy decay and secret growth. Apart from the occasional scurryings of small animals and creak of tired branches, their movement was the only sound of life.

"Can't we stop yet? I feel as if I'm sleepwalking," Ussu complained.

She stopped so suddenly Ro could not avoid bumping into her and waking Lalli, who immediately set up a thin wail.

"That's it!" Ussu exclaimed. "No further!"

Dovinna and Lar held a whispered consultation. The healer led the way deeper into the undergrowth.

"We'll rest here," she said.

"Where?" Ussu demanded. "I see nowhere that's not either covered in mould or thorns."

Dovinna carefully parted the long outer shoots of a huge bramble. "In here," she said, and ducked underneath.

Ussu hesitated but Lar and Raimi followed the healer, leaving her no choice but to follow. Ro was last to enter. Under the prickly canopy there was room enough for them to sit upright, and if they curled up, room enough to sleep. It was not ideal, but at least it was dry, and the brambles would deter any animal which might be on the prowl, while hiding them from unfriendly eyes. They set no guard: if anyone discovered their hiding place during the night, there was nowhere they could run.

When Ro woke she thought for a moment that she had been struck down by some mystery disease. Then she realised that the reason she could not turn over was because Ussu's feet were firmly wedged against her back, and her jaw ached due to the root that was her pillow. In the double gloom of the forest and the bramble cave it could have been a few minutes since Ro closed her eyes or a few hours. She gradually eased her body outside their thorny shelter. The air was clearer with shafts of pale sunshine sharpening the edges of the trees. Ro stretched and breathed deeply. The light warmed the colours of glossy ivy leaves and purple berries. Ro's mouth watered: breakfast!

She turned and looked back at their shelter, fixing its image in her mind, then headed for a tree with a twisted trunk, collecting the seasonal bounty on the way. Soon she was engrossed in the sweet taste of the fruit bursting on her tongue and the pale patches of sunshine. The animal scurryings of the night were joined by the chirrings and whistles of birds invisible in the canopy. Taking care to fix her bearings by oddly shaped branches and patches of colour, Ro scoured the area for berries and soon had enough for the whole party scooped in her cumbersome skirt.

She turned to retrace her route. A sudden movement caught the corner of her eye. Ro scanned the area. Perhaps its was a bird flitting from tree to tree. Finding her way back needed concentration despite her precautions. As the sun rose, the shadows changed shape, barring the forest floor with different patterns. The undergrowth seemed to have crowded closer requiring Ro to unsnag her skirt every few steps, as if the bushes were trying to make her spill her harvest. Scurrying sounds and the occasional grunt of unseen animals made Ro start and pause, although whatever caused them fell silent whenever she stopped. It was not until she saw Dovinna waving to her that Ro felt the tension melting from her shoulders.

The healer answered Ro's smile with a frown. "It's dangerous to wander off," she scolded.

"I was perfectly safe," Ro answered her, dismissing the noises. "And look what I've got for us."

Dovinna remained serious. "Those berries might have cost you dear. The forest has a habit of playing tricks on you. The inhabitants don't like disturbance." She looked nervously at the path Ro had taken. "We'd best get back."

The healer's unease seemed unwarranted by their experience of Kabonn so far, but with all that had happened to them over the past few days Ro allowed that it was better to be overcautious. The others had risen in her absence and were trying to ease the night out of their cramped limbs. Their conversation was confined to muttered necessities, as Ro shared out the berries. They set out with Dovinna and Lar in the lead once more, and Ro fell back to where Raimi was stoically bringing up the rear. His hand repeatedly went to the haft of the hunting knife strapped to his belt.

"Are there any big animals in the forest?" Ro whispered.

He glanced at her sharply. "Deer, I should think. Why? Have you seen something?"

"No, I just wondered what everyone's so tetchy about."

"We're being chased by the king's soldiers. Isn't that enough?"

Ro looked steadily at him, waiting for more.

"You'd better watch where you're going or you're likely to trip up," he said sourly.

Ro sighed and followed his advice. If even Raimi was in a bad mood about something, then she had better stay alert. Whenever Ro turned at an unexpected noise it ceased, as if whatever caused it turned to stone under human gaze. All around was the wild tangle of the forest. When the undergrowth drew back from their path, Ro took the opportunity to move up beside Dovinna.

"Maybe I'm imagining it, but... "

"We're being watched," Dovinna finished for her. "Treat it as though you are imagining it."

Ussu protested. "But they're not friendly. Who are they?"

"The Kabonni, Varda's people. They don't welcome intruders since they have a habit of regarding them as little better than herd beasts. While they leave us alone, I suggest we do the same." Dovinna increased her pace, leaving their questioning and the exposed space behind.

"But," Ussu persisted. "If they know you, surely they'd help us. Give us a decent place to rest and something hot to eat." She turned to the unnaturally quiet undergrowth. "After all, we mean no harm and the quicker we find your teacher, the quicker we'll be gone."

There was no indication that anything except the trees and the birds had heard her. Ro looked at Lar for guidance, but her mother's thoughts appeared occupied elsewhere.

Dovinna shook her head. "I knew when Varda returned here that I wouldn't be welcome." She raised her voice for their unseen audience. "If coming here wasn't essential for your safety and I wasn't under an irredeemable obligation I would never have disturbed her peace again."

Raimi's voice from the back of the line settled it. "As long as we get a move on, I don't care whether we see any of the Kabonni or not."

Their progress was slow, hampered now as much by their desire to tread carefully. In the deep cover of the canopy the air was stuffy and still, so that the occasional streak of sunshine falling across their path was as refreshing as a cool drink. A muttered curse behind Ro made her turn. Raimi's pack had caught on a long springy arm of bramble which held him tighter the more he struggled.

"I'll get it," Ro said.

As fast as she released the thorns from Raimi they caught at her, dragging on her sleeves and viciously tugging at her hair. Raimi's struggles became wilder as he tried to shrug out of his pack and gain some measure of freedom.

"Be still!" Dovinna hissed a warning. Too late. Raimi's arm burst free striking Ro in the ribs and knocking her breath out as it sent her tottering off the path. She sprawled in a mound of old twigs and leaves. She had barely registered surprise at the softness of her landing, when a screech pierced the forest. A figure erupted from the mound beside her, scattering a fountain of leaves.

"Help! Fire! Murder! Help!" From the pitch of its voice Ro guessed the figure was female. Its rough seamed skin was the yellowy brown of old acorns and its grey hair stood out from its head in tangled waves. Its coarse clothes covered stick-like limbs. The woman was no taller than a child and appeared to be on the verge of throwing a childish tantrum.

Ro struggled to her feet, discovering shattered bowls and upturned furniture in the wreckage of the mound.

"Help! Fire! Help!" The figure began to pelt Ro with sticks and debris from its home.

Raimi tried to stop her. "Hardly that, ancient one."

"Look what you've done to my house!" The woman tore at its hair."

"I'm sorry, it was an accident." Ro tried to stand a low table upright.

"Don't touch! Leave it, leave it!" The Kabonni's voice began to swing between angry screeches and moans.

"Let us help you, we meant no harm," Ro tried again.

"No, you never do, do you?" The Kabonni caught sight of Dovinna as the others gathered around. "You! Traitor!" she hissed. "Back to cause more trouble? You'll pay this time. Oh yes, you'll pay!"

The Kabonni dashed into the undergrowth with a speed and agility they could not hope to match. She leapt and dodged past the obstacles which had all but barred their path.

Dovinna sank to the forest floor with her head in her hands. "Oh, no."

Ussu glared from Raimi to Ro and back, but for once said nothing, merely pursing her lips.

"Where has she gone?" Lar asked.

"To fetch her nephew, Bissig. He's as short-tempered and self-important as his beloved aunt, Wey, and his word carries weight in the forest. We could hardly have chosen a worse home to wreck."

"Perhaps if we try to straighten things up a bit," Ro suggested, all too aware that her clumsiness had landed them in trouble again.

Dovinna shook her head.

Raimi placed a reassuring hand on Ro's shoulder. "It was my fault. I shouldn't have been so impatient. It's the way these trees suck everything into them. There should be vibrations everywhere, but all I feel is one great pulse of trees."

Ussu interrupted. "Why don't we just go? I don't see why we should wait here for trouble."

"And how far do you think we'd get?" Dovinna asked.

Lar agreed. "We need these people's help, Ussu, or at least not their hindrance, if we're to find Dovinna's teacher. Besides we have destroyed the old one's dwelling and must make amends if we can."

"Very noble!" A thickset Kabonni appeared soundlessly from the undergrowth. His short limbs looked as solid as tree trunks and his brows were drawn together over a beak-like nose that ill-matched his other features. Movement in the undergrowth around them showed they were surrounded.

"Bissig," Dovinna murmured.

"Yes, Citylover. Thought you could sneak past, did you? Should've known better. You know what the penalties are for entering Kabonn uninvited, and now you've turned wrecker too." He strutted back and forth in front of the ruined mound.

"It was an accident," Raimi repeated.

The elderly Kabonni, Wey, emerged from the brambles. "Don't you let them get away with it–smashed everything they have." She buzzed about her nephew, plucking at his sleeve.

"All right, Auntie." Bissig shook the old woman off. "I know what's due to you." He turned back to the waiting Iyessi.

Lar spoke up. "Of course, we'll do all we can to restore the old one's home. All we wish is to pass peacefully through this place to seek Varda's help for the little one."

It might have been Lar's quiet authority or the mention of Varda's name, but for a moment Bissig hesitated. Then he jutted out his chin.

"Not so easy to replace a home–takes skill, takes time, takes barter goods. Where's she to live in the meantime, eh?"

Ussu exploded. "You should be ashamed of yourself! What were you thinking of letting her live alone in a hovel like this, when she should be with you being looked after?"

If the situation had not been so serious, the sight of Ussu towering over the belligerent Kabonni, who looked up at her with his lower lip thrust out and hands on hips, would have sent Ro into giggles. It was like watching a rooster threaten a swan.

"For your information, Wrecker, Auntie prefers to live alone. Little palace, wasn't it, Auntie?" He turned to the old woman, but her attention had been caught by Lalli, who had been woken by the fuss. The baby watched solemnly as the old woman made nonsense sounds and pulled faces at her.

"Nice babe," she said, turning sparkling eyes on Bissig.

Ussu's expression remained cold. "Thank you."

"Now, what have you got to offer as compensation?" Bissig signalled the Iyessi to open their packs, but his aunt tugged at his arm and began speaking in hurried whispers.

Dovinna rose and looked questioningly at Lar.

The hearer shook her head. "I can't make out the words, but I don't like the tone."

"And I don't like the way she looked at Lalli," Ussu added.

"Neither do I," Dovinna agreed. "Better give her to me."

Bissig kept glancing at the baby and shaking his head while his aunt alternated between pleading and angry gestures.

"But I'm lonely, nephew. It would be company for me."

"How will you feed it, Auntie? How will you raise it? It'll be me and mine has to do the providing."

"It could help when I get too old to do for myself. Could make the difference between staying here and having to move in with you."

Bissig's frown changed to a grin. He stepped forward. Raimi started opening their packs for the Kabonni to see, but Bissig waved him away.

"We've decided. There's only one thing you've got that's worth having–hand over the babe."

Ussu and Raimi immediately stepped between Bissig and Dovinna. Without changing his expression, Bissig made a chuckling noise in his throat, like a game bird. The heads of several Kabonni appeared around them.

"Do as I say and hand the brat over or you'll regret it."

Ussu took a step towards him, but Dovinna's voice stopped her.

"Aren't you forgetting something? These people are here to seek help for the child from Varda. She'll hardly be pleased when she finds out you prevented them."

"We'll take her to Varda ourselves," Bissig blustered.

The old woman nodded. "Oh, yes, we'll take care of her, we'll take very good care of her."

"But you don't even know what's wrong with her," Dovinna said.

Bissig's grin changed to suspicion. "She ain't contagious, is she?"

"She don't look ill," the old woman said.

Dovinna shrugged. "It's beyond my skill to cure. Do you really want to risk upsetting Varda for a sickly child that might bring you nothing but trouble and hard work?"

Bissig regained some of his bluster. "Go on, we're not falling for that. Hand her over."

"All right for you to say, but what about everyone else here? Why should they risk Varda shunning them?"

There were one or two murmurs from Bissig's supporters.

Dovinna continued. "No one's saying you don't deserve compensation, Wey. Why don't we all take the child to Varda and let her decide?"

"Sounds reasonable to me," one of the supporters agreed.

"But I want it!" Wey stamped her foot, fist clenched.

Bissig held up his hands. "Enough, Auntie. We'll take them to the healer, and then we'll see. I've wasted enough time on this. Besides... " His face took on a crafty expression. "You know the wise one sent this citylover packing before. We may yet come out of this richer." He rubbed his hands and nodded to his supporters.

The Iyessi and Dovinna found themselves being herded deeper into the forest at a pace which their larger size and unfamiliarity made dangerous. It soon became apparent how the Kabonni could appear and vanish so suddenly. Their way led through tunnels of undergrowth and maze-like hedges of intertwined branches. Their speed made it hard to look about them, but occasionally they came across a cluster of leafy mounds, or bramble huts and enclosures, which denoted a small community of Kabonni. Instead of attracting curiosity, abandoned baskets and tools showed that people fled at their arrival. When Lalli's hungry wails persuaded Bissig that they should rest for a few moments, Ro took the opportunity to question Dovinna about it.

"They don't have any government or communities as such– only clans scattered so that they don't interfere with each other. The only real contact between them is when representatives gather at the quarter feasts to discuss any grievances or news–and barter any spare produce. They all know and respect Varda because of her healing skills and her travels, but they have no desire to see or know about anything beyond the borders of Kabonn themselves, and they feel that outsiders should stay that way–outside Kabonn."

"But this may work to our advantage. We'll reach Varda far quicker this way." Ro hoped Dovinna would agree, but the healer sighed.

"With a grievance against us."

"But it was an accident. Varda surely won't think they have a right to Lalli."

"No, but we did destroy Wey's home and Kabonn's few laws are quite clear. Equal reparation must be made."

Her words gave Ro unpleasant thoughts for company as they continued their journey. At length the undergrowth gave way to form a clearing around an ancient yew tree. Its branches were

adorned with ribbons, woven dolls and scraps of mirror, but its
real glory was its size; at least six people would be needed with
arms outstretched to span its girth. A brown figure detached itself
from the folds of its bark.

"At last," she said, but without a smile.

Bissig began a blustering explanation, but the figure swept by
him to stand before Dovinna. Her appearance was similar to that
of Wey, except that she plaited her hair about her head like the
veins of a leaf. Her tidiness extended to her quiet manner. So this
was Varda. Ro found herself thinking of Verron, the vitae-hearer.
Varda surveyed Dovinna in a silence that made the others fidget.
Ro wished again that she had the Iyessi ability to feel the
vibrations of emotion. It was impossible to judge whether Varda
was pleased to see her former pupil or not. Dovinna stood in a
tension that was somewhere between apology and defiance.
Varda's eyes slid from her former pupil to the baby in her arms.

"We've brought you a patient," Dovinna said.

"And Bissig and Wey escorted you here out of kindness to
make sure you didn't get lost." The master healer's irony made no
impression on the Kabonni.

"They wrecked Auntie's home."

"I wrecked Auntie's home," Ro corrected, then wished she
had not as she felt the force of Varda's gaze. "It was an accident."

"You shouldn't be so quick to take blame on yourself."

"We want compensation," Bissig demanded.

Varda turned a stern frown on him. "Be sure you'll receive
exactly what you deserve, Bissig. Meanwhile, wouldn't your
energy be better spent preparing somewhere for your aunt to spend
the night?"

"But the baby... " Wey wailed.

Varda spoke softly to her. "Come back tomorrow at noon, and
you'll have your answer. There's much to consider, not least how
you could dare to detain anyone who came seeking my help."

Bissig drew himself up to his full height. "Come on, Auntie,
we'll get no justice here today. But tomorrow... " He left the words
hanging as he and his followers were swallowed once more by
Kabonn.

Varda shook her head. "You always were a troublesome
child," she told Dovinna. "I've missed you."

"That's why you came back to live in Kabonn, no doubt."
Dovinna spoke lightly, but her smile was brittle.

66

Varda shrugged. "Sometimes people have to be alone to discover what they're made of."

"You already knew, surely!"

"It wasn't me I was speaking about." Varda surveyed the group. "Time for old arguments later." She stretched out her hands for Lalli. "Now, little one, what can I do for you?"

"She's mine–ours." Ussu took Raimi's hand. "She can't hear."

Varda rocked the baby in her arms. "Can she not? Well, well, we shall see, shan't we, we shall see." She turned and stepped into the tree.

The voices ceased as Anni entered King Channan's sitting chamber. Little had changed since the last time she was there. Channan was seated behind a table covered in papers and the remains of an impromptu meal, with his head in his hands. Ersilla stood behind him like his bad angel and Torslin was seated at one end of the table, the only one of the three who looked entirely comfortable with his situation. The momentary interest that made them look up at Anni's entrance vanished almost without comment.

Ersilla looked as if she wished to box her brother's ears. "You can't invite Darian to father's funeral, have you no sense? He'll just use it as an opportunity to grab some more of our land while your attention's diverted."

Anni joined them at the table. "But we must invite all the neighbouring kingdoms to send a representative, it's only what's due to our father."

"And since when have you known anything of statecraft?" Ersilla sneered.

"I may know nothing of politics, but I do know about courtesy, Sister."

Channan added his argument. "If we don't ask him, King Darian will think we're afraid. Besides it would be an opportunity to improve relationships between Ortann and Amradoc." Channan looked hopefully at Torslin.

The adviser paused before answering. "It would also be an opportunity to flood the city with foreign spies. I strongly advise that we keep King Berinn's funeral an Ortanian occasion. Your father never was one for pomp and spectacle, after all.

Channan hesitated. "Oh, I don't know, my head's buzzing. There are so many things to think of and none of them simple. How did Father cope?"

"He delegated, Sire," Torslin answered.

"As you should do, Brother," Ersilla added, all honey where a moment before she had been vinegar. "Our sister has no doubt come to suggest you should get some rest. Why not leave these trivial details to us?"

Channan's shoulders sagged. "Maybe just for an hour." He rose slowly. "But I at least want the neighbouring kings told when the funeral's to take place. Wake me if anything happens."

Torslin froze the comment Ersilla was about to make with a look. "Of course, lad."

The familiar term made Anni shudder. She said nothing until they had left the room. "You know Ersilla's never forgiven King Darian for turning down Father's offer of her hand."

Channan nodded. "But there's sense in what they say."

"I wish you wouldn't be so close with them."

"Who else am I to turn to? Torslin was Father's closest adviser and he confided in Ersilla as if she was our mother."

"Who indeed? Dovinna is fugitive and Fordel is sent to chase her."

Channan's face filled with misery. "Why did she do it, Anni? I still can't believe it."

"Neither can I."

Channan did not notice the irony in her voice. "What did she think to gain? And then, to run..."

"Perhaps she has powerful enemies–maybe she felt she had no choice but to run."

"I know what you're thinking, but the evidence was against her."

"Well, you still have me to talk to, even if, as our dear sister was so pleased to point out, I am unused to matters of state."

Channan smiled and planted a kiss on her forehead. "I value your judgement very highly, you may be sure."

Anni returned the smile. "I had rather you would value your own judgement. Think for yourself, Channan, and don't trust people just because Father did."

They had reached his chamber door. "My judgement! We've seen how good that is. I hope Fordel finds her and brings her back."

"Do you?" Anni asked. "I wonder, and what will you do then?"

But Channan was already closing the door behind him.

Fordel reined in his horse at the edge of the Forest of Kabonn and wondered the same thing. Rain hurled itself down on them and the slopes of bracken, making the dry leaves crackle and snap. It plastered the horses' manes to their necks and soaked through cloaks to add to the general ill-humour. There was no way he could come out of this mission smelling sweet. If he caught Dovinna and took her back to Najarind, Channan would be forced to sentence her to death. Something he, Fordel, would be bound to be blamed for afterwards. But if he did not catch her, Torslin would see to it that he was posted to the furthest outpost of the empire in swampy Gindul, where he would spend his life fending off voracious insects and snakes. Captain Pachand would be only too willing to point out his shortcomings as leader. The impenetrable face of Kabonn gave Fordel no answers.

"The chances of us finding them in there are virtually nil," he murmured.

"We'll never get the horses through, but we should be able to cut a path—one of the men says he's been in there before, he can lead." Pachand looked as fresh as Fordel was weary.

Fordel's eyebrows raised. "He knows the way?"

Pachand shifted in his saddle. "No, but we're agreed they're heading for the bitch's teacher—we just grab the first Kabonni we come across and shake it out of them."

"Hm... I'm not so sure. Still, I see little choice." Fordel glanced back at his troop. There was a way that he might wriggle out of the blame for failure and success. "Send someone back with word to Najarind: you're taking half the men to patrol the area where Kabonn comes closest to the Amradoc road—if we miss them in the forest, that's the nearest border. The rest of us are going in."

With any luck Dovinna and the Iyessi would evade him and run into Pachand's arms instead. Let his second have the dubious honour of taking them back to the city. He watched as Pachand prepared to carry out his orders. Provision had to be made for the horses, packs had to be redistributed, but eventually Pachand rode out and there was no further excuse to wait. At least the canopy should protect them from the worst of the downpour. Fordel signalled his men to advance.

The warmth and silence of the forest soon lost its appeal. Despite hacking at branches and creepers, the undergrowth still grabbed at clothes to detain them. The effort required by each step had them panting and sweating. The rain was trapped in a heavy mist by the branches adding to their disorientation. They left daubs of red along their route in case the destruction they wrought should not be sufficiently visible to find their way back, but when Fordel turned even these marks were hard to spot. He called a halt. The Kabonni were not renowned for their sociability and the patrol's appearance was not likely to inspire trust. The forest dwellers could easily avoid their clumsy approach. Fordel had no wish to wander around in the forest forever.

"Which one of you has been here before?"

A soldier attempted to snap to attention. Me, Sir, when my mother was ill, Sir. She didn't hold with those new healers–sent me to Varda for a cure."

"And you found her?"

The soldier hesitated. "Not exactly, sir–some of these forest monkeys took me to her."

"Forest monkeys? And isn't the healer herself a 'forest monkey'?"

The soldier swallowed and avoided Fordel's frown.

"How exactly did you find the Kabonni to take you to her."

Again the soldier swallowed. "More like they found me, Sir. I didn't know where to look, so I just called the healer's name and someone came."

"But you can find your way back?"

"Well... "

Fordel sighed. "Never mind. We'll rest here."

There was no sense in continuing to thrash about the forest. Instructing the soldier to keep him in sight, Fordel went further into the forest alone. Putting himself at risk would, he hoped, demonstrate his peaceful intent.

"Kabonni, hear me. King Channan of Najarind, Emperor of Ortann, has need of the healer, Varda." His voice was absorbed by the forest like a stone sinking in mud. He struggled into the undergrowth in a direction parallel to the camp and tried again. Eventually he had completed a full circle, but there was no sign that anything lived in the forest, let alone had heard him. He returned to his men.

"We'll wait an hour, then we'll move on and try again."

They moved and rested a further three times before Fordel decided to give up for the day. As he settled down wrapped in his damp blanket for the night, Fordel considered his options. If his strategy had not worked by the end of the next day, he would have to think of something else, otherwise their search for Dovinna and the Iyessi might well turn into a search for a way out of Kabonn.

In the middle of the night Fordel was shaken awake. The sentry had risked lighting a covered lamp. In its glow, Fordel saw what appeared to be an ancient child, with wild grizzled hair and wide eyes. Fordel looked a question at the sentry.

"Name's Wey, Sir. Says she knows how to find Varda."

"I see. Well, Madam Wey, we have need of a guide to take us to the healer as quickly as possible. Can you do that?" Fordel looked at the Kabonni's stick-like limbs and doubted she would be able to totter more than a few paces. But however slow or frail, she was the best chance they had.

The old woman nodded eagerly and a crafty look came into her eyes. "I can take you there, but there's something I want."

"Of course, we'll pay you anything within our power." Fordel felt an itch at the nape of his neck, and the same uneasy feeling he got when someone looked over his shoulder.

"Oh, it's within your power, all right; it's within your power." The old woman rubbed her hands together and skipped from one foot to the other. Fordel was regretting his promise already.

Ussu inhaled with a hiss as Varda vanished with her baby. Unconcerned, Dovinna followed. Closer to, Ro saw it was not magic but a fold of the massive yew trunk which hid the entrance to Varda's abode. The tree was hollow, divided horizontally to form two irregularly shaped rooms. The ground level one was lined with jars and hung with pungent leaves as Dovinna's had been. In the dappled light from gaps in the ceiling and reflected with mirrors, a Kabonni girl was studiously measuring various powders into a bowl. She broke off at their entrance.

"My new apprentice. Make us some brew, dear, then you can go 'til morning."

The serious apprentice handed them bowls of a bitter-sweet drink. Dovinna watched her closely. Ro stroked the rough wooden walls. She had not felt so welcome nor so safe since leaving home. She could appreciate why Dovinna would regard her teacher's home as a sanctuary. Seated on a root with her back leaning against the wall, Ro closed her eyes and let the voices of Lar and Dovinna lull her as they explained their predicament. The words blurred and lost meaning becoming a flowing ripple which suddenly stopped. Ro opened her eyes and found everyone watching her.

Varda gestured for her to come close. The elderly healer grasped Ro's head firmly with both hands and drew it level with hers. No sooner had Ro recovered her balance, than she was released and Varda grasped her again, front and back, level with her heart. Bewildered Ro looked at Lar for an answer, but the healer snatched up her hands and placed them against Ro's temples.

"Well?" Ussu demanded as Varda released Ro once more and sat back wearily.

"So impatient for one who believes in the rhythm of all things," said Varda drily. "Now, what I have to say, you will not want to hear, but listen you must and pay heed you must. There is nothing I can do to cure Lalli or Ro because there is nothing wrong with them."

Ussu's mouth opened but she found no words. Raimi held her hand. Lar and Dovinna were motionless.

Ro filled the space. "I don't understand. Lalli doesn't hear vibrations and I can't feel them, how can you say nothing's wrong?"

"Because you are as you're meant to be–and not much is according to the tales you bring me. Seasons out of time, the changing course of the elements, suspicion and treachery in the city. It all smacks of the worm."

"The worm? What has Lethir to do with us?" Ro's disappointment welled up to choke her.

"Patience, Ro." It was Lar's subdued voice.

Varda nodded. "It's impatience which has brought things to this state–Ondd is sleeping and it shouldn't be, all isn't ready, and the worm, Lethir, is taking advantage."

Dovinna frowned. "But what has this to do with Lalli and Ro?"

Varda looked expectantly at Lar and then at each of them in turn. "Well? Don't you listen to the words of your songs any more, or do you think they're just pretty tunes?"

Ussu stiffened indignantly, but Lar considered. "The song of Ondd's scales." She half-closed her eyes and began the familiar refrain. "Once there was one of us who was not one of us who played on Ondd's scales a tune that was not a tune and while the worm wept the whole world sat up and sang... "

"So you're saying Lalli is the 'one who is not one' because she can't hear," Raimi said.

Varda shook her head. "I'm saying the 'one who is not one' is two."

They all turned to look at Ro and she felt her ears turn red.

"I'm saying," Varda continued. "That Ro and Lalli have to be deaf in their own ways, and that they will be the ones to wake Ondd and restore the balance."

"But Lalli's only a baby!" Ussu protested.

"As I said, these things are happening out of cycle. Nevertheless, it lies with these two to set things right."

"And then we'll be cured?" Ro tried to hold some comfort as her world flew to pieces around her.

"What would you call a cure, Ro?" Varda looked intently at her and Ro suddenly felt unsure of the answer.

"To be as other Iyessi are."

"But then you wouldn't be Ro. Are you seeking to lose yourself or find yourself?"

Ro turned away and leaned her cheek against the wall. The rough trunk was comfortingly real and stable.

"I'm not convinced." Ussu's voice had a hysterical sharpness. "You're not the only healer, we should take Lalli to the Sud-Iyessi at the Singing Lake, as I said we should all along. They might have strengths we don't even know of."

"And they might throw us out like our neighbours did," Raimi reminded her.

"It's worth a try," she appealed to Lar.

The Earth-hearer shook her head. "So far all my decisions have taken us into greater danger."

"Danger can't be avoided," Varda said.

"What does Ro think?" Dovinna asked gently.

Ro turned to face them again. "We can't stay here, can we?" She looked hopefully at Varda's noncommittal face. "No, eventually the soldiers will find us here and there's Bissig and Wey–no, we have to leave, and we have to clear Dovinna's name. What would you do?"

Varda shrugged. "You must follow the path that seems right to you. As for Dovinna–head for Amradoc. Ortanian soldiers can't cross the borders without risking war. You should find safety there until you can prove your innocence."

Dovinna squeezed her teacher's hand.

"Then we should go with her," Ro said. "Varda says 'be patient' and I think it would be worth the delay in getting to the Singing Lake if we can find a way to clear ourselves of poisoning King Berinn. Then we can travel without fear."

Dovinna grinned. "But what about Ondd?"

"What about it? If Varda's right and Lalli and I are going to wake it, or whatever we're supposed to do, it will happen whatever choice I make."

Ussu made a noise of derision. "You seriously expect us to believe that my sister, who causes chaos wherever she goes and has done ever since she was born, will be the one to restore harmony?" Ussu's sarcasm produced an awkward silence. No one except Varda could meet Ro's eyes. "I still say we should go to the Singing Lake. At least we'd be with our own kind. What have all these intrigues and myths to do with us?"

"No one can avoid the calamity that will happen if Ondd's not roused–no matter how far you may run, Ussu!" Varda scolded. "You think Najarind's troubles are the source of the evil? They're nothing compared to the devastation to come if you turn your backs."

"But why go to Amradoc? We'd be in no danger if we weren't with Dovinna." Ussu stuck out her chin. Ro knew the look of old. It would be difficult to shift her.

"But they're looking for us," Ro objected.

Ussu looked away.

Raimi spoke. "I'm sorry, Ro. We have to put Lalli's safety first."

"You're right, we're both putting you at risk. Dovinna and I'll go on to Amradoc alone." Despite her words she looked hopefully at Lar.

Her mother shook her head. "You're both my children; how can I choose between you?"

"Time enough for that tomorrow," Varda said. "We have the matter of Wey's compensation to consider first."

Raimi spoke without hesitation. "We could help Wey rebuild in harmony with the elements."

"Or teach her songs to balance," Lar offered.

Dovinna shook her head. "Bissig will want something with material value that he can brag about." Throughout the discussion she had been twisting the ring on her finger. Now she slipped it off and placed it in Varda's lap. "This should do."

Raimi and Ro both erupted in protestations, but Varda nodded and clasped Dovinna's hands between her own.

"Hurry! Hurry!" Wey hissed at Fordel, gesturing with arms like dead branches tossed by the wind.

Fordel took a deep breath before answering. "How do you expect us to hurry and be quiet at the same time? Especially as you won't let us cut this mess out of the way." He detached a bramble from his tunic.

The journey was turning into a nightmare. The Kabonni woman knew where she was heading well enough, but the way she muttered and groaned made Fordel doubt it was where they wanted to be. She might look decrepit, but the tired soldiers with their clumsy gear found it hard to keep up with her, and in the poor light of covered lamps they were in constant danger of losing their guide. Now, at Fordel's mention of cutting the undergrowth a look of alarm came into Wey's eyes.

"No, no, you mustn't." She glanced about her as if expecting devils to seize her and carry her off.

"Then we must go more slowly. My men are in need of rest." And, he added to himself, I won't let them be rushed headlong into what may prove to be a trap.

Fordel's unease grew the further they went. Their guide seemed more afraid of the forest than of them, odd enough in itself, but Fordel caught occasional words in her constant mumbling: "Ruined! My baby!" Perhaps this raddled old pile of twigs had once lost a child and her wits along with it.

A lieutenant pushed his way through the file of soldiers. "Lord Fordel, if we carry on at this rate we won't be fit to fight when we get there."

"You fear a handful of women with a baby will cause us problems?"

The lieutenant's eyes slid uneasily to the dark forest. "Who knows what help they may have?"

"All right, half an hour, no more." He dismissed Wey's protests. His men sank gratefully to the floor and broke out some rations. Despite their aching legs there was not one who was not eager to move on once more when Fordel gave the command. The forest watched them too closely.

"It's time to decide. You should be ready to leave as soon as Wey and Bissig have been. There's something going on and I don't like it," Varda warned.

Lar nodded. "I can feel–unease–more than we caused, and it's growing."

The others looked expectantly at Lar, who turned away. Ussu made to speak, but Varda intervened.

"This is a decision Lar should make on her own–if it's not yet made."

Lar turned to Ussu. "You're determined to go directly to the Singing Lake?" Ussu nodded. "This choosing splits my heart. If my daughters must go separate ways, then I must go with the one who is alone. Ussu you have Raimi and your affinities with the elements to protect and guide you."

Ussu pouted. "Ro wouldn't go to Amradoc if you came with us."

Lar shook her head.

"What's this, what's this?" It was Bissig. Absorbed in their troubles they had not heard him approach. "Talk of leaving when my compensation's yet to be settled?"

"Your aunt's compensation, Bissig, not yours–and although it is yet two hours before noon you might as well know that this is offered in compensation." Varda held Dovinna's ring out for him to see while keeping a firm grip on it. "That should be enough compensation to build the snug dwelling within the clan compound your aunt needs." Bissig reached for the ring. "Where is Wey?"

"I couldn't find her. I thought she might be here."

"Unlike you to be so concerned," Varda observed.

Bissig retreated outside into the clearing. "Just because I don't fuss around her!" They followed him out. "Independent, Auntie Wey is, she wouldn't thank me for it. Where can she be then?" He frowned.

"Where might she be, Bissig?" Varda's tone demanded the truth.

He blustered. "Well, you know Auntie's not as sharp as she once was–tends to wander a bit these days... "

"And?"

"And there's wreckers in the forest," he said in a rush. "What are two sets of wreckers doing in Kabonn within days of each other, that's what I'd like to know?"

But Varda was no longer listening. "Tsh!" She silenced him as there was a crackle of dry twigs. "Wreckers indeed, and you brought them straight to us! What did they promise you, hm?"

"Not me," Bissig declared as Fordel's soldiers burst into the clearing around Varda's tree.

Fordel strode up to Varda with Wey at his elbow. "Madam Varda, my apologies for disrupting your home, but I have orders to take Dovinna and her companions back to Najarind to be tried for the murder of King Berinn."

"Now, Fordel, I've known you since you were a babe in napkins and I know you're not such a fool as to believe Dovinna would do such a thing."

His men smirked at Varda's scolding.

"The charge has been made and must be answered."

"And as for you, Wey!" The old Kabonni hid from Varda's anger behind Fordel's sleeve. The Lord signalled his men to secure the fugitives.

Wey started to screech. "The baby, I must have the baby. You promised!"

"I certainly did not." Fordel shook her off.

"Auntie, what have you done? They offered us an adamant ring and you throw it away for a brat!" Bissig shook his aunt sending her spinning into the soldiers. Fordel was caught between protecting her and fending her off.

"You promised to give me what I asked for!"

"If you want the child you'll have to come to Najarind with us first."

Wey launched herself at him and Fordel pushed her roughly.

"You leave my auntie alone!"

Bissig barrelled into Fordel's stomach with his bullet head. Soldiers rushed to their commander's aid and Bissig's clansmen joined in. Suddenly the fugitives were dodging flailing arms and charging headbutts.

"Quick!" Varda signalled her apprentice to lead the fugitives into the forest's embrace. Dovinna hesitated.

"I'll be all right–go!" Varda reached up to give her a snatched hug and watched as they vanished into the tangle of brambles and branches. As they fled, the teacher's voice reached them, ostensibly refereeing the fight.

"Bissig, would you have the whole army down on us? Wey stop pulling Lord Fordel's hair." Somehow, the more she helped the soldiers the more ensnared in roots and burrs they became.

From under the heaving pile of bodies Fordel roared in fury. "Secure the prisoners, you idiots! Get off me!"

He stood up panting and bruised. His soldiers and the Kabonni faced each other as if all it would take to start the violence again would be one sneer. He glared at his men.

"You're meant to be an elite fighting force, not clowns." He turned to the Kabonni. "I shall hold your leaders here until you bring me news of the fugitives. Go!"

Bissig's clansmen melted into the forest.

The lieutenant stood to attention. "Don't you want us to go after the prisoners, Sir?"

"There'd be no point in trying, would there?" Fordel asked Varda.

She folded her hands in front of her. "You'd better let me take care of your men's wounds since it appears we're all going to be here for some time."

As if by magic, Varda's apprentice appeared from behind the tree. She gave Varda a nod that could pass for a bow.

"Make us all some brew, there's a dear."

While attending to a long scratch running down Bissig's cheek–a scratch which looked suspiciously as if it could have been made by Wey's fingernails–Varda again showed him Dovinna's ring on the finger where she had slipped it during the fight.

"You still want this?"

He nodded.

"But your aunt's actions have forfeited compensation."

He groaned.

"It can still be yours if you help me get rid of these wreckers."

Bissig looked at her with a greedy glint in his eye.

Deep in the forest the fugitives ate a frugal meal in the smoky interior of a Kabonni hut. Varda's apprentice had left them with her father after a hurried explanation. He and her two brothers now waited impatiently for the fugitives to follow them once more.

"It's time. My girl worships Varda, but I'll not put her at more risk than I need. You must say your good-byes."

Ussu's eyes filled with tears.

Lar clasped her close. "Feel my love for you now, as no words can tell you. May Ondd and all the elements protect you."

Raimi and Lalli each received hugs too. "Ondd protect."

Then Ussu stepped in front of Ro. She struggled for a moment trying to find words, then clasped her in her arms. "I only wish you could feel how much I'll miss you. Join us soon."

All Ro could do was nod, and then the apprentice's brothers spirited Ussu, Lalli and Raimi off down one of the forest's labyrinthine paths. Ro only had time to attempt a smile to reassure Dovinna and it was their turn. There was no need for their guide to enjoin silence. Their hearts were too full for speech. Their route twisted and turned until Ro had no more idea of their direction than of how long they had been walking. When the forest began to get lighter, she thought at first it must be the dawn. Then she noticed that the canopy was thinning and there were gaps in the knotted growth. Their guide pressed on until they reached a band of trees with nothing beyond except grassy slopes. They breathed deep of the air, enjoying the feel of the breeze.

When Varda was apparently asleep, Bissig shook Fordel awake. He put his finger to his lips and jerked his head for the Lord to follow him outside.

"Look, I'm no lover of those strangers, all I want is my compensation."

Fordel waited for him to continue.

"You promise me that when you catch them, you'll make them pay and I'll help you find them." Bissig toyed with the ring in his pocket. He was no lover of soldiers either.

Fordel regarded him coolly. "I suppose you're going to lead us here, there and everywhere then say you've lost them."

Bissig put on an innocent look.

"Very well, I'll tell the men we're moving out."

As they followed the blustering Kabonni, Fordel wondered who was fooling who. He called over his lieutenant. "Keep a watch on him, we don't want to be stranded in the middle of nowhere."

Bissig led them into the embrace of the forest. More importunate than a spurned lover, it grasped at shoulders and ankles, tugged hair and trailed long scratches over exposed flesh. Yet there was no sign of their prey. They stopped for a meal break. Fordel chewed over how long he should play this game along with his food. There was a sudden outbreak of curses, and the lieutenant marched Bissig over, flanked by two men.

"Found him with this, Sir." He handed a small hard object to Fordel that sparkled and blazed even in the dim forest. Fordel recognised Dovinna's ring.

"So, they paid you to keep us busy while they escape. Do you know what Ortanians do to traitors?"

Bissig's curses died.

"Now, you're going to take us out of this forest, without any more tricks–or we'll give you a demonstration." Fordel pocketed the ring. The search was up to Pachand's patrol now.

# Chapter Six

Four riders passed through Najarind's main gate and set off two
abreast on the road to the Abbey of the Patriarch. The two behind
kept a respectful distance between them and their masters. The
autumn sunshine flashed off the jewels in Princess Ersilla's hair
and the buckles fastening Torslin's cloak. Ersilla's chatter rose on
the air like an alarmed bird's.

"Thank goodness we're free of that stuffy palace! If I'd had to
endure my darling brother's moping or Anni's fussing one more
minute, I'd have shrieked until the ceiling fell in."

Torslin cast a warning look in the direction of the servants.

"Don't worry. They know too well what happens to
chatterboxes." She kicked her horse into a canter, cutting off
Torslin's rebuke.

When they arrived at the abbey, only Ersilla's heightened
colour and quickened breathing indicated that their visit was
anything other than a sad necessity. The Patriarch of Ondd greeted
them with sober dignity as they dismounted.

"Princess, Lord Torslin, welcome to this place of study and
prayer to the greater glory of Ondd. May its breath heal and its
wings protect you."

He guided them along stone-paved corridors. The simplicity
of the Patriarch's garb was deceptive. He bore no adornment, but
the cloth was finely woven and cut, and his beard and nails were
carefully groomed. His apartments were furnished with the same
refined simplicity. A junior priest finished laying a table with
refreshments and bowed himself out as the distinguished guests
seated themselves.

"You honour me with your visit, Princess, especially at such a
sad time. I'm sure you are a great comfort to your brother, King
Channan."

"I doubt it." Ersilla took a delicate bite from one of the
proffered sweetmeats.

The Patriarch looked taken aback. "I assure you that all the arrangements for your beloved father's funeral are in hand. Perhaps after you have seen them, it might amuse you to be shown around the abbey. Our wall paintings are said to be... "

"What would amuse me, Patriarch, is to be shown your little project."

"Princess?" The Patriarch glanced at Torslin for guidance.

"There's no need to be coy. Torslin's told me all about your little experiment. I want to see it!" Her last words could have cut glass.

Torslin nodded, his expression wary.

"Well, if you are sure, Princess, but it's not a sight for those with delicate sensibilities."

"I am sure, Patriarch, and I'm also sure I don't need to remind you that I am my father's daughter and quite equal to anything that I choose to undertake."

The Patriarch bowed and led them out. They left the stone cloisters and crossed the vegetable garden and orchard where a few late bees still hummed around the fading leaves. Beyond was a stubby tower that looked little more than an untidy heap of rubble. The Patriarch produced an elaborate key from the folds of his robe, and fitted it in the rusting lock. It turned with a well-oiled click.

"The acolytes believe I study the stars here to determine the moods of Ondd–and so I do, but there is also this." The Patriarch ushered them through a small study littered with scrolls and charts. He took out another key and opened the door to a long low chamber lined with cages.

Ersilla hastily snatched a handkerchief to her nose. "Faugh! Don't you clean them out?"

"Oh yes, Princess, and I study what they produce. The droppings are quite toxic."

The Patriarch's elegant features showed no offence either at the stench or the repulsive sight of the occupants of the cages. Heaving masses of grub-like lizards whose spindly legs and transparent wings supported semi-opaque bodies, rippled and pulsed as they digested the rotting meat they lay on. Ersilla was drawn closer.

"I wouldn't get too near, Princess. They eat anything, even certain metals, as I discovered only just in time to avert disaster.

Their appetites are voracious–if they run out of other food they'll turn on each other."

"They're quite revolting," Ersilla breathed, her eyes fixed on the cages. "But surely, no matter how greedy, such small creatures can do little harm unless we have them in great numbers."

"And we shall have them in great numbers before long–they produce another generation every ten days–but these are not fully grown. If you would care to look at the end cages–but do stand further back," the Patriarch called a warning as Ersilla swept past.

"Oh my, these are as long as my arm!" Her eyes shone.

"They're not fully grown yet," the Patriarch called, then hissed at Torslin. "Was this wise?"

The lord shrugged. "She insisted. It was safer to bring her than leave her."

"Forgive me, Torslin, I know she's your protégée, but she appears... unstable."

"She's more than that, but we need her. I can't just take over the country. The people are still loyal to the royal house. Once they're plagued with your fal-worms, and Channan's occupied fighting Amradoc it'll be a different matter. Then we shall have the power and Najarind will head a great empire once more."

"And the people will return to Ondd. We wouldn't have all these troubles if people would believe as they ought."

"Quite so, and you'll command the respect you crave."

The Patriarch stiffened.

Torslin cut off his objection. "Let us be clear, we may cite Najarind's greatness or Ondd's deserts, but we both have much to gain."

"No, Princess!" The Patriarch's alarm spun Torslin round to see Ersilla hastily snatching her finger from the bars of the cage.

"Did it bite you?" The Patriarch hurried over, grabbing Ersilla's hand as if he expected to see half of it missing.

"I was too quick for it." She smiled. "You know, they have a certain charm. Perhaps I should keep one as a pet." The look of horror on the Patriarch's face sent her into uninhibited giggles. She recovered her composure slowly. "When shall we use them?"

"Not yet, Princess. I'm still cross-breeding to increase their flight and size, and I have yet to develop a means to control them. At present they'll settle on anything warm or moving and will only leave when the food supply's exhausted."

Torslin nodded, but Ersilla's face darkened. "A pity, I'd like to see them in action."

"These are only planned as a last resort, Princess. Let's hope we won't have to use them."

"Aye, let's hope," Torslin agreed, but with less conviction.

"Ah, well." Ersilla brushed dirt off her hands. "I've seen enough." She looked pointedly at Torslin and walked out.

The Patriarch's gaze followed her. "I hope we won't regret this."

Torslin put a hand on his shoulder. "Don't worry. Should she ever prove a greater danger than an asset, what served for her father can serve for her too."

They followed the Princess out. In the end cage the fal-worm stopped eating and tremors began to pass through the gross body. Moments later, the base of the abdomen split like the skin of an overripe plum and a glistening egg plopped to the floor. It was followed by another and another until they formed a sticky heap. The parent shuddered and sagged to the floor.

Raimi tried to untangle the disparate strands of vibrations as he peered over the lip of the hollow towards the road. Even the flow of energy from Ussu sheltering behind him was confused. Only the rhythm of Lalli flowed contented. Their journey since parting from the others two days before had been largely silent, except for the unvoiced clamour which made them stumble. No words were needed: both doubted their choice as much as their route and missed the reassuring presence of the others. When they had felt the approach of a patrol trotting briskly back towards Najarind they had moved in unison and placed the protective bulk of some tumbled boulders between them and the soldiers. When the last ripples of their passage had faded, Ussu had stood up and shook herself.

"They were looking for Ro." The certainty in her voice had not convinced Raimi. "I hope they're safe."

Now they were in hiding again. On the road before them a long file of dejected mules bearing heavy loads was passing. At its head were half a dozen riders and behind were two wagons. One of these was richly painted with a wavy-line design reminiscent of the Iyessi house paintings.

"What do you feel?" Ussu whispered.

Raimi shrugged. "I suppose we'll have to reason it out the way Ro has to."

Ussu blushed as if accused.

Raimi continued. "They're heading in the right direction and that wagon looks as if it could be Sud-Iyessi. On the other hand the patrol must have stopped them. They'll know the king's men are searching for us."

"But they're not, they're looking for the others–and if they were looking for us, what better place to hide than somewhere the patrol has already searched?"

"But... "

"Besides, look how contented Lalli is. If Ro and Varda are right, surely she'd be uneasy."

"As we are?" Raimi asked drily.

"We wouldn't have to walk all the way."

Raimi looked at Ussu's hopeful face. There were dark smudges around her eyes. "Come on, then."

He helped her out of the hollow. At their approach one of the wagon drivers whistled and two riders peeled off from the head of the train to meet them. One was as sleek and well fed as his horse, and as richly attired. He scrutinised his bejewelled fingers as his far plainer companion addressed them.

"Ho there, strangers–where did you spring from?" His voice was harsh and flat.

Raimi and Ussu saluted him formally with fingertips to lips.

Raimi answered. "We were resting when we heard your train approach. Forgive our caution, but not all travellers are honest."

The plain rider grinned at his companion. "Why should we trust you? You could be decoys for a gang of bandits."

"Preposterous!" Ussu blurted. "As if you could have anything that we want!"

Raimi sighed, but the rich rider laughed. "Well, you want something, otherwise why are you here?"

"We're heading in the same direction. Safer for both if we travel together."

"And while your wife and babe rest on one of the wagons, you'd get a rest from her tongue, eh?"

Ussu drew herself up and pursed her lips.

"What do we get out of it?"

"We have our own supplies," Ussu said coldly.

"No need for that. We'd find your presence at supper—entertaining." He turned to his companion. "Tell Jassi to let them ride with her on our wagon, Tolar."

"Yes, Othar." He rode off and Othar gestured for the Iyessi to follow.

By the time they had caught up with the ornate wagon, their host was back at the head of the train. The driver of the wagon was a girl who could be little older than Ro.

"Sit in the back and don't touch anything." She flicked her hand making her bracelets jangle.

Tolar laughed irreverently and she shouted a curse after him as he rode to rejoin Othar. "Pig! I'll have Othar put you on the midnight watch!"

He laughed all the louder. As Jassi turned her scowl on them Raimi and Ussu took Lalli to the rear of the wagon. The baby began to grizzle as it jolted forward.

"Keep the brat quiet, can't you?" Jassi shook the reins making the horses pick up their pace.

Ussu gave her a sour look in return and began crooning to Lalli. But Lalli would not be appeased. Ussu's voice grew sharper and her gentle rocking jogged as much as the horse's gait.

Raimi reached out. "You're too tired."

Ussu handed the child over. Lalli's face grew redder and her wailing louder.

"For pity's sake!" Jassi turned. "Don't either of you know anything about babies? Here, take the reins." She thrust them towards Raimi and took Lalli from him.

The baby gazed at her glinting jewellery. Within minutes she was dozing again.

Jassi caught Ussu's look. "I'm the eldest of ten children. You have to be calm yet firm. They always sense when they can play you up, even when they're this small."

"Sense?" Ussu looked sharply at her.

"What?"

Ussu shook her head. "Nothing. Thank you."

The girl watched her calmly as Ussu settled further back into the soft embrace of her seat and allowed the rhythm of the horses to lull her. Her gaze settled on the now contented baby.

"So, what are you doing in the middle of nowhere with this little one?" Jassi asked.

"Visiting our kin in the south," Ussu yawned.

"You're not very well provisioned for a long journey," Jassi pointed out.

Ussu shrugged as if too weary for talk.

"Othar would never travel without all the comforts of home," Jassi continued, surveying her jingling bracelets with a look of satisfaction.

"Does he count you among those?" The question was out before Ussu could stop it, but Jassi neither reacted to the sharpness in her voice nor the implied slur. She gave Ussu a superior smile.

"He calls me his little homemaker. I can have whatever I like–the finest cloth from Najarind, painted furniture from Sud-Iyessa, perfumes and lotions from Gindul... " She counted them off on her fingers.

"You're not from Sud-Iyessa then?" Ussu asked, stifling another yawn.

Jassi blushed. "Not any more. Life there was cooking meals, washing napkins, wiping snotty noses, and what would I have got if I'd married? More of the same. But now..."

"Now you cook meals and wash clothes for Othar instead," Ussu sniped. "Perhaps I should take Lalli from you. I wouldn't want you to risk soiling your nice clothes."

"No." Jassi put a possessive arm around the baby. "Besides, she's asleep."

Ussu allowed her eyes to close, and for a while heard nothing but Raimi singing softly to the horses with the rattling of the wagon for accompaniment.

At the head of the train Othar looked pleased with himself, despite Tolar's grumbling.

"What did you take them on for? They don't look as if they've ever seen a coin let alone have enough of them to pay for the ride."

Othar winked. "Oh? They look like pure gold to me." He rubbed his thumb and forefinger together. "Najarind gold. Tell me, Tolar, how many Iyessi have you seen on this road?"

"Lately?"

"Ever."

The plain rider considered. "Come to think of it, none."

"Exactly! Now, here's what I want you to do... "

Minutes later, Tolar trotted away from the road on a fresh horse and waited in the cover of a copse for the mule train to pass. When the last wagon was well ahead, he trotted into the open again, then kicked the horse into a gallop back down the road they had just travelled.

The sound of unfamiliar voices woke her. Ussu opened her eyes and stretched, enjoying the feel of velvet against her skin and the luxury of soft cushions. Then she remembered where she was and jerked upright.

"Lalli!" The wagon was stationary and there was no sign of either Raimi or Jassi with her baby. The light had faded, blurring the edges of the furnishings. Jassi's face appeared around the back of the wagon.

"Relax, I've got the child. Your man's tending the horses. He said to wake you, but I saw no point."

Ussu rose. "Can I help with anything?"

Jassi shook her head. "The men know what to do."

The pair stood together for a while watching the muleteers erecting a gaudy communal tent and setting up a temporary oven, using the contents of the other wagon.

"You'll sleep in there tonight." Jassi nodded at it. "It's not as nice as Othar's and mine, but you should be comfortable enough– not like that, fool!"

One of the men had upended a box of utensils. Jassi dumped Lalli in Ussu's arms and stormed over to him. Ussu wandered in the direction of the tethered horses. She found Raimi running his hands appreciatively over one of the mules.

"I might have known you'd be fussing over the animals."

Raimi started.

Ussu lowered her voice. "What are you up to?"

The protective oilcloth on the pack nearest the mule was pulled aside.

"Raimi!" Ussu hitched Lalli onto her hip and hurriedly covered the pack again. "Are you trying to get us thrown out?"

"That might not be such a bad idea. I don't trust these people."

"The girl's all right. A bit full of herself, but basically decent."

Raimi nodded. "I grant you, but from what I heard the other drivers saying, she's not been with Othar long. Apparently, he trades his women for a new one every couple of journeys or so, and he always makes sure he profits..."

Ussu looked over at the young mistress of the camp and shook her head.

Raimi continued. "I haven't seen his second-in-command since we stopped."

"Perhaps he's been sent ahead to make arrangements."

"Or perhaps he's been sent back to see if there's profit to be had from us."

Ussu rested her head against the mule. "So what are our choices? Stay and try to convince the Najarind soldiers we aren't the ones they seek, or slip away and have the caravan searching for us too?"

"Or make it more profitable for Othar not to trade us to the Najarindians."

Ussu laughed; a loud emphatic 'hah!' without mirth.

"I thought maybe if there was something in the packs that Othar shouldn't have–contraband stimulants or rare plants perhaps–we could persuade him that silence would be best for all."

Ussu's eyes narrowed. "I never appreciated before how devious you are. There was no sign of this in Iyessa."

"In Iyessa everyone can hear a lie shouting at them, however innocent your face. Out here it's different." He began to unwrap what he could of the packs. There were perfumes and silks, spices and curios.

"Anything?"

The slump of Raimi's shoulders was answer enough.

"We'll have to think of something else, then. Lalli wants feeding." Ussu turned back to the bustle of the camp. A split second later an angry wail confirmed her judgement.

The evening meal was spent in luxurious discomfort. Othar called for his guests to sit near him and plied them with delicacies and wine while questioning them about their journey and their home.

"I've never been to Iyessa. Perhaps I've been missing an opportunity. Tell me, do you think this wine would go down well there? It's from the high vineyards of western Amradoc." He poured a goblet for Raimi, but Ussu swiftly put her hand over hers.

"Forgive me, but while I feed the baby, I can't drink fermented juice." Her heart hammered fit to shake the tent walls. Courtesy did not allow an outright refusal.

"Fermented juice." Othar stared into his goblet. "I think I've just gone off it." He smiled at Ussu with wolves' teeth.

Seated beside him, Jassi leaned over and whispered in Othar's ear. He shrugged and turned his smile back on Ussu.

"Jassi has a fancy to hear some music after dinner. Iyessi are supposed to be good at that, aren't they?"

"Our instruments are in our packs." Raimi made to rise, but Othar gestured him back into his seat. "My men'll fetch them." Still the smile. It vanished as he gave a brusque nod to one of the men who leapt to obey. A moment later he returned, and the Iyessi were forced to open their gear in front of Othar's acquisitive gaze.

"Amazing! You carry barely enough to make life comfortable, and yet you lug these awkward things with you." He flicked the skin of Raimi's hand drum, which responded with a resonant thrum. Ussu stiffened, as for a moment Othar's and Raimi's eyes locked.

Jassi broke the tension. "Can you play a dance? Something wild and lively." Her face shone.

"Like you, my dear." Othar was all indulgence.

Without conferring, Ussu picked up her flute and the Iyessi began a tune of celebration. The men joined in clapping and even Othar tapped the table with one finger following the rhythm. Ussu's fingers kept wanting to pull into another tune and their rhythm's were a blade of grass's width apart. The music was not helped by Lalli's fractiousness or the way Othar's gaze kept sliding towards the tent flap. Even Jassi noticed it and followed his look with a frown. The tune ended and the Iyessi acknowledged the cheers of the men. Jassi's frown cleared.

"Where's Tolar?" she demanded.

Othar continued to applaud. "Oh, I sent him on an errand. Perhaps our guests will play again, and you can dance."

"As you wish."

The Iyessi launched into another lively melody, but now as well as Othar's gaze, Jassi's and theirs turned repeatedly towards the entrance. Finally, Othar rejected the men's cries for more.

"Enough! We start out early tomorrow." With that he dismissed them all.

As Raimi and Ussu clambered into the baggage wagon they heard Jassi's voice.

"Why won't you tell me? I'm supposed to be your woman, we should share everything."

There was the sharp clap of flesh on flesh. "Share that then! I won't be bothered by a whining woman!"

90

Raimi quietly drew up the tailgate. "If there should be trouble, Ussu, I tethered a couple of horses on the edge of the camp. Take Lalli and one of them and go. Don't wait to see what happens."

Ussu opened her mouth to protest, but subsided. She gripped Raimi's hand. "Only a little longer. Once we reach Sud-Iyessa we'll be safe."

Even to someone without Iyessi sensibilities the words would have sounded empty. Raimi kept watch while Ussu slept. By the time he woke her the sky had paled enough to show blooms of heavy clouds whipping across the sky. He answered her questioning look.

"Nothing. No one came into camp, no one went out."

"Perhaps you were mistaken."

"Perhaps, but if Othar was keen to make an early start where is he?"

Ussu joined him at the front of the wagon. The men were shambling about their chores, yawning and talking in murmurs. There was a meagre cooking fire where a kettle hissed, its steam mingling with the men's breath in the morning chill. Anything less inclined to move in a hurry would be hard to imagine. The Iyessi had washed and breakfasted off their supplies before the leader of the mule train emerged from his ornate wagon. The men immediately straightened their shoulders and picked up their pace: his expression was darker than the clouds. Jassi emerged from the rear of his wagon and approached Raimi and Ussu.

"They'll be wanting to pack everything in here. You'd better come to our wagon." Her speech was hampered by a blotchy red swollen cheek. She dropped her eyes unable to meet their unspoken disapproval. "I have a toothache, perhaps you could sing something to soothe it," she said.

Ussu reached out and matched her fingertips to the red blotches. Jassi snatched her face away and turned abruptly back to the ornate wagon. The Iyessi followed. Like Jassi, they had no desire to bring themselves to Othar's attention. They set out once more with Jassi at the reins, occasionally aiming slaps and muttered curses at the horses. Raimi caught up on some sleep and Ussu struggled to amuse Lalli until the midday break. They lunched off what was left of their provisions, preferring to remain in the wagon. Othar's voice could be heard bellowing orders and demanding Jassi's presence.

When she returned and took up the reins again, Jassi was more subdued than ever. Raimi rose.

"See what you can find out," he whispered, then went forward and offered to drive.

Jassi looked inclined to resist, but shrugged and joined Ussu. She eased herself onto the cushions, arranging one carefully under her cheek. Each jolt of the horses made her wince.

"That toothache seems to have spread," Ussu observed.

Jassi ignored her.

"I wouldn't put up with it."

Jassi cast her a thundery look.

"Toothache can drive you mad," Ussu added.

"So can people who talk too much," Jassi complained.

"Is that why he did it?" Silence. "Come on, Jassi, I may have led a sheltered life by your standards, but I'm no fool."

Jassi sat up. "Is that so? Then how come you walked right into Othar's greedy hands? You could have stayed clear. Now... "

"What about now?" Ussu's heart set up a beat as if mice were scurrying in panic at the scent of a cat.

Jassi shook her head and winced. "I don't know, he wouldn't tell me—but he will, and whatever he's up to, he'll regret being unkind to me, you may be sure." As she spoke Jassi's cheek burned flame red, but no brighter than the angry fire in her eyes.

Despite the jagged vibrations of anxiety and anger, Lalli slept on calmly. It was only after Ussu had fed her that evening and they were seated again by Othar in the communal tent, that the baby's serenity was replaced by inconsolable sobs.

Ussu apologised. "I'm sorry, perhaps I'd better take her back to the wagon."

"No, I'll take her." Jassi held out her hands, glaring at Ussu to comply.

Instead of quieting, Lalli screamed all the louder as Jassi carried her out. As the tent flap closed behind them, Ussu could just make out voices above the din. The tent flap was swept aside and Tolar entered, made plainer than ever by a heavy coating of road dust. As he let go of the canvas a gauntleted hand caught it. The mailed figures of two Najarindian patrolmen followed him. Captain Pachand's gaze brushed over Othar and fixed on Raimi and Ussu.

# Chapter Seven

Lar gasped and clutched a hand to her heart.

"What is it?" Ro supported her, but Lar straightened and waved her away.

Ever since they had begun travelling along the wasted remains of the river, Lar had looked ill. They were following the former watercourse, which Dovinna said had once been full of lazily flowing water fringed with willows and so clear that it was possible to see the fish hanging buoyed by the current. That was before Channan's father had been persuaded to divert it. Now the river was channelled to irrigate the fertile lowlands of central Ortann, tamed and lifeless.

"Just one of the reasons why there's no love lost between Ortann and Amradoc," Dovinna had explained as they had half slid, half jumped down the steep bank. "The river used to flow broad and unfailing into Amradoc. Now that country's been left barren, with poor soil and skinny flocks where there were once lush meadows."

At Lar's cry Dovinna turned back, touching her fingers to the Earth-hearer's forehead to test her temperature.

Lar drew back. "I'm not ill."

"But something's troubling you," Ro persisted. A real Iyessi would have felt whatever was amiss without the need to ask. Images of Ussu, Raimi and Lalli flitted across her thoughts, and she clenched her fist against the guilt that tormented her with each step further from her sister's family.

"Yes, Ro," Lar explained wearily. "This troubles me." She waved a hand encompassing the compacted earth, jumbled rocks and bleached roots of dead trees which surrounded them. Occasional green scummed pools in the shade of the banks gave off a smell of slimy decay and attracted buzzing clouds of insects.

"All this unnatural destruction," Lar continued. "The earth remembers this place as it should be, and the silence of it is an ache."

Ro bowed her head, but Dovinna looked resolute. "I'm sorry, Lar, I had no idea this route would cause you pain, but I see no other way of reaching Amradoc without being caught by... " she hesitated. "The king's men."

"I know," Lar managed a smile. "We should continue. The sooner we move on, the sooner I can leave this poor place behind."

Dovinna led the way and the others followed in silence. Even without the threat of discovery, the landscape discouraged talk. As they walked, a thought grew in Ro's mind so that despite all, when they made camp she had to ask Lar about it. They were huddled under the protection of a massive fallen tree, finishing a cold supper.

"Why did you cry out this afternoon?"

Lar sighed and set down her plate. Ro remembered the lessons when her mother had patiently repeated the tune of a song one more time, explaining again why the notes should flex this way or that depending on the occasion. Her patience was the reward for Ro's effort, or so Ro had thought, but maybe Lar had regarded it as a penance for her mistake in going to Najarind.

"I told you–it's this deserted land."

"But why cry out then? Something must have happened."

Dovinna was suddenly alert. "Yes, the pain must have become intense for some reason."

The Earth-hearer hesitated. "I was thinking of Ussu and Raimi and Lalli. There's a bond–a thread of barely heard music which connects parents to their children, no matter the distance. Today, I felt a surge of panic–enough to bring bile to my throat. I don't know why." Her eyes met Ro's.

"Something's happened to them," she said.

"Perhaps not. Perhaps they just thought something would."

"Maybe you should have gone with them." Ro stabbed at the cracked earth with a stick from the fallen tree.

"No, Ro. The decision's made. I can't be in two places at once no matter how much I might wish to. Get some rest."

The autumn sunset came even earlier to the overhung watercourse. They did not sing comforting songs or whisper stories into the night, but wrapped themselves in their blankets and fled into sleep.

The next morning they trudged on, much as before. The lazy winding of the old river and the uneven footing made progress slow. At intervals Dovinna clambered up to the lip of the bank to check their whereabouts with the landscape beyond. It was late afternoon when she scrambled back down from one of these surveys.

"Shouldn't be long now before we come to the tributary–perhaps tomorrow morning. It's only a trickle, but we shall have fresh water."

"Can you feel it?" Ro asked Lar.

Her mother shook her head. "Too far away perhaps."

Unless it's dried up too, Ro thought. If it was, they would be forced to rejoin the road at one of the waystations and hope no one else using it had been in Najarind lately to hear about the Iyessi and the healer who had poisoned the King. The weather changed to match Ro's gloomy mood. Dark clouds bloomed in the distance behind them, and even in the hollow of the riverbed they felt a damp wind pushing them onwards.

Lar turned her face to the clouds. "Rain."

"Perhaps we should find shelter now, before it reaches us," Dovinna suggested.

Lar headed for the bank without answering. Dovinna looked at Ro for an explanation. Ro shrugged. A faint rumbling reached them.

"Thunder?" Dovinna asked.

"No." Ro's ears were quick enough to detect the difference. "Come on."

She grabbed Dovinna's arm and they raced for the bank. Lar helped them to the top as the sound became a roar. A tumbling mass of angry water swept dead branches and stumps towards them. It hurled itself at the banks, flinging up silt-laden spray and snatching at the crumbling overhang. They drew back.

Dovinna's face was as grey as the clouds. "The river wall must have burst at the diversion. We could have been killed."

"But we weren't." Lar was matter-of-fact.

They watched the swirling water, which was rushing ahead to meet its tributary, free at last. Swept along with the flood were the remains of a cart and its load of vegetables, bobbing and twirling. There was no sign of the driver or the horse.

"Let's hope they managed to get clear as we did. This will mean hardship for many–the loss of food, the loss of land. Poor

Channan, to have to deal with this on top of everything else."
Dovinna shivered as the first hard splats of rain hit them.

Ro tried to lighten the mood. "I'll tell you what else it means:
we're going to get very wet!"

Recalled to their immediate situation, they headed for higher
ground. There was little hope of finding shelter in that dead
terrain, and they were soon soaked. Growls of thunder warned that
worse was soon to follow, and the weight of the sky pressed heavy
on their shoulders. Every few steps, Lar flinched and glanced
upwards.

"What is it?" Ro asked, expecting lightning to stab an
accusing finger at them.

"I'm not sure. Something's scared," Lar answered.

"An animal scared of the storm?" Ro suggested.

Lar called forward to Dovinna, who still led the way. "We
need to find shelter." The heightening wind snatched her words
away from her.

Dovinna nodded. "There used to be a ferryhouse further on."

Lar's wary skywatching made Ro jumpy. She found herself
casting anxious glances at purplish thunderheads.

"There it is!" Dovinna pointed to a low stone building with
gaping windows on either side of an empty doorframe like a
startled 'oh'. They increased their pace until they were splashing
through the downpour at a jog. Ro hunched her shoulders against
the sky. Tumbled stones marked what must once have been the
boundary wall of a busy compound. Ro gasped and swallowed:
one last dash.

A rush of air bore a sharp scream that buffeted her head and
scratched and fluttered around her. Ro tried to beat off the attacker,
the materialisation of the storm's anger. Her unseen assailant tore
at her hands, gripping with dagger-like talons and tangling wings
in her hair. A tail lashed stinging blows to her face and shoulders.
Through her panic, Ro became aware of other hands trying to drag
the creature away, and of Lar's voice, an incongruous pool of calm,
saying, "soft! soft!" The tail wound itself about Ro's throat. She
clutched at it, feeling faintness loosening her fingers while the tail
tightened and the claws scored her scalp. Above the commotion a
fluting whistle sounded. The beast responded with its shriek that
pained the ears. As Ro began the descent into comforting darkness
she saw tongues of flame approaching through the rain. Had the

worm come to take her to its lair? She wondered if that was why she felt no pain. Then there was black.

Colour returned slowly, and with it, feeling. The intense sting and burn of Ro's injuries clamoured above the sounds around her and she struggled to divert her attention to what was happening outside her battered body. The pressure on her throat had eased, but her head still felt the weight of the beast. She was half reclining in the mud and puddles, supported against something warm. The faces of Dovinna and Lar, one with her bottom lip caught between her teeth and the other full of steely calm, were before her, but their attention was focused on something beyond.

"Still now, Pirik." She felt the breath of the deep voice on her neck. She was leaning against the owner of it. "Soon have you free."

"Be as quick as you can," Dovinna urged as a shudder of pain passed through Ro.

"I think we'll have to cut her hair." The deep voice again.

Dovinna looked at Lar. She nodded. How about asking me? Ro thought, but without energy. She watched listlessly as Lar produced a knife from her pack and a strong, long-fingered hand reached past her shoulder to take it. The ragged hiss and tear seemed unconnected to her. Hanks of hair landed in the muddy puddles. She watched unmoved. The sight of Lar's hair plastered to her head and the rivulets of rain running down her nose to drip off the end brought the word 'undignified' into her head, but she neither felt an urge to laugh or to regret. Her whole body was being rhythmically shaken. Ro looked at her hands, they were trembling violently.

"We must get her to shelter." Dovinna held her hands and Ro felt warmth creeping up her arms.

"Done!" The hand passed the knife back to Lar.

As Dovinna and Lar hauled Ro to her feet she heard a groan and was intrigued to recognise her own voice. The world see-sawed for a few moments.

"Try to walk, Ro," Lar urged.

Between them they stumbled the last few paces to the abandoned ferryhouse. Behind them Ro heard the fluting whistle again and the flapping of wings. The ferryhouse had been stripped of everything that could be used, but it still had a reasonably waterproof roof and a serviceable fireplace. Ro felt herself gently lowered against the wall. Dovinna set about collecting the broken remains of furniture and the dead brush which had drifted through the open doorway to make a fire, while Lar undid their packs for dry blankets and clothes.

"There's no need to grip so tightly, Pirik."

Ro turned her head to try to see the owner of the deep voice. She could make out dancing flames. A fluting whistle rising to a shriek seemed to emerge from them.

"Kettle's boiling." She smiled to herself. Dovinna and Lar looked anxiously at her.

"Let me help." The owner of the deep voice moved towards Dovinna at the hearth. He was covered all in red and gold tongues of flame, and appeared to have a second head growing out of his shoulder. As he spoke he pointed at the hearth and a sphere of fiery light shot from his finger and burst the brush into life. Ro wondered why he bothered; they could simply warm themselves on him. She closed her eyes.

When she opened them again she was wrapped in a soft white sheet and Dovinna was applying a salve to her scalp. The crackle of the fire had replaced the insistent beat of rain. Lar was humming a soft melody beyond the steam of wet garments propped before the fire. In fact, steam was coming off the fire too, but that was impossible. Ro struggled to shake off the miasma of pain and see clearly. It was not a fire, but a coat of reds and oranges. The owner of the coat and, she assumed, the deep voice was sitting on the other side of the room, stroking the beast perched on his arm. The man was perhaps younger than Lar, although his hair and luxuriant moustache looked a little too black. His face was unlined, but his manner was weary.

Dovinna noticed the line of Ro's gaze. "That's Edun–or, I should say–the Incredible Edun, and the creature on his arm is an onddikin, it's what attacked you."

Ro's gaze slid to the creature. Edun's second head was a lizard-like bird or a bird-like lizard. It had scaly grey feathers starting in a ruff around its neck, along its back ridge and ending at the base of its flexible tail. A few long feathers like fingers punctuated its wings. Its glossy black skin was leathery and it had a translucent beak and claws whose delicacy belied their rending power. Its eyes swivelled independently this way and that, as if fearing that the sky would fall in one minute and that the earth would swallow it the next. Ro tried to pinpoint what it reminded her of, then it shook out its wings and she saw again her father's musical dragon in Ondd's temple.

"Poor beast." Now she could see it, it was obvious that it was fear that had driven its fury. "Why did it attack me?" Only then did Ro realise that her mother's song was intended to soothe the onddikin and not her. Her breath snagged on self-pity. Of course, the music would be wasted on one such as she, who could not feel it. She picked at the sheet searching for something to forestall the tears.

"Where did this come from?" she asked.

"A parting gift from Varda." Dovinna smoothed the cloth. "Blankets are too rough on injured skin. She said a healer should always have a sheet, if nothing else to make bandages with." She paused and when she spoke again she wore her healer's persona. "Some of the cuts are nasty, but between Edun's salve and my herbs we should get them to heal without scarring."

"My hair... " The tresses which had floated away in the rain suddenly seemed far more important.

Dovinna hesitated. "We'll trim it into shape as soon as you're feeling better."

"So now I look like a freak too." Ro felt tears rising to choke her again.

She turned to watch the onddikin. Why me? She wanted to ask. Lar's song was having an effect. The animal's eyes were half-closed and it was chirring an accompaniment.

"I might be able to risk going back to my wagon now. When they make that throaty noise they're content." Edun rose and the onddikin sidled to a more secure position on his shoulder. "Now, aren't you ashamed of yourself for all that fuss, Pirik?" He hesitated as he came level with Ro. "I'll be back soon." He hesitated a moment longer, and then vanished through the doorway.

Lar stirred from her seat and came over to inspect Dovinna's handiwork.

"Do you think he will come back?" Dovinna asked her.

"I felt no discord in the words."

"Besides," Ro butted in. "He's left his coat behind." She had thought him a harbinger of Lethir, and he was just a man after all.

Jingling harness and oiled wheels heralded his return. Ro caught a glimpse of paintwork as colourful as Edun's coat. The

Incredible Edun strode in with his arms fully laden with food. Three onddikins hopped behind him.

"Where shall I put this?"

Lar hastily spread a ground sheet near the fire.

"I thought I'd make one of my special stews." His face wore a bright smile. The onddikins swivelled their eyes and flapped up into the rafters. "Don't worry," he assured Ro. "Pirik will be fine now he's with Quinik and Finik again. Of course, one should not really give one's real name to strangers, but after Pirik's bad behaviour, I think he deserves to take the risk."

"Bad behaviour?" Ro's torn arms and bruised face shouted that the words were inadequate.

The magician turned to her. "There's no way I can apologise enough, but I hope you'll understand: Pirik was mad with fear. I'd been exercising the onddikins as I do each day. Quinik and Finik were already back in their cages when something disturbed all three. Then the storm came and Pirik streaked off as if the great worm itself was about to swallow it.

"If it was scared of me, it could have just flown away," Ro said.

"I've been thinking about that. I don't believe Pirik was attacking you. He was holding on to you so desperately, I think he sought your protection." There was no hint of mischief in Edun's face.

Ro looked up at the onddikins where they sat with tails wrapped around the wooden crossbeams. Her hand touched the sore weal on her throat.

"I'd have trouble protecting it when it had choked me," she grumbled.

Edun sighed. "Onddikins aren't overly blessed with brains."

He began preparing the meal, chopping up vegetables and depositing them in a blackened pot at a speed which had Dovinna reaching for her bandages. Ro did not dare to distract him until he had finished. As the pot began to bubble and waft inviting aromas around the ferryhouse, the atmosphere became relaxed. The onddikins glided down from the rafters and took up position in a semi-circle around Edun, making chirruping noises. Edun filled a platter and handed it to Ro. The onddikins followed it, swivelling their whole heads and not only their eyes.

"Ignore them, they only think they like what I eat. Really they prefer ground bugs." He directed his words at the beasts, who fluted at him.

"Are they pets?" Ro asked.

Edun looked scandalised. "Pets? I'm a magician, my dear. Whoever heard of a magician without onddikins?"

"What do magicians do?"

"What do....? You mean you've never seen a magician before?"

Ro tried to shake her head without making the throbbing worse. Edun turned to the others. Lar frowned and shook her head.

Dovinna shrugged. "I've never seen one, but I've heard tell they can produce onddikins out of hats and make people disappear," she sounded sceptical.

Edun waved his hand. "That describes the average run of our kind, but I am the Incredible Edun! Renowned in all the glittering cities of the globe, I have performed before kings and received an encore; I can make flowers bloom in your hair and conjure onddikins from thin air–I can even turn onddikins into bouquets." He ended with a flourish and a bow, glancing up when no applause came. "I can see I shall have to show you."

He pushed his plate aside and strode out to his wagon. A moment later his fluting whistle summoned the three onddikins, who rolled their eyes longingly at the leftovers but obeyed. He returned with poles and cloth and began to assemble a makeshift stage, assisted by the onddikins. They flapped up to the cross-poles above the platform, hooking catches and threading pulley strings. Seeing the fascinated stare of Ro, Edun drew a curtain across the front so that only his face poked out.

"No peeking!"

"Ro should get some sleep anyway," Dovinna said.

"I'm not tired," Ro insisted. The noises behind the curtain, and toings and froings intrigued her. How could a person be made to vanish? Or an onddikin be made to appear? Unless the magician and his beasts had powers she had never heard of.

"If you're not tired you can help to clear up this." Lar indicated the wreckage caused by Edun's cooking. The sight of the dishes made Ro wish she had kept silent. "The activity will do you good, otherwise you won't be able to move when we want to get going tomorrow," Lar added.

"Couldn't we ask Edun to magic them clean?" Ro asked without much hope.

Dovinna laughed. "He's an entertainer, Ro. His type are full of tricks and illusions–like getting someone else to do his dishes."

The glow of hope Ro had begun to feel became a hard cold lump.

"I'd surely have felt it if there was something special about him," Lar reminded her gently. "I hear nothing in him except a nimble tongue."

Eventually, the commotion behind the curtain ceased. One of the onddikins, from the colour of its beak Ro guessed it was Quinik, which had been keeping one eye on them and one on the proceedings behind the curtain, now swooped down to join its master. There was a drum roll and the curtain drew back to reveal a table with a casket on it, a golden perch and at the back, a cabinet of a black lacquered material inscribed with symbols in red and gold, and representations of moons and stars.

A bang startled a cry from her as Edun emerged from an eruption of smoke, swathed in his fiery coat.

"Nobles and gentles all–welcome to this command performance by the Incredible Edun–that is to say, myself. Behold!"

Dovinna sighed at his flowery speech, but Ro found herself smiling. There was something in the magician's smile and extravagant gestures which invited her to be part of his elaborate game. He drew his sleeves up his arms to his elbows on both sides, showed them the backs and palms of his hands, then, with a flourish produced a bouquet of paper flowers. Dovinna's polite and Ro's enthusiastic applause were curtailed by Lar's disapproving "tut". The magician's smile faltered for a heartbeat. He presented Ro with the paper bouquet, then gestured elaborately before producing a rope of silk kerchiefs from his mouth. Next he showed his hands again, tossed the nothing they contained into the air and caught an egg, almost the size of his fist.

"Now, ladies, this is no ordinary egg. Please examine it." He handed it to Ro, who turned it over. There was no sign of a crack or even a pinprick in the smooth shell. As she passed it to Dovinna, Edun continued talking.

"This is an onddikin egg." He retrieved it from Dovinna and set it on the table on the stage. He covered it with another silk kerchief and passed his hands over it, muttering an unintelligible incantation.

"And so!" He whipped the kerchief away and there sat Pirik. The onddikin yawned and settled its wings as though it had just woken. Edun held out his arm for it to hop on and settled it on the golden perch. "But onddikins don't only hatch from eggs." The magician took a dramatic tone and drew his eyebrows together.

He pointed suddenly at a spot on the stage, there was another thunderclap of smoke and Quinik appeared. Before they had time to recover from the bang, Edun repeated the gesture on the other side of the stage and Finik appeared. The three took off and circled above his head before flying off. Ro was almost too puzzled to clap. The magician continued doggedly.

"And now, I shall perform for you perhaps the greatest illusion of all. I have here a vanishing cabinet from the far reaches of Gindul—where this ancient trick was taught to me by a master of the mystic arts." He manoeuvred the cabinet to the centre of the stage. He turned it around and tapped each side, then opened the door and rapped again. "For this illusion, I shall need a volunteer from the audience." He looked directly at Ro, who prised her sore body from its seat. As he handed her into the box he whispered. "Don't worry, my dear. All will become clear. Await my signal before you reappear."

She followed his gaze to the floor of the cabinet, then the door shut and she was left in stuffy darkness. While his muffled voice continued to tell the story of the mystical history of the cabinet, Ro felt about the floor; it rocked when she pushed one side. There was just enough room to slide through the tilted opening. Beneath it, a trapdoor had been opened in the stage to a compartment deep enough for her to crouch in or for an onddikin to stand upright. The trapdoor was fixed by a bolt. Finik jumped up and drew it shut using its talons, as she entered. So that was how! She was so taken aback, that she almost blurted it aloud.

"Now we must all concentrate hard," she heard Edun say.

He began a droning hum. Quinik and Pirik joined in. Ro heard Dovinna gasp as the cabinet door was thrown open.

"Your companion is even now resting on the mystic plane. Shall we leave her there, or shall we bring her back?" He waited for an answer which did not come. "Yes, of course we must bring her back."

The rapping of knuckles against lacquer told Ro the whole process was being repeated. Her heart beat faster waiting for the sign. Finik jumped up and slid back the bolt once more, and Ro scrambled through the tilting floor. Hampered by her injuries and her unfamiliarity with the tricky balancing act required, she only just managed to straighten up before Edun began his droning hum again. The door was thrown open again and Ro could not restrain her laughter as Edun handed her out to take a bow.

"Well, my dear, and what do you think of magicians now?"

"Ingenious. Mother, it's really clever, there's... "

"Ah-ah." Edun wagged a finger at her. "Those who have been to the mystic plane should never talk about the experience."

Ro nodded solemnly, then could not resist clapping her hands together like a child, despite Lar's disapproving look.

"Thank you, Edun, for your performance, but we've a long way to travel and need our rest," the Earth-hearer said.

The magician cleared his throat as if reprimanded. "Of course. I'm rather tired myself–exciting day." He whistled the onddikins to him and began to back out of the doorway.

"What about all this?" Lar waved at the stage.

"Oh, I trust you not to peek until morning." The magician slipped out of the house, winking at Ro as he went.

Settling down for the night, Ro found she could close her eyes without seeing herself fending off an airborne attack, or picturing Ussu, Raimi and Lalli surrounded by unfriendly faces. Her mind was full of the magician's performance. Now she had a key to one illusion she should be able to reason out many of the others and who knew what else besides?

She was woken by the unaccustomed sound of snoring–a tooth jangling rasp followed by a wheezy whistle. She opened her eyes and cut back a cry. Inches away from her face was that of Pirik. The onddikin was curled up with its beak resting on its tail. Hardly daring to move, she looked further down her bed. Quinik had fitted his back into the crook of her legs and Finik lay stretched out on his side with his head dangling over the edge of the pillow, his parted beak letting the awful noise escape. Ro turned her head warily to look at where Lar should have been asleep. Her mother was sitting with her knees drawn up and her hands over her ears, glaring at the sleeping animals. The light had the fuzzy quality of dawn. Dovinna was out of sight, but from the steady sound of her breath, Ro guessed the onddikins had not woken her.

How long they remained so, Ro was unsure, but the light was casting long fingers of shadow across the room before she heard stirrings in the wagon outside. Footsteps approached and a soft whistle. Pirik opened one eye, but did not move. Then the magician's head appeared in the doorway.

"Would you please remove these creatures?" Lar hissed.

"Woke you up, did they?" Edun asked jovially. "You should have pushed them off."

"After yesterday?" Lar reminded him. His smile disappeared.

"Come on, my lovelies. Time to get up. They seem to have taken to you. They usually sleep with me–that's what woke me, I was cold without them."

Ro was unsure whether she should feel honoured or guilty. Edun shooed the onddikins off Ro's bed. They shambled outside after him, stretching their wings and giving them a desultory flap. By the time Edun returned, Ro, Lar and Dovinna were almost packed.

"Honey cakes for breakfast?" Edun suggested, wafting the honeypot under their noses.

"It would give me time to check Ro's wounds." Dovinna looked at Lar. She acquiesced. As they ate, Edun talked.

"Where are you heading? I'm going to King Darian's capital in Amradoc. I've heard the city of Mandur is a centre of culture. If you're heading the same way we could travel together. That way Ro's injuries would have a chance to heal."

"Thank you," Lar said. "But we have our own path to follow."

"Yes?" Edun smiled encouragingly, but no more information was forthcoming. "Well, it just remains for me to pack up."

As he started to dismantle his gear, the others found themselves with the breakfast things to clear away again.

"We could just leave them." Dovinna sounded dubious.

Ro defended him. "I think you're being too hard on him, he means well."

"You forget, he lives by deception," Lar warned.

"Only on stage, and the answers are there for those who want to look." Ro tried to stalk off into the open air. Her bruises would not let her cut a dignified figure, but she hobbled to the remains of the compound wall. Even now they were so far from Iyessa that they might as well be on the other side of the globe, no one took notice of her opinion–simply because she could not feel what they did. With a mixture of self-pity and indignation occupying her thoughts, Ro did not immediately register the blur of movement in the distance. When she did her heart thudded in her ears. Moving as carefully as she could to avoid attracting attention, Ro returned to the ferryhouse.

"Riders! There are riders heading this way." She attempted to keep her voice level, but still caught Edun's sharp glance, first at her, then Lar.

"Perhaps I'll have a paying audience before Amradoc. I'll go out and meet them." He returned a moment later. "It's a patrol. They're not renowned for their courtesy to women, especially in remote areas. You'd better keep in the background. I'll try to get rid of them."

Dovinna turned to Lar. "What do you think? Can we trust him?"

"Yes," Ro answered before Lar could say otherwise. "He owes us for the trouble he's caused us–why else share his food and secrets?"

They heard hooves and the jingle of harness.

"You there! Stay where you are!" A voice barked.

"Certainly, Officer. How can I help you?"

"Who else is with you?"

"No one. I merely stopped here to shelter from the rain. I was about to be on my way."

"Search the wagon!"

Edun's cabinet was still on the stage. Ro gestured to the others to follow her. "Quick!"

The same high-pitched shrieking which had heralded Pirik's attack, set up. For all their sakes, Ro hoped that Edun had had time to put the onddikins in their travelling cages. Hurriedly, she showed Lar and Dovinna the tilting floor. They squeezed through the gap into the confined false floor of the stage. She slid the bolt to and they crouched hardly aware of the discomfort as the voices entered the room.

"What's this? I thought you said you were alone."

"Just practising my act–sleight of hand's like playing a musical instrument–you don't do it for a day or two and your fingers seize up. And I needed to check my equipment–wouldn't do to have it fall apart in front of a paying audience."

"Hm!" Heavy boots thudded onto the stage. "What's in here?" There was a rap on the cabinet.

"Nothing." They heard the creak of hinges. "See for yourself."

"This is one of those tricks, isn't it? How does it work?"

"I can't tell you. The secrets of magic are inviolable. I've sworn an oath not to reveal them. If I should break it, Lethir's ravening hordes would sweep me off to the void."

"And if you don't, I shall take each stick apart until I'm satisfied that you're not hiding anything."

There was a silence in which Ro had the urge to throw open the trapdoor and surrender. Then the cabinet door slammed.

"You couldn't hide all of them anyway. Count yourself lucky, Magician, that I'm not in the mood for delays. We're searching for a Najarindian woman with a party of Iyessi–three women, a baby and a man.

"I've seen no one since leaving the village to the south of here."

"They're wanted for treason and murder. Just remember–if you help them you're guilty of the same charges, and I don't think you're capable of magicking your head back onto your body."

"Treason and murder? Whatever did they do?"

"Poisoned King Berinn." The soldier's voice was moving away.

"Poisoners!" Edun's voice was shocked. "A moment, Officer... "

Trapped in their hiding place, the fugitives heard Edun's footsteps hurrying after the soldier.

# Chapter Eight

Othar put on his best smile, but did not rise. "Welcome! You're just in time to hear some genuine Iyessi music!"

The soldiers pushed past Tolar, ignoring Othar's welcome, and hauled Ussu and Raimi to their feet.

"Where are the others?" Captain Pachand pushed Ussu's chin up so that she was forced to meet his gaze.

Othar's voice lost its silky good humour. "All in good time. You and I have some business to conduct first."

There was a rustle of movement behind the soldiers as Othar's men loosened their weapons.

"Obstruct us and the rest of my patrol will see to it that your train is confiscated and your trader's pass revoked," the Captain warned.

"If I'd wanted to obstruct, I wouldn't have had my man bring you here–but I'm sure you'll appreciate that I have a living to earn, and you did mention a reward when you passed by before."

"I'll be sure to tell King Channan he owes it to you." Pachand jerked his head in the direction of the exit, and his subordinates shoved the Iyessi towards it. Othar's men sprang to block their path, swords drawn.

"I think not, I think I shall hold on to these two until I've seen the colour of his money." Othar's smile made Ussu shudder.

"They aren't the ones we're looking for."

Othar shrugged. "Then why do you want them?"

The Captain looked at the men around him. "All right. I'll question them. If they're any use to us, you'll get your money."

Othar yawned. "Frankly, I'm in no mood for bargaining right now. Take them out, Tolar. Put them in the pack wagon and set a watch. We don't want anyone stealing them away before we've concluded our deal." He turned back to the soldier. "I intend retiring for the night. Tempers tend to fray when people are tired. I wouldn't want any misunderstandings. I'm sure after you've slept on it, you'll come to the right decision."

Raimi and Ussu were herded out to the wagon.

"Sleep well." Tolar gave them a shark's grin as he left them under guard. Ussu and Raimi wrapped their arms around each other, holding tightly as if trying to synchronise heartbeats.

"Lalli!" Ussu's whisper was a cry of pain.

"Jassi won't let her be harmed."

"Jassi can't prevent herself being harmed." Ussu turned her head so that Raimi could not see her anguish.

"Maybe we can convince the soldiers our being here's just a coincidence."

Ussu stroked Raimi's face. They both knew there was little hope of that. The wagon creaked as their guard leant against it.

"Perhaps while they're delayed with us the others will be able to reach safety," Ussu consoled herself.

"Perhaps."

There was nothing they could do, except listen to the sounds of the camp settling down for the night. The wagon shook as their guard stood up. Raimi and Ussu became very still. There was a disturbance in the flow of the camp.

The guard's gruff voice called a challenge. "What do you want?"

"To bring back the brat. You don't think Othar wants to be woken by its squalling, do you?" It was Jassi's petulant tone.

There was a chuckle and the tailgate was released. Ussu immediately moved forward to retrieve Lalli, but Jassi held on to her and clambered inside. The smile she had worn for the guard vanished. With her free hand she gestured for them to stay silent.

"Be ready," she whispered. "I've put a sleeping draught in Othar's wine. It would take a hurricane to wake him. I'll distract the guard. When he moves, get out of here and head for the trees to the right of the road–while Othar was talking 'business' I tethered horses there for you."

"Oh, Jassi." Ussu's eyes filled with tears.

"It'll serve him right. With any luck each side'll think the others have betrayed them." She turned to go.

"But you... " Raimi's eyes went to Jassi's bruised cheek, and she touched a hand to it.

"Don't worry–as soon as we get near Sud-Iyessa I'm going back home to my brothers and sisters." She gave Lalli a last smile and slipped out.

"Phoo– babies! I thought once I was with Othar I'd escaped the stink of them!" She sat on the tailgate, preventing the guard rebolting it. He laughed.

"Stay with Othar much longer and you'll be having some of your own."

Jassi pouted. "Oh, all Othar's interested in is turning a profit. No sooner does he go to bed than he's snoring." She rose and stood very close to the guard, who swallowed. "I tell you, it's not what I expected." She began to run her fingers along the front edge of his jerkin. "Young girls need a little more, you know?"

The guard ran his tongue over his lips.

"After all, it's not as though I'm not beautiful." Jassi leaned forward so the guard could see a hint of cleavage. "You think I'm beautiful, don't you?" She slowly began to raise the hem of her skirt revealing her slender legs.

"Wouldn't these keep you awake at night?"

The guard swallowed again. "But... Othar... "

She grasped the edge of his jerkin and pulled him towards her. "He wouldn't know." As the guard made a grab for her she whispered: "Not here" and began dragging him away.

Raimi slipped out of the wagon, paused as he landed to make sure the guard had not heard and pulled out the rock which wedged the wagon's wheel. Two quick steps, a sharp downward blow and the guard was crumpled at his feet. The enormity of it made them freeze. Then Jassi hissed: "Go!" and headed back to the ornate wagon. Ussu jumped after Raimi with Lalli and they fled towards the hidden horses.

Two figures detached themselves from the shadow of the communal tent. The dying camp torches snagged on their mail.

"Should I follow, Sir?"

Pachand's face twisted into a smile. "Make sure they don't see you; with any luck they'll lead us to the others. I'll join you after I've dealt with our greedy friend."

One of the horses whickered a greeting at the Iyessi's approach. They led the animals until they were well away from the camp, expecting to hear the sounds of pursuit at any moment. When they did mount they picked up speed, risking waking Lalli in an

110

attempt to put as much distance between them and their would-be captors as possible. The direction did not matter as long as it was away from the reverberations of guilt and fear which snaked out from Othar's caravan. They risked pausing only when the horses were too exhausted to go further.

"Have you any idea where we are?" Ussu asked Raimi.

"Does it matter?" He continued rubbing down his mount with more vigour than it warranted. "Othar knows we were headed for Sud-Iyessa so that's out. We can't go back to Najarind, and if we head after Lar and Ro we risk bringing pursuit down on them."

"Surely they'll have reached safety by now–they only had to travel to the border. For every step we've headed south they'll have gone east."

"Unless they also met unforeseen difficulties. I think the best we can do is trust our senses and hope we come across somewhere that feels safe."

"Then we'd better move on." Ussu pushed herself wearily to her feet. "I can't shake off the echoes of danger; they've been with me since we camped last night."

"Me too."

"It's almost as if we hadn't escaped at all." Ussu turned frightened eyes on Raimi with sudden awareness.

He held the bridle for her to remount, his hands shaking on the harness. Ussu had one foot in the stirrup when Lalli began to grizzle and the horse danced her round in a circle. A mounted figure appeared over the slope ahead of them.

"What was that you were saying about not having escaped at all?" It was Captain Pachand. His men fanned out in a circle around them. "You might as well stop hopping around that horse, because you're not going anywhere until I'm ready."

He dismounted and strode up to Ussu until he was close enough for her to feel his breath as he spoke. "I believe you mentioned your companions heading east for the border."

Ussu remained silent.

"You'll show me on the map where they intend crossing."

She glanced down at the map but was otherwise motionless.

"You will show me, I promise you." Pachand's smile threatened.

"Leave her alone, we don't know... "

The Captain's mailed fist caught the side of Raimi's mouth. Lalli screamed as Ussu gasped and reached out to him.

"That's only a beginning." Pachand let his gaze drop to the terrified baby.

Raimi shook his head at Ussu. She sobbed. "I have to."

"Good. I always knew you Iyessi barbarians were intelligent enough to understand where your best interests lay. Now, show me."

"I can't," Ussu began.

The Captain raised his fist towards Raimi once more.

"Not on this." She pointed at the map. "I'll take you there. Only let my husband and baby go."

Pachand tutted. "Please don't underestimate me. You'll take me to the murderers or you'll find out whether all those stories about Najarindian soldiers eating babies are true."

They remounted. Raimi's hands were tied to his saddle pommel. As the soldiers were about to follow suit with Ussu she objected.

"I need my hands free for the baby."

The Captain nodded. That small freedom was little enough. Their horses were led by members of the patrol and sandwiched between them. The weather reflected their misery. Insistent rain closed in, punctuated by sword-thrusts of lightning and great slaps of thunder.

"Sounds as if Ondd has indigestion," one of the men joked, but only received muttered insults for his trouble.

The land began to be criss-crossed with water channels, many of which crept over their bounds drowning the crops on either side. That night the patrol commandeered a farmhouse. While Pachand and his men ate in the main building, Ussu, Raimi and Lalli were left under guard in one of the barns. The rain had let up, but the sky was still heavy. The guard leaned in the doorway looking at it. Ussu joggled Lalli to wake her up. The baby let out a whimper. The guard hunched his shoulders against the noise.

"Oh no, she's awake again. A lullaby might work." Ussu began a gentle sing-song while Raimi tapped out a pattering rhythm on the floor. The nonsense words tripped up and down a tune that breathed peace and contentment. Very soon it was not just Lalli's eyes which began to close; the guard's also became heavy. His head began to dip and every few breaths he had to catch himself upright. Keeping a careful watch on him Ussu began to intersperse other words with the childish nonsense of the lullaby.

"It's raining, it's pouring," she sang. "It'll carry on 'til morning."

"The lakes will fill," Raimi's voice harmonised with hers. "The rivers will flood."

"And when we cross."

"We must take care."

"That only they... "

"... get washed away."

The guard jerked upright and Ussu's song became the rhyming nonsense it had been before. He wrapped his cloak around him, unaware that anything had taken place except that the baby was now blessedly quiet.

Sweat trickled down Ro's face, getting into her cuts and making them sting. After Edun had followed the officer out of the ferryhouse, she could hear no more, no matter that she listened with her whole being. The panicked shrieking of the onddikins overlaid all. The air grew stale and her battered limbs felt set forever in her crouched position. Then there was the shudder of a footstep on the stage.

"Time for the travellers to return from the mystic plane." Edun rapped on the floor above them. Ro drew back the bolt and a hand reached through the trapdoor to haul her out. She emerged into the daylight expecting to see half a dozen soldiers watching.

"As you see, there's no audience for you to curtsy to."

"Thank you." She would have held on to his hand, but he was turning to help the others.

"Thank you? I should think so!" he exclaimed.

"You've risked your life for us." Lar saluted him with fingertips touching her lips.

"That's putting it mildly. If the mystic brethren discover I've caused the secret of the vanishing cabinet to be revealed to three non-magicians they'll probably turn me to toast and eat me." He winked at Ro.

As he handed Dovinna out of the cabinet, he paused and searched her face. "You don't look like poisoners and rebels."

"We're not," she said quietly.

"You can tell me all about it on our way to Amradoc. The soldiers tell me the tributary is too flooded to ford. We can either wait for it to subside, or we shall have to travel around. My vote is to keep moving." Without waiting for a reply he continued dismantling his stage.

Lar put a hand on his arm to stop him. "I owe you an apology. I'd thought that an accomplished deceiver couldn't have a noble spirit."

"Is that a compliment?" he asked Ro.

"We owe our lives to your ability to lie. In Iyessa that's inconceivable–I certainly never managed to get away with it." She blushed; she had not meant to admit so much.

Edun smiled. "The secret is to believe what you're saying while you say it." He hefted his gear and headed out to his wagon.

Ro gasped when she saw it. Clothes, books, pans–all were scattered on the ground. She began picking them up.

"It's no worse than after some celebrations I've held," he assured her.

"But why? Why protect us at such risk when for all you know we might be everything the soldiers claim?"

"Trust a liar to spot a liar, Ro. Besides, they teased the onddikins."

Ro peeked inside the wagon at the cages. There were feathers on the floor outside and Pirik was missing part of his ruff.

"Poor Pirik."

The onddikin pressed itself against the wire for her to fuss it.

"Poor Ro," Edun laughed. "You match now."

Ro's hand flew to her head. Dovinna had combed her hair for her that morning, insisting that she would be better able to avoid her cuts, so Ro had not seen herself. Once underway she insisted on being given a mirror. They had travelled many miles before she had reconciled herself to her spiky-haired reflection.

The gloomy skies opened again before they had gone far, confirming their decision to find another crossing point. The sun was nearing the horizon beneath the clouds by the time they reached a bridge.

Dovinna shook her head at the sight. "Like everything else in this area, it's neglected. All the prosperity has moved west."

Neglected was an understatement. To Ro it looked as if the bridge was held together by no more than faith. The sodden ropes and timbers smelled of decay. Mud and reeds sucked at the wheels of the wagon as they approached.

"You'd better walk across first," Edun advised. He loosed the onddikins which flapped over and perched on the wooden pilings on the other side.

Lar stepped up to the edge. "I'll go first." She stood with eyes shut concentrating, then set her foot on the first plank. It squeaked a protest but held. The wood played a tune of old age and better days, and then Lar was over. Ro had watched each careful footstep, remembering the melodic paths of Iyessa.

"Come on, Dovinna, just step where I do." They joined Lar on the far side.

Edun whistled to his horse and flapped the reins. The hollow clatter of its hooves made it balk, but Edun urged it on.

"Is it strong enough?" Ro whispered to Lar, but her mother stood as if willpower alone could make the planks strong. The noise was a torment of splitting grain and overstretched ropes. The pilings groaned and leaned towards the middle of the tumbling water, making the onddikins flutter into the air. It was too much for the reluctant horse. It bolted, sending the wagon swaying and crashing against the pilings, and then The Incredible Edun's magic show was safely across and careering off without them.

"Whoa, there! I've had enough for one day even if you haven't." The horse came to a standstill. Edun mopped his forehead, then waved the kerchief at the others as they caught up. "Congratulations, ladies. We are now in Amradoc."

The following morning the sun sparkled on pools of flood water and streamlets. By midday these had become wallows of mud. One unwary step and they would find themselves up to their knees in it while they struggled to push the wagon out. The pretensions of the tributary to be a grand river dwindled and it became an innocent stream again, but the sky was still barred with grey and the air felt heavy as they drew opposite the ferryhouse.

"Two day's travel and here we still are," Ro said. "I wonder whether the others are in Sud-Iyessa yet."

They turned away from the tributary and headed towards King Darian's city.

"What's Mandur like, Edun?" Ro asked the magician as they ate their evening meal in the wagon, listening to the insistent tapping of rain on the roof.

"Like any other city," he said, and her heart sank, remembering Najarind's welcome.

"And King Darian?" Dovinna asked.

Edun shrugged. "I've never heard any bad said of him–unless I was in Ortann."

It did not sound encouraging. Ro could not sleep for speculating about their destination. She knew her unrest must disturb Lar, but could not help it. She almost wished for Ussu's sharp tongue to tell her to stop fidgeting.

Despite the cold rain, Ro felt she had to get out of the wagon the next morning. She ignored the wet grass that whipped stinging trails across her legs and strode up the nearest hill. The countryside was all undulating slopes of dead grass, beaten down by the weather. Had it not been for the pall of rain over everything, Ro thought she would have been able to see far enough maybe to catch sight of Mandur's rooftops. As it was, she sighed and turned to look back at the way they had come. At the rate it was raining, it would not be long before the ford was impassable again. Closer to, the magician's wagon looked sad and bedraggled. Sadder still was the figure of Lar. Ro's mother approached, retaining an authoritative dignity despite the rain. She smiled as she stood beside Ro.

"Your poor hair." She touched the slicked down remains.

"It'll grow." Ro tried to sound cheerful. They watched the distance in silence for a moment.

"I feel your regret. Even Ussu can't hide her feelings from me," Lar sighed. "Today I feel she's very close, I can't account for it."

"You think she's in trouble?"

"It's possible, but this isn't like before, it's... "

" ... close," Ro finished. "Perhaps that's because she is nearby. She and Raimi would be drawn to the water." A surge of excitement sent her running down the slope.

"Ro, be careful!" Lar called, hurrying after her.

They passed the wagon. Ro was vaguely aware of the astonished faces of Dovinna and Edun. Their excitement infected the onddikins, who took off and wheeled above them. Suddenly, Ro stopped and dropped flat in the mud and stringy grass. Behind her she heard the others following her example. A patrol was approaching the ford.

The riders stopped near the ferryhouse.

"This area's already been searched, Sir," one of the patrolmen informed Pachand.

He nodded. "Perhaps they gave them the slip–or perhaps they didn't come this way at all." He turned on Ussu.

"Perhaps. I can only tell you where they told us they would go." She lifted her chin. "If we're going to cross, we should do it now."

"I'd advise against, Sir, it looks as though it's flooded once already."

"Don't worry–our guides here are going to lead the way."

Ussu and Raimi's horses were led forward. The Iyessi scanned the water. It was dimpled with raindrops but otherwise calm. As they urged the horses in, it only reached up to their hocks. Ussu glanced upstream and then at the small currents which began to swirl around the horses' legs. The soldiers' horses splashed nervously behind them. When they reached the middle, Ussu paused allowing Raimi to pass, then half-turned her horse to block the path of the patrol.

"We'll have to go in single file."

She urged the horse on a few more paces. A smooth wave the width of the tributary that was no more than a ripple to the untrained eye, overlaid the jumbled currents of the ford. Ussu kicked her horse into life. At the same instant, Raimi's horse bounded forward and a wall of debris-laden water swept through the channel around the laggard riders. Raimi's horse kept its footing to scramble out on the far bank, but the angry swell slapped the hind legs of Ussu's horse from under it, turning it around so that it was in danger of being pulled away rump first. In the confusion of shouts from the soldiers and the terrified neighing of their mounts, Ussu's clear voice sang encouragement to her floundering beast.

The sound had Ro and Lar on their feet silently adding their urging to hers, heedless of the danger. Then the horse's hooves met stone and it gained a purchase on the bank. Raimi leaned over and grasped the bridle to help it. Unable to do anything but watch, Lar and Ro saw Pachand drag himself back onto the ferryhouse bank. He snatched a bow from one of his men, aimed–fired. Ro's warning shout died as Ussu's arms flung wide and she toppled back into the current. Still strapped in her sling, Lalli fell with her, but as they tipped over she slid free and the water snatched her into its embrace.

Ro blinked and stared, willing what she saw to be different, but Raimi was still clutching the cheek-strap of the riderless horse.

Then she was running again. The onddikins streaked overhead. Quinik and Finik began harrying the surviving soldiers, while Pirik flew downstream where the waters tumbled the bodies of those caught in the flood. Raimi was off his horse and would have flung himself after Ussu had not Lar interposed herself.

"It will do no good, Raimi–she's gone." Her voice held a quiet finality.

Ro leaned out as far as she could. There was no hope for the soldiers burdened with their armour, but Ussu and Lalli... She could see nothing except Pirik sweeping back and forth, making keening noises as it darted and swooped. The soldiers had fled for cover from the onddikins, but one loosed a parting shot. There was a shriek as an arrow tore through Finik's leathery wing and it tumbled towards the earth. Quinik flew to its aid, and half-dragged it back to Edun. He murmured something and Quinik flew off to join Pirik. Suddenly the searching onddikins dived. For a long moment in which the blood beat in Ro's temples there was neither sight nor sound of them. Then they flapped into view, clumsily staggering under the weight of the bundle of cloth they clutched in their  talons.

"Lalli!" The cry burst simultaneously from Lar and Raimi.

There was no sound from the baby. Ro looked from one to another of her companions. Their set faces gave her no reassurance. The onddikins descended slowly and gently laid their burden before them. Their talons had torn the baby's clothes but there was no mark on Lalli herself. The child looked utterly peaceful with a bluish tinge to her lips. Raimi snatched her to him. There was a small cough and a trickle of water ran from her mouth. He looked at them, his face caught between disbelief and despair.

"Quick!" Dovinna's professionalism shook them out of their dumbstruck shock. "We must get her to the wagon."

"Yes," Edun agreed. "I don't fancy still being here when this weather lets up. What's left of the patrol will want to avenge their comrades."

"They're not the only ones," Raimi's good-natured face was dark. "I can't just leave Ussu here."

Lar spoke quietly. "She's already gone–you must feel it–her song has ceased and there's Lalli to think of. Come."

"Is she to have no music to mark her passing?"

"We'll sing her home and honor her and ask the waters which have claimed her as their own to carry her gently." As she spoke, Lar drew Raimi away from the stream's bank.

Dovinna and Edun hurried ahead to tend the injured. Ro was left alone, hearing in the flood Ussu's triumphant shout. Her throat filled with the need to moan and wail or scream out her anger, but she could make no sound. Tears ran down her face in silence, mingling with the rain as she forced herself to follow the others. The moment she hauled herself onto the wagon, Edun slapped the horse into a canter. While Dovinna dried and warmed Lalli, Lar tended to Raimi. Ro felt superfluous. She sank onto a seat oblivious of her soaked clothes and the uncontrollable shuddering throughout her body. Dovinna looked up from the tiny pinched face of Lalli.

"Ro! Ro!"

Ro drew a stuttering breath. Dovinna shoved bandages and salves into her hands.

"Can you tend to Finik? The onddikins trust you."

Ro stared at the medicine. A thin keening was coming from the front of the wagon under Edun's seat. Yes, the onddikins. The brave efforts of the creatures had more than paid for the scratches Pirik had given her. Without them they would have lost Lalli too. She stumbled forward. All three onddikins were huddled under the seat; Quinik and Pirik supporting their injured fellow. Ro went down on hands and knees to encourage them out. Quinik shuffled to put itself between Finik and Ro, flapping its wings and stretching its neck in a warning gesture. Ro tried to make gentling noises, but knew she had not the knack.

Edun spoke over his shoulder. "How bad is it?"

It was too much. Ro hid her face in her hands and wept, wishing the cold water of the tributary had swallowed her instead. Something light and feathery brushed against her hand. She moved and saw Pirik's face tilted to watch her. It made a small chirrup and scrambled onto her lap. Quinik relented, folding its wings and nuzzling at Finik to encourage it out of hiding. The onddikin's condition was not good. The gloss had left the leathery skin and it looked folded. The damaged wing trailed on the floor leaking an inky fluid from the tear.

Ro gently raised it and cradled the beast in one arm while she smeared salve onto the injury. She felt along the wing. There appeared to be no other damage. She bandaged it against the onddikin's body to prevent further harm. By the time she had finished, Finik's eyes were half-closed and its keening had subsided to an occasional whine. She took a deep breath.

"They'll be all right, Edun, don't worry. I'll take them inside to keep warm."

The magician nodded, and some of the strain smoothed out of his forehead.

Ro returned in time to see Dovinna pass the now sleeping baby to Raimi. A little life returned to his eyes.

"There don't appear to be any bumps or cuts and her lungs are clear of water now. All we have to do is watch she takes no hurt from the cold. It's a miracle."

Raimi made a noise somewhere between scorn and a sob. Ro could not bear to meet the sorrow in their faces. As soon as the onddikins were settled she rejoined Edun.

"How far to Mandur?" she asked.

"A week or more. We can't keep this pace up."

"What of the soldiers?"

Edun looked grim. "Let's hope it keeps raining and we can get too far into Amradoc for them to follow."

Ro watched the horse, trying to blank out all thought in the rhythm of its gait. Whichever way her mind turned pain lurked. They finally stopped when the darkness and the horse's exhaustion made it impossible to do otherwise. Little was said. Mundane details seemed too trivial and the events at the tributary too big to be faced. The immediate problem was finding a way to appease Lalli's hunger. Edun sweetened some water with honey and Raimi struggled to get her to take it. Eventually by patiently dipping a finger in it and placing it against her lips, sufficient fluid was got inside her, but she was still fractious and refused to be rocked to sleep until Ro had the idea of wrapping her in Ussu's shawl, which was still in the pack on her horse.

Sleep was hard to come by and short-lived. Ro dreamed she was standing on the riverbank watching the horses gallop but make no headway against the current. Then as Ussu's horse scrambled onto the shore she heard the thud of the arrow hitting Ussu's back and saw her topple, feeling the moment she met the water as a physical blow that doubled Ro over. She turned and met the accusing stares of the others. Lar, Raimi, Dovinna, Edun–even Lalli–gathered around her.

"Cursed! Cursed!" The words echoed inside her head. She felt a tap on the shoulder, turned and there was Ussu with her annoying superior smile.

"Fooled you! If you had any feeling you would've known I wasn't dead. Well, aren't you pleased to see me?"

They flung their arms about each other and for a moment Ro experienced the rippling bubbling joy of Ussu's laughter. She woke. Lalli was screaming. For an instant Ro wondered why Ussu did not pick her up, then reality rushed in.

Somehow they managed to get through the morning chores and set off again. The rain had eased off, so Raimi and Ro mounted the saddle horses ostensibly to ease the burden on Edun's nag, but also to relieve them of any attempt to divert their thoughts. Ro tried to keep close to the wagon out of Raimi's sight as he rode ahead, conscious that each time he caught a glance of her he must expect to see Ussu. Occasional shafts of weak sunshine poked through the heavy clouds, spreading a pleasant warmth throughout her body. She gripped tightly on the reins; what right had she to take pleasure in anything? She scanned the sky behind them. It shone a clean blue drawing a thick mist off the land.

They had not progressed far when Lar clambered forward to Edun's side. "Fly! We're followed!"

Edun hesitated. "So far into Amradoc?" He slapped the reins and the poor horse broke into a canter. "She can't keep this up—my old nag's got a brave heart but she's used to an easier life."

Raimi reined in his horse. "I'll slow them down." His face was twisted into a smile that chilled Ro.

"No!" Ro turned in her saddle. She could make out the glint of sun on metal where the mist thinned. "You should ride ahead for help." She slapped the rump of Raimi's horse and it sprang forward. By the time he had the beast under control once more they had reached a wide roadway.

"The highway to Mandur. We may be in luck," Edun called. He slapped the horse's reins again, but the gallant beast was sweating and its pace began to slow.

Ro could now make out a band of horsemen gaining on them. She cast about for a hiding place. Perhaps if they could make it past the next bend in the road...

"Whoa, there!"

She looked around in astonishment as Edun hauled on the reins.

"What are you doing?" she demanded.

Edun nodded in the opposite direction. Another band of horsemen was bearing down on them. They were trapped.

# Chapter Nine

"Where did they come from?" Ro could not understand how the patrol had managed to get ahead of them.

Raimi drew his knife. "Get ready."

"It's madness, Raimi, you can't fight them!"

There seemed no course other than for Ro and Dovinna to give themselves up. She steeled herself to take the first steps, squinting to see the approaching riders more clearly. Turning in her saddle, she took another look at those behind them. They were different.

Edun's quiet voice held them all. "Of course! I should have expected this. Let me do the talking."

The second band of riders surrounded them and flowed on a short distance to await the others.

"Explain yourselves!" The leader gave their party an appraising look. His armour was lighter than that of the soldiers Ro had previously come across and his helmet bore an unfamiliar crest. Before Edun could answer they were hailed by the pursuers.

"Hold them fast!" The voice was Pachand's.

The first soldier frowned as the Captain rode up.

"So, Magician, it looks like you'll get a chance to perform for King Channan." Pachand took the reins from Edun's hands. The onddikins began to shriek. "Fresh meat for the journey home too."

"Not so fast." The first soldier placed his gauntleted hand on top of Pachand's. "These are not Najarindians and they're on Amrad soil. What's more they're in our possession."

Their eyes locked.

"No need for them to pollute Amrad soil any longer. These fugitives are responsible for the death of King Berinn." Pachand waited to see the effect of his words. "You must have heard of his death."

"We've been on patrol in this sector for several weeks. We saw no messengers from Najarind."

"Can we be blamed for poor Amrad communications?"

"Enough!"

Pachand stiffened at the other officer's tone.

"You're violating Amrad soil."

Pachand adopted a conciliatory pose. "I've explained. These fugitives must be returned to Najarind for punishment."

His soldiers moved forward. Behind the Amrad officer there was a rattle of swords being loosened in scabbards. At that moment there was a squeal of delight and Lar appeared with the baby in her arms at the front of the wagon. Lalli's attention was firmly fixed on the antics of Pirik as it fluttered around her.

"What crime has the baby committed?" the Amrad soldier demanded. "If your king wants these people tell him to send an embassy to Mandur for them."

"You're making a mistake," Pachand warned.

The officer stared back impassively. "Back off, Najarindian. Unless you want to start a war."

Pachand hesitated. The Amrad officer nodded at one of his men, who placed a great horn to his lips. The brazen upward blast made Ro fear for the other Iyessi's ears, but Raimi's eyes were sparked to fire. There was a response from further off.

Pachand scowled. "This insult won't be forgotten!"

"Move, Najarindian, or I'll do you the honour of an escort."

Another party of riders appeared around the bend in the highway. Pachand yanked his horse's head around and kicked the beast to a canter. They watched the Ortanian patrol head back towards the border.

Raimi could not keep silent. "You can't let them go–they killed Ussu."

The officer was impassive. "Make sure they cross the border," he told one of the newcomers, then signalled his second-in-command. "Secure these people–take any weapons–I want no tricks before we reach Mandur."

"Thank you, Captain." Edun used his professional voice.

"Save your thanks for King Darian–if he frees you."

They rode off surrounded by soldiers. The uniforms might be different but they were still captives. At least this time they were heading where they wanted to go.

When they reached Mandur the sky was brushed with stars. A haloed half-moon lit the way and edged the blocks and towers of the city with silver. Ro did not see the beauty of it, only that the shapes were plain. They had stopped at several holdings along the way, which had been able to provide goat's milk for the baby, but it was not to her liking and throughout the journey Lalli's hungry whimperings had alternated with outraged screams until their nerves were strung tauter than an Iyessi viol. They had given the days an eerie unreality. At least the city looked solid, as if it would obey the laws governing the world and be unchanged in the morning. Once, Ro had taken such laws for granted, as she had taken it for granted that she would always have a sister. Now, anything was possible. She could only guess at the pain Lar and Raimi felt, but at least they could share it. Ro was more alone than ever. She heard Ussu's voice and envisaged how she would have stood with hands primly folded.

"If you spent less time feeling sorry for yourself, you might not always be in such trouble. Try paying attention for once!"

Good advice. As the wagon clattered past Mandur's walls, Ro set herself to fixing as much of the city in her memory as she could. The main street ran broad and straight to the heart of Amradoc's capital. Minor thoroughfares radiated from it lined with buildings whose flat-roofed rectangular shapes made them appear squat, no matter how many stories they had. The unlit windows were small and barred, but sounds of laughter and music and the smells of the evening meal mitigated their forbidding appearance. Few people were abroad, but those they came across called greetings to the party before disappearing behind the high gates each building had let into the walls instead of a door.

"What news, Officer? What news?"

Never 'hello' or 'good evening', and although the people were smiling and unhurried, the officer answered each one with a serious "All's quiet" as if news was the last thing anyone in Mandur truly wanted.

They entered the gates of a building taller than any other they had so far passed and found themselves in a cobbled courtyard bounded by stables and long barracks on either side with a high blank wall between. The officer dismounted and strode into a lit room next to the barracks. He emerged a few minutes later with a younger soldier.

"Are you sure King Darian needs to be bothered with this? He's only just returned from the southern reaches." The younger officer looked them over dubiously.

"Unless you don't mind being held responsible for what might turn out to be a major diplomatic incident."

The other officer's face fell. He led them into the main building. The corridors were plain and sturdily built, with clean paint and polished wooden doors testifying to homely care. The contrast with Najarind was like night and day. Everything in the Ortanian capital spoke of neglected grandeur. The fugitives were left under guard in the corridor while the officers went inside. The thick wood let no sound through that Ro could detect. She looked at Lar, but her mother's thoughts evidently were elsewhere. Then the door was opened again, and they were ushered inside an antechamber as simply decorated as the corridors. The only objects it contained were what were serviceable: a table strewn with papers, straight-backed chairs, a brazier. It was like the inside of a tent that might have to be packed up and moved at a moment's notice.

In addition to the fugitives and their escort, the room contained three men. One was obviously a high-ranking soldier by his decisive bearing and short-cropped hair; the second wore a long robe in a dull indiscriminate colour, and stroked his beard as if it was a pet while he listened to the officers. The third was a short man who might have been on a level with his companions if his spine had not had a twist to it. His limbs seemed capable of individual thought as they twitched and gestured at random. The man's necklace of beads jangled and clicked with each jerky movement. Edun groaned.

"What's the matter?" Ro whispered. "I thought we were to be brought before the king."

Edun tried to hide his face behind his hand.

The older officer finished his report and the beard-stroker turned his attention to them. "It's customary to bow when in the presence of the king."

The fugitives hastily obeyed and gave him the formal salute. The high-ranking soldier let out a bark of laughter.

"Not me, you fools!" The bearded man coloured.

The soldier clapped him on the shoulder. "Perhaps I should take your advice, Uwert, and dress as befits my rank as king rather than head of the army."

So this was Darian. Ro looked more closely. His face had the ruddy tint of someone used to being out in all weathers. The lines suggested ready laughter, not age, and his eyes were a blue that immediately made Ro think 'water affinity', yet his body had the solidity of earth.

"Well, well... so we have the most wanted criminals in all of Ortann in our midst, and what are we to do with them?" He looked from one to another of them.

Ro glanced expectantly at Lar, but the Earth-hearer remained silent; listening, Ro thought, to discover if he played clear and true.

"Send them straight back, Sire. Why risk antagonising Ortann when we already have trouble with her Gindullan minions to the south?"

Darian nodded, but continued his scrutiny. The third figure copied, thrusting his face close to each one in turn. Ro felt an urge to laugh.

"Or perhaps you could make their return part of a pact with Najarind to keep its vassals from harrying our borders."

"Do you think they'd keep such a pact, Uwert?" Darian raised his eyebrows.

The adviser shook his head. "What else are we to try, short of outright war?"

"Patience," giggled the third. "Try their patience!"

"You try my patience, Jubb!" Uwert, snapped. "Why do we need this fool here?" he appealed to the King.

"Would you prefer another?" Jubb answered, his face innocent.

Darian laughed as Uwert reddened. "There are no fools here, Uwert, only trusted advisers. So, we'll start with patience and hear what these people have to say. Who'll speak for you?"

For a moment there was silence. Ro looked to Lar, but the Earth-hearer continued rocking Lalli, whose lip trembled on the verge of another hungry outcry.

"Sire," Ro blurted, then stopped amazed at hearing herself speak. The blue eyes immediately pinned her to the spot. "We'll gladly tell our story, but first we need to find a wet-nurse for Lalli. She hasn't been fed properly for days." She was so conscious of how much depended on what was said, that Ro could barely make her lips move.

The King turned his penetrating blue gaze on the baby and stroked her cheek.

"You are the child's mother?" he asked Lar. She shook her head.

Raimi's voice cut in. "She's dead."

Darian frowned. "Very well–you will stay." He pointed at Ro. "Put the rest under guard in the guest quarters and find someone for the babe."

The officers saluted and led the way out to the waiting guards. As the others followed, Edun allowed his hand to drop. Jubb let out a cry.

"It's you!" He plucked at the magician's sleeve gesturing like a broken doll with the other arm. "It's him! The magician who gave me my Words of Power. It's him!" He would have fallen to his knees and kissed the hem of Edun's flame-decked coat if the magician had not snatched it away.

"Get up–I did nothing," he muttered.

"Everything, everything. Your words have protected me from beatings, brought me food and drink and helped me find my good friend the king." As proof he drew a tattered piece of paper from the breast of his tunic and opened it reverently in his palm.

King Darian's face was stern. "Is this true?"

Edun hung his head. "He begged me–I meant no harm."

Darian positioned himself directly in front of the magician. "Some people treat those whom Ondd has blessed with simplicity with scorn; they ill-treat them and ridicule them. I've seen the words on that paper."

Edun stared at the offending scrap. "I didn't think he'd keep it. I meant no harm." He blushed deeply. Ro did not understand. 'Words of Power' must be real magic, but Edun's wagon contained mere illusions.

"Whatever you meant, no harm has been done." Darian turned and Edun sagged. "Count yourself lucky."

"Oh, it's me who counts himself lucky. Blessed indeed the day I met The Incredible Edun." Jubb beamed at the magician. "Now I know you shouldn't send them back."

Uwert shook his head. "Sire... "

"Edun let us ride on his wagon–that's all," Ro cut in, trailing off as Uwert tutted. "He wasn't with us in Najarind."

Darian nodded at the officers to carry out his orders. Jubb looked desperately from Darian to Edun. He grasped his hair firmly in both hands and squeezed his eyes shut, then opened them again.

"No, I'll have to stay here, but never fear, friend, I'll come to see you as soon as I can," Jubb assured Edun.

Darian gestured for Ro to sit. He leaned back in his chair. "So, tell us your story. No doubt you're innocent." From his direct gaze Ro guessed that Darian was no liar, but the clear steadiness of his expression warned her that he was used to spotting them and expected her to try to deceive him.

"Yes, what happened to your hair?" Jubb ruffled the ragged tufts making her wince.

"Peace, Jubb. I'm sure she'll come to that in due course."

Ro took a deep breath and plunged into the tale, starting with the discovery of Lalli's disability and their expulsion from Iyessa. She kept the tale as simple as she could, concentrating on it as hard as if trying to set it to music so she would not be distracted by Jubb's grimaces or the reaction of Uwert, just visible from the corner of her eye. She described the scene in King Berinn's sickroom and their imprisonment, the drugging of the guard and their flight from Najarind. The only part she left out was Varda's prediction that she and Lalli were destined to wake Ondd. She was not sure how much she believed that herself. Finally, she related their pursuit and the death of Ussu at the river. She had to focus hard and dig her nails into her palms to keep her voice steady, but Jubb's eyes filled with tears and he sniffed loudly.

"Your claim that Edun did nothing but let you ride with him wasn't strictly true then?" Darian commented.

"Indeed not–he saved them!" Jubb puffed up with pleasure.

"But he committed no crime," Ro said quickly.

"Harbouring criminals, helping them escape justice... " Uwert listed the charges.

"We aren't criminals."

"That remains to be determined," Darian silenced them. "Why did he help you? The magician doesn't strike me as one to risk his neck for strangers."

Jubb opened his mouth indignantly, then snapped it shut again as Darian gave him a warning look.

Ro considered. "It was the onddikins, I think. He trusts their judgement. The onddikins chose me... "

"Attacked you," Uwert corrected.

"They chose me," Ro repeated. "And they disliked the soldiers."

"I remember the onddikins," Jubb reminisced. "They had wonderfully soft skin and ... "

Uwert tutted.

"Sometimes these simple creatures have truer instincts than we who believe ourselves so clever." Darian steepled his fingers. Ro was unsure whether the 'simple creatures' he referred to were the onddikins or people like Jubb or both. "You say you believe Lord Torslin and the physician Ayif are behind King Berinn's death and seek to blame Mistress Dovinna to divide her from the new king, Channan."

Ro nodded.

"How?"

She returned Darian's gaze. "Somehow Ayif put the poison into the goblet he handed to Dovinna–I don't know how."

"But you were watching him," Uwert objected.

"Magic," breathed Jubb. Ro felt the blood rushing in her ears.

Darian shook his head. "There are too many unanswered questions. Why, having accused you, would Torslin let you go? Why was no embassy sent here with the news of King Berinn's death? Protocol demands that heads of state be invited to pay their last respects... "

"Since when have Ortanians bothered with courtesy?" snorted Uwert.

"And you haven't given sufficient explanation why you came here. Are you in the pay of our enemies, sent to implicate Amradoc in a plot against Ortann?" Darian searched her face.

"Why take the risk?" Uwert urged. "Send them back and let Najarind's courts decide."

"Courts?" Jubb parroted. "But Lord Torslin's already declared them guilty."

Darian ran a hand over his forehead. "This deserves more thought. Have her put with the others," he instructed Uwert. "And stay away from them for now."

Jubb pushed out his bottom lip.

"I'll make my decision tomorrow."

Ro was escorted by two guards to rooms off the courtyard. From the outside they did not look welcoming enough to be called guest quarters. Inside they were surprisingly cosy, if not lavish. Edun was brewing something aromatic over a lively fire in a broad chimney, while Dovinna questioned him about the ingredients. Lar was towelling her wet hair and Raimi watched as a woman cradled a sated Lalli in her arms. The sight made Ro start, thinking of Ussu, but then the plump figure and rosy cheeks of the woman registered themselves. They all looked expectantly at Ro as she entered.

"King Darian will decide what to do with us tomorrow." Ro slumped in a chair, the tension of the interrogation flooding out of her limbs, leaving her feeling empty. Now, she had their anxious questions fired at her.

"Did he believe you?"

"What about avenging Ussu?"

"Will he risk offending Ortann?"

She turned her head away as if they were blows.

"Enough." Lar hugged her. "You've done your best, Ro. Now rest. We'll just have to wait until morning."

As if to give her statement emphasis, Lalli let out a contented burp. Ro giggled, but Raimi was instantly on his feet and snatched the baby away from the wet-nurse.

"Not like that! Ussu always burped her like this. Look!" His anger wiped the pleasure from Ro's face. The wet-nurse bore the criticism with a placid expression.

"This is Mirri. She has three children of her own, and was wet-nurse to the King's cousin," Lar told her.

"We're very grateful," Ro said.

The wet-nurse blushed. "It's nothing. I've got plenty of milk and cuddles to spare–why waste them?" She watched Raimi soothing Lalli. "Now isn't that a picture! I'll be off then, until the morning feed." She smoothed out her apron and knocked to be let out. If she had felt any qualms about being surrounded by alleged murderers she had given no sign. Would that Darian would accept them as easily!

Ro was still struggling to make her hair look presentable the following morning when the door was thrown open. Uwert entered, standing just inside the doorway to survey the domestic scene. Jubb pushed past him.

"Brr... it's cold, it's cold. Cold enough to freeze... "

"Jubb!" Uwert rebuked him. His hands were tucked inside a fur-trimmed robe.

Overnight the weather had returned to the seasonal norm, catching the last remnants of the downpour and holding them fast as icicles hanging off gutters and dazzling crystal sculptures on the small square windows. The open door let the first of the winter sneak in to bite at their ankles.

"I haven't come here to discuss the weather," Uwert announced as he took up a warmer position with his back to the fire. He stroked his beard a few times, so that Ro almost expected it to purr. "King Darian has asked me to convey his decision to you."

"Yes, he would have told you himself but... " Jubb subsided under Uwert's frown.

"The King is called to attend to more urgent matters, you may be grateful that he saw fit to give so much of his personal attention to you at all." The sight of Mirri putting Lalli to her breast momentarily disconcerted him. "Do you have to do that now?" he asked, curling his lip with distaste.

"What a question!" she scolded. "Time, the tide and babies wait for no one–not even perfumed courtiers."

The adviser rolled his eyes. "Very well. You're to know that King Darian thinks you should be tried with all the evidence for and against brought before your judges before you're sentenced. He's sent word to Najarind to that effect." Uwert headed for the door.

Ro stopped him. "Exactly what does that mean?"

"That's easy," Jubb answered, hugging himself with pleasure. "It means you get to stay here with us, and I get to thank my old friend and play with the baby for at least a double-week–even longer if everything freezes."

"At the end of which time you'll have to hope you can convince ten worthy citizens of Amradoc that they should let you go." Uwert's words left a chill in the room after he had left that no amount of fuel on the fire could disperse.

Anni's teeth chattered. The palace balcony provided a clear view of the city spread out below them and beyond the gates to where the road was no more than a faint wrinkle in the landscape. The sun caught on the pennants and gilded litters of the last of the departing mourners, and further. It also suffered the full blast of a raw wind which sent the Najarindians scurrying about their business with shoulders hunched, and shook out the canvas roofs of the stalls. Despite this, Channan, Ersilla, Torslin, Fordel and Anni lingered on the balcony in regal immobility–apart from Anni's teeth.

Ersilla spoke without turning or spoiling her serene smile. "If you're too weak to stand properly, go indoors."

Channan turned. "Surely that'll do? I'm getting out of this damned wind!" He turned to Fordel. "Come on, there's a bottle of wine I've been wanting to try."

Fordel hesitated. Since returning empty-handed from the hunt, but for Dovinna's ring, his position had been precarious. Channan and he had been friends since childhood, but Anni was not sure whether that made him safer or placed him at greater risk. Channan might be king, but Torslin ruled.

"What's that?" Ersilla's sharp voice interrupted. Too regal to point she narrowed her eyes the better to see what was moving in the distance.

Riders were approaching the city. Anni held her breath forgetting the cold as she waited for them to come close enough to identify. The disciplined trot at which they travelled two abreast was unmistakable.

"Pachand's patrol," Fordel said quietly.

What little colour there was, drained from Channan's face. His hand shook as he reached for the casement to go inside.

Ersilla's voice oozed concern. "Are you all right, Brother? Perhaps you need a glass of that wine."

Channan ignored her. "Is she with them, Fordel?"

The Lord shaded his eyes. "I'm not sure, I... no, I see only soldiers."

A look passed between Ersilla and Torslin.

"Escaped?" suggested the Princess.

"Or dead."

Channan sagged. "Dead."

"I share your disappointment, Brother. The chit's cheated us of our right to punish her for Father's death." The satisfaction in Ersilla's voice brought Channan's head up sharply.

He straightened his shoulders. "It wasn't revenge I wanted, but answers."

Anni took his hand. "There's no point in speculating, Channan, we'll know soon enough." She was rewarded with a wisp of a smile.

"Poor Anni. We forget how much you must be suffering." Channan put his arm about her. As they went inside, Anni could not meet his gaze and felt a guilty blush spread across her cheeks.

Glancing over her shoulder as they entered the welcome warmth of the audience chamber to make sure the others did not follow too closely, she whispered: "My sole grief, Channan, is seeing you so unhappy. Why should I grieve over Father when he could barely remember my name?"

Channan kissed the top of her head.

"If only you'd eat a decent meal and get some sleep instead of drinking the night away..." She broke off as he flung himself onto a chair and started fiddling with the embroidered upholstery.

"So Fordel keeps saying. What none of you seem to understand is that I drink because I get no sleep. When I lie abed all I hear is 'why?' Why did she do it? Why did she run? Why didn't she trust me?" His fist clenched on the adamant ring, which he had taken to wearing on his little finger.

"Perhaps it was her ambition to be queen," Ersilla answered scornfully as she came in behind them and took up a position to the right of Channan's chair.

"It will be some while before Pachand gets here yet–at least get some food inside you in the meanwhile," Anni suggested without hope.

"I agree, lad." Torslin strode into the room. His presence seeming to Anni to leave no room for anyone else. "There's no reason why you should hear all the tedious details of Pachand's report. I can deal with it and give you the salient points after you've rested."

"No." It was the first time Anni had heard Channan directly refuse one of Torslin's suggestions, and the adviser stiffened. "I'll wait. The rest of you may be dismissed if you please." Channan's face was set as if the roof could cave in and he would not move.

Torslin made a stiff bow. "As you wish, Sire, of course."

He stood on Channan's other side, and there they waited, unmoving and unspeaking. Only as they heard the sound of booted feet approaching along the corridor did Anni raise her eyes and catch Fordel's fixed on her. The nonchalant veil had slipped and she saw concern, but for Channan or himself?

Captain Pachand was admitted still wearing the stink of the road, and made his report uninterrupted until he reached the part where Darian's patrol intervened. Ersilla's cry of outrage made him falter.

"We were outnumbered and on foreign soil, Highness. I had no instructions and I'm a soldier not a diplomat. I thought it best to return."

"You say they headed straight for the Amrad patrol–as if they were expected?" questioned Torslin.

Pachand hesitated. "Maybe."

"It seems you have your answer," the adviser told Channan. "Amrad spies and assassins. Thank you, Captain." Torslin dismissed him.

The King's fingers tightened on the arms of his chair. "Wait!" He struggled to speak. "Did you see her? Mistress Dovinna?"

"Oh, she was there all right, Highness."

"No." Channan gestured impatiently. "How was she, how did she look?"

The soldier looked uncertainly at Torslin. The misery on Channan's face was too much for Anni to bear.

"Brother, I'm sure Captain Pachand's exhausted."

Channan waved him away.

Almost before the door had closed behind him Ersilla burst out: "Insufferable! How dare Amradoc insult us so?"

"It's as I feared, lad." Torslin put a fatherly hand on Channan's shoulder. "They're plotting to take over the empire and they don't even have the honour to do it openly."

"Surely not." Anni looked at Fordel for support.

"Aren't we reading too much into the actions of one patrol officer?" he drawled, as if the matter was all too boring.

"Then why haven't we heard from Darian?" Ersilla demanded.

"Perhaps because we didn't have the courtesy to inform him of Father's death," Anni countered.

"News he was already aware of, it would seem." Torslin's face was grim.

"You surely can't consider war with Amradoc?" Anni appealed to Channan.

"If he attacks us we have no choice." Ersilla snapped.

"But if he really wanted Ortann he would have... " Anni stopped, suddenly aware of where the words were taking her.

"Yes?" Ersilla's eyes would have frozen lava.

"He would have married you when Father offered him your hand. It would've given him a stronger claim." Anni held up her chin, but Channan intervened before Ersilla could strike.

"Father wanted half of Amradoc in return–Darian would've been a fool to accept," he said.

There was a nervous tap on the door and a servant edged into the room.

"Apologies, Sire, but a carrier-bird has arrived... " The servant kept clearing his throat and flicking his gaze anxiously about the room. "Didn't quite believe it, it's been such a long time, but I've checked and double-checked and there's no mistaking the bird's wing bars... " He caught Torslin's thunderous frown and held a scrap of paper at arm's length. "It's from Amradoc."

Torslin snatched it from him and read as the servant made his escape.

"Well?" Ersilla demanded.

"From Darian," Torslin said. "He 'regrets' the border incident and would like to assure us that he has the fugitives safely under lock and key. To make amends and save us the expense, he intends putting them on trial. He requests that we send him our evidence. Our observers are welcome to attend." Torslin's voice was calm, but the paper shivered in his hands.

"Ridiculous!" Ersilla exploded.

"Channan?" Anni prompted gently.

He slumped. "I don't know." He looked at Torslin.

"It could all be a trick to fool us into thinking he's a friend, so we aren't prepared when he makes his move. He executes the murderers and prevents them revealing his secret," Torslin said.

"You mean they wouldn't get a fair trial?" Channan's face flushed.

Torslin realised his mistake, but it was too late.

"Then we must certainly send an embassy, someone who won't be fooled by him." Channan considered.

"Certainly, I'll... " Torslin began.

"Ersilla," Channan said. "You have the rank to be respected and it'll show how serious we are."

"Sire," Torslin protested, but Ersilla was all smiles.

"Don't worry, I know how to discover the truth."

"The Princess can't go alone, I... " Torslin persisted.

"You'll be needed here to help me prepare the country if you're right. We need to be ready if Darian decides on more direct action. But we should send a strong escort." Channan rose and faced Fordel. "You shall go too."

Torslin protested. "Lord Fordel's hardly distinguished himself so far."

"All the more reason for him not to fail now. Don't let me down." Channan clasped his shoulders.

Fordel swallowed, avoiding Torslin's furious look. "I won't."

Anni let out a sigh. She felt as if she had been struggling for days to unravel a ball of tangled embroidery silk and now at last could see the twists and turns that would undo it. Startled heads turned her way as she poured herself a goblet of wine and drained it.

# Chapter Ten

King Darian waited at the top of the broad steps to his palace as the embassy approached. Princess Ersilla rode at its head, flanked by Fordel and Pachand and followed by her maids and a contingent of soldiers in their brightest armour. Fordel could see by Princess Ersilla's disdainful expression that she thought the city plain and uncouth, but its simple grandeur dressed in sparkling robes of winter beneath the sharp blue of a frosty sky made his breath catch in his throat. King Darian descended a few steps to greet the party as it dismounted. His jaw clenched momentarily as he recognised the woman at its head. Ersilla carefully lifted her riding skirt so that its rich hem would not be fouled by Amrad soil. Her face danced with girlish smiles as her gaze met Darian's and she held out her hand to be kissed.

"Welcome, Princess." Darian's lips brushed her fingertips. "Your brother does me great honour sending his most priceless treasure on this errand."

Ersilla blushed at the compliment and inclined her head. "You flatter me, Sire. My presence here shows the importance which Ortann places on bringing our father's killers to justice. Thank you for apprehending them for us." Her eyes were hard despite her smiles. "When may we take them back to Najarind?"

"When they're found guilty." Darian drew her arm through his and led the party into the palace before Ersilla could protest. "You must wish to relax and refresh yourselves after your long journey."

They were shown through lofty halls and stairways to their apartments. Fordel found he was quartered with Pachand.

"You don't mind if I take the bed furthest from the window, do you? Daylight always seems to arrive before I'm ready for it." Fordel stretched out on the couch in question and yawned.

"It's of no consequence to me," grunted the Captain as he divested himself of his mail and set about a brisk but thorough toilette.

Fordel watched through slitted eyes, pretending to doze. Instead of resting, the Captain donned a fresh civilian outfit, moving quietly with many glances in his direction.

"Going out?" Fordel asked, yawning and stretching.

Pachand started. "I want to find out the lie of the city. If this is a trap we may need an escape route."

Fordel rose. "Good idea. I could do with stretching my legs after all those miles on horseback. Give me a minute and I'll come too."

Pachand shrugged. "As you wish."

A few minutes later they were tramping the orderly streets of Mandur, having dismissed the offer of a servant to guide them.

"Wouldn't it have been better to let him accompany us? If we get lost we could wander for hours before anyone gives us directions," Fordel drawled as a family of Mandurians hurried past them, the mother shooing her children out of their path as if they were contagious. "We're not exactly popular."

"Go back if you wish. A guide wouldn't show us what we need to know," Pachand growled.

Fordel frowned. "I fear I'd need you to find my way."

Eventually, they headed back towards the palace. They turned a corner and found themselves in the street facing the rear of the complex. The strong gates stood open but guarded. Pachand grunted satisfaction. He nodded to the guard and they passed inside while the soldier hesitated. Fordel quickly took in the scene as Pachand checked his pace. To one side there were stables and storehouses, to the other what Fordel guessed to be barracks and married quarters. Nothing remarkable. Pachand suddenly moved on.

"This way."

He headed for a building of more humble proportions with cheery smoke rising from the chimney and a guard at the door.

The window squeaked as Ro rubbed the misted pane with her sleeve, drawing disapproving glances from Mirri.

"Really!" the wet-nurse scolded. "Just when I'm trying to get Lalli down for her nap!"

"It won't disturb her, Mirri, Lalli's deaf," Ro snapped back.

"It does bother me, however." Lar's rebuke brought Ro to the edge of tears. She stared hard out of the small window, determined not to let the others see, even if her mother could feel her distress.

Outside, a narrow strip of shiny cobbled courtyard and high red stone walls bounded her vision. The city still sparkled under a hard frost which caught the sun as if all the stones were studded with crystal. So still and clear was the weather that the clatter of horses' hooves and the greetings of passing Mandurian citizens could be heard from afar. In the three weeks since they had arrived in the city this had been their sole sight of it along with the enclosed quadrangle where they took their exercise twice a day. Occasionally, a curious citizen would approach, unable to resist delaying their business for a look at the fugitives. They would exchange pleasantries with the guards, their words hanging frozen in the air. Not all the looks were friendly.

"Why do we fascinate them so, Mirri?" Ro had asked one particularly trying afternoon when it had seemed there was always at least one face staring in at them.

"Because you could be the death of us all." Mirri was given to colourful exaggeration, but this had seemed too extreme even for her.

"What do you mean?" Dovinna had joined the discussion.

"War, my dears. You could bring war with Ortann, not that that band of cutthroats in Najarind, saving your young prince, that is, hasn't been spoiling for it long enough. Just waiting for an excuse, if you ask me, and you're it. Well, how's a poor country like Amradoc to defeat Ortann that's got all the wealth and manpower of an empire behind it?"

"It's an empire in little more than name," Dovinna protested.

"Nothing like a war to unite people, eh, my sweet?" Mirri asked the baby cradled in her arms. "Not that King Darian's not a clever man and a brave, with an army of the best-hearted men you'll find anywhere on this earth." She dabbed at her eyes. "What's to become of us? My Praidis was a trained soldier, one of the best, but that didn't stop him getting killed."

Ro and Dovinna had looked at each other with eyes full of guilt.

Edun broke the mood. "Less of that now, Mirri, you'll sour the milk. Did I ever tell you about the time I performed for the Caliph of Hemdulla? No? Well... " He winked at them as he embarked on another outrageous tale to leave Mirri saucer-eyed and open-mouthed, but ever since then Ro had felt hostility underlaid Mirri's scolding.

"Perhaps there won't be war," Ro muttered to herself now. "Perhaps King Darian will send us back–or perhaps we should offer to go."

"Offer?" Mirri's voice was as high-pitched as an excited onddikin's. "I've never heard such nonsense–and what about your baby niece? And your mother?"

The words may have been meant to reassure, but instead Ro felt selfish. She sighed and turned her back to the window, ignoring the sound of approaching footsteps. It was no doubt another curious Mandurian. As the footsteps drew closer something about them caught Ro's attention. They were not the familiar skip and tiptoe of Jubb, who could not forbear from visiting his hero, Edun, despite his master's warning. Nor were they the regular tramp of the soldiers going to or from their duties. Yet there was something. Then Lalli shrieked as if Mirri had stuck her with a pin. Ro's heart responded with an extra thump. She glanced back at the window and started. On the other side, so close that had the pane not been there she would have felt his breath on her cheek, was Pachand, his expression grimly satisfied. Beyond, she caught a glimpse of Lord Fordel.

"What is it?" Raimi tried to see past her. His bouts of fierce restlessness alternated with periods of lethargy. These had become so extreme since their arrival in Mandur that even Lalli's windy smiles could not relight the spark in his eyes. Ro feared the consequences if he was to see Ussu's killer. An attack now would only confirm in King Darian's eyes that they were capable of the crime of which they were accused.

"Nothing–a spider–I wasn't expecting it." She held her breath as her marriage-brother pushed past her, but the faces had disappeared. She craned her neck to see further. They were gone as if they had never been there. Her heart was recovering its usual rhythm when her attention was snagged by more footsteps. This time there was no mistaking them–the erratic stuttering gait of Jubb played a descant over the more considered steps of Uwert. The door was thrown open and the pair entered. Ro's welcoming smile faded as she saw the agitation on the fool's face.

"They're here!" Jubb announced. "The embassy from Najarind."

Uwert tutted. "King Darian sent me to deliver the news. Look at the fright you've given them!"

Ro sat down heavily as her blood plummeted to her feet. So, she had seen Pachand.

"Time's run out," Edun sighed.

"It's running out for them too." Raimi clenched his fists at his side.

"Who's King Channan sent?" Dovinna asked, blushing as she said Channan's name.

"His sister, Princess Ersilla, Lord Fordel and a Captain Pachand–all of whom claim to be material witnesses."

Lar put out a restraining hand to Raimi whose knuckles whitened.

"Ersilla!" Dovinna said. "She despises me. We'll never convince her we're innocent."

"Ah, but it's King Darian you have to convince." Jubb sat down next to Mirri with his knees tucked up under his chin.

"I feel Darian's a just man," Lar said. "He may not be Iyessi, but he is sensitive to emotion and must read people well to govern."

"However adept His Highness is at reading people, as you put it, it won't be enough. You must offer your evidence to the Council of Citizens." Uwert smoothed his beard. "In the interests of justice, King Darian has appointed me to put forward your case."

"You?" Ro asked.

The adviser bowed.

"I thought you wanted us sent back."

Uwert swelled at the implication. "I still think it would have been wiser, but now this course has been decided on, I'll do everything in my power to see that Amrad laws and justice are upheld. Now, since I have other duties to perform, let's get down to work. I'll need to hear each of your stories in turn–separately."

The light had faded by the time it was Ro's turn. The lamplight and fire threw sinister shadows onto the hollows of Uwert's face as he tossed question after question at her, making her repeat details, trying to trip her up with things the others had said. At first bewildered and upset, Ro found heat rising in her chest and threatening to spill scorching words from her throat.

"You said you're on our side."

"So I am." The adviser sat back and stroked his beard wearily. "But I need to be sure you've told me all. For instance–you say, King Berinn's physician," he checked his notes, "Ayif, must have administered the poison–how?"

Ro's anger seeped away, leaving her dry and exhausted. It was the question she kept asking herself. "I don't know. I wish I did. But it must have been him."

Eventually, Uwert gathered them again. "I can't say I'm hopeful of acquittal, but the charges against some of you are tenuous. I shall do my best." Uwert prepared to leave.

Lar gave him the formal salute with fingertips to her lips. "Dance to Ondd's music."

The adviser cleared his throat. He looked at Jubb. "Are you coming?"

The fool shook his head. He was joggling Lalli on his lap in a way that had Mirri on the edge of her seat. After the door shut behind Uwert there was silence.

Jubb broke it. "I don't know what you're all so gloomy about. All you need is for Edun to give you some Words of Power like mine, then everything will come out right."

Edun looked awkward. "What we all need is a little diversion."

He began rummaging in his box of equipment, making the onddikins twitter expectantly. Ro sighed. Whenever she had tried asking him about Jubb's talisman he had hastened to change the subject. Yet it seemed nothing short of magic could save them. She watched half-heartedly as Edun asked Mirri to choose a playing card from the pack. How had the physician put poison in the medicine goblet without anyone seeing? How had he hidden the evidence? Mirri clapped her hands with delight as Edun produced her chosen card seemingly from thin air. He then began to draw a chain of coloured scarves from his mouth.

"And now... " The magician made an elaborate gesture, bundled the scarves tightly into one hand, blew on it, then opened his fingers–they were gone! Ro's jaw dropped.

"That's it!"

Edun's showman's patter faltered.

"Please do that trick again."

Edun shrugged and complied. Ro watched with all her concentration.

"How did you do that?"

She watched again in her memory as Ayif carefully raised the goblet to the light and handed it to Dovinna.

"Magic," breathed Jubb.

"Like the cabinet trick?" Ro asked.

Edun looked haughty. "Illusion, please, and you know I'm sworn not reveal the secret of my magic."

"But it's the answer–don't you see?"

The magician sighed. "Watch... "

He performed the trick again, more slowly this time, explaining each stage as he did so. "You know this is going to ruin my reputation. I won't have an act left soon," he complained.

"But you have at least one more show to perform–before the King and council of citizens tomorrow," Ro said.

Minutes later the scarecrow figure of the fool was galloping and skipping through the palace corridors. He threw open the door to King Darian's audience chamber.

"We've got it! We know how King Berinn was poisoned." He skipped round in a circle.

"Of course." A cool female voice halted his dance. He blinked at the tableau of Princess Ersilla and King Darian seated opposite each other in front of the fire. "The so-called healer in league with Iyessi malcontents gave it to him instead of medicine." The ice in her voice did not penetrate the fool's glee.

Jubb hugged himself. "Oh no, that's not it at all. You'll see tomorrow, you'll see." He ignored Darian's warning look. "It's magic."

"Thank you, Jubb. That will be all." Darian smiled at the Princess. "I'm sorry. Sometimes Jubb forgets his manners."

The fool hopped from one foot to the other, eager to tell the King all about it.

"You may leave, Jubb."

"That's quite all right, King Darian." Princess Ersilla rose with an understanding smile. "I was about to retire." She dipped a curtsy and left.

As soon as the door closed behind her, Ersilla's smile vanished. She swept along the corridors, pausing before the door to her quarters only long enough to make sure she was not watched before hurrying on. Her tap at the door of Pachand and Fordel's quarters was light enough for Fordel to pretend that it had not disturbed his doze. Pachand answered it. Fordel heard the Captain come to attention.

"I have a job for you, Captain."

Fordel recognised Princess Ersilla's voice. It dropped to a whisper.

"But, Highness... "

Whatever she said made Pachand uncomfortable.

Ersilla cut off his protests. "No buts, Captain. I have given you an order."

Through slitted eyes Fordel saw his roommate bow. The door shut, and he heard Pachand come to stand over him. There were sounds of furtive movements and a minute or two later, the door opened and closed as Pachand went out. Fordel toyed with the idea of following. Whatever he was up to, Fordel was probably safer not knowing. By the time the Captain returned, Fordel had dozed off in earnest. He felt only moments could have passed, but there was a reddish dawn-like glow outside the window. As Pachand stood over him, he detected a smell no dedicated carouser like himself could fail to place. Spirits! So the upright Captain was a secret drinker. Fordel allowed himself a smile. As he began to drift once more a sudden clatter, seemingly outside the window, snatched him awake.

"Fire!"

Shouts and clanging alarms brought Fordel scrambling to his feet and to the window. The courtyard was full of frantic activity. Flames darted through the stable roofs. Guards and servants struggled with terrified horses and water pumps. Fordel turned to haul on his clothes and found Pachand half-dressed–or was it half-undressed–watching him.

"We should help."

The soldier nodded. They hurried out into the cold night air, now awhirl with motes of soot and plumes of smoke. As they crossed the courtyard, a soot-blackened figure dashed into them, arms whirling wildly.

"Fire! Fire!"

"Idiot! Do you think we're blind?" Pachand pushed Jubb out of his way. The fool lost his balance, tumbling over the cobbles. He clutched at the arm of a groom struggling to calm a white-eyed horse.

"Over here! Fire! Fire!"

The groom shouted to his comrades. "It's caught the guest block. Quick!"

"Where's the guard?" someone shouted. It was Darian, clothed only in shirt and breeches, his short hair dishevelled.

Cries and thuds and the shrieks of the onddikins could be heard from within the burning building.

"My friends!" Jubb cried. He began beating on the door.

Darian snatched an axe from one of the soldiers. "Stand back!"

He aimed a few sweeping strokes at the solid wood, creating a gap large enough for the prisoners to slip through. He dropped the axe and took Lalli from Ro's arms. The others stumbled through after her. Fordel turned and saw Pachand walking away. Through eyes streaming from the smoke, Ro saw him too. Beside her, only the support of Raimi kept Lar on her feet. Her mother's breath came in choking wheezes and beneath the fire's grime she was as grey as ashes.

"Mother?"

The Earth-hearer waved a dismissive hand feebly.

"She needs my help," Dovinna told the King.

Darian nodded and beckoned to Jubb, who was running about the courtyard flapping his arms in an attempt to help Edun catch the onddikins.

"Take them to my quarters–I'll not be needing them tonight." His face was grim as he surveyed the mayhem around him.

For once, Jubb became almost businesslike. As he guided them through the corridors to the royal apartments, Ro felt she was walking through a nightmare once more. Sounds and images bombarded her; being torn awake by Lalli's screams; struggling to rouse Lar; Raimi and Edun's desperate attempts to break down the door; onddikins screeching and flapping; smoke streaming out of the fireplace reaching hungry fingers out to them. Were they cursed to be trapped, or lucky to escape the flames? No matter what they tried to do, Ondd seemed to have other plans in store.

"Why struggle?" she thought and settled onto a soft mattress between clean sheets.

Ro felt worse. "I suppose I'm not used to soft beds any more," she told Dovinna. She struggled to breathe past the tight bands around her chest.

The healer stroked salve onto her forehead. "This will help purge your lungs of smoke. Thankfully, it's not in short supply here–all our gear is ashes."

The smell was so strong it made Ro's eyes run.

"How are the others?"

"Lalli screamed so much I don't think she paused to breathe in the smoke," the healer hesitated. "Lar isn't as strong as she'd have me think." Seeing Ro's look she hurried on. "Oh, I'm sure she'll be all right, providing we can persuade her to rest."

"You forget... " They looked up as Lar entered. "We have to face our judges today." The Earth-hearer's face still wore an ash-tinged pallor and her voice was a rough whisper.

"The fire," Ro said. "Perhaps they'll postpone it."

Lar shook her head. "Lord Uwert is waiting for us outside."

The adviser's face was subdued as he led them to the audience chamber. The Najarindian embassy and King Darian were already there. Ro looked for the ten Mandurian citizens who were to be their judges. Darian nodded to Uwert, who directed the fugitives to seats placed opposite the King. Princess Ersilla sat next to him with Pachand and Fordel behind her.

"You offer them seats?" Ersilla demanded.

King Darian ignored the comment. "I've been questioning my men about last night's fire, and there are several things that puzzle me."

"Indeed, it's a miracle that no one was hurt," Princess Ersilla said as if discussing the weather.

"Indeed," Darian agreed. "Especially as it spread so quickly. Strange how the fire erupted in two buildings so far apart when there was no wind to speak of."

"Who can explain coincidence?"

"The man who left this in his gear, perhaps." Darian nodded at Jubb, who had been waiting as unobtrusively as he was able to by the window. He now placed a bundle of rags and an empty spirit bottle on Darian's table.

Ersilla shrugged. "Then ask him."

"Thank you, Princess." Darian turned to Pachand. "Captain, what have you to say?"

"Pachand? I find your joke tasteless, King Darian."

"No joke, Princess. Jubb here likes to say 'goodnight' to the horses before he goes to bed. Last night he saw the Captain waiting in the shadows."

Ersilla's smile tightened. "That means nothing."

"These were found in his gear," Darian added.

"You had the nerve to search my people's possessions?" She stood stiffly.

"Well, Captain?"

"Don't answer. He has no right to accuse you."

"You just gave me permission," Darian smiled.

"This is an insult! Someone's planted these things to throw suspicion on us."

"Perhaps."

"You can't possibly hold us responsible for what would be attempted murder on such flimsy evidence."

"Yet you would have me punish these people on no greater evidence," the King argued.

Princess Ersilla hesitated. "But... their motives... this is entirely different."

Darian looked at Uwert.

The courtier cleared his throat. "If you wish I can read the relevant codes of law to you, Highness. Essentially both cases have similar circumstantial evidence, but no proof. Find one guilty and you must find the other guilty also."

"Ridiculous!" Ersilla hissed. "If you take the side of the guilty that makes you guilty too, and the guilty must be punished–with an army if need be."

"Who exactly is guilty: he who set the fire, or the one who told him to do it? The guilty must be punished, you say, but I'd be loathe to keep you in an Amrad prison, Princess, fond as I am of your company."

"This is an insult, Darian. It won't be borne!"

"No, Princess. It's Amrad law. All must obey if from the humblest peasant to the highest noble, especially its king. My hands are tied."

For a moment Ro expected Princess Ersilla to shatter into shards and fly off in all directions. Instead she turned, sweeping several small items from the table with her skirts, and stalked out, speaking over her shoulder.

"This isn't the end of this matter–of that you may be sure."

Uwert looked at the King.

"Provide them with an escort to the border–make sure they know it's an honour."

So that was it. After weeks of searching for proof, none was needed. Ro stepped forward to thank the King. He waved her silent, slumping in his chair.

"Not now. You're sick and I'm weary. There'll be time enough for explanations."

"You hope," said Uwert.

Darian smiled for the first time that morning. "Never fear, Uwert, we'll be safe until the spring."

As Uwert directed them to new quarters, Ro asked what the King meant.

"War, my dear. You heard the Princess. We can look forward to a return visit, but with an army at her back.

Dovinna leapt to her lover's defence. "Channan would never sanction such a thing."

"Are you sure?" Uwert asked. Dovinna did not answer. "But no one offers battle in winter. For the time being at least, we're safe."

# Chapter Eleven

"You failed then," said Lord Torslin.

His calm irritated Princess Ersilla yet further. They were in her sitting room in the palace in Najarind. Despite the blaze of logs filling the fireplace and the luxurious cushions and rugs, the room was chilly and uncomfortable. Ersilla's agitated pacing threatened to sweep porcelain from tables.

"You might at least sound surprised," she complained. "How that man had the nerve to treat me so–me! Princess Ersilla of Ortann, the highest ranking lady in the empire!"

Torslin let her run on. "Darian will soon discover his mistake."

"The man's impossible!" Ersilla threw up her hands, then turned on Torslin. "He must be made to regret his insult–bitterly, you understand?"

"Oh, don't worry. Darian's arrogance will simply make the next stage in our plans more easy.

"Explain."

"He forestalled the fugitives' trial. Whatever they know or think they know, he denied them the chance to speak publicly, and he's shown himself no friend of Ortann in the process. Present Channan with the news in the right way and it shouldn't be hard to convince him that Darian was behind the plot all along, and that we must act to curb his ambition now. Providing no embarrassing evidence comes to light. We may have to deal with Pachand and Fordel." Torslin frowned. The former had proved a competent if unimaginative officer, just the sort of combination that was useful in a war; one who would do his job without asking questions. He would be a loss. Fordel was another matter.

Ersilla waved dismissively. "Pachand believes he acted to punish the murderers and avert a war. As for Fordel–he drank well at supper and snored through the whole episode until the alarm was loud enough to wake the dragon."

Torslin winced at the comparison. "I'll keep an eye on them just the same. Now we must decide exactly what you're going to tell the King."

"How is dear Channan?" Ersilla asked without interest.

"The betrayal by the healer has shaken his faith in himself, never very strong thanks to your father. He sits in his chambers and weeps into his wine."

Ersilla made an impatient gesture. "How can he show such weakness? Does he care nothing for the reputation of our family? No wonder upstarts such as Darian dare to insult us and flout our wishes. He's not fit to rule."

"And indeed he doesn't, Princess." Torslin grinned. "He's quite happy to leave matters of state to those of us with more experience. Only mention of his beloved healer rouses him. We shouldn't find it difficult to turn this setback into an advantage."

"Hmm... my darling brother has an irritating tendency to dig in his heels when you least expect it." She gave Torslin an arch look. "We wouldn't want two failures, would we?"

"Then we shall have to be careful... " He broke off as voices were raised outside. The door was flung open and Channan entered a little unsteadily, followed by a flushed maid.

"Careful about what?" he demanded.

"Listening at keyholes, Brother?" Ersilla took in his dishevelled appearance.

"You know this chit tried to stop me coming in? You should teach your servants who's king here."

"She probably didn't recognise you," Ersilla retorted. "You should have a shave."

Channan rubbed his hand over his chin. "Thought I'd grow a beard," he mumbled and slumped into a chair. "Why didn't you let me know you were back? Instead I had to overhear one of the servants talking about it." He noticed Torslin for the first time. "What're you doing here?"

"Like you, Sire, I heard of the embassy's return," Torslin said.

"And unlike you, he had the grace to ask how I am." Ersilla pouted.

Channan sighed. "How are you, Ersilla?"

"I am most fatigued. The journey was dirty and tiresome and I had hoped to make myself presentable and compose myself before facing you with the bad news."

Channan's bloodshot eyes suddenly came into focus.

151

"Yes, Brother. I had a wasted journey–there was no trial. All that way for nothing!"

"Then... then you've not brought... " Channan hesitated. "You have no prisoners?"

"No. And I very much doubt that Darian does by now. He said we had no real proof against them–without even hearing our testimony–and then used a fire at the palace as an excuse not to take the matter further." She sat in front of Channan and placed a hand on his knee. "I'm sorry, I did try, but not even my rank could persuade him to reconsider."

"Her Highness is trying to spare you, King Channan. From what she's told me, King Darian was so abrupt as to be rude. His treatment of her was not only insulting to her person, but to Ortann."

Channan appeared not to have heard him. "So we're no closer to knowing the truth."

"I wouldn't say that." Torslin and Ersilla shared a look. "We know that King Darian's protecting your father's murderers."

"Supposed murderers," Channan interrupted.

Torslin bowed. "There can be little doubt, but even if there was, it seems most likely that Darian never intended putting them on trial."

"Then why ask us to attend?" Channan protested.

"Because with the disruption caused by your father's death and the flooding he didn't think we'd be able to respond. But we called his bluff and this is the result."

"He takes us for fools." Channan got up and paced to the window. "But why would Dovinna go along with it?"

"With your father out of the way there'd be no obstacle to her becoming queen. People have turned to murder for less." Torslin was fatherly, understanding.

Channan reasoned with himself. "She could easily have met with Amrad agents. All and sundry made their way to her door."

"Like the Iyessi," Torslin agreed.

"But Fordel introduced them to each other," Channan protested.

"Perhaps they were meant to meet the healer in the temple of Ondd and got arrested first," Ersilla put in.

"It would've been a coincidence. I thought you used to say there was no such thing."

Torslin shrugged.

Channan's fingers tightened on the windowsill. "We should increase the border patrols and send representatives to keep an eye on Iyessa."

"A wise idea."

Ersilla's face darkened. "Keeping an eye on Amradoc won't be enough. That insolent, arrogant, cowardly man who calls himself king there will see it as weakness. We should chastise him for his behaviour."

"Declare war?" The thought drained what little colour there was from Channan's face.

"We're not ready for such a move," Torslin said quickly. "We should use the winter to prepare ourselves. I doubt Darian will show his hand before then. Besides, he's shown little inclination for anything as honest as an outright declaration of his intentions."

"Next spring or next decade, we will know the truth, we will be avenged, even if I have to trample Darian's palace into the dust," Channan ground out the words, staring out of the window as if seeing very different scenes from the routine bustle beneath.

Behind his back Ersilla could not keep the smirk from her face.

Anni walked rapidly along the corridor towards Ersilla's chamber then stopped suddenly. There was no point in asking her older sister for information. At best she would feed her a few patronising platitudes, at worst she would instruct her maid to send her away. When Channan had returned to his suite his cold quiet had alarmed her. It was as if all the alcohol he had consumed in recent weeks had turned sour. All he would tell her of his interview with Ersilla was that they had been betrayed, and honour demanded that Darian and all those who sided with him should learn that Ortann was not to be abused lightly. She had looked at him aghast, too shocked to try to cajole him into a lighter mood. Could this be her easygoing brother, who avoided disputes wherever possible, defusing arguments with a smile and his self-deprecating jokes? It was as if another creature was walking around in his body, one who had been taught how to think and talk by Lord Torslin. Anni shuddered. Ersilla was already under the adviser's influence, but they had always been like-minded. Now, it seemed, Anni was about to lose her brother to him. She saw again the look of contempt on Channan's face when she had ventured to suggest he should hear what the other members of the embassy had to say.

"Enough, Anni. There was no trial, because Darian feared his part in our father's death would be revealed. There's no other explanation."

Anni had swallowed her protest. Channan was not listening and she could not bear the emptiness in his eyes.

A servant left Ersilla's chambers and looked curiously at Anni hesitating outside. She would follow her own advice and seek out Fordel. She had glimpsed something underlying his carefree demeanour when she had last seen him that made her think he might be an ally. She found him haphazardly sorting through the reports that had arrived on his desk during his absence. An open flagon and half-empty goblet stood amongst the papers. As Anni entered he stood, knocking the goblet and showering spatters of red onto the documents. He waved away a servant who tried to mop up the mess.

"Leave that and fetch Princess Anni a goblet." He held a chair for her.

"No, thank you," she said. "I apologise for interrupting your work."

"Not at all. Any excuse to delay facing this." Fordel gestured at his chaotic desk.

"I don't suppose there's a report of what happened in Amradoc amongst it?"

Fordel turned on the servant. "Don't just stand there, man–fetch something to dry up this mess." He waited until the man had gone. "No, Princess, there isn't. I'm sure your sister will be able to tell you all."

"Able, but unwilling. I want to know what happened–without a lot of talk about insults." Anni looked Fordel in the eye.

He looked away and poured himself another drink. "Your sister found certain suggestions by King Darian called Ortanian integrity into question."

"That tells me nothing," Anni pressed. "What insult could be so bad that it's worth going to war over?"

"War?" Fordel set down the goblet untouched. "Has Channan agreed to this?"

"He claims it's inevitable."

Fordel hesitated, then lowered his voice. "While we were in Mandur there was a fire in the palace. There was almost no need for a trial, there was almost no one to try." He waited while Anni registered the implications, then picked up his goblet. "You know,

154

I always thought Captain Pachand disapproved of my taste for wine, but I do believe he likes the odd drop himself."

"I don't follow."

"Why else would he leave our room in the middle of the night?"

"You think... "

"I think there's no more loyal soldier than Captain Pachand. He certainly would never disobey an order."

"I see." It confirmed Anni's worst suspicions. Far from revealing a plot by King Darian, her sister's embassy had all been part of a design by Torslin and Ersilla. War with Amradoc was a gamble, but it might not come to that. Perhaps all they intended was to distract Channan from what was happening at home.

"You must tell Channan," Anni insisted.

"Of course, I'd been drinking myself and couldn't swear to any of this. In fact, I may have dreamed it," Fordel concluded.

Anni's tart reply was forestalled by the re-entry of the servant with a cloth.

"There you are! Some of these are already soaked beyond reading."

Anni stood and took Fordel's hand. "Thank you for your time. Channan can take comfort in knowing that he has courageous friends such as yourself." Anni was gratified to see Fordel look self-conscious. He pressed her hand.

"I am indeed his friend." Then raising his voice for the benefit of the servant. "Perhaps we should drink a toast–to the health of King Channan and all his brave friends." He gestured to the servant to refill his goblet, but the flagon was empty.

The air in the chamber was so hot that it hit those unprepared for it like a blow on the chest, but Torslin had been there many times before. He slipped through the curtain to the alcove with surprising quiet for one of his heavy build, and waited. Standing with his back to him was the flamboyantly dressed figure of Ayif. There was barely enough space for them both. The Gindullan physician swayed and muttered, his concentration wholly centred on a representation of the worm, Lethir, carved from jade set in a velvet draped niche. It coiled upwards to a gaping mouth holding a small brazier. Flames leapt from this and the candles on either side of the altar making its topaz eyes glitter with malevolent life, greedy to consume its worshippers. The physician's bald head wore a sheen of perspiration. He bowed and cast something into the brazier. It sizzled, releasing fumes of burned flesh in blue smoke. Ayif bowed with his fingertips to his lips three times, then sank to his knees and repeated the gesture. Then he brought both arms above his head with a flourish, clapped once, stood and blew out the candles.

"I hope that wasn't Ersilla's crimson finch that went in the flames; she's threatened to cut off the ears of the maid who let it out if the bird's not found, and we both know that she's capable of carrying out the threat." Torslin's drawl surprised Ayif into spilling hot wax down his robes.

"Lord Torslin, it is not good to mock our Master's devotions."

"It wasn't Lethir I was mocking, but you." Torslin moved back into the room and kicked one of the logs in the fireplace so that it sent out a spray of sparks. "I've come to tell you that you're safe. Not only are the fugitives out of the way, but Channan's convinced that he has Darian to blame for his troubles. They could say now that night follows day and he wouldn't believe them."

The physician turned back to the altar and cast another morsel into the flames.

"It's me you have to thank, Ayif, not the worm." Torslin grinned at the look of shock on the physician's face.

"Lethir is the all powerful, the mighty... "

"Who is it who's lulled the dragon and who will confound Lethir's enemies until It can return to rule in chaos for the era to come? It needs us to carry out its wishes." Torslin's chin jutted.

Ayif snatched up another offering and cast it to Lethir's image. "There are always others to take our place. Please, Lord Torslin–Lethir could crush us with barely a ripple."

"Don't worry, we aren't the ones who'll be crushed. It's time for the next step in our plans. Channan himself has given us the perfect opening. Your people in Gindul will have to step up their attacks on Darian's southern borders–keep him occupied there while we prepare the main blow, and give the Patriarch time to perfect his greedy pets. Meanwhile, you'll have to ensure Channan remains malleable."

"My Lord, I'm not sure... " Ayif protested.

"Then you'd better be–we need him eager to fight, but ready to follow our lead."

"It requires a delicate balance. Too much aggression and he'll become uncontrollable, too much indecision and he may follow another's lead, and whatever I do must be subtle enough to escape notice."

Torslin clapped him on the shoulder and Ayif winced. "I'm sure you're up to it, and soon there'll be so much going on that if anyone notices anything they'll merely think Channan's not settled into his kingship. Lethir's relying on you." Torslin's fingers tightened on the physician's shoulder.

Ayif swallowed and nodded. At that moment facing the worm seemed less dangerous than Torslin's smile.

# Chapter Twelve

The marks on the paper began to crawl about as if they had developed insect legs. Ro rubbed her eyes and looked again. She was beginning to wish she had never started. When she had discovered the library she had hoped one of the books might hold some clue to a cure, or maybe tell her more about the one who was not one, or at least some Words of Power like Jubb's. Ro had immediately seen their potential. Now the year was at the turning and the days were at their shortest and darkest, but despite weeks of searching she had found nothing that helped. She blew on her hands and began to trace the first line with her finger once more.

The library was cold. The bright frosty weather had given way to a spiteful wind that pinched any exposed flesh, sawing at wrists and ankles and bringing tears to eyes. Not that it chased the sword practice inside. For hours the clang and clash could be heard outside the window as one class after another brushed up on its technique. She knew that at some point Raimi would be among the swordsmen. After the weeks of wandering, Ussu's death had left him unable to rest. Even if Amradoc had not been constantly at threat from Ortann and its minions, Ro was sure he would have sought release in physical activity. When they all came together for the evening meal in their new quarters, it was as much as he could do to make the traditional responses in the song of bounty. To look at Lalli seemed a torture, and he escaped whenever he could.

Perhaps Ro's efforts in the library amounted to the same thing. They still could not return to Najarind either to prove their innocence or to root out the evil which was turning the world awry. Dovinna felt this more keenly than any of them. She was another who sought relief in work. There now seemed little hope of being reunited with Channan. On the one occasion when Ro had ventured to mention him Dovinna had studiously continued sorting herbs.

"I'm not sure that I want to any more, Ro. How could he be so ready to believe the worst of me?"

"We don't know what poison Torslin has poured into his ears." Ro could hardly believe her tactlessness. "I'm sorry, I meant... "

"I know. You're right, there's more than one sort of poison and Channan's so little aware of his worth that he'll readily question his own judgement. But–he knows me–he loves me, or so I believed. Surely that should wipe away the doubt?" Dovinna spoke briskly, then paused and pressed a palm to her forehead.

"Perhaps that makes it harder," Ro said.

"Well, at the moment it's not worth worrying about." Dovinna had wiped the remaining bits of herbs from her workbench as if brushing the conversation aside. Nonetheless, Ro often caught her glancing at her finger where Channan's ring had once been.

At least while she was in the library Ro was not disturbing anyone with her unguarded words or movements. The fire had affected Lar badly. Dovinna said her lungs and air passages had been scorched by the smoke and would take time to recover, but it was her mother's mood that worried Ro. The damage had affected her voice, so that she could neither project it nor sustain it with her customary power. All too often she would be reduced to a rasping whisper. Unless obliged to talk she spent her days with her eyes closed in a frown of pain listening to the thin wheeze of air as she breathed. Ro pushed back her chair. Perhaps she studied here because she could not bear to hear her mother so weakened. She should go back and at least relieve her of the need to listen to Mirri's banal chatter. If it had not been for Edun's efforts to build new tricks, and Jubb's attempts to assist him there would have been no relief for any of them.

A loud crack made her start as if the ceiling was about to collapse.

"Got you!" Jubb skipped up to the desk, a thick volume clasped to his chest. "Didn't hear me come in, did you? Would you like me to show you how I did it?" Jubb balanced the open book on his flat palms.

"No, thank you." Ro did not trust herself to say more. She restored the book to its shelf and dragged Jubb into the corridor with her.

Jubb took her arm and started hopping and skipping with her, as if following an invisible pattern of Iyessi planks and paving.

"Still looking for Words of Power? Why don't you just ask Edun?" He patted his chest where Edun's paper was safely stowed in his robe.

"He's busy at the moment." Edun had changed the subject so often that Ro dared not introduce it again. "Why were you in the library anyway?" she said, changing the subject herself.

Jubb froze, hand over mouth and eyes wide. "I forgot. Darian sent me to fetch you."

The King was in his antechamber with Uwert. A map was spread out on his table and they leant over it conferring. A food tray stood unheeded to one side. Sitting opposite the King was a man of middle years whose girth proclaimed him to be comfortably off. He leapt to his feet as they entered and stood turning his hat round by its brim.

Darian looked up. His welcoming smile was replaced almost instantly by a frown. "You're here, good! Sit down."

There was something in Darian's manner that made Ro's spirits sink.

"I've had news from Najarind that I think you and your kin should know about."

"King Channan has contacted you?" she asked.

Darian smiled grimly. "Little chance of that. No, our information comes from traders crossing the border. Tell them what you told us."

The man cleared his throat. "Well, as I told His Highness, me and my son were in Najarind a double-week or so ago. We came from the coast." He pointed on the map, next to a large patch of blue, but it meant little to Ro. "We import spices from the sandy continent, then transport them across Amradoc and on to Najarind. There we trade them. We always get enough profit to stock up on fancy goods and fine cloth to trade on our way back. Some say 'Why bother going all the way to Najarind?' but the profit's better there and... "

"Yes, yes," Uwert interrupted. "Stick to the point."

"Begging your pardon, Highness. As I was saying, trade's normally good in Najarind, but this time it was as if they might never see spices again. We could have asked whatever we wanted– the people kept outbidding each other, and when our stocks began to get low, scuffles started. In the end soldiers of the guard had to break it up. Well, I asked the landlord at our inn what was going on and it seems there's a rumour that war's brewing. 'Never

thought I'd say it,' he said, 'but thank Ondd I only have daughters.'
Seems recruiters have been sent out to every region–even remote
places like Iyessa–to get men for the army. Seen them come round
the inn and drag off some likely looking young men, myself. They
don't take no arguments. The priests are just as bad–even barging
into the inns demanding offerings to help Ondd's battle against
evil–that's you, begging your pardon, Highness. They've got the
king's backing to go out into the provinces and step down hard on
any practices don't suit their rules. Say that backsliders like me are
the cause of the trouble and must be 'brought back to the fold'.
There's at least one goes out with every recruiting party. Now, I'm
not the most dedicated attender at temple, but I don't consider
myself no 'evil'. That's when I says to my lad–'We'd better make a
dash for it, Son. Don't want to get caught up in no army–whether
they be priests or soldiers–not unless we've got boots to sell 'em.' I
reckon we only just got out in time–border patrols stopped and
questioned us as it was." The trader finished, and looked hopefully
at the King. Jubb mimicked his pose.

"Thank you. Uwert, see that he's recompensed for his
trouble." Darian nodded for the trader to leave. He turned to Ro.
"If they're closing the borders, it's to stop us getting information,
which means they definitely intend striking as soon as their army's
mustered." He hesitated. "And there's more. This talk of
re-establishing the 'Rule of Ondd'. You know what it means?"

Ro remembered the priest in Ondd's temple. She could see
him ordering Verron and the others put in chains, whitewashing
the Iyessi houses, making them sing strict songs–crushing all the
music and laughter out of them. She nodded, clamping her lips
tight to prevent them trembling.

"I know you didn't leave Iyessa in happy circumstances."

"They don't deserve this. They're not warriors or rebels. None
of this would have happened if not for me. I jinx everyone who
comes near me," Ro said bitterly.

Darian sat on the edge of the table. "Don't you think you're
rather overestimating your importance? Torslin would've found a
way to gain control of Ortann one way or another. Your arrival in
the city at that time was just a coincidence, unless... " He left the
word hanging until Ro blushed. "Unless Varda is right and you
really do have a role to play in waking Ondd."

Ro tried to speak, but Darian waved her silent. "Dovinna told me. She also told me that Lar believes the solution to your problem lies in the city, and Amradoc's too maybe."

"But I don't know how... "

"... to get back to Najarind?" interrupted Jubb. "That's easy. Follow the map."

Ro was about to protest that she did not know how to find the solution, when the intent look on Darian's face stopped her.

"I'll go with you," Jubb offered. "With my Words of Power we'll be safe enough."

"I dare say we will," Ro answered slowly, and saw Darian's tension ease. "You'll need to know what's going on–perhaps we can even get through to Channan." A voice inside her shouted. "What are you doing?"

Uwert was talking. "I've offered to go, but King Darian feels my face is too well known in Najarind. In happier times I went there on many embassies. If the one who goes is caught they must appear to be acting independently. We want to add no more persuasions to Torslin's call for war."

Darian added. "You don't have to go. You know Torslin won't let you slip through his fingers a second time if you're discovered."

"Who else can go?" Ro said, trying to give herself reasons as much as him. "Lar's too ill, Dovinna too well-known and Raimi... " Her marriage-brother was too eager for blood, his own if need be.

"Raimi has a child to care for," Darian finished for her.

"I can go, that's who else," Jubb added, crossing his arms with a look of triumph.

"You're just as likely to be recognised as Uwert, surely?" Ro protested.

"Not me, I'm a master of disguise."

"And who pays any attention to a fool?" Uwert said drily.

Darian put a hand on Jubb's shoulder. "And believing him a fool–as I do not–no one would believe I would entrust him with such a mission."

Jubb's face broke into a broad grin. "And there's my... "

"Words of Power," they answered in unison.

Darian straightened. "If you're to go, it should be as soon as possible and there's much to arrange first, but before you decide finally you should discuss this with the others."

As Ro was about to follow Jubb from the room, Darian stopped her.

"I would place more trust in his opinion than his scrap of paper," he whispered.

Ro nodded. A fool and a freak–a winning combination indeed!

Ro breathed in the smell of the books one last time. The leather and parchment dampened the noises of preparation outside the library and the air was hushed. Everything was ready outside. It was only the day before yesterday when she had agreed to return to Najarind, yet it was a different lifetime. Then she had been a clumsy freak, neither use nor ornament; now she was about to become a heroine, brave and capable. The trouble was, she still felt like the girl who sensed and understood nothing. She closed the door behind her, and joined the others in the courtyard.

Jubb was already mounted and Dovinna, Lar, Raimi, Darian and even Mirri with Lalli were there to wave good-bye despite the cold air. There was no excuse to delay their farewells. The crate of four geese which were to be their carrier-birds was loaded. They were less obvious than pigeons were, but would fly home to the lake outside Mandur as surely as the smaller birds. She did not look back as they rode out with their cavalry escort. Her last image of Mandur was of Lar holding Lalli up in her arms and softly singing Ondd's blessing.

The priest took the best seat by the fire making sure his leather satchel was within reach.

"You can leave that," he told his host, who bustled about preparing a meal and a room for his unexpected guest.

"It's been a long time since one of Ondd's holy men has paid us a visit." His host set a goblet of wine before the priest. The visitor drew his heavily embroidered robes closer about him. Despite the effects of the weather, the priest looked better fed and dressed than his host, whose best coat had frayed cuffs and tarnished gold thread.

The priest smiled. "The Patriarch's mindful of the lack of spiritual guidance among the communities on the further reaches of the empire. If a priest of Ondd had been in Iyessa, the evil which led one of their number to murder our late beloved King

Berinn could not have prevailed. He's sending priests such as myself far and wide to remedy the situation."

"Then I wish you the best of luck. It's as much as people around here can do to fill their bellies. They've little time left over for temples and talk of sin."

The priest tutted. "You can go now."

The man cleared the plates and took his leave for the night.

The priest stirred up the fire and settled back in his chair. His full belly and the warmth soon dispelled the irritation of his host's obvious displeasure at his arrival. He could not resist picking up the satchel and taking out one of the eggs with which he had been entrusted. These holy symbols of Ondd would soon persuade doubters back into the temple. Although warned to keep them hidden in his pack where they would be undisturbed, he preferred to keep such a precious cargo close to him. He replaced the egg and satchel at his feet. Images of how the people for miles around would come to hear him preach and of how the temple here would be restored to golden splendour began to dance in the flames. The priest's head fell forwards and his breathing took on a snorting regularity. Before the fire had subsided into red embers, the satchel began to twitch and jump. There were creaking, cracking sounds and a hole appeared in the leather.

"Why don't you sing us a song?" Jubb turned in his saddle and gestured so that his reins flapped. "It would make the journey go quicker."

Ro shook her head. On the first day of their journey back to Najarind she had been certain that Jubb would either knock himself off his mount or startle the poor horse into bolting. Now, they had left their escort behind and were deep into Ortanian territory, but nothing seemed to subdue her companion.

"I'm meant to be dumb, remember? What if someone should hear me?" she chided, but Jubb grinned.

"Then they'd think a morning bird had taken human form."

Ro shook her head. She could hardly feel less like singing. Every step they took increased their danger. So far Darian's advice had held true and Jubb had proved a safe companion. He stuck to their story that he and Ro were a brother and sister whose parents' farm had been drowned in the recent flooding, and were seeking their fortunes in the city. It was not that his sincerity was beyond question, but that his behaviour was so eccentric, no one bothered listening after the first couple of sentences. Thankfully, they had not yet needed to put Jubb's Words of Power to the test. Tomorrow, however, might well prove different.

"Are you sure we'll reach the city tomorrow?" she asked as they settled down for another cold, comfortless night.

"As sure as I am that horses have four legs."

As the towering buildings of Najarind came into sight the next day, Ro clamped her teeth on a feeling of dread. She had lost a sister in the attempt to escape the city's grip and now she was walking back in of her own accord. They joined the melée as dusk was deepening into night. The press of people was worse than she remembered. The guards on the gate made little attempt to regulate the flow of people, occasionally grabbing someone within arm's reach of their post to check their papers.

"What's the hurry?" Jubb asked a harassed looking man determined to push his way past them. Another voice answered, belonging to a flower-seller vainly trying to protect her basket of tired looking stock.

"Where've you been? There's a curfew and no one wants to get caught outside the walls–not after what they say happened up north."

Ro poked Jubb to urge him to ask her more, but the press of people bore the woman into a different channel.

"Oops." Jubb turned to her. "Better hold tight to the horses."

He led the way further into the city. When Uwert had suggested she should pretend to be dumb to avoid her Iyessi voice betraying them, she had readily seen the sense of it, but now she discovered the flaw in the plan; she had no option other than to follow wherever the fool chose to lead her. The first whirrings of the chimes began and the gates swung closed behind them.

Anni took a quick look over her shoulder, swept up her skirts and ran along the corridor. No one ever thought to tell her when something happened. She only knew that a rider had arrived from the north and that Channan had insisted on seeing him straight away, because she had caught two maids whispering about it. If the rumours they had heard were true, a horror was loose on the land, and Anni was determined that at least one person should be present who had the empire's, and therefore Channan's, best interests at heart.

She reached the audience chamber door, paused for a moment to adopt her usual meek demeanour and entered. A mud-spattered man tried to rise from his seat.

"Sorry to be late," she said innocently, taking a seat near the window where she could see everyone.

Channan was sitting forward gripping the arms of his chair as if he would squeeze the life from them. Ersilla lounged at his side, casting Anni a small frown of annoyance at the interruption. Fordel stood by the window looking out.

Torslin ceased pacing before the fireplace. "Princess Anni, my apologies." He looked at Channan. "I hadn't sent for the Princess, Highness. I thought you wouldn't want her to hear possibly disturbing details."

Anni returned his smile. "If you think the news is too awful, Ersilla and I will withdraw, of course."

"No!" Ersilla sat upright. "I won't be sent out like some silly girl. I'm King Berinn's daughter." Her eyes flashed Torslin a warning.

"Well, then." Anni smoothed her skirt. "Please continue."

Torslin looked to Channan for support, but he nodded at the rider. Anni was aware of Fordel trying to hide a smile.

"Go ahead," Channan said.

The rider's face was grey. "There was nothing living–nothing! It seemed to start around the manor house and move on through the fields. Not many of the villagers escaped. The creatures attacked everything in their path, gorged themselves and moved on. Didn't even leave any bones to bury. The whole swarm swooped down on a horse and stripped it to nothing, just like that." He snapped his fingers.

"Swarm of what?"

"Flying monsters with claws and pointed teeth that could rip open armour. Not many who saw them lived to tell it."

"But you did," Channan said.

"I live further up the mountain. I'm marriage-contracted–was marriage... " the rider choked on a painful memory.

Channan nodded and clamped his lips tight.

"Where did they come from, man?" Torslin asked.

Channan interrupted. "More importantly where did they go?"

"They just appeared."

Torslin gestured impatiently. "Nothing just appears."

Before the rider could answer, Ersilla fired another question at him. "You say they devoured a horse–how many were there? How big were they?" Her eagerness brought heads round to stare at her. Torslin stepped in.

"This is useless. We must send a patrol to find out what's going on. This man's obviously seen nothing himself."

Channan nodded. "Go and get some rest, friend."

As the rider left Channan strode restlessly to the window and Anni was shocked to see how all traces of boyishness had vanished.

"Murder, war and now wild beasts," he said. "Even father never had to face as much."

Torslin thumped his fist on the table. "King Berinn's great strength was his decisiveness. When threatened he wouldn't hesitate to act."

Channan turned, his expression grim. "But first we have to find out where the threat is. Send the patrol. These creatures have to be destroyed."

"That's my lad. We'll make a king of you yet." Anni winced at Torslin's praise. "It wouldn't surprise me if all our troubles turn out to come from the same source."

"Amradoc?" Channan looked incredulous. "Aren't they accused of enough already?"

"Those poor people, Channan." Anni tried to divert the flow of thoughts that she knew would lead back to Dovinna's treachery. "The villagers."

"Yes, Anni, you're right. Send supplies with the patrol. If Amradoc is behind this Darian will pay dearly for the suffering he's caused our people." The set lines of his face made her turn away.

"I'll see what we can spare from the palace stores."

Anni closed the door behind her, wishing she could shut out the events of the past few months as easily. Channan's grief ate away at him so that the slightest push would send him whirling away from the line of reason. And then there was Ersilla: there was an unnatural eagerness in her manner, as unsettling in its way as Channan's, as if she was permanently on the edge of a fever and that she would embrace the fall. No one it seemed could see the approaching disaster except for her, Anni, to whom no one would listen. At least organising supplies for the survivors would allow her to feel she was making a difference somewhere.

As she entered the laundry, Anni caught sight of a cropped head and almost cried out. But no; surely no one could be that foolish.

# Chapter Thirteen

"I'm not one of your soldiers, Torslin, and I don't take kindly to being bullied." Ersilla sat stiffly in her chair, trapped there by Torslin leaning menacingly over the table. Her face was pale, but she held and returned his glare.

The Lord relaxed. "Your pardon, Princess, but this carelessness could ruin us. If you're involved in it, I need to know before the patrol returns."

"I don't see what all the fuss is about. You must have intended putting the fal-worms to the test at some point. Maybe the Patriarch decided to go ahead without telling you. It's only a few peasants in a remote village, after all." She brushed invisible crumbs from her skirt.

"We'd intended a controlled experiment when all was ready. Then the threat of having the monsters turned loose upon them would be enough to subdue our enemies. But all isn't ready and this was no controlled experiment. I ask again–was this destruction your doing?"

"How could it be?"

"I've spoken to the Patriarch," Torslin said. "He assures me that none of the priests knew of the fal-worms, and if they had, the keys to his tower are always kept on his person."

"Then someone must have broken in." Ersilla shrugged.

"Indeed. Perhaps one of the missionaries the Patriarch sent to the outlying regions. A certain zealot was bound for Iyessa. The village would have been on his route."

Ersilla nodded, wide-eyed. Torslin suddenly leaned forward.

"What did you tell him? That he was punishing the unbelievers? Did you promise him eternal glory? Did he even know what he carried?"

"I don't know why you insist on asking me." Ersilla got up and walked to the window, turning her back on him with an irritated sweep of her gown.

"Princess, I need to know what the patrol will find. We may be able to use this incident to our advantage, but if its cause is traced back to us... " He left the rest to Ersilla's imagination.

She made no answer.

"We'll have to move our plans forward and trust to luck."

Ersilla giggled. "You, Torslin? Speak of luck? I'd never have thought you superstitious."

"I'm a soldier, Princess. We're all superstitious." He bowed and left her to her amusement.

As he walked to Channan's private chambers, people ducked out of his path. Channan turned a weary gaze on him as he entered without waiting for an answer to his knock.

"More trouble?"

"No news from the patrol yet." Torslin signalled a body-servant, who was preparing to shave the King, to leave. "Glad to see you taking some trouble over your appearance. People need to see you looking fit and confident."

"Was that what you came to tell me?"

"No. I've come to suggest we should march on Darian now, without waiting for the muster from the far provinces." He held up a hand against Channan's protest. "We already outnumber his forces and the longer we wait the more likely it is that Darian will hear about the creatures–and if they are under his command they may attack again at any time."

Outside the chamber a laundry-maid stood with her ear to the door, clutching a bundle of linen. As Anni's quick step approached she hastily moved away, but not before the Princess caught a glimpse of the face beneath the ragged hair. Anni followed her around a turn in the corridor, a rebuke on her lips, but the maid had vanished. There were too many doors she could be hiding behind for Anni to continue her pursuit. She turned back to Channan's chamber intending to have words with Mistress Hexem, the laundry-keeper, about the girl later. Outside her brother's door she hesitated, then put her own ear to the wood, with a frown of concentration. A few moments later the frown was replaced by a look of horror.

Ro waited until the sound of Anni's footsteps receded, struggling to hear over the pounding in her ears. When all was quiet she hurried back to the laundry with her burden of linen. A sturdy young woman with blonde hair escaping from its plaits looked up from a heap of fresh sheets as she entered.

"Manage?" she asked. Tillenne had been assigned to Ro to show her what her chores entailed and help her find her way around the meandering back stairs and corridors.

Ro nodded. She liked Tillenne, whose hearty untroubled nature shone in her rosy face. The Iyessi girl had to battle her instinct to speak to her. It was all the harder because Tillenne would good-naturedly try to interpret Ro's gestured responses as if they were part of a game, whereas others often turned away before she had finished. Over the week since she and Jubb had arrived, Ro had become increasingly certain that she would slip up and say something. It had been a relief to be allowed to tend the chambers on her own at last. Until now, Tillenne's presence had made it impossible to discover anything more secret than which maid fancied which steward. Today was only the second time she had been unsupervised. She felt the words she had overheard burning through her chest as she set about helping Tillenne to fold the sheets.

"Are you all right?"

Ro fanned herself with her hand and pointed to the door.

"Some fresh air?" Tillenne suggested.

Ro nodded.

"All right, I'll cover for you. Don't let Mistress Hexem see you, though."

Having dodged Anni and any number of courtiers who might have questioned her presence in the royal wing, Ro felt escaping Mistress Hexem's notice ought to be child's play. She slipped into the huge washroom, where the laundry-keeper supervised the tubs of soapy water and alleyways of ironing boards. The slop and slurp of wet cloth on ribbed boards and the hiss from the irons hid the sound of Ro's footsteps as the thick mist of steam hid her from the laundry-keeper's view. Even if she had caught sight of her across the room, the laundry-keeper's starched skirts would not allow her to move quickly enough to stop her.

Outside, Ro ducked through flapping forests of wet washing on lines, only stopping on the boundary to make sure there was no one who could recognise her between the yard and the stables where Jubb should be helping to tend the beasts. The head ostler had recognised the fool's ability to commune with the horses and had readily taken him on despite his lack of other accomplishments. Jubb had been delighted, assuring Ro that the stables were the ideal place to hear all the soldiers' gossip, but Ro could not help thinking that the main advantage might turn out to be access to good mounts if they had to leave in a hurry. She slipped between the stalls, enjoying the warm smells of hay and well-kept beasts. Jubb was in one of the furthest stalls rubbing the occupant's nose and murmuring reassurance to it.

"This is Ro," he told it as he caught sight of her. "She's a friend and she looks as if she's got some news for us."

Ro's heart almost stopped beating. "Shh... others might hear," she whispered.

"The horses won't tell." Jubb's face was infuriatingly innocent.

"I have to get back to the laundry before I'm missed." Ro sat in a corner of the stall and took out a notebook Uwert had given her. She thought carefully before writing a few words in the smallest letters she could manage. She tore out the page and gave it to Jubb. "You must send one of the geese with this as soon as you can. Torslin's persuaded Channan to march on Amradoc."

Jubb's face fell, then brightened again. "Does this mean we can go home?"

Ro shook her head. "Not yet–not me anyway. I have to prove that Dovinna and I are innocent."

"Why bother if there's going to be a war?"

"Perhaps there's still a chance of stopping it. I must go." Ro gave Jubb a hug. He looked miserable. "What?"

"Do we have to keep the geese in the Garden of the Dead?"

"They'd be noticed anywhere else. Few people go there, and if anyone sees you, you can say you're paying tribute to your forebears."

"I know, only... I don't like it there."

"If I could leave the laundry long enough, I'd do it, but I can't. Darian is relying on you, Jubb. Besides, you've got your Words of Power to protect you." She smiled encouragement.

Jubb placed his hand over the spot where his precious paper was hidden.

"Don't lose that message. I'll come back as soon as I can."

Ro slipped back across the yard and in amongst the billowing washing lines, trying to quell her unease by reminding herself that Jubb was good with animals. She slapped irritably at a towel which blew in front of her.

"Where do you think you've been, Miss?"

At the end of the alleyway of lines stood Mistress Hexem with hands on hips, as stiff and white with rage as if she too had been bleached and starched.

The patrol rode in silence. Only the sound of the hooves and harness and the occasional snap of ice echoed across the empty landscape. The drovers of the supply wagons quelled their usual quips and encouragement to the dray-horses. Nothing else moved: no bird, not even a breeze. Frost sparkled and flashed off the roadway and distant stone roofs. The scene would have been one of calm had it not been for an air of watchfulness.

Pachand narrowed his eyes against the low winter sun. Some of the mounds and protrusions in the fields were not the remains of last year's harvest, as he had at first thought, but the remains of herd beasts and their keepers.

The rider beside Pachand murmured: "It all looks so clean." It was Natann, who had brought news of the disaster to Najarind.

Pachand nodded and turned in his saddle to face his men. "Keep your eyes and ears open. These creatures could be anywhere." The Captain did not like this. Unseen enemies created fear. Imagination made them bigger and more ferocious. It led to ill-discipline and mistakes. The horses picked up the tension, shying at nothing and whickering their nervousness.

"There's no smell," Natann said. "The survivors spoke of a smell the creatures carried about them, like putrid flesh and rotting vegetation."

Pachand nodded. "But by the time we smell them they may be too close for comfort."

By now they had reached what had once been a thriving settlement. The doorways gaped, and Pachand doubted even a cockroach would find a living there. The very land seemed dead.

"When I left, the survivors were sheltering further up in the hills. They won't last long there in this weather."

The terrain became increasingly difficult as the patrol followed Natann into the highlands. Loose stones made the way treacherous for the horses and their progress slowed. The sun was retreating towards the horizon when there was a "Holla!" above them. They were pelted with small stones as several ragged people scrambled down the hillside to greet them. Natann dismounted and threw his arms about a sturdy man of middle years.

"Are these all that are left?"

The villager returned his embrace. "There are others in the old ore workings." He turned to Pachand. "Thank Ondd you're here, Captain. Have you killed them, the beasts? Our people are without food. Few dare leave the protection of the workings."

Pachand noted the uneasy glances he and his companions kept casting at the sky. "All in good time. We have supplies for you."

The villager shook his head. "No use–we're all dead unless you destroy the devourers. You too. You haven't seen them."

"You can tell me about them as you show us the way."

"No." He began to back off. "You can't get the horses inside the workings, and the monsters'll smell them. They'll bring them down on us again!"

"Very well, my men will unload the supplies here and we'll carry them to your base. Then you'll tell me all you know." Pachand's tone left no room for argument.

Fit and well-fed as the soldiers were, they could not match the fear-fueled stamina and strength of the survivors. As they worked, the villager constantly urged them to hurry. Despite his warning, Pachand refused to abandon the horses altogether and left two of the patrol to tend them until morning. Once in the safety of the ore workings, with the sorely needed blankets and food distributed, their host showed Pachand to the corner he had made his own and invited him to sit. As he looked about him, Pachand saw the same haunted expression in the eyes of all the survivors. Each noise made them start as if they expected the roof to cave in.

"They've seen things no one should expect to look on outside of a nightmare. There were three of the beasts." Their host described them and Pachand's jaw tightened. "They fell on all who came in their path–old, young, fat, skinny. At first they flew back and forth striking victims with their claws and snatching flesh into their mouths as they flew. The taste of blood seemed to madden them and they began gorging themselves on the fallen. Some were still living when they began their feast." His voice dropped to a whisper. He shuddered. "There were more than enough dead to sate them, but they began squabbling and slashing at each other over the same corpse. That was the only reason we managed to escape. While they were occupied, those of us here managed to run."

"And afterwards?" Pachand asked.

"We hid. I don't know where they went." The villager passed a weary hand over his brow. "If it's any help, the manor house was struck first–it's set back from the village overlooking the road."

Pachand considered. "You think that's significant?"

"Who knows? But a priest arrived there a few days before. No one's seen him since." He caught Pachand's look. "I know, there's no reason to connect the two, but when the horrors of myth come to life, then people are bound to become superstitious– anything's possible."

The villager's words made uneasy companions for Pachand the next morning as he and his men scrambled back to the place where the horses had been left. Many of the soldiers had a white-eyed look. Their shivers were not all due to the deep frost.

"Who goes there?" The challenge brought grins and murmurs.

The villager's prophesies had been false. All was as they had left it. They mounted and retraced their steps to the village. Sending a couple of riders to scout the road beyond, Pachand and Natann turned their attention to the remains of the manor. Beneath their coating of frost the ruins were blackened and crumbling.

"Fire!" Pachand kicked through the ashes. What did other beasts do when they were gorged? "They'd surely have been too heavy with food to fly far," he told Natann. "They'll have found somewhere sheltered close by to sleep."

Natann considered. "Elmett's Fort–it's an old mound, wooded now."

The earth was too churned up to show clear tracks, but once Natann pointed out the wooded mound, like some giant hedgepig further along the line of hills, Pachand could see evidence that something big and heavy had been that way. The brush fence was flattened and a black hole like a startled mouth showed where at least one of the beasts had entered. They proceeded slowly, striving to muffle the rattle of armour and avoid the crackle of frozen undergrowth. The stench told them they were on the right trail. It had the soldiers reaching for kerchiefs to muffle their noses. Pachand raised a hand and they halted. Silence. They started forward again. Suddenly the trees cleared and an odour that was almost visible buffeted them. Before them was a tangle of wings, claws and bulbous bodies sheened with slime. Pachand raised his spear. Something was wrong. He stepped closer. It was not slime, but ice. The fal-worms were frozen. Cautiously,

Pachand made his way around the heap of bodies. Even with eyes frosted over and icicles hanging from their mouths they were terrifying.

Natann came up beside him. "Are they all here?" he whispered.

"Looks like it. Perhaps they killed each other."

There was a sharp crack from the trees behind them. Pachand jerked round, crouched to meet an attack. There was a whimper.

"Have mercy! For Ondd's sake, have mercy on me."

The soldiers dragged a blood and soot-smeared figure from the undergrowth. His face paled as he saw the bodies of the fal-worms. He howled and covered his eyes.

"It wasn't my fault, I didn't know."

"Didn't know what? Who are you?" Pachand demanded.

"Mercy, have mercy." The figure fell to his knees, his blackened robes in shreds.

"I think we've found the priest." Pachand lifted part of the tattered sleeve.

"Yes," he began to snivel. "The Patriarch himself sent me here, you must have mercy."

"Why should you need it?" Pachand waited only an instant before grasping the remains of the priest's robes at the throat and tightening them.

"I didn't know, I swear. She told me they were holy relics."

"She—who?" Pachand demanded.

"The lady. She'd been to see the Patriarch. She said they'd help me in my holy mission."

"Who, man?" Pachand shook him. The cloth disintegrated in his fingers, leaving them smeared with black.

The priest wiped his nose on what remained of his sleeve. "I hid in the chimney. It was too hot for them, too hot for me, see?" He showed them palms that were blistered and oozing. "They found other prey, and they grew with each kill." His eyes widened as if seeing them again. "They couldn't reach me then and I escaped. They smelled me, but the cold came—it made them slow. I outran them. And then, and then they laid down, slept and now... " The priest threw his arms over his head and wailed. "Mercy, mercy... "

"I'll give you mercy—a clean death—more than my poor darling got." Natann snatched a sword from one of the soldiers and raised it above the priest's bowed head in one smooth movement. Pachand grabbed his arm.

"No! There's a conspiracy here. We need this... this... " Pachand spat on the ground at the priest's feet. "We'll take him back to Najarind, see how high the rot goes. He said the Patriarch was involved. We'll take one of those back too." He jerked his head in the direction of the dead fal-worms. "Rig something up to put it in, Sergeant, so we're not all killed by the stench."

The sergeant jerked to attention. "What about the others, Sir?

"Burn them."

The soldiers immediately set about cutting wood to start a blaze and sealing one of the corpses in oiled cloth. They had to take turns at the work. The reek from the beasts made them stumble and retch. Flanked by two soldiers, the priest shivered and muttered for mercy throughout. When all was ready Pachand lit a brand and thrust it into the piled firewood. The flames fizzed and sparked upwards melting the ice on the nearest trees and turning the ground to mud.

"No!" shrieked the priest. "You'll wake them."

He struggled free of his guards and grabbed for Pachand's arm. The Captain dodged. The priest scrabbled at air and fell into the flames. The blazing mound heaved and there was a weird whistling shriek. Then nothing but the comforting crackle and spurt of the fire.

"Ondd is merciful after all," said Pachand drily.

"What was that sound?" Natann's face was white.

"Trapped gas," Pachand answered with a shrug.

The glassy looks of the soldiers showed they shared Natann's fears. Pachand cursed. News of a possible religious plot should be taken to Najarind as soon as possible. He had hoped the priest might let slip some clue on their way back.

"You should have let me kill him, then justice would've been carried out, not some accident." Natann stared at the flames.

"I have another task for you, if you'll do it."

Natann looked up eagerly.

"Ride for Najarind; take news of our suspicions. Mind, tell only King Channan himself or Lord Torslin." Of all those in Najarind they were the only two he could trust.

Ro's ears were scorching from the chastisement of Mistress Hexem as if she had held the flat iron to them.

"There's no room in my laundry for shirkers or lovestruck maids who keep slipping out to see their swains. Understand?"

Ro had nodded vigorously, but the laundry-keeper's mouth remained a thin seam.

"Very well. You're on washing the kitchen cloths until further notice." Mistress Hexem gave her a strong push in the direction of the steaming tub and a great mound of stained tablecloths and aprons.

There was nothing for it but to roll up her sleeves and attack the pile with soap and washboard. All hope of further spying that day was gone. Every time Ro showed signs of flagging, Mistress Hexem gave her a reminder with the flat of the tub stirrer that she expected hard work. Tillenne cast her sympathetic looks. What trouble had Ro landed her in? By the time Ro had finished work for the day her arms felt heavier than boulders and her fingers were rubbed raw. She dragged herself to her cot in the maid's dormitory and knew no more until she was shaken awake the next morning.

She struggled to coax her stiff fingers and shoulders into movement. So much for waking early and slipping out to discover how Jubb had got on! Another morning was spent pounding soiled clothes on the washboard until her blisters made her wince with each scrub. Mistress Hexem leaned as far over the tub as her stiff gown would allow.

"Enough! You're making the water bloody."

Ro found herself back helping Tillenne.

Her friend tutted. "Your poor hands."

Ro had no chance to do more than smile her gratitude, when Princess Anni burst in. Ro hastily bent over her work, as Mistress Hexem hurried to greet her.

"Highness, we're honoured." The laundry-keeper bowed, prevented by her stiff skirts from curtsying.

"There's no time for pleasantries, Mistress Hexem. I need enough linen for an army... " Their voices were lost in the hiss of steam.

"Oh-oh," Tillenne murmured. "Old Starch-breeches will be in a fine fit if her warming shelves are raided. Thank goodness the visitors' wing still needs doing." She picked up a basket and gestured at Ro to follow as the laundry-keeper began organising a chain of maids to load the stacked linen into trunks.

"Where do you think you're going?" Mistress Hexem's crisp voice almost made Ro drop her burden.

"We were just... " Tillenne began.

"Hoping to get away without me noticing. I can't spare two of you on the rooms. You stay here."

Tillenne rolled her eyes. Ro hastily snatched up her basket and escaped into the corridor. Heart thudding in a way that would have brought Iyessi running from miles around, she headed for the royal apartments. Torslin's room first. If the army was about to move he was unlikely to be lounging there. She walked purposefully, as if she had every right to be in that wing and paused outside his door. There was no sound within and no response to her knock. She entered and scanned the interior. It could as easily have been a guest room, for all the personal items it contained. The only luxury appeared to be a massive rug of soft animal skins slung across the bed. Ro touched it and shuddered. It was typical of the man that he should choose to wrap himself in the remains of the innocent dead.

Flinging the covers back to make it look as if she was changing the linen, Ro set about searching every drawer and niche in the room, pausing frequently to listen. Oh, for the sensitivity of the least among the Iyessi, which could have warned her before someone came! She was flicking through the pieces of paper in the last drawer when she heard booted feet approaching. Torslin! Ro tiptoed to the bed. Her hands trembled as they smoothed the sheets. She bent her head, hoping her rough hair and maid's clothes would disguise her. The latch rattled.

"Lord Torslin!" A breathless male voice called. "Your pardon, Lord. King Channan sent me to fetch you... "

The latch dropped and the booted feet retreated. Ro sat heavily on the bed, combating the bile which had risen to her throat. Time to leave. The paper appeared to bear nothing more than neatly written lists with Torslin's signature at the bottom—inventories and reports. Silly to have hoped for more. Torslin was far too wily to keep anything that could damn him. Ro set the room to rights and left. Maybe she would have better luck in Ayif's chamber.

The Gindullan physician's room was above the royal apartments where it benefitted from heat from the main chimney. Getting to it meant a heart-stopping walk, expecting to be challenged at any moment. Again Ro listened outside the door.

There was a hiss from within that almost made her start back. She waited. There were no sounds of movement, no variation in the hiss, no pause for an intake of breath. Expecting some monster to strike at her, she entered.

The room was gloomy and smelled foul. It looked as if it had not seen a chambermaid for months. The hiss came from a bubbling pot set over a brazier. Ayif could not be far away. Fearful of touching anything which might be smeared with poison, Ro used her apron to sort through the bottles and jars of medicine. Where better to hide something than in full view? The trouble was, Ro had no idea what she was looking for. Anyway, Dovinna had said that the substance that had killed King Berinn was sometimes used as a medicine. She turned her attention to the cupboards and bedside, carelessly strewn with discarded clothes and papers. The fear which had made her breath swift and shallow threatened to turn into giggles. The Gindullan's writing meant nothing to her. She could decipher the letters, but the words must be in his own language. Ro sat on the bed. To have risked so much for nothing. Her weight on the mattress allowed the corner of a book to slide from under the pillow. She drew it out. The leaves fell open where a note had been placed between the pages. Her eyes caught on Torslin's name.

Something brushed against the door. She shoved the book into the linen basket, snatched it up and stepped behind a curtain. The alcove was barely big enough to hide her and her burden. The rank smell was stronger there, but movement outside helped her to hold back a cough of disgust.

Ro heard Ayif's syrupy voice. "Sit down, my Lord, I congratulate you on the good news. Now Lethir's kin are abroad wreaking havoc on the unrighteous once more, who shall stand against us?"

Peeping through the curtain Ro saw the physician stoking up the fire. His companion was out of sight, but there was no mistaking his voice.

"Save your flattery for someone who believes it," snarled Torslin. "I ought to have your throat cut right now, traitor."

The smile slid from Ayif's face. "Traitor? How can you say so? Haven't I done everything you've asked? I've risked everything."

"For your own purposes and don't pretend otherwise. Someone with your conjuring skills will have found the Patriarch's locks no trouble, I'm sure."

Ayif's eyes bulged. "Why should I do so?"

"Maybe you've decided that the servant should be master. You're treading in very dangerous water, Ayif. As yet you're in the shallows but one more step and... " There was a rustle of movement and Torslin erupted into view, grasping the physician's robe at the throat.

The physician swallowed. "As dangerous to you as me–if you denounce me, I'll take you down with me."

Torslin loosened his grip slightly. "Who'd believe your word against mine?"

"They wouldn't have to, I've got proof."

Doubt flickered in Torslin's eyes. Ro felt a surge of hope: she swayed back from the curtain and felt something brush against her back. Carefully turning so as not to disturb the cloth her eyes met the awful stare of Lethir. She started, stifling a squeal. At the same instant there was a clatter and thud. She froze.

"You dare threaten me?" Torslin growled.

Ro held her breath and peeped out. Ayif's chair was on its back and the physician cowered on the floor protecting himself with an outflung arm from Torslin's threatened blow.

"You misunderstand me, Lord. I meant only that we are bound to each other as brothers. I'd do nothing to risk our partnership."

A sly look crawled onto Torslin's face. He helped the doctor to his feet. "Enough. I needed to be sure of your loyalty, that's all. I have another task for you."

The Gindullan regained some of his ebullience. He inclined his head as if granting a wish. "Who?"

"I fear Princess Ersilla is about to succumb to some malady."

"Princess Ersilla?" Ayif's eyes widened.

Torslin nodded. "She's been under such a strain, I'm sure her nerves are about to give way. Others have remarked on it."

"Don't we still need her?"

"Some friends are more dangerous than enemies," Torslin said drily.

"Indeed."

"Then I shall expect her to need your ministrations very shortly."

"But what of the King?"

Torslin smiled. "Many things can happen on a battlefield. Now, you'd better supervise the medical supplies. Channan's army marches within the hour."

He disappeared from Ro's view and she heard the door close after him. Ayif held the edge of the table for support. His eyes fixed on the curtain and Ro felt certain he must have heard her thoughts willing him to leave. Her only hope lay in using the linen basket with its secret cargo to barge past him and escape while he was off balance. She tensed as he stepped towards her. As his hand reached for the curtain he hesitated, turned and picked up a bottle of blue liquid. He poured a small glassful, tossed it back and poured another. Soon the bottle was half empty and Ayif was slouched brooding in his chair. Relief made Ro's legs shake so that she could barely stand. Despite Torslin's warning that the army would leave shortly, Ayif made no move. Ro's feet grew numb. If he did not go soon she would have to take the chance and barge past him or fall over. There was a knock at the door.

Ayif stirred at last. "Yes, yes, I'm coming." He snatched a few bottles and salves together, seemingly at random and left.

Ro's legs demanded that she sink to the floor, but somehow she controlled them enough to reach the corridor. Her steps quickened with a rush of triumph. She had it! The evidence that she and Dovinna were innocent. The paper now nestling in the laundry basket was the only one with Torslin's name on it. It had to be Ayif's threatened proof. But what to do with it now? It was unlikely that Mistress Hexem would take her eyes off her once she returned to the laundry, but she had to see Jubb. She had not even managed to find out whether he had sent the last message without mishap. She decided to bypass the laundry and go straight to the stables. Ro hesitated halfway down a flight of stairs, closing her eyes to remember the route she would have to take.

"Hsst!"

Ro's eyes flicked open. Tillenne stood at a door opening off the corridor, gesturing urgently.

"For Ondd's sake, hurry up! Did you get lost? Old Starch-breeches'll put you through the mangle this time!" Tillenne held out her arms to take the basket from Ro, who clasped it tightly to her. "Come on, let me take the basket, it'll be easier."

Ro shook her head and tried to tug the basket out of Tillenne's grasp.

"I'm trying to help." Tillenne pulled harder.

They struggled unaware of a door opening further along the corridor. The weave of the basket cut into Ro's blistered fingers and her grasp slipped. The suddenness of her victory knocked Tillenne off balance and the basket tipped spilling sheets and pillowslips to the floor. Ayif's purloined book landed with a clatter. Torslin's signature was visible on the paper which poked out.

"How dare you!" It was Mistress Hexem, and she was not alone. Anni stood beside her, astonishment replacing the memory of Channan's face as he rode out at the head of his army.

"Brawling in the corridors!" Mistress Hexem caught hold of the pair by the ears. Neither Ro's wild gestures nor Tillenne's protests persuaded her otherwise. "Your pardon, Highness. I can't think what's got into them. This one's a bit featherbrained." The laundry-keeper pulled Ro's ear. "But Tillenne's always been a steady girl."

Anni bent and picked up the book. Mistress Hexem gasped horror-struck. Anni looked at the book, then closely at Ro.

"A thief!" the laundry-keeper finally managed. "I'll dismiss her straight away."

Ro returned Anni's gaze. As anxious to guess her thoughts as the Princess appeared to be to analyse hers.

"I'll deal with this." Anni's words stopped the laundry-keeper in full flow.

"But... "

"You have much to do repairing the inroads the army's made on your linen. I might as well make myself useful. Stop crying girl and pick up these things," she told Tillenne, who obeyed with trembling hands. "Don't be too hard on her, Mistress. I think you'll find she wasn't at fault."

Mistress Hexem gave her a stiff bow, took a firm grasp of Tillenne's ear again, and marched her back to the laundry. When they were gone, Anni turned to Ro.

"Now, what am I to do with you?"

Ro remained silent.

Anni tapped the book. "A strange thing to steal. Are you Gindullan?"

Ro shook her head.

"No, you're Iyessi, aren't you?"

Ro took a breath to speak, then let it out. She looked to left and right pointedly. Anni's eyes strayed back to the book. Her fingers fiddled with the corner as if eager to open it.

"Perhaps we should return it to Ayif and ask him why you would take it." Anni waited.

Lar would have known whether she could trust her. She would have felt it in her bones without having to think about it. All Ro had to go on was the Princess's face and the conviction that Ayif's book contained the words with the power to exonerate her.

She took another breath. "Don't do that, Princess. You'd be putting yourself in danger."

Anni bit her lip. "Why should I trust you?"

"You shouldn't, Princess. Trust no one."

Slowly, the Princess nodded. "Then I shall just have to find the answer myself. Come."

# Chapter Fourteen

Anni led Ro to her chamber and took out the paper. It was thick and so yellow that it was turning brown at the edges. It appeared to have been torn from a journal.

"Our work is begun," the Princess read. "The young conqueror bears us nothing but contempt. His disgust is evident in the way he will touch nothing but the bland fare of his own land, hear only its own music. He would rather suffer the torments of celibacy than touch the flesh of one of our Gindullan beauties. Not so his second-in-command. Torslin also holds us in contempt, but his contempt for King Berinn is greater. The Lord believes that the purpose of conquest is to crush your enemies and take from them whatever you desire–and the lord's desires are great. He has no scruples about spending his days and nights lying with our trained courtesans, sampling the exquisite torture of senses intensified by Gindullan drugs or experiencing the pleasures of inflicting pain. His feet are already on the path to Lethir, it is merely that his head does not know it yet."

Anni flipped the page. "It is done: Torslin is bound to Lethir hand and heart and soul. We will help him lull the king and kingdom so that Ondd may sleep soundly and Lethir's arrival will find his servants unprepared. When the Great Worm nears, the one we send will help Torslin rid himself of our enemy. Then the Lord will welcome Lethir's chaos and it shall last five hundred hundred years."

Ro watched Anni's face. The Princess said nothing, but the colour faded from her cheeks, only to return in a rush. She shook the book by its covers as if it was a wild thing that had attacked her. Another sheet fell out.

"Death to all enemies of Lethir! Let those named here be crushed entirely." There followed a list of names. Underneath them was a row of bloody thumb-prints. Anni choked back a cry.

"What is it?" Ro asked.

"A list of those Torslin and his co-conspirators intend killing. Here's my father's name." She pointed. "Here's the Patriarch's. There are others I don't know, and some that make no sense. Who's the one who is not one? "

"Lalli–Lalli's in danger." Ro shivered, trying to discount the fact that she herself was the other half of the 'not one'.

"Lalli?" Anni asked.

"My baby niece."

Realisation made Anni sink back in her chair. "You were Dovinna's accomplice. I knew there was something familiar about you, but I'd thought it merely because you're Iyessi."

"We were wrongly accused. You must see that. You have the evidence in your hand."

Anni looked at the paper. "Do I? Just because this says Torslin's guilty, doesn't make him so."

Ro's heart beat faster as Anni tried to fit her own thumb over one of the prints. She could try to run, but if Anni called the guards how far would she get?"

"Your father was ill before we arrived in the city. It was only by accident that I was at Dovinna's house when Fordel fetched her. It was only because Fordel insisted that I went with her at all."

Anni passed a hand wearily over her face. "Sit down, I'm not going to give you to the guards. I have no doubt one of these marks is Torslin's."

Ro hesitated. "There's more, Princess. I overheard Torslin and Ayif talking. Your sister's life's in peril." As Ro explained the colour came and went in Anni's cheeks again.

"Are you suggesting Princess Ersilla was a party to her own father's death?"

Ro flinched expecting a blow. None came. The Princess stood as if she was the one who had been struck.

"What shall I do?" she said to herself.

"Ayif is bound to miss his book. It won't take him long to hear about the laundry-maid caught stealing, or your involvement."

"You must leave the palace, get away from Najarind."

"I can't, Princess. That paper proves King Darian's innocence too. I have to know what you intend, and besides," Ro hesitated. "There's another I have to consider."

"Very well." Anni began to scribble a note. "Give this to Mistress Hexem. It says I've decided to give you another chance. I'll find a way of getting word to you."

Ro took the note and surveyed her sore fingers ruefully. No doubt Mistress Hexem would make sure her blisters acquired blisters by morning. She gave Anni a formal bow and left.

Anni watched her go. She felt as unable to move as if her blood had turned to ice. The sound of tramping feet and the jingle of harness as Channan and the Ortanian force had left still filled her head. The sight of the army pouring through the gates on the road to Amradoc had stirred her spirits despite its desperate purpose. It had been fiercely beautiful, and Channan had borne himself like a hero from a fireside tale; his face pale but determined, the lively step of his horse adding to the courage of his bearing. Then, Anni had felt her throat tighten with love and pride. Now, all she felt was dread. Each time the scene replayed in her head the figure of Torslin seemed to ride a little closer to him, the lord's smile increasingly sinister.

She shook herself. She could not afford to give way to panic. They would soon see that she was as much her father's daughter as Ersilla. Thought of her treacherous sister made her fingers tingle to slap the superior look off her face. How could she have been so selfish and stupid? Anni could not look far along that path. Ersilla deserved whatever Torslin had planned for her, and Anni was afraid that she would get it.

Outside in the courtyard, there was the sound of laughter. It was so out of place with Anni's gloomy thoughts that she went to the window. Lord Fordel was exchanging a few encouraging words with one of the young soldiers who, along with some grey-haired veterans, were all Torslin had left behind to defend the city. She opened the window.

"Lord Fordel! Levity at such a time? Kindly come up and explain yourself." Anni stood at the window long enough to see the lord bow and head for the palace. Perhaps there was one person in the city she could trust.

Anni had not been the only one caught up in the excitement of the army's departure. Jubb had watched along with all the other stable hands who were not travelling with their charges. He saw pride and one or two tears in the eyes of his colleagues. It was a brave sight: the horses' coats gleaming and the tack sparkling to rival the sun. As the walls hid them from view, Jubb felt a hand on his shoulder. It was the head ostler.

"How many of them will be back, I wonder? It's bad enough men have to fight each other without dragging the poor beasts into it. Left to their own devices they've got more sense."

The pair walked back to the stableyards. They were quiet now, with a haunted, echoing feel. There were no whinnied greetings, no rustles or stamps in the stalls. Only the courtiers' horses and those of the guard remained. Jubb wandered from one empty stall to another, bereft.

"Go on, lad. Take the rest of the day off. There'll be little enough to do here for a while." The head ostler slapped him on the back to send him on his way.

For a while Jubb hung about the laundry like one of the rumpled shirts, lacking a breeze to lift it. There was no sign of Ro. He had sent the message as she had asked, but had not seen her since. Eventually, some of the laundry girls spotted him. They giggled and pulled faces at him until Mistress Hexem shooed them away. Knowing Ro would worry if he drew attention to himself, he wandered off. Outside the palace compound, the city was as echoing and subdued as the stables. He peered through the window of an inn, but the customers were staring into their drinks as if they contained some oracle of the future.

Jubb found himself heading up out of the usually bustling thoroughfares towards the Garden of the Dead. At least the geese would be pleased to see him.

They honked and flapped their wings on his approach.

"Shh... my beauties. Jubb's brought you a little treat." He had saved the crusts from his breakfast. Now he tore them up and fed them to the greedy beaks. "No need to snatch, my pretties, Jubb needs his fingers."

He fetched them water from one of the elemental fountains.

"There you are, I bet you'd like to have a paddle in the pool, feel the mud beneath your feet."

The geese honked.

"Poor things."

There was barely room in their cage for them to stretch their wings without damaging their feathers. It made Jubb's shoulders feel cramped to see them. He looked again at the elemental pool and back at the geese.

"Why not?"

Jubb hefted the cage. It was awkward to carry and see over with the geese's flapping and shifting unbalancing it.

"You stop that now, you'll hurt yourselves." Jubb paused to check his bearings. He needed to adjust his course to the right. As he did so, he caught the cage on the corner of one of the monuments, lost his balance and fell. The cage fell with him, the door sliding open allowing the occupants to waddle out. The geese strutted with necks outstretched and bills raised, testing their wings.

"Nothing broken, see?" Jubb brushed himself down. "Now, be good birds and come back here."

But they were not good birds. They seemed to enjoy testing Jubb's legs almost as much as their wings. Every time he thought he had one, it would flap off to another part of the garden. For a while they bobbed about on the elemental pool and Jubb's flailing attempts to catch them soon had him soaked.

"I know." The birds had only eaten a few crusts so far. It should be possible to tempt them back to their cage with a trail of bread.

Jubb waited. His wet clothes hung heavy and cold on him, but he dared not move and risk disturbing the geese. Eventually, they too seemed to tire of the joke and left the water. They took it in turns to eat so that while one head was down another was stretched high watching.

"A little further, my beauties," Jubb breathed.

The first of the birds reached the edge of the cage. Suddenly there was an explosion of fur in their midst and a clamour of barks and hisses. At the end of it, Jubb found he had a skinny snarling mongrel in the cage and a few feathers. The geese were high, high in the sky heading away from the lengthening shadows.

"Oh no." Usually Jubb's heart would have soared with them, but he was going to have to explain this to Ro, and not even his optimistic spirit could convince him that she would be pleased. He looked at the mongrel. It cowered in the cage as far from his reach as possible. It looked half-starved.

"Come on, you can help me explain." He picked up the unwieldy cage and headed back to the stables.

Anni waited for Fordel to finish reading. He put the paper down.

"I swear to you, Princess Anni, I knew nothing of any of this."

Her mouth twisted into a bitter smile. "I'm not accusing you of anything, Fordel, except perhaps, turning a blind eye." She held up her hand to forestall his objections. "I want to know what to do about it. You must choose. Will you remain 'fuddled with wine', or will you help me?"

Fordel blushed and Anni knew she had hit her mark.

"Channan's my friend as well as my king."

"Then tell me what you think. Should we warn Ersilla? Knowing her, she'll either take no notice or throw us in the dungeons. And what about Channan? We must prevent this war."

Fordel paced to the window. "What we must ask ourselves, what I have asked myself ever since Channan told me, is why I was left here in charge of the city's defences."

"Channan trusts you," Anni answered.

"Exactly. Channan trusts me and Torslin thinks I'm an incompetent baboon. By leaving me here, he separates me from the King and prevents me getting in his way there, and also leaves the city vulnerable, or so he believes, for him to walk into when he returns."

"You think he'll strike at Channan?"

"People do die in battles, Anni. What could be easier for him than to make sure of it? Then Ersilla wouldn't just be regent, but queen. Who knows? He may even have intended marrying her."

Anni shuddered. "But he's commanded Ayif to kill her."

"Yes. Why?" He paused. "I don't think we need to worry about her safety just yet. Put yourself in Ayif's place. There's no guarantee that Torslin himself won't be killed if there's a battle. Then he'll need someone else to protect him. No, I think all we need to do for now, as far as your sister is concerned, is to keep an eye on her. Ayif won't make a move until he knows Torslin's returning."

"But he'll know I have his book."

Fordel shook his head. "He may suspect, but unless he finds it here or we give the game away, he can't be sure. He can hardly ask you, can he?"

"Then we must make sure he can't find it, and that Channan's warned. I think I know how."

Ayif sagged as he re-entered his chamber. He reached out an unsteady hand for one of the bottles of medicines, extracted a crystal and placed it on his tongue. He closed his eyes and a smile spread over his features. After a few moments savouring the effects, he replaced the bottle. His hand hovered over the cluster of pots and jars. A frown wiped away the look of contentment. He turned full circle until his eyes met the curtain before the niche. It was not completely pulled across. He checked the shrine. All was as he had left it. He bowed to the image of Lethir, turned and caught sight of his bed. Almost tripping over the curtain in his panic, he checked under the pillow. Gone! Gone! It was gone! His sole protection from Torslin. But how did the Lord know where to look? Ayif poured water into a basin and splashed it over his head. It could not have been Torslin. Ayif himself had seem him engaged in organising the Ortanian forces when he arrived with his medical supplies, and he had watched him ride out at King Channan's side. It was not something Torslin could trust to an agent, who might get nosey. He splashed himself again, then grabbed a towel. He sniffed it. It was clean.

He arrived at the laundry only to find his way barred by the press of maids who were trying to get a better view of the cause of a commotion.

"What's happening?" he asked the nearest one, a woman of matronly years and build, but with a distinctly unmatronly glint in her eyes.

"It's that new maid again. How stupid can you get?" She drew Ayif closer to her and mouthed a loud whisper in his ear. "They say she was caught stealing earlier and only Princess Anni's soft-heartedness saved her from a beating from Mistress Hexem."

Ayif looked scandalised.

"No sooner has Mistress Hexem finished giving her a telling off that'd scour the dirt off a roasting pan, than that simple brother of hers comes looking for her. Well, he only brings a filthy flea-bitten mongrel with him, and it only goes and lies in the fresh table-linen Mistress Hexem had all ready for the evening meal."

"She's had it now," joined in one of her colleagues.

"Tch!" Ayif disengaged himself from them and searched for a way through the throng. He spotted a channel opening up and made his way towards it. Ahead of him, Princess Anni's arrival quelled the gossip.

"Well, Mistress Hexem, I come to check on the preparations for tonight and I find the laundry in chaos."

Mistress Hexem gave her a stiff bow and an accusing look. Ro stood with head bowed.

"I see the cause is the same as before," the Princess continued. "It seems my kindness was ill-placed. One chance is all you get, girl." She brushed past Ro to face Jubb. The mongrel struggled in his arms. "And who... what is this?"

"Your pardon, Lady." He bowed.

"Princess," hissed Mistress Hexem.

"Your pardon, Princess. I came to check on my sister. She's not that bright, you see, and I hadn't seen her for two days."

This was greeted with laughter from the maids, which quickly petered out under Mistress Hexem's glare.

"Where do you work?" Anni snapped.

"Stables, Princess."

"Well, it's not as if we're short-staffed with half the population following King Channan. You're dismissed–both of you. I won't have anyone creating havoc at a time like this. Collect your things and go!" Anni stepped backwards, treading on Ro. She swung round on her. "Understand?"

Ro nodded vigorously and dropped a curtsy. Her 'brother' helped her up, fumbling with the struggling mongrel. Among the tangle of limbs Ayif caught a glimpse of something straight-edged. He stepped forward for a better look.

"What are you doing here?" Mistress Hexem's whole manner spoke of disapproval for the Gindullan's exotic and less than spotless attire.

He puffed himself up to his most dignified bearing. "I came in search of my... "

"Ayif! Is Ayif here?" There was a stirring in the throng, as a maid pushed through. "Princess Ersilla has need of him urgently."

The doctor muttered something that would have shocked Mistress Hexem had she caught it. "I'm here."

"Quickly, Sir. She said you were to come at once." The maid took hold of his sleeve and began pulling him after her. Ayif looked back, but Anni was right behind him, blocking the view.

"Is she ill? In Ondd's name, what's the matter." All the colour had drained from her face.

Ayif was hustled out of the laundry. Before he had reached the door, Ro and Jubb had gone.

"I'm sorry, Ro. I've messed everything up." Jubb dragged his feet as they headed back to the stables.

"No, you haven't." Ro looked straight ahead, determined not to keep looking over her shoulder.

"But the geese–and now we've been thrown out. What're we going to do?"

"Wait until we're safely in the stables and we'll see."

Jubb led the way to the nest of hay that had been his sleeping place since their arrival in Najarind, and began playing with the dog while Ro took out the book. Anni had pressed it into her hands when she had bumped into her. Tucked inside it was not only the yellowed paper incriminating Torslin, but a note from the Princess.

"Channan must know the truth. There's no one else I can trust to take it to him. I know this will place you in further danger, but I have to ask you to try to catch up with the army. You'll find horses and supplies at the Fat Man Inn near the main gate. You'll find pedlars' wares too, in case you're stopped. Of course, they are yours wherever you decide to go. May Ondd's wings protect you." It was unsigned. Unused to statecraft as Anni claimed to be, she was no fool.

Ro distracted Jubb's attention from his new friend and explained.

"What do you want to do?" she asked him.

"I want to go home to Amradoc," he said.

The tension in Ro's shoulders eased. Here was the excuse she needed to refuse further heroics.

"I want to go home, and Darian wouldn't ask me to do any more, but if it was him, I know he'd do anything to prevent this war. Chickens and I'll come with you."

Ro smiled in spite of herself. "Chickens? Isn't that a strange name for a dog?"

"He chose it himself, didn't you, boy? I suggested lots of names, but when I said 'Chickens' he barked. See?" he said as Chickens barked agreement.

"And you think Chickens would be better off with us than lounging by some inn's fireside, being fussed and fed scraps?"

"He chose us."

Ro knew that tone of voice: there was no point in arguing. "Come on then. We'll have to be quick if we're to get out before the gates close."

Despite all Ro's efforts to hurry him, Jubb had to double check that he had packed everything. Then he had to say 'good-bye' to the head ostler. By the time they had reached the Fat

Man Inn and had fended off the curious enquiries of the landlord, there were only a few stragglers left passing through the gate, and those were going the other way.

"Hey! Where'd you get those horses?" One of the guards stepped across their path.

"They were a gift from the Princess," Jubb answered.

Ro held back a groan. If the guard should take it upon himself to check.... Instead he took a bored look through the pots and trinkets Anni had provided as trade goods.

"Oh yes? And my comrade here can whistle out of his backside." He winked at the other guard, who sauntered over from his post.

"What proof have you got that they're yours, eh?"

"This." Jubb slid his hand into the breast of his jerkin and pulled forth his precious Words of Power. He unfolded the page slowly, as if expecting the words to fly off it, and showed it to the guard. He threw back his head and roared with laughter. Ro's jaw dropped.

"Truer words were never written!" The guard laughed and slapped the rump of Jubb's horse. "Off you go, then, before the chimes ring."

Jubb refolded his paper with a smug expression. Much as Ro wanted to take a peek at it, they had no choice but to hurry out of the city. They were not many yards along the road before the mechanical chimes began and they heard the gates creak to behind them.

Pachand held a vinegar-soaked cloth in front of his face as he took a closer look at the patrol's putrid cargo. Despite having packed the remains of the fal-worm about with ice from the high slopes, it was rotting fast. The sudden change in the weather had not helped. There was now no more ice to be found, and the milder temperatures were causing problems on two counts. Streams that had been no more than icy trickles when they had passed before were now gleeful torrents that leaped over rocks and raced along widening channels. Frosty meadows had become quagmires that held on to the horses' legs and cartwheels like misers to their hoard. As the fal-worm's decomposition accelerated, the stench grew worse. At first it had merely made those closest sick and lightheaded, but the effects were intensifying. The carts which had carried supplies on the way out were now full of soldiers too weak or delirious to ride.

The sun was well risen and they should be on their way again, but the whole patrol seemed infected with lethargy. Apart from the horses. When the handler had tried harnessing the team to the fal-worm's cart, they had shied and frothed at the mouth. One had succeeded in snatching its reins from the handler's grasp and smashed through the camp. A soldier caught in its path was trampled and there was a sharp crack as his leg snapped.

Pachand turned his head and spat on the ground. Wrapped in oiled cloth though it was, the rotting package had begun to leak a sickly yellow liquid.

"Burn it," he told the sergeant. "Wagon and all."

The soldier lost no time in obeying. Pachand strode on to the wagons holding his sick men. Now he would have no evidence to offer King Channan except hearsay, but at least he would have some of his patrol left. Assuming that the sickness would wear off once out of the fal-worm's proximity, and that it would not spread and infect all.

Pachand gave the soldiers a businesslike nod. "Soon have you on your feet again now."

As the flames leaped up around the stinking corpse, Pachand mounted his horse at the head of the column. War was one thing; terrible, but clean in its way, but this... Pachand spat again. If the Patriarch was behind this, he would take great joy in putting his fingers around his throat and squeezing until they met.

# Chapter Fifteen

At first, Natann thought the sound was thunder, but the sky was clear, and instead of rumbling through the air the noise came up from the ground. If he had still been in the highlands, he would have expected an avalanche. Riding on, the cause became clear. A river of men, wagons and horses was pouring out of the far-off city. Sun flashed off helmets and swords. At the head of the army the wind caught the royal banner. Even at that distance, Natann saw the glint of gold on the dragons as they writhed and clawed the air. Natann kicked his horse to a canter.

It was nightfall before he caught up with the flow of men. The rapidly moving army had pooled into a lake spreading over either side of the road and surrounding fields. Tents were being thrown up, fires lit and horses rubbed down; bustle and activity met the eye in all directions. Already the excitement of being on the march was punctuated with grumbles about blistered feet and flavourless rations. No one challenged the exhausted messenger. He led his horse through the sprawling camp, ignoring the smells of cooking and the invitation of the fires.

Set on the crest of a gentle slope overlooking the camp, Natann came to a village of tents more luxurious than those below. The royal banner hung outside one. Squires criss-crossed the open space leading to it, bearing flagons and dishes. A sentry wearing the uniform of the elite palace guard checked each one in and out of the tent. He stepped in front of Natann.

"I have important news for the King," he explained.

The sentry held out a mailed hand. "I'll see that he gets it."

Natann shook his head. "My orders are to give it to King Channan or Lord Torslin in person."

"Whose orders?"

Natann hesitated. News that a rider had arrived from the patrol would spread like blood in water.

"Captain Pachand's."

The sentry looked him up and down. "Wait here."

He entered the tent where King Channan watched his generals arguing over a map in front of him. Torslin sat back, as the sentry approached. He listened to his news, then quickly bowed to the King and left.

"Well, man, you come from the patrol?" the Lord demanded as soon as he caught sight of Natann.

"My Lord." Natann bowed, so tired he could barely keep his balance.

"This way." Torslin caught one of the scurrying squires and relieved him of a tray of food. He led the way to a tent furnished with a bed, camp table and chair. He set down the tray and nodded at Natann. "Well?"

The sight of the food flooded Natann's mouth with saliva and he had to swallow before he could speak. He began to relate what the patrol had found, prompted by Torslin's brusque questions. The memory of the fal-worms took away the desire to eat.

"The priest—he confessed it was a religious plot?"

"He mentioned the Patriarch and a woman—it wasn't clear who—maybe that murdering bitch who killed King Berinn."

"Hmm... " Torslin's eyes narrowed. "Who else have you told?"

"No one. Captain Pachand's orders."

"Good." Torslin's manner suddenly relaxed. "You're exhausted, man." He slapped Natann on the back. "Sit. Eat. Leave this to me now. I'll have a fresh horse and supplies prepared." Torslin's expression made the protest die on Natann's lips. "As soon as you've eaten you can be on your way."

Natann sat in the empty tent, ears buzzing with exhaustion. He ate slowly, starting at noises outside of the camp settling for the night. On the whole, he would be glad not to stay, although Pachand trusted the Lord. He stumbled to attention as Torslin returned.

Before long he was in the saddle riding into a night that seemed clearer than before. He did not stop until lack of sleep threatened to throw him off the horse's back. There was no telltale sound of hooves following. He found a sheltered spot out sight of the army and the road. Too tired now for anything but sleep, he ignored the flask and packed food, rolled himself in a blanket and was soon unaware of the noises of the night.

"Come on, Jubb. Let's find somewhere to camp."

Jubb had been nodding in the saddle, and Ro found her own eyelids closing.

"I'm not tired." He had immediately jerked upright.

"Well, I am, and no one's going to believe we're pedlars if they catch us travelling at night."

They dismounted and led the horses off the road looking for somewhere safe from view. The sound of regular breathing alerted Ro. Someone else had got there first. Ro turned to signal Jubb to stay back, but he had set Chickens down so that the mongrel could stretch its legs. Before he could grab it again, the dog ran up to the sleeping figure, sniffing cautiously at his face, then turning its attention to his saddlebags, dumped on the ground next to the tethered horse. It whinnied and stamped. Instantly, the rider was up; his hand on a knife at his belt.

"No!" Jubb ran to scoop up the dog. "Don't hurt him, please!"

Ro stepped forward. "Your pardon, Sir. We hadn't meant to disturb you. We were looking for somewhere to sleep." Too late, she remembered her pose of dumbness.

The rider eyed them but said nothing. Chickens began to squirm in Jubb's arms, licking his face until he had to laugh and set him down. The dog immediately ran back over to the rider's bags.

"Are you hungry?" the rider asked.

"We have food with us," Ro answered, but the growling of Jubb's stomach seemed to contradict her.

"Sit down then, eat, and you can tell me what you're doing here." The rider sat, but retained hold of his knife.

"That's easy," Ro answered, busying herself with unloading their provisions and bed rolls. "We're pedlars trying to catch up with the army. No better customers than a load of bored soldiers."

"Your accent seems familiar." The rider frowned, trying to place it.

"From the Singing Lake," Ro blurted. "Best fancy goods you'll find anywhere. What about you?"

For an instant, Ro thought she saw a familiar consciousness pass across the rider's face. "I'm Natann, heading back to my village in the hills before the thaw makes the way impassable." He hauled his bags over, watched keenly by Chickens, and began pulling out the wrapped food. "Might as well have something myself now I'm awake."

Ro's pulse slowed to a more measured pace. Apparently, their new companion had secrets of his own. It should be possible to deflect uncomfortable questions by returning them. They were soon sharing a welcome meal, the conversation becoming easier as the food relaxed them.

"Here." Natann poured them all a cup of a dark red liquid from the flask Torslin had provided. "If my nose doesn't deceive me this is wine from the summer country. It should warm hearts and spirits."

They raised their cups in salute. Natann drained his in one go and poured another. Jubb would have followed suit but Chickens, not wanting to be left out, jumped up and knocked his hand spilling most of it down his jerkin. Natann laughed and refilled the cup, while Ro sipped at hers politely. She had yet to acquire a taste for the woody tang of the drink. Natann upended the dregs of his third cup and yawned.

"That's it, I could sleep forever." He crawled back into his blanket. "Torslin's wine makes up for his inhospitality. Never even a 'thank-you'," he murmured.

"Torslin?" Ro's voice was sharp.

"What? Oh–his wine, that's all," Natann's words slurred and his eyes closed.

Ro threw what was left of her wine into the bushes and snatched away the cup that was slipping from Jubb's limp fingers.

"Nah? Wotya doin'?" The fool slid down until he was curled on the ground. Chickens curled up next to him and licked his fingers. Through a shimmer of dizziness, Ro realised that Jubb did not move.

"Jubb?" She bent to check his breathing and fell to her knees. Drugged! The rider had drugged them. She shook Jubb making his arms and head flop. Chickens began to whine. Ro tried to focus. The rider had drunk more of the wine than any of them. She crawled on limbs that insisted on moving in their own directions to Natann's side and placed her head against his chest. There was no movement, no sound of air gliding in or out of his lips, no beat of life. Dead: the word appeared in her brain but it had little meaning. She knew she ought to move, but resting her head on Natann's chest was so comfortable. Poison: the thought spurred Ro to make the effort to rise. Torslin's wine, Torslin's poison. He had killed the rider, for what reason she did not know, and oh, how he would laugh if he knew he had hit Ro and Jubb with the same shot.

"Jubb! Jubb! You've got to wake up!" Ro shouted, but only a murmur came out. As she closed her eyes, Ro thought she heard barking.

Anni pulled her cloak around her and stepped out into the rose bower. At this time of year the branches thrust outward in supplication for the return of spring. Even the gardeners hardly came there. It was depressingly bleak but for the glow returning to some of the stems and the swellings where soon there would be buds. Anni felt an affinity with the abandoned place. It was the best spot in the whole of Najarind to watch for the first streaks of golden dawn in the sky. She closed the door to the private apartments behind her and settled into a skeletal arbour to wait. Her eyes were not turned towards the sunrise but strained in the direction of Amradoc. A streak of rose-tinged light barred the sky: Ondd's tail, a good omen.

"Great Ondd, speed their journey to Channan. Don't let my trust be misplaced." She closed her eyes against the thought of all that might go wrong: horses going lame, capture by Torslin as spies or worse, Channan's refusal to believe. Yet what else could she have done?

She sat struggling to control her turmoil until the streak had bled into a diffuse glow catching on the edges of roofs. Anni sank back into the arbour, breathing in the peace of the moment. The gate-latch creaked. The Princess quelled her indignation as she saw the intruder. He too was wrapped in a heavy cloak and had muffled his face with a scarf, but there was no mistaking the haughty deportment of the Patriarch. His eyes darted about the twilit garden. Apparently satisfied he tapped lightly at the door to the private apartments. It opened only enough to allow him to slip through, but Anni caught the greeting whispered by Ersilla's body-maid. She waited long enough to allow them to clear the corridor, then followed.

It was not unknown for the Patriarch to visit the palace to offer spiritual guidance to the royal family, but it was rare and never like this, as if he was a thief. Ersilla had never shown herself much interested in religion before now either. Anni considered briefly, then hurried past Ersilla's room and up a flight of stairs to the old nursery. She tiptoed across the floor to the chimney. The same one served this and Princess Ersilla's sitting room. She had virtually to climb into the hearth, but she could hear voices funnelled up to her.

"This is most unwise, Highness." The Patriarch's voice grew louder and faded as he paced back and forth in front of Ersilla's hearth.

"Do be still, you're making me giddy."

"Apologies, Highness, but what you ask is suicidally dangerous." The voice halted by the chimney.

"What I order, Patriarch, what I order, and I assure you I am far from being suicidal." Anni could imagine Ersilla's haughty expression. "It can't be long now before Pachand's patrol returns and who knows what he's discovered. If he links the arrival of the fal-worms to the arrival of your priest, there will be no option but to search your abbey. I should be forced to order it. Far safer for our experiment to be kept here in the palace vaults."

Despite the warmth from the chimney, Anni felt a chill creep over her.

"Lord Torslin would never approve," the Patriarch said.

"Lord Torslin's not here. In fact, he might never be here again. The same goes for my brother. Consider that, Patriarch."

"Indeed, Highness."

"Good. We understand each other. There will be provisions coming in from the regions to feed the city should there be a siege. You can arrange for our experiment to be part of them. I leave the details to you."

"Very well, but... "

"Now go. I have other matters to deal with. The seamstress will be arriving shortly with my new gown."

Anni heard a door close, punctuated by a shrill burst of laughter. She shuddered and tiptoed back out of the nursery. Like dough in a hot oven, her problems had just ballooned.

# Chapter Sixteen

The daily journey to the lake had become a ritual. When the shadows were at their longest and about to fade with the setting sun Lar, Dovinna, Raimi, Edun and Mirri carrying Lalli, would accompany Uwert to check the tame geese for messages. Yesterday, their devotion had been rewarded with news from Ro and Jubb at last, but it had brought little comfort: Ortann's army was about to move.

"Really, there's no need for this procession every day," Uwert protested as they neared the feeding place.

The wooden platform had been built at what was once the water's edge before King Berinn had diverted the river. Now the pilings strode across a wasteland of mud. The topping of frost made it look like a huge iced festival cake, but beneath this sparkling crust the mud waited to embrace the unwary. The geese congregated like a noisy audience waiting for the curtain to rise on Edun's magic act. The goose-keeper, a small man with peat-coloured skin as leathery as his jerkin, allowed the party to reach the platform before spreading the bird's grain. He waded into the froth of white feathers and snapping beaks, bent and withdrew one honking its protest. He handed Uwert the capsule from its leg.

"Empty!" He showed it to Lar, but the goose-keeper had not finished. He repeated the process twice more. Each time the capsule was empty.

"What does it mean?" Lar whispered.

"Either they're on their way back, or that fool Jubb let them escape."

"In other words, there's no way we can know," Raimi spoke with bitterness.

"There'd be no point in staying without the geese, would there?" Mirri asked.

The others turned back to the city without answering.

"Well, would there?" she insisted, touching Lar's arm.

The Earth-hearer's face wore a look of strained concentration, which was rarely absent now. "I don't know. It's too far away to hear."

"But... " Mirri persisted.

"Leave her," Raimi interrupted. "It's enough to lose one daughter."

Mirri's mouth formed a round 'O'. She dabbed at her eyes with her sleeve. "I'm sure, I never meant to upset anyone."

"No one thinks you did, dear." Edun pulled a face at Lalli, who chuckled. The baby had a knack of raising all their spirits. "If Ro and Lalli are connected, as the healer Varda says they are, surely the little one would feel it if something happened to Ro," he suggested.

Raimi took the baby from Mirri, holding her out of reach of both the wet-nurse and the magician. "I don't believe it. Ussu would have none of it."

Mention of Ussu silenced them all. Dovinna walked a little apart from the others. Since Ro had left the healer had grown increasingly silent, becoming animated only when playing with Lalli. The stiffness of her shoulders and the jut of her jaw showed more determination than confidence. Occasionally, she sighed. Edun looked from one to the other. He could almost wish for Jubb's chaotic presence. Even the onddikins were listless, and when he let them fly free for their exercise they tended to circle back in the direction of Najarind. He had to call them several times before they returned.

At the door to their quarters Uwert parted from them, refusing Lar's polite invitation to enter.

"I must report to King Darian." He hesitated, as if he would say more. Instead, he bowed to Lar and left.

"So, it's come on us at last." Mirri spoke as she bustled about preparing for Lalli's bath and feed. "Our brave soldiers are going to have to march off and fight Ortann's soldiers, else what's to become of us?"

No one answered. Dovinna moved restlessly out of Mirri's path. Raimi set Lalli in her cot and stood gazing moodily at the fire.

"Now would you look at that? What a forward babe it is!" Mirri gushed. Lalli had succeeded in levering herself into a sitting position and was trying to catch the painted butterflies Edun had hung above her cot. "Why, if she carries on at this rate, she'll soon be talking."

Lar flinched and Raimi's face darkened.

"In her own way, perhaps," Edun tried to smooth the situation. "I've met deaf people who are as fluent with gestures as most are with speech."

Lar rewarded him with a sad smile, not so Raimi.

"If she's such a prodigy, no doubt she'll soon be weaned and we'll have no more need of a wet-nurse."

Real tears started to Mirri's eyes. "Aye, and then I'll be able to spend time with my own children. They'll be pleased enough to see me."

"Oh, Mirri... " Dovinna sounded exhausted. "We're all at our wits end with worry. Things get said that aren't meant."

Mirri blew her nose loudly. "It's not as though I haven't lost anyone myself."

There was an almost solid silence. Raimi broke it, speaking more gently this time.

"It would be better if she was weaned."

Mirri gasped.

"Because I shall be taking her with me when I leave with the army, and you'll be needed here with your family."

"Whoever heard of such a thing?" Mirri turned to the others for support. "Take a baby to a battlefield? It's mad! No, it's criminal! Lar, you can't let Raimi do this."

"I haven't the right to prevent," Lar returned. "She's his daughter, and since I intend going with him he'll have no kin left here to look after her."

"You! But you're not well!" Mirri protested.

"Quite well enough to find my daughter. I should never have let her leave without me."

Mirri made an indignant sound.

Dovinna clasped the Earth-hearer's hands tightly. "No, Lar, it isn't you who's at fault, but me. I was the one who led Ro into danger, I was the one who should've mended things."

Lar smiled as if Dovinna was also her daughter. "Some things can't be mended, not even by a healer such as you."

"I have to try though. If nothing else, the army's bound to be short of healers."

Mirri stood with hands on hips, her mouth pressed into a line. "You've all gone moon gazy! You've no more sense between you than that stewpot! What about you, Master Magician? Have your wits done a vanishing act too?"

"I've always made it a policy to avoid trouble wherever possible." Edun shrugged. "But I need the onddikins for my act and, you see, they insist on going to Najarind. I believe that means I too will have to accompany the army. If nothing else it'll give me a captive audience to perfect my new tricks on."

"Very well, then you'll need someone with some practical sense to take care of you. I shall just have to go too!"

There was an explosion of protests, but no matter how many times the others pointed out that she had responsibilities in Mandur, she refused to be swayed.

"I'm not letting my Lalli go traipsing around the countryside without someone to make sure she has a fresh supply of napkins and has her sleep in the afternoons." She stuck out her chin as if daring one of them to hit it. Into the sudden lull came a knock at the door.

"May I come in?" King Darian poked his head into the room. The others hastily rose to salute him formally. His face was grey with lack of sleep, but he wore a grin. "No need." He waved away the gestures. "Forgive me, but I couldn't help hearing as I approached a discussion remarkably similar to the one I've just been having with Uwert. You intend travelling with the army?"

Lar answered. "Yes."

"All of you?" He looked from one to another. As his gaze touched them they nodded. "I'd thought to offer you the choice of remaining here, or supplying you with the means to continue your journey. Well, it seems we're to be quite an unstoppable force then. We leave at daylight."

Perhaps the air was fresher on the road. Everyone's steps gained something of a spring, and their shoulders a more purposeful set. Raimi was even seen to laugh as he prepared the horses, despite the fact that Darian had refused to give him a place in the ranks.

"I don't doubt your bravery or your ability. You've proven both getting to Mandur, but you have other concerns and talents that I may want to draw on."

Raimi had accepted the King's verdict with a shrug. He had spent the morning's march riding either alongside the wagon conveying Dovinna and his family, or that of Edun. The magician had refused to leave it behind.

"It's my home and the onddikins are used to it," he had protested when Uwert had tried to persuade him to travel in something less colourful.

"Make it easier for him to run when things look dangerous too," Mirri had whispered to Dovinna. The healer had pointedly walked away. "I'm only saying what others might think," she persisted. "Oh dear, Lalli. I can see everyone's nerves are still bothering them. They'd be far better off if they were placid creatures like you and me."

Under the circumstances, Lalli's burp seemed a most appropriate response.

Lar and Dovinna did not have to put up with Mirri's chattiness for long. The jolting of the wagon disagreed with her, and her complaints about the roughness of the ride and the bruises she had acquired swiftly changed to groans as she struggled with motion sickness. Dovinna treated her with as much sympathy as she could muster. The healer sat down next to Lar, who guided the horses as much by humming to them as with the reins.

"We should get some peace now, I've given her something to make her drowsy."

"I'm sure she's a good soul. She didn't have to come with us."

"Mm.... Once this is over, I think Raimi had better watch out," Dovinna giggled. Raimi had escaped Mirri's moans some time earlier by finding an urgent need to speak to Edun.

"Once this is over," repeated Lar.

They continued in silence, watching the horses plod on.

Dovinna stirred. "Do you think Ro and Jubb are on their way back to Amradoc? I mean, I know all King Darian wanted was news of Channan's plans with the army, but... "

"But you'd hoped she'd find a way to prevent it marching?" Lar questioned gently.

Dovinna nodded. "Unreasonable of me, I know, but Channan isn't violent or vindictive. I'm certain he'd prefer not to go to war if there was any way he could see to avoid it."

"Like discovering your innocence?"

She blushed.

"I have no doubt the same thing was in Ro's mind when she left. I was too full of my weakness then to offer her much counsel." Although Lar's voice had regained much of its power, it was still prone to becoming clogged with smoke that had to be coughed out.

"What counsel could you give? I'm the one who knows Najarind."

"And now the Ortanian army is marching, you think that Ro's failed and that maybe you should have gone in her stead."

Dovinna hung her head. "I started this trouble."

"I think you'll find it started long before you were born, Dovinna. Since leaving Iyessa, I've discovered that trying to find a place to lay blame sets nothing to rights. Besides... " she added in a lighter tone "... as Edun is so fond of telling us: everything depends on how you look at things. Ro may not have succeeded yet, but that isn't the same thing as failing." Lar turned her attention to the horses.

Dovinna watched her curiously. "Forgive me, Lar, do you... ?" She paused, knowing that the Earth-hearer would be able to feel her uncertainty. "Do you think Ro will follow Channan's army? Is that why you've come? Because you think you'll be able to 'hear' her?"

Lar did not answer straight away. "Perhaps."

"But there'll be so many people and beasts, such turmoil... it's impossible!"

"How many times have we seen Edun perform the impossible?" Lar answered mildly.

"Tricks."

Lar smiled. "Don't worry. I know I'm hoping for a chance in a million, and what else am I to do? At least this way I might play some useful part."

There was a commotion behind them, and Mirri's voice crying out for a basin. Dovinna sighed and went back inside.

Life on the journey fell into a regular pattern with few incidents. It was almost possible to believe that they were not marching to meet war. King Darian led his men as if riding to a wedding, taking care at each rest period to visit the various tents and share a few encouraging words with his soldiers. Only the arrival of the scouts sent to detect signs of the Ortanian force made their hearts jump. The fugitives found themselves retracing much of the route of their flight. Finally, with the late winter sun burning its brightest above them, they arrived at the same farmstead which had sheltered them on their first night in Amradoc. By the evening halt, they would be nearing the river and a few miles north they would reach the ford and the border with Ortann. Raimi became increasingly silent and pale as the day faded. When Darian called a halt for the night, he strode off on his own.

"Isn't anybody going to stop him?" Mirri demanded. "He ought to eat a decent supper and get some rest. He's thin as a tent pole!"

"Here, Mirri, let me help you with Lalli." Dovinna took the baby from her. Lalli had grizzled much of the afternoon. Mirri declared she must be getting a tooth, and tried pacifying her by laying a cool cloth against her cheek, but Lalli remained fractious. Usually a change of view in a different pair of arms would soothe her, but even taking her to see the horses did not work today. She kept turning in Dovinna's embrace and reaching out for something. Whichever way Dovinna turned, Lalli reached towards the same spot.

Dovinna called Lar over. "What do you think it is? Something's upsetting her."

"Maybe she wants her father," Mirri interrupted.

"He went off in the other direction," Dovinna observed.

"She seems to be reaching towards the river," said Lar. "Perhaps the water pulls her."

Mirri muttered something, of which the only audible words were 'nonsense' and 'superstition'. She bustled about banging pots and plates as she began 'helping' Edun prepare the evening meal.

Edun looked up. "Perhaps you should take her for a walk. The onddikins could do with some exercise too."

With Pirik, Finik and Quinik wheeling and swooping overhead, they followed Lalli's insistent tugging, until they came to the edge of the river. It looped in lazy meanders fringed with reeds and trees leaning out to see their reflections.

"Here we are then, Lalli. We've seen the river, now we ought to go back," Dovinna told the baby. As soon as the healer turned, the baby screamed. Mirri snatched Lalli from her.

"What did you do to her?"

"Nothing." Dovinna looked at Lar for support.

Mirri began searching the chubby arms and legs. "You must have pricked her or something."

Lar held out her arms. "Give her to me."

Mirri looked about to object, but saw Lar's expression and handed Lalli to her. The Earth-hearer waded into the water. Lalli's lip stopped trembling and she began crooning.

"If you think I'm going in there, you're seriously mistaken," Mirri snapped.

"That won't be necessary, Mirri." Lar was staring at a reed-choked bend where the water pooled outside the main flow. "I want you to find Uwert and ask him to fetch Raimi here." There were tears running down her cheeks.

For once, Mirri did as she was bid without argument. Lalli was cooing and leaning forward on Lar's arms. Dovinna waded out, the icy water making her gasp. She followed the Earth-hearer's gaze and immediately forgot the cold. They were still there when Raimi arrived minutes later. He ran straight into the water, and began tearing aside the reeds.

"Gently, Raimi," Lar whispered. "They've been her bower all this while."

He sank to his knees in the water. His shoulders shook, but no tears came as he looked on Ussu's dead face. "I'd never thought to see her again," he said, as both Uwert and Darian hurried to the riverbank.

Mirri struggled breathlessly in their wake. Darian looked questioningly at Dovinna.

"It's my daughter, Highness," Lar said, her voice so full of pain that Dovinna felt she could not bear it. "The river has cradled her here, so gently she might only be sleeping."

"The ice, Sire," whispered Uwert. "This slow stretch of the river would have frozen over and... " He broke off.

The ice had protected Ussu. Her face appeared almost to be smiling, as if listening to a favourite melody. Her hair billowed about her and her arms were stretched wide as if to welcome someone into them. Darian and Uwert stood with heads bowed, until Raimi stirred. He took Ussu in an embrace and lifted her clear of her bed of reeds. Darian waded into the river to assist him. No one seemed to know what to say. At sight of the body, calm and untouched as it was, Mirri fainted, breaking the tableau. Dovinna tended her, desperate to prevent the hysterics that would inevitably follow when she woke.

Raimi and Darian laid Ussu reverently on the bank. Darian gave Lar his arm and helped her from the river.

"Whatever you need, if it's in my power I'll provide it, but I can't delay. The army must move on, and with me at its head."

Lar bowed. "We'll bury her here, where the leaves will rustle over her and shade her in summer, and the murmur of the water

will soothe her. Once we've sung the Song of Passing, we'll
follow."

"I'm sorry, Lar." Darian clasped her by the shoulders.

"Don't be, Sire. This is a chance to perform one last service
for my daughter. One that I'd thought beyond hope."

Raimi and Lar spent the night preparing the body and sitting
vigil over it. The customary noise and restlessness of the army
camp grew respectfully quiet around them. The dignified grief of
the Iyessi inspired an awed hush.

Watching, Dovinna said: "I feel I should be helping, but that
it would be an intrusion."

Edun swallowed hard.

"Maybe now he'll begin to heal," Mirri sighed and retired to
the wagon where Lalli was now sleeping soundly.

The gentle song of Lar over her dead daughter held Edun and
Dovinna spellbound by the fire, until the night faded and the army
began to rise. Then they stirred themselves to prepare a breakfast
and freshen themselves for the coming ceremony. As the soldiers
set off on another day's march, those that passed made the Iyessi
party a formal salute, fingertips pressed to lips, and some left
sprigs of sweet-smelling winter herbs to garland the grave. The
mourners waited in silence for the noise of wheels and booted feet
to fade. Lar and Raimi were still listening long after the others
thought all was quiet. While they waited, Uwert joined them,
making his own offering of scented oil to sprinkle over the site.
The sun was halfway up the sky before Lar rose. Edun and Uwert
shouldered the bier, and Raimi turned to Mirri for Lalli.

"You're not wanting the baby to go to a funeral. Oh, that
would be bad luck!"

Raimi was in no mood to argue and took the baby, who was
already reaching for him. The mourners followed the bier to the
river's edge where Ussu was found. Dovinna hastily put her arm
around Mirri.

"We must respect their customs–and you see? Lalli's quite
content."

Lar sang: "May the winds blow softly over you... "

Raimi's clear tenor joined in: "Cooling the heat of the day."

"May the fire bring warmth in the night... "

"And light to guard your sleep."

"May the earth guide your way... "

"And the water refresh."

"May your spirit be bright with vitae restored."
"Let all bring delight in the land you now tread,
Not lost or alone, but cherished forever,
In songs and in hearts and by Ondd ever blessed."

As Lar and Raimi sang the Song of Passing, Lalli's chubby
fingers reached out to Raimi's lips and she joined in with her own
rambling sing-song. It formed a moving counterpart, and the tears
flowed. Even Uwert and Mirri, who had never laid eyes on Ussu
before, felt the song sweep their souls to a place where tears and
rivers ran clear, where waters and hearts were untroubled. Lar's
voice faded on a last pulsing beat and the mourners covered the
body with the herbs and branches of willow, before wrapping her
in a blanket of earth. They turned back to the wagons in silence,
until Lar spoke.

"We've tended the needs of the spirit, now we must tend to
the body. We'll eat and rest, then move on."

The conversation was quiet.

"How do you feel?" Edun asked Dovinna.

"Exhausted, sad, but somehow lighter."

He nodded. "I know. I couldn't sing that melody, but I feel it's
in my bones now, there forever."

Uwert made ready to ride on. "Forgive me, I must catch up
with King Darian."

Lar gave him a formal salute. "Ussu would have been
honoured that you chose to attend her."

"What will you do now?" he asked.

Lar frowned. "We'll follow you, of course. Our purpose hasn't
changed. If anything it's stronger now. We must find Ro."

The wild barking bothered Ro, but she did not have the energy to
move. It grew more insistent.

"Shh... " Chickens greeted the barely audible command by
licking Ro's face enthusiastically.

"Gerroff... " Ro waved her hand feebly.

Chickens began alternating the licks with tugs at her hair and
fingers and stinging nips. Ro managed to roll onto her side. The
mongrel jumped and darted at her, setting up an excited yapping
again. To Ro it seemed as if there were three of him, the sight kept
fading out of focus. Her eyes locked on the dead body of Natann.
Soon she and Jubb would join him, and poor Chickens would be

211

masterless again. Unless Jubb was dead already. Poor Jubb, poor Ro. She began to cry, then gritted her teeth.

"No! I will not let Torslin win!" She hit her forehead with her knuckles hoping the pain would help her to think more clearly. She did not know what the poison was, but there might be something in the supplies Anni had provided for them that would help. Ro crawled to their packs, while Chickens started whining and licking at Jubb. There were salves for bumps and grazes, herbs to cure headaches–salt. She tipped some into a cup with water, swilled it around and swallowed it as fast as she could. It came back almost immediately. The retching felt as if her stomach was being torn out, and the bitter taste was foul, but as soon as the spasm passed she repeated the process. Then she filled the cup again and stumbled over to Jubb. The fool had drunk more of the wine than she had, but Chickens had succeeded in spilling quite a lot and Jubb had a larger frame than she. If she could get him to swallow some of the brine there was hope.

Chickens's antics caused barely a flutter of the fool's eyelashes. Ro added her pestering to his, clumsily trying to raise Jubb's head and pour the brine between his lips. He spluttered. She poured some more. There was no sign of consciousness, but his body automatically reacted. Fighting off the dizziness and lassitude which whispered seductively about the pleasure of curling up and sleeping, Ro made him swallow some more. It had the desired result.

"That's it, Chickens, I can't do any more." Ro allowed herself to sink down beside Jubb. The darkness rushed in until only one small point of bright light remained. It seemed to Ro that she was floating through a dark green tunnel, which resolved into the copse near her village. She emerged on the level green border of the pool that had always been her sanctuary. Calm and still, the water hardly rippled. Ro lay down to look into its depths, seeing the circle of blue sky and clouds floating in it. All the clamour and indecision and disjointed thoughts floated away with them. There was silence, and then Ro heard a voice. Its familiarity made her frown, trying to place it.

"Ussu?"

"You're not going to die looking like that, are you? Look at your hair, and there's vomit on your gown."

She tried to ignore it, but the voice continued drily.

"Some friend you are! You'd let Jubb be found by strangers without even laying him out tidily. Fool he was indeed for relying on you."

"What would you have me do?" Ro asked and found the earth pressing uncomfortably hard on her cheek. The vision had gone. She looked at Jubb. The voice had been right, she could not leave him to be found looking as if no one had cared about him. She forced herself to move again. She bathed his face and hands, straightened his clothes and brushed away the dust. While she worked she began to sing. When she realised, she broke off. She had never sung before unless forced to; it made her lack of sensitivity all too evident, and why choose the lullaby about Ondd's scales? It should have been the Song of Passing. Whatever the reason, her song seemed to calm Chickens, who laid down by Jubb's head. Ro listened to Jubb's shallow breathing.

When she woke the sun was shining full in her face. The glare as she opened her eyes set off fireworks in her head. Coming to her knees the world rocked under her and she scrambled into the bushes to retch out what remained of her stomach. Chickens greeted her reappearance in the camp with a couple of thumps of his tail, but remained by Jubb's head. Ro picked up Jubb's hand: still warm. The fool's cheeks were as white as Mistress Hexem's laundry, but breath passed through his parted lips.

"Jubb?" Ro called gently. "Jubb!" She shook him and he sighed. "What now, Chickens?" Ro's head felt stuffed with goat's wool and she could barely speak, her throat was so dry. No doubt wherever Jubb's spirit was wandering, he also was thirsty.

Ro forced herself to drink some water slowly. She had been careless pouring it last night and the bottle was half-empty. Supporting Jubb as best she could, she moistened his lips and managed to get him to swallow a couple of mouthfuls. Rummaging through their pack, Ro found a biscuit to nibble on, hoping it would settle her stomach rather than cause another revolt. She continued searching the pack. Last night she had been sure she had seen some herbs for headaches. Instead her fingers closed around some unprepossessing stems with tiny brown leaves. She crushed a leaf between finger and thumb. The air was suddenly full of the scent of spring fields: the same smell had helped to call King Berinn's spirit back before Ayif's treachery. Chickens sat watching her with his head on one side and crooked ears cocked.

"You stay with Jubb, Chickens. I'm going to find some more water to put these in. If anything can bring Jubb back, they can."

Ro wandered quite a way before she realised she was heading for the road. She hesitated. Perhaps someone would come along who could help them. On the other hand they might be suspected of murdering Natann; even taken before Torslin. That would not do. She closed her eyes and wished for a water affinity.

"I've found water before, and I'll do it again," she told herself.

Turning her back on the road, Ro set off in what she thought was the most likely direction and soon came to a fast-running brook. Filling the pots she had brought with her, Ro headed back to camp. Before long the water was bubbling over a fire. Ro took a few of the precious stems, crushed them and scattered them on the water. Immediately, the smell of death and despair was banished. Breathing in the steam, Ro felt like laughing. She placed the pan close to Jubb's head where he would receive the full benefit of the herb. His eyelids began to flutter.

"Jubb?" Ro called again. His lips moved, but no sound came out. He turned on his side, towards the pan, and drew up his legs into a more comfortable position. Chickens settled into the hollow they formed and Jubb put his arm over the dog, a sleepy smile on his face.

"Thank Ondd!"

Despite the joyous aroma that now pervaded the area, Ro found herself in tears once more; they seemed to wash away the last of the cloud that was in her head. When he woke Jubb would need something to eat, but now the crisis had passed, Ro knew there was an obligation to another to fulfill before that. Natann's body had been lying neglected all day and could not be ignored. Ro forced herself to look at him. The rider's face was peaceful. At least Torslin had spared him a painful death.

"What did you do to make him your enemy?" she asked the dead rider. "Are there people waiting for news of you? People who love you?" Ro thought of her own family, as desperate to know what was happening to her, as she was to hear that they prospered. "We can't just leave you."

She was too weak to dig a proper grave, but scraped a shallow hole in the lea of a bank of earth. Dragging the body to it was almost beyond her and she had to keep stopping. She smoothed Natann's hair and clothes as best she could. Her fingers hovered over his tunic.

"Forgive me." She began searching the folds and pockets, hoping to find some clue to his loved ones, and why he should have died so far from home. All she found was a lock of hair in a folded piece of paper. Taking care not to touch anything with her bare fingers in case the wine was not all Torslin had poisoned, she then did the same with his pack. There was nothing to help identify him or his mission. When all was ready, Ro stood by the graveside.

"I swear to you, one day Torslin will pay for this, and for all the pain he's caused."

She sang as much as she could of the Song of Passing. The sun was creeping towards nightfall once more, and seemed to be taking Ro's strength with it. She filled in the grave and covered it with stone, then returned to the camp. The scent of the herb still hung in the air, softening her mood, but more comforting yet was the sight of Jubb struggling to sit up.

"Jubb!" If she had had the energy she would have bounded around him like Chickens.

"Got a hangover," he said.

"A bit more than that. Rest while I get something to eat, and I'll explain."

Progress was slow. At first Jubb could stomach no food. A few sips of water were enough to cause discomfort. Ro forced herself to eat what he left, knowing that if she did not regain her strength they would both die. On the second day, Jubb managed to keep down some broth, but each spoonful had to be coaxed into him. The spark that had made him such an engaging companion had gone out and Ro did not know how to reignite it. The only time he showed signs of his old chaotic humour was when Chickens got up to some mischief. More worrying was Jubb's claim that something was wrong with his legs.

"You're just weak still, once you've got some food into you, you'll soon get better." Ro held up another spoonful of soup.

Jubb shook his head. "No, they feel all sort of tingly, and I can't make them move how I want."

Ro could not hide a smile. The fool's limbs had always seemed to move any which way.

"I know, I'm always clumsy, but this is different." Jubb hung his head.

"You've been lying there too long. Let's try getting you on your feet for a few steps."

It was easier said than done. Ro would have found Jubb's weight difficult to balance when fit, and was more likely to fall on top of him than get him upright. Chickens darted around them barking his encouragement. Thus distracted, Jubb managed to stand and totter a couple of steps before his knees crumpled and Ro had to catch him.

"There, you see? You did it!" Ro sounded as cheerful as she could.

Jubb sank back onto his makeshift bed. "You'll never catch up with King Channan with me holding you back. You should leave me here and go on."

"Rubbish! Tomorrow you'll be stronger still, and maybe the next day you'll be able to ride–that horse loves you too much to let you fall." Ro's joke plummeted.

"We must have eaten our way through most of our supplies," Jubb answered.

"There's plenty left yet," Ro lied.

Jubb shook his head. "You should leave me."

"And let you starve? I don't think King Darian would be very impressed. Anyway, you're supposed to be looking after me. How can you do that if I leave you behind?"

It was the sort of logic that Ro had known Jubb to use himself on occasion. The look he gave her told her he knew very well how upside down it was. He fumbled in his tunic and produced his precious piece of paper from Edun. He took hold of Ro's hand and pressed the paper into it.

"Here, take my Words of Power. I'm sure they'll look after you better than I can."

Tears stung in Ro's eyes. "Oh, Jubb."

He waved away her protest, leaned back and closed his eyes. He was right, the chances of he and Ro finding Channan in time were about as good as finding one particular snowflake in an avalanche, but the delay was so great that Ro doubted she could make up the time even on her own. She looked at Jubb's tired face, so open and innocent despite all that life had shown it.

"Now you listen to me, Jubb. I will not leave you here, so you just make up your mind to get better."

She made to put the Words of Power back in his tunic, but pulled a blanket over him instead. The chance to learn the magic which protected him was too great. Ro unfolded the paper and read. Blood crept up her cheeks. On the paper, written in Edun's ornate hand, were the words: "This man is a fool!"

"And so am I for believing in them," she muttered.

No wonder Edun had always tried to wriggle out of talking about them. Yet Jubb was adamant that they worked. It was not the words that held the power, but the simplicity of his trusting heart. Ro refolded the paper and placed it back in Jubb's tunic.

Two days later, they set out once more.

# Chapter Seventeen

"I tell you, it's giving me a headache, Fordel. Get it changed!"
Princess Ersilla paced about the audience chamber. She stopped
and rubbed her temples. "Fetch Ayif, Anni. I must have something
to get rid of this... this... noise."

"If you would try to relax... get some exercise in the fresh
air," Anni suggested.

"Did I ask for your advice? Go and get him!" Ersilla stamped
her foot, on the verge of tears.

Anni had no choice but to obey. She exchanged a worried
look with Fordel as she left.

The Lord cleared his throat. "As to the chimes on the citadel
gate, Princess, I'm afraid there's nothing that can be done about it."

"You'd do well to be afraid if you're going to argue with me."
Ersilla's smile sent a shiver down Fordel's back.

"I'd do what you ask if I could, Princess, but the chimes are
part of the locking mechanism linked to the citadel and city gates.
They can't be changed without dismantling the whole thing, and at
such a time... "

"Are you suggesting my brother might be defeated?" Ersilla
used a dangerously silky tone.

"We have to make sure he has a city to come back to."

Ersilla stopped pacing and threw herself down on a chair.
"Why will people argue with me when I have such a headache? I
can't think." She closed her eyes.

Fordel was beginning to wonder if he should take his chance
to leave when a servant announced the arrival of Captain Pachand.

"At last!" Ersilla sat up as the Captain strode into the room
and saluted. "You may go," she told Fordel.

"But, Princess, as commander of the city's defences I must
know if what he found poses a threat."

The Captain agreed. "We should make preparations, Princess.
The beasts responsible for destroying the village are dead, but

218

where they came from and whether there are more of them we don't know." Pachand's face was impassive.

Ersilla smiled. "You must tell me all about it." She patted the seat beside her, then clapped her hands. "Bring refreshments."

When the servant returned, he had Ayif with him. Anni hovered behind.

"Oh, there you are. I don't need you now. My headache's quite disappeared." She waved him away. The physician bowed and gave her a smile full of teeth. "You can go too, Anni. This is going to take some time, and I'm sure you have plenty of housekeeping to do."

Fordel gave Anni the merest nod.

"Whatever you say, Sister." She turned to the physician. "My apologies, Ayif."

"Not at all, Princess, I'm here to serve." He gave her a bow and smile the twins of those he had given Ersilla and headed back to his apartments.

Anni watched him out of sight, then headed for the vaults. She and Fordel had tried to keep track of all the crates and barrels which had arrived in the palace over the past week, but between their duties and the constant additions and rearrangements they could not be sure they had not missed something. Since they had discovered nothing untoward so far, Anni was certain that miss something they had. It would have helped if she had known what she was looking for. Whatever it was would need to be kept somewhere that could be visited by whoever was attending to it without attracting comment, and yet be out of the way of the routine traffic to and from the stores. She walked between the walls of boxes, consulting her tally lists at intervals to satisfy the curiosity of the guards placed there to discourage pilfering. Anni tapped her list and walked back to them with a puzzled expression.

"I was expecting a consignment from the Abbey of the Patriarch, but it doesn't appear to be here."

"Ah, that must be the stuff the acolytes brought in yesterday." The guard looked to his colleague for confirmation. "Now, where did they take it? I know, it's down the end of this corridor. There's a cell on the right with a trapdoor and steps to an under-cellar. Said the stuff had to be kept really cold. Wine is it?" he added, in time for Pachand to hear as he entered.

"It's no concern of yours what's in any of these containers. You're here to guard them, not sell them."

The guard jerked to attention.

"Captain Pachand. I hadn't expected Ersilla to finish with you so soon." Anni cursed the blush which rose to her cheeks.

"There was little to tell, Princess. Her Highness has given orders for my men to be given a barrel of spirits as her thanks," he told the guard.

"And then, Captain?"

"We're to patrol the city's outer defences."

"Wouldn't your experience be better used assisting Lord Fordel?"

"I believe Princess Ersilla feels the patrol is due for some lighter duties." His face was unreadable.

"As indeed you are, Captain." Anni kept her smile until the door had closed behind her. She must find Fordel.

He was in his wardroom finishing a goblet of wine when Anni entered.

"Your sister saps a man's courage," he said by way of excuse. "I take it you found nothing?"

"Not exactly." Anni sat down and poured herself a goblet. "The Patriarch's 'supplies' are being kept in an under cellar away from the rest, but I couldn't look. Pachand came in. You know Ersilla's set his men to patrol the outside walls?"

Fordel nodded. "I don't know what to make of him. His report was too full if he and Ersilla are in cahoots, but I got the feeling he was holding something back."

"Well, there was no chance to find out what's down there with him around."

"I think I already know." Fordel downed another goblet as Anni waited for him to explain.

So, Princess Anni had been asking about a consignment from the Patriarch. Pachand was waiting for the promised barrel of brandy to be brought. If the Patriarch was a traitor, did that mean that Anni was the 'she' of whom the priest had spoken? Where had the guard said the consignment was kept? Pachand considered searching himself. What had happened to Natann? If he had caught up with Lord Torslin and King Channan, why had no measures been taken to curb the religious conspiracy? Pachand knew that the soldiers who survived a battle were most likely to be those who kept a stony calm. Until he discovered otherwise, he would suspect all and bow to all. Being posted outside might not be a bad thing. If they thought to keep him out of their way the same could work to his advantage.

"Fal-worms," Fordel said. "But huge. Big enough to fell a horse, eat it in one go and look for more."

Anni stared at him with her mouth open.

"I know it's incredible, but one thing Pachand isn't given to is exaggeration." Fordel looked grim.

"But why would my sister want such things? Why would anyone?" Anni finally managed to ask.

Fordel shrugged. "I don't know, but you didn't see her face when Pachand spoke about them."

"And these monsters are under the palace now? Great Ondd! If they should escape... " Anni could not think clearly. "Perhaps she doesn't intend using them. Maybe she wants them to protect herself from Torslin."

"Perhaps," Fordel returned.

"Don't humour me. I've had enough of being patronised. What are we to do?"

"Watch and wait. First we have to be sure what's in that cellar, and if we're right, find a way to destroy them."

"And hope Ro gets through to Channan," Anni added.

"It's all we can do, unless... "

Anni looked at him sharply.

"Unless Ersilla's headaches get worse. If she's not up to being regent, then as her sister, you're next in line," Fordel spoke cautiously.

Anni giggled. "And who, pray, do you think is going to take any notice of orders from me? Besides, she's my sister. No, no I won't hear of it." She thought a moment. "Not yet."

The wagons halted. In Edun's onddikin-cluttered vehicle Dovinna grumbled.

"What now?"

"Perhaps Mirri's 'you knows' are causing her trouble again," Edun joked.

They had already made three stops for Mirri to relieve herself. The wet-nurse's delicacy in finding a place that was completely unexposed before doing what she had to slowed them down still further.

"I wish she'd get on with it then. We'll never catch up at this rate."

Edun gave her a sideways look. "What's the matter?"

"Nothing. I just don't want to get left behind." Dovinna jumped down from the wagon and went forward. Raimi and Lar were also dismounting. Lar took a few steps away from the road and turned towards a distant hill. She began a low hum. Raimi came to her side, turning slightly away and back again as if testing the direction of the wind. Dovinna looked questioningly at Mirri, who had come to the front of the wagon.

She shrugged. "They say something's pulling them."

Lar and Raimi returned.

"I'm going to ride to the hill," said Raimi. "I'm no earth-hearer, but it's so strong even I can't lose the line."

"What is?" Dovinna asked.

Lar smiled. "There's resonant stone. We can work with it." Her manner was more decisive than it had been since the fire.

"While Raimi's exploring, do we just sit here and wait?"

"No, we carry on. Be patient a little longer, Dovinna, the army's not far ahead. We should all be able to hear it soon."

Dovinna blushed and ran back to Edun's wagon as Raimi cantered away. They set off again. Dovinna now strained her eyes between trying to see signs of Darian's army and watching for Raimi. They had set up camp for the night before the sound of hooves signalled his return. Raimi dismounted and helped himself to food, trying to eat and talk at the same time.

"There's a huge marker stone in a basin at the top of that hill– and the vibrations! They ripple in a broad band–the strongest I've ever felt." He almost choked in his eagerness.

"Can the wagons get up there?" Lar asked.

He nodded. "It's ideal, Lar."

"Good. Then we must start early tomorrow, so we can stop King Darian before the army moves too far on."

"I know I'm just a simple Mandurian mother, but would someone please explain what's happening? All this talk about stones. Let's just get to the army where we're safe." For once Mirri spoke for Dovinna too.

"It's not something that can easily be explained. Perhaps you'll feel it when we get there," Lar said. "We've found the place for King Darian to meet the Ortanian army."

Dovinna's smile faded. She rose.

"Are you all right?" Edun asked.

"Tired. I think I'll go to my bed," she spoke with her head down and hurried off. Lar gave her a minute, then followed. Dovinna continued shaking out her bed things.

"It's all becoming real, and I can't stop it. How can I hope for Channan to win? Yet if he loses? There should be some way I can stop it."

Lar took the healer's hands and waited until she looked at her. "There's still hope–especially now."

Dovinna choked on a sob. "Because you've found a good place for them all to get killed?"

"It's a strong place, not a bad one. Everyone will play their part in their own way. You'll help lessen the death and pain with herbs and potions, Raimi and I will seek the help of the stone. It's the best we can do."

"I know, I'll be all right."

Lar left her then. For a few minutes Dovinna tossed and turned, then outside, Lar began a soft lullaby accompanied by the crooning of the onddikins. Previously, Dovinna had claimed Lar sang for her own comfort rather than Lalli's. Tonight, however, she was not so sure.

The next morning they wasted no time in catching up with Darian's force. Leaving Mirri and Edun with the wagons they went in search of the King. Many of the men called greetings as they passed.

Darian reined in his horse when he saw them. "Good! I was about to send a rider back to find you. We've had news of Channan's army. It's less than a day's march away. I didn't want you to fall foul of any of his scouting parties." He clicked his tongue for his horse to move on, but Lar caught hold of the bridle.

"We've discovered something. It's important."

"Tell me when we make camp. There's need of haste if we are to be the ones to choose where the armies meet."

"That's what we need to discuss," Lar answered calmly.

"Discuss?" Darian's eyebrows quirked upwards. "The decision was made last night, and it isn't one I care to speak about in front of so many."

"If your chosen place lies in that direction, it's wrong." Lar pointed ahead. "I'm an earth-hearer, King Darian. When I say I know the place where you should await Ortann's force, I'm not mistaken." She looked steadily at Darian.

"I don't have time for argument. How long will it take to get there?"

"Four hours there and back," Lar estimated. "You must know the place of the standing stone."

Darian frowned. "Ondd's Basin? Yes, I know it." He turned to Uwert. "Take a rest here. Use the time to get the men to check their kit. I'll get word back in no more than two and a half hours."

"But... " Raimi and Uwert protested almost in unison.

"You'd need wings to get back by then," Raimi said.

"Did I say that's what I'd do?" Darian asked with a smile, and held up a hand to cut off Uwert's argument. "I know what you're going to say, and I shall be perfectly safe. We'll take half a dozen riders with us." He pointed at the handful of riders closest. "You men, with us."

No sooner had Lar and Raimi remounted than he kicked his horse to a canter back along the road. At a high point, approximately half an hour into their ride, Darian signalled one of the riders to wait there.

"Keep a look out."

This he repeated at intervals until only two soldiers remained with them. They left the road, slowing their pace as the ground rose. When they reached the brow of Ondd's Basin they dismounted. The basin and much of the stone were thrown into shadow by the higher ground. Only the top of the vertical marker stone caught the sun, turning its mottled grey surface a warm honey.

Darian walked around it. "I admit it's impressive to look at, but what makes you think it's so special?"

"Touch it," Lar said.

The King placed his palm on the rough surface. "It's warm," he said.

Lar nodded. "Despite being in shadow. But what's important is its relation to the land around."

She led Darian to the brow of the hill where they could clearly see the countryside stretching into the distance. There were uneven ridges radiating from the basin, almost as if the slope had once been terraced by farmers. The route they had taken had been easy enough, but it was narrow and easily defended. The pale dry grass of winter was beginning to green up with the new spring shoots, but a few yards from the foot of the slope there was lusher growth.

"It's boggy ground. A spring which has become choked perhaps. It will be reluctant to let go of those who tread in it and will slow them down."

Darian nodded. "It's not a bad position, but what about the right flank? Those trees come too close for my liking–too much cover for an attacking force."

"You could place some of your own men there, although we should be able to hear them approach," Lar suggested.

Darian walked once more around the site.

"And there's the stone," Lar added. "It fairly makes the air crackle."

"How does that help us?" Darian's expression was dubious.

"Maybe it won't," Lar said. "But the stone here is part of the bones of the earth which hold everything together and give it shape. Change the bones, change the shape. Given the right circumstances... "

"And a squad of engineers, eh?" Darian interrupted. "At least there's little habitation here, less to be destroyed by a battle." He drew himself up. "I suppose if people are to die, one place is as good as another."

Lar and Raimi prepared to remount, but Darian pulled a mirror from his pocket.

"Stay, the army will come to us." He squinted up at the sun to test the direction, then began tilting the mirror. When he finished, they all gazed in the direction they had just travelled. A few moments later, a series of flashes answered his signal.

"Well, as we have nothing to do now except wait, I suggest we eat something and give thought to the troop disposition."

By the time the vanguard approached, they were ready. The flashes of sun on arms and armour stretched into the distance. Tiny flying creatures circling above a wagon showed where the rest of the exiles' party followed the main force.

"A brave sight," Raimi said, his eyes glittering. "One to inspire courage."

"You think so?" Darian's voice was flat. "Tomorrow we'll have another such sight before us–only then it will be our foe. Ortann can put many more men in the field than Amradoc. I doubt many here will find it uplifting then."

The sounds of Darian's camp were hushed as if someone lay sick nearby. The Ortanian army had arrived. The dawn mists hid the extent of it from view, but magnified the sounds, funnelling them into the basin. Darian had taken Lar's advice and placed a small force in the wooded area, which was the site's main weakness. It was enjoined to silence, as was the reserve force sheltered within the basin, rather than formed on the outer slopes.

"When the sky clears we should be able to see the full extent of Channan's army, but we'll have this surprise waiting for him," Darian explained to the men.

The wagons were on the far side of the slope, ready to flee back to the road for Mandur should the need arise. Here, Dovinna had worked with the Amrad surgeons to set up an area where the injured could be treated. She had checked her preparations and rechecked them, but could not be still. She wandered over to Edun's colourful wagon where Mirri was rocking Lalli as if they were on a picnic, but her blank eyes as she turned to greet Dovinna showed that only the normality of the mundane actions was keeping the horror of battle at bay. Edun was rummaging through his magic equipment.

"What are you doing?" Dovinna asked.

"Darian's not the only one who can plan a few surprises," he answered, barely pausing to look around.

She was not needed there either, and so she climbed to the brow of the hill to stand beside Darian, Uwert and the Iyessi. At that moment the sun vaporised the last of the mist and all the colours jumped out vivid in the clear light. Dovinna's breath caught. Spread out on the ground before them like a meadow full of summer flowers, was Channan's army. Gay pennants and tents rose brilliant above the crop of men. She tried counting one small square and multiplying. There were so many of them. A rustle travelled the length of Darian's lines.

"And so it begins," Dovinna whispered.

Uwert heard her. "Not quite. Warfare is a kind of elaborate game or a dance. You have to follow all the right steps in the right order. First the heralds will ride out and offer a parley, which both kings will feel obliged to honour. One side will make an offer and the other a counter offer, but sometimes one and more often both will have no intention of abiding by it. The offers will be rejected. Then King Darian and, I am sure, King Channan will give their troops a rousing speech. Next the posturing will start when both sides try to scare the other with their defiance. Only then will the battle begin."

"But surely, if there's an offer to parley a battle might be averted."

"I've never known it yet." Uwert turned in the direction of the Ortanian force, where King Channan's banner could now be seen following a chestnut horse caparisoned in the royal green and gold. "What did I tell you?" He turned back, but Dovinna had gone.

Uwert looked over his other shoulder, but she was not there either. Instead, he saw Lar with eyes closed, raise a peremptory hand against something Raimi was saying. His manner was urgent. He turned away and strode off in the direction of the reserve's horses. Pain settled into lines on Lar's forehead and at the corners of her mouth. She too turned from sight of their waiting opponent and took up position by the marker stone.

Uwert's eyes travelled its length. Legend had it that the stone had been placed there at the dawn of humankind, when the world was full of wonder, to mark the place where Ondd had alighted during its struggle against Lethir. The land should have been green and full of life, but the worm had scoured the earth and devoured all the creatures which abode there. The sight angered Ondd, who flicked its tail, causing the dent in the hilltop where it landed and making ripples in the earth. It flicked its tail again, striking the valley, and a spring burst forth making the land fertile again. So life was born of chaos and the force of good was hard to distinguish from evil. The story had once appealed to Uwert's cynical wit. Now, he looked at the stone and shivered.

Ro crouched behind a bush watching. In front of her was a cluster of tents on a knoll surrounding the one flying the dragon pennant of King Channan. If only she could get past the guards, she might be able to catch the King alone. She flattened herself on the ground as two squires hurried past, their arms laden with armour. She had crept into position hidden by the dawn mist, but now the sun made her feel as conspicuous as brambleberry juice on a white cloth. When they had moved away she risked changing her position. The air was full of barked commands and rattling weapons. There was a heart-stopping thud beside her. Something cold and wet touched her cheek. It was Chickens's nose. The dog struggled in Jubb's arms.

"Sorry, Ro, I couldn't leave him behind, he'd bark," the fool explained.

Ro put a finger to her lips. "That's why I told you to stay back."

"But... the armies are forming up. We have to speak to Channan now."

Her heart hammered. Thinking about it was getting them nowhere. One of the squires emerged from Channan's tent and hurried towards one nearer the perimeter. Ro took a deep breath.

"You stay here. If something goes wrong, find a way to get to Darian and let him know what happened."

She clasped Jubb's hand, then began worming her way to the tent. She peered under the canvas, then wriggled inside. The squire was preoccupied and Ro too skilled at masking sound to notice that he was not alone in the tent. He bent over a trunk of gear. Ro picked up a lamp from the table, and a moment later the squire lay unconscious on the floor. A minute or so later anyone looking that way would have seen a slightly built squire with untidy hair, who was almost hidden by a pile of clothing, emerge and walk purposefully towards the royal tent. Ro was still a few paces away when King Channan came out clothed in gleaming armour and a crowned helmet. Torslin stepped to his side and Ro's pace faltered, but he appeared oblivious of the activity around them.

"Channan, my boy. Please take my advice—don't wear the crown, it makes you too easy a target."

Channan did not warm to his adviser's fatherly approach. "I will not hide my identity. My army deserves to know that I'm fighting at their head, and that I'm not afraid."

Torslin bowed and followed Channan to the spot where his chestnut horse was saddled ready.

Too late! Too late! Ro dropped her burden and ran towards him as he mounted, heedless of the danger of recognition. Channan kicked the horse and it bounded forward. From the vantage point of the knoll, Ro could see both armies spread as rigid and close-ranked as the palings of a fence. Those of Ortann stretched beyond Amradoc's as if the ends would turn and grasp the opposition in a fatal embrace. A small group of riders from each side rode towards a canopy roughly halfway between them. A blur caught the edge of Ro's vision. Another rider was converging on them from the far side. It bore no banner and there were no telltale glints of metal, but the rider's appearance was enough to bring Channan's party to a halt short of the meeting point. Darian's party slowed and a rider detached itself, heading towards the newcomer. A rider shouted, and Channan kicked his horse towards the lone rider. Torslin gestured and one of their escort rode after him, drew his short throwing spear and launched it at the perceived threat. A roar went up from the Amrad army and was answered. The sound that came from those thousands of throats made Ro cover her ears. It reminded her of wild dogs fighting over a kill. There was no way to reason with it. The negotiators were already heading back to their respective armies.

"Too late," Ro muttered. And yet, she could not look away.

# Chapter Eighteen

Dovinna watched the riders head out from the Ortanian army. Beneath each soldier's metal shell was soft flesh; hearts beat with dreams of the future and present fears. How many of them would be stilled forever by the end of the day? All because of her. Tears blurred her vision as she looked at the green and gold rider on the chestnut steed. She mounted her own more modest horse and kicked it into a canter. Her shout made the converging riders draw rein.

"Channan! Stop! There's no need for this! Do what you will with me–I surrender!" At least that was what she had intended saying. She saw Channan's head turn in her direction, and his horse spring forward. He shouted something–her name? Dovi–yes, that was it. Then another cry went up–treachery! Another rider spurred towards her, spear raised. The roar she heard could have been the opposing armies or the pressure in her ears. She could barely keep in the saddle. A hand caught her horse's bridle and steered it out of danger, back towards the Amrad ranks.

Uwert snarled at her. "Fool, girl! Do you want to get yourself killed?"

At that moment it did not seem such a bad option. They dismounted behind the lines. Dovinna leant against her horse for support.

"I've made it worse," she murmured. "They were going to talk until I messed it up."

"Don't you listen to anything?" Uwert demanded. "I told you, the forms have to be gone through and one is the pretence of parley. All you did was speed things up a little," he added more gently. "Stop feeling sorry for yourself and go and do something useful."

He strode off to take up his place near Darian. Dovinna brushed her tears away and straightened her shoulders. He was right. Nevertheless she could not take her eyes from the scene below.

Trumpets brayed their brassy defiance and the Ortanian front lines detached themselves from the rest as they began to advance. It was as if someone had shaken a kaleidoscope and a new pattern was forming. The boggy area about halfway across forced the troops on that wing to wade and flounder in grasping mud and the line began to break and bunch at the centre. Still they came on. There was no movement from Darian's army. His troops were sheltered by the ridges of the slopes. Behind the front ranks were archers, protected by the shields of the infantrymen. Channan's force reached the foot of the slope. Finally, Darian gave the signal and the air hummed with arrows. Holes appeared in the Ortanian ranks and were swiftly closed. The cries of the stricken rose on the air like weird birdsong. Dovinna hurried away. She would be seeing the wounded much closer to ere long. As she neared Edun's wagon, she met Lar hurrying away from it.

"Have you seen Raimi?" The Earth-hearer's eyes scanned the figures around them.

"No. Is something wrong?" Lar and Raimi had been so encouraged at finding the marker stone, that it had not occurred to Dovinna that something could be amiss.

"There was some discord between us. I'd thought he might have come back to spend some time with Lalli."

"He's bound to show up here eventually."

Lar nodded. "If you see him, tell him I need his voice. He knows where I'll be."

It did not need Iyessi sensibility to know that the plans so carefully made with King Darian were already going awry. The Earth-hearer strode back towards the marker stone. A few moments later, Dovinna heard a low droning hum penetrate the shrieks and clashes of battle. Whatever Lar hoped to achieve with the stone, she had begun. The sound collected in the basin and was thrown outwards, strumming up backbones and making the hairs on arms and necks stand up.

"Now we shall see." King Darian eyed the battlefield grimly.

Despite Lar's warnings not to advance beyond the furthest ripple in the slope, Darian had been forced to order his centre forward. The press of men grew closer; arms rose and fell, bodies jerked, so that the battle appeared to be between armies of automata rather than men. Those Ortanian troops who had been hampered by the marshy footing had now crossed, adding their weight to the attack, and Darian's men were giving ground step by step. Lar's drone set teeth on edge and unsettled horses but nothing more. The fighting became more tumultuous as Channan ordered more men forward. Darian rode up and down his lines encouraging the men to stand firm. Still Lar's voice had no effect other than to add to the tension. The note changed pitch and intensity. A shudder seemed to go through Darian's forces. Perhaps sensing their hesitation, Channan launched his cavalry, riding at its head to pound down all in its path. Darian gave the order for his infantry to form into porcupines; ovoid ranks bristling with spears and swords to prevent the horses getting close enough for their riders to strike. It would hold the tide of hooves and steel off for a while, but each wave would erode the men like pebbles on a beach.

Darian called to Uwert. "Tell Lar–now would be a good time."

He flipped down the visor of his helmet and formed up his own cavalry. Unless Lar could coax the earth to co-operate, a counter-charge was the sole hope of saving his men and beating the Ortanians back. Uwert ran to do his bidding as another clash of cavalry against infantry shook the hillside.

Lar was in the basin with forehead and palms pressed to the marker stone. Sweat collected in the lines about her mouth and in the notches of her collarbone. She showed no awareness of Uwert's presence. He found himself holding his breath waiting for the Earth-hearer's voice to break off as she gasped in air. Instead there was only a small flicker in the sound.

"Lar, it grows urgent that you act."

The Earth-hearer continued the murmuring hum.

" Lar," Uwert insisted.

"I hear you," she broke off. "Find Raimi–bass and treble are needed here."

She took up the hum once more, extending the 'eer' of 'here' to infinity. Uwert ran back to the wagons. Mirri was hidden beneath a pile of bedding with Lalli and would not come out.

"I haven't seen him. Ondd have mercy on us!" she shrieked as there was a renewed roar from the battlefield.

Lalli gurgled to herself and played with strands of Mirri's hair. Uwert paused an instant to wonder at her serenity, before finding Edun. The magician was crouched inside his wagon crooning reassurance to the onddikins, which fluttered and whistled their agitation.

"No one's seen him since the parley, but if my marriage partner had been killed by the Ortanians I think I know where I'd be."

Uwert ran back to deliver the news to Darian, but he reached the vantage point too late. The Amrad and Ortanian cavalry met with a clash that sent a jolt running back up the slope. The standard of Darian's house snapped and fluttered bravely as it followed the King about the field. Amradoc's cavalry was lighter and quicker than Ortann's. Uwert saw the king's horse dart this way and that, wherever his men were hardest pressed. The enemy was checked, but Darian's army only had an instant of relief before shouts went up from the flank nearest the wooded slope.

It was as Darian had feared. Channan had sent a force creeping through the trees. They had silently overwhelmed the sentries and now overlooked Darian's right wing. That section suddenly found itself under a mortal fire of arrows and sling shot. The attackers burst from cover virtually on top of the defenders, occupying them so that those coming up behind could slip round to their rear. Channan's cavalry attack had been a ploy to coerce the main Amrad forces out. There was no time to consider or to wish for help. Uwert signalled a section of the reserve cavalry to follow him and rode off to scatter the enemy before it could drive the defenders back into the basin. If the Ortanians once managed to establish themselves behind the Amrads, Darian's army was finished.

Raimi squinted against the sun, trying to pick out the emblems of the Ortanians closest to him. He had reached the edge of the marsh and solid ground, his water affinity enabling him to move swiftly through the sodden channels. The Ortanians who had blundered into it were distracted by trying to keep their footing. So far his sword was still clean. There was only one man Raimi sought to make war on. He prowled the battlefield, so intent on his prey that much of the fighting seemed to flow around him. A soldier sprang up in front of him, and he barely had time to register the colours of Najarind before a vicious jab of the man's sword made him jump aside. The move unbalanced his attacker and Raimi brought the heavy pommel of his own sword down on the exposed back of his neck. The soldier crumpled. Raimi's expression was impassive as he moved on. The evenness of Lar's hum penetrated through his feet, despite the shudder as the momentum of Ortann's cavalry was halted on porcupine spears. It was like a slow simmer that only needed a little more heat to become a rolling boil, echoing Raimi's state of mind. Until he found Captain Pachand and avenged Ussu it would remain a blank, unmoved by screams of pain or the tug of duty. Sun flashed off the gold of King Channan's banner. Raimi headed towards it, certain that someone so trusted by the King would be kept close by.

The King's horse was on the Amrad side of the marsh, and Darian's cavalry was bearing down on it with the speed of the slope to give it extra impact. The Najarindian banner wavered perilously close to the sodden ground. In the clash that followed, Raimi saw Channan's horse rear. The King kept his seat but his crown was thrown off his helmet. Raimi dodged a maelstrom of hooves, yanking one Najarind rider from his saddle as he swung his sword at the Iyessi. He plunged his own sword under the rider's breastplate and saw the look of surprise in his eyes as he sighed a last breath. The pattern of blood on Raimi's blade held his gaze, suddenly seeming of the greatest significance. The world had gone quiet, listening.

The scream of a horse driven crazy with pain and terror yanked Raimi's attention back to his situation. He looked up in time to see Torslin withdraw his sword from the belly of Channan's mount. The Lord's horse hid the action from the view of Channan's comrades. Spurting blood, the horse crumpled landing heavily on its side in the mire. Channan was trapped. He sought to free himself, struggling with the stirrup and pushing against the ground, but it gave way under pressure, making him sink further. Torslin glanced round, and tugged at his horse's head until the unwilling beast was forced to trample the fallen horse and rider. Raimi blinked, unsure momentarily whether he truly could have seen what he had. He cried out, flinging his arms wide in some vague attempt to startle Torslin's charger away, but the move was unneeded. Encouraged by a savage dig of Torslin's spurs, the horse bolted and carried Torslin from the scene. All was confusion, and Raimi was standing at the still centre of the whirlpool.

He moved closer to the fallen king. The horse's sides heaved like bellows trying to compensate for the loss of blood, but Channan did not move. His armour was dented and where his

helmet had rolled off there was blood on his head. Raimi leant
down to him and felt a faint hush of breath on his cheek. Torslin's
treachery replayed itself in Raimi's head, breaking the spell he had
been under. The Iyessi began a soothing song to the fallen horse,
stroking its neck. With a swift movement his sword ended its
suffering. Unstrapping the armour which was pulling Channan
down, Raimi braced himself against the firm ground and used it to
help lever the weight of the horse off the King enough to pull his
legs free. Channan's forehead creased in pain and his lips moved.
Blood seeped through the King's torn jerkin.

"Wake up." Raimi shook him gently. A groan was the only
response. Raimi grabbed the King under the shoulders and
dragged him further into the marsh. Without his armour to identify
him and unconscious Channan should be safe enough. The Iyessi
ran lightly from tussock to tussock in search of a riderless horse.
There were many scattered throughout the field. Some stood
trembling with heads hanging, others ran helter-skelter dodging
invisible predators. Then he found one, a proud roan stallion
standing head up and ears pricked beside its dead rider. It snorted
as Raimi approached. Raimi halted, singing the same gentling
song he had used with Channan's dying chestnut. The roan tossed
its head and walked a couple of grudging steps towards him, then
halted. Still singing, Raimi turned back to the marsh and the horse
followed.

Channan was lying as Raimi had left him. The Iyessi
manhandled him over the horse's back, securing him there with his
belt, and steered the stallion back onto firm land. He was about to
mount behind the unconscious burden when the horse's head came
up, nostrils flared. Raimi looked around: an Ortanian soldier was
stalking towards them in a half-crouch.

"Nice 'oss. Yours, is it?"

Raimi said nothing.

"Ner, I dun't think it is. Tell yer 'oo I think it b'longs ter... "
The soldier started weaving circles with the tip of his sword. "Me!
'And it over!"

"What about loyalty and honour?" Raimi draped the reins
over the saddle pommel and stepped back from the horse.

The soldier's face twisted into a grin, showing rotten teeth.
"Me loyalty's ter meself, and me honour's in makin' sure I comes
out on top." He spat in his palm and took a double grip on his
sword. "Now, we cun do this easy, or... " He lunged at Raimi, who

slapped the horse's rump. It leapt forward in the direction of the Amrad lines, almost knocking the soldier over. He was quicker on his feet than his appearance suggested.

"So, that's the way yer wants it, eh?"

Raimi drew his sword and began to sing the song of the invulnerable soldier: death. His face was fierce and his voice was joy.

"What are you doing here?"

The voice made Ro's steps stutter as her heart skipped. She had dumped her burden and was heading back to Jubb's hiding place, before the squire whose clothes she had stolen regained consciousness.

"I, er... " She tried to make her voice deeper.

"Where's your unit?" The officer who had accosted her was in his middle-years with cheeks scraped rosy and shiny by his razor. He shook his head. "Don't know what the army's coming to, taking babbies like you from their mother's arms. Well?"

Ro pointed vaguely further along the lines.

"What're you doing here then?"

"I've, er... " She clutched at her stomach and hopped from one foot to another.

"Turned your bowels thin, has it? Not to worry, lad. You're not the first to find battle gives them the shits. It's nothing to be ashamed of."

To Ro's horror, he began to accompany her to the sheltered area behind the tents. She tried desperately to think up another acceptable excuse. Perhaps if she pretended she was the sweetheart of one of the soldiers, who had wheedled her way past the sentries. Luckily, the officer had launched into a tale about his first battle and was not looking about him. Ro felt her blush burning the roots of her scalp, as the officer relieved himself behind the bush where she had instructed Jubb to wait. Where was he?

"What're you waiting for, lad? There's no point in being bashful."

She had left it too late. The officer had finished and was now watching her expectantly. Ro fiddled with the front of her trousers and turned away.

"Best be lively about it," came the officer's voice. "Your commander's probably looking for..."

There was a clatter. Ro risked a peep over her shoulder. Jubb was standing over the officer, who now appeared to be taking a catnap on the ground while Chickens licked his face. The fool held a fist-sized stone and had tears in his eyes. Ro took the stone from him and dropped it.

"Thank you, Jubb. It's not easy to do that–hurt someone who isn't trying to hurt you, but he would have if he'd found out the truth."

Jubb nodded.

"You'd best call Chickens away. There's nothing for it now but to try to find a way through to King Darian and the others."

At mention of his friend, Jubb brightened. Ro led the way around the edge of the army to the place where their horses were cropping grass. All attention was focused on what was happening on the field ahead, and they managed to reach the road without being accosted. Jubb kicked his horse to a canter.

"Wait!" Ro called him back. "Not too fast. We should behave as if we have every right to be here. We're just neutral civilian pedlars trying to steer clear of the fighting, right?"

"Right," Jubb agreed. "Only... " He looked pointedly at Ro's clothes. She was still wearing the squire's uniform.

"Great! Now we can be killed by Ortanians as spies or deserters, or attacked by Amrads as the hated enemy."

They would just have to make the best of it. Happily the road skirted the marsh and little fighting spilled into that area. They had left the road again to cut across to Darian's position when a roan horse pelted across their path, making their mounts shy. There was a body strapped to its back. The horse halted a few yards away and stood looking at them with nostrils flared. Ro managed to get her horse under control, but as she urged it towards the roan, the stallion stepped back. She twisted her head to get a better look at its burden.

"Is he dead?" Jubb whispered.

"We'd better hope not," Ro said.

"Why not?"

"Because–I could be wrong–but I think that's King Channan."

Jubb's jaw dropped. Without hesitation he slid from his saddle and strode up to the roan. Either sensing his incapability of doing it harm, or reassured by his confidence, the stallion allowed itself to be caught.

"He's still breathing," Jubb confirmed.

Leading the roan, they set off, this time at a jaunty trot that swallowed the distance. Despite the need for haste, they approached the Amrad position from the rear, expecting to be challenged at any moment.

"There's Edun's wagon!" Jubb jumped down and ran towards it. Suddenly he vanished in an explosion of smoke.

"Got you! Attack the Incredible Edun, would you?" The magician emerged from the cloud with his eyebrows singed and the flaming coat edged with scorch marks. His eyes locked on Ro.

"What have you done?" Ro cried.

Edun gestured at a hole at his feet. "Jubb?"

She nodded. He peered in. There was a joyful shout. Edun closed his eyes and placed a hand over his heart.

"I'll get him out, don't worry. He's the third one I've caught so far."

"I hope the others were Ortanians," Ro said. "Where's Dovinna?" Her heart hammered at the prospect of how the healer would react when she saw the roan's burden.

She hurried in the direction that Edun pointed. The encampment looked like a disturbed ants' nest with blood-soaked orderlies, white-faced squires and soldiers running in all directions. She reached what served as a hospital. Ro spotted Dovinna immediately. She was the one calm spot amongst the chaos.

"Dovinna?"

The healer looked up from an arm she was bandaging. Her face lit with a tired smile. "Ro!" She began making her way through the pallets of wounded towards her, then saw the figure slung over the roan and stopped, hand to mouth.

"It's all right, Dovinna. He's not dead, but he needs your help." Ro dismounted and shook her gently by the shoulders.

Dovinna nodded and called an orderly to assist her. They got Channan to a treatment couch.

"How are things going?" Ro hardly dared to ask.

"Not good," Dovinna said quietly. "Lar needs Raimi, but no one can find him. Without his voice... " She shrugged.

It was only then that Ro realised that underlying all the clamour of the battle she heard a hum. The voice was amplified and blended by the stone, but it was unmistakably Lar's. Ro hurried towards the source, bowling into Uwert as she ran over the lip of the basin and tumbled towards its centre. He helped her up.

His immaculately groomed beard had a red sword slash through it. Helping to raise her to her feet almost pulled him over.

"What news?" he asked in a low voice.

"We couldn't reach Channan in time, but we have proof of Torslin's treachery." Her gaze kept flicking to her mother.

Lar was as grey as the stone and appeared to be melting into it, as if it would absorb her completely and leave a mere husk.

"How long has she been like this?"

"Too long. Have you seen Raimi?" Uwert's voice was eager. Ro shook her head and his jaw tightened.

"Are things going so badly?"

"We're outnumbered. Our only real hope was that Lar... " He braced his shoulders. "Still, it's better to end like this than to live to a great age and do nothing." He smiled and clasped her hand. "Better get your people away while you can." He strode back towards the sound of fighting.

"Wait, maybe I... "

Uwert raised his hand in salute, but did not turn around. Ro swallowed a sob and went up to Lar. She wanted to hug her, but feared to touch her.

"Mother? How can I help? Tell me what to sing and I'll do it." Tears spilled onto her cheeks.

"I don't know what to sing," Lar answered in the same droning tone, making it hard for Ro to decipher the words.

"There's no sign of Raimi," Ro said. "Uwert thinks we should leave while we can."

"Noooo... " Lar drew the word out. "Not until I am on my knees with no voice left."

Ro balled her fist to hit the rock, but at the last moment realised the shock waves it would cause and swung aside, ending up sitting on the grass at the foot of the stone. She looked up at it. The sun was already past its zenith and the stone cast a long shadow across the basin, but at the top it was warmed by the light.

"What are these marks?" The angle of the sun threw a series of wavy lines into relief. "It's a song." Realisation turned her voice to a croak. "Mother! Mother! It's a song!"

Abruptly, Lar's hum ceased. Slowly she drew herself away from the stone. Without its support she swayed and dropped to her knees.

"What?" she whispered.

"Quick," Ro urged, holding out her hands to her. "Quick, before the sun goes."

Lar crawled next to Ro and looked where she pointed. "Help me up."

Ro did as she was bid, supporting her mother as she placed her palms against the stone once more, and with head thrown back, began to sing the melody marked on it.

On the battlefield, the sudden absence of Lar's voice sent a shiver through both armies. What did it signify? Darian wheeled his horse around, calling his men to him with a great shout of defiance. Watching at the top of the slope, Uwert settled his helmet on more securely and readied himself. So, Ro had persuaded her mother that they should flee. He lifted his arm. When he dropped it again, he and the reserve would make one last desperate charge down the slope. As he paused to take one final look at the sky, another song began. He grinned: a song of farewell.

"Wait! Wait!" It was Ro, breathless from running, hanging on to his bridle as if it was all that could save her. "Lar says you must call all the men back as quickly as possible."

"Let go, Ro. Nothing's going to happen. Lar's been trying all day."

"This is different. We've found the right song. You must get Darian to retreat. Please, or they'll be caught too." She was sobbing now, looking from Uwert to the carnage below, as if she would fling herself down the hillside if he did not agree to do as she demanded.

Uwert turned to the horseman next to him. "Signaller, you heard her–sound the retreat."

The signaller blew a piercing series of notes on a whistle. Men began to fall back. Others hesitated. The thick knot of soldiers around Darian held their ground. The horses at the hilltop became increasingly restless, neighing and trying to break free of their reins.

"Keep signalling," Uwert commanded.

It seemed that Darian turned in his saddle and looked towards him. Uwert took the chance and pulled out a mirror to flash the message: "Lar has woken the stone." There was no way to tell whether he had seen it or not, but moments later the king's standard was seen in the middle of a group of men making an orderly retreat. A wave of dizziness flowed through Uwert ending with a sour taste in his mouth.

"Did you feel that?" he asked Ro. The ground had throbbed.

Lar's voice rose until it seemed to be in the air and the ground under their feet, to pulse through them. Ro felt the shifting of the ground, but not the sensations it produced in the others. At first, each step of the retreat was slow with Darian's cavalry mounting a rearguard to hinder the jubilant Ortanians. As the pulse reached them, many of the Amrad soldiers turned and ran for the safety of the slope's ripples. Momentarily caught off-balance the Ortanian army hesitated, then the lines advanced inexorably, accompanied by boastful trumpets.

The first pulse was rapidly followed by another, and another, each intensifying in strength and gathering speed. They accelerated down the slope, tumbling loose rocks and tilting bushes. The watery marsh shivered under their influence. Darian's rearguard raced up to Uwert's vantage point. They watched in silence, struggling to stay upright under the intense pressure of Lar's song. Below them, Channan's army found the ground rumbling and rolling underneath them, casting them on their faces and scattering cavalry. Suddenly an immense crack and tearing sound as of the world splitting apart made Ortanian and Amrad alike hold their hands over their ears. The moisture was sucked from the marsh. All was still for an uneasy moment. Then men and horses began to scream as giant arrowheads and blades of rock thrust upwards from the lowest part of the battlefield. Some were swallowed in the rift, others tossed in the air or shaken down cliffs and crevices that had not been there a moment before. It could only have continued for seconds, but when the earth settled, there was a ring of stone around the hill of Ondd's basin and the Ortanian army was      scattered.

# Chapter Nineteen

The song ceased. Its echoes vibrated through the uneasy ground. Distant shrieks of the dying made the silence deeper. Lar remained welded to the stone so that Ro did not dare speak to her. She waited with anxious eyes, searching for a sign that her mother was coming back to herself. As Uwert approached she looked around. The courtier took off his helmet and gauntlets and ran a hand through his hair as if waking from an exhausting dream.

"Lar, the enemy's routed," he said. He looked questioningly at Ro, who shrugged, trying not to let her bottom lip tremble.

"Mother?" she whispered. "She must have felt the ground being torn almost as if it was her own body," she told him.

She touched Lar's arm. A shudder went through the Earth-hearer. She drew a long breath and opened her eyes. When she saw Ro, she smiled.

"It's all right, Mother, the battle's over, you can rest."

"Rest," Lar repeated, a long shivering sound. She pushed away from the stone, struggling to stand. Her legs buckled and had Ro and Uwert not caught her she would have fallen.

"Forgive my doubts, Lar." Uwert saluted her, fingertips to lips. "You've fulfilled your promise and more."

At what cost? Ro wanted to add. Lar was as grey as the stone, but she managed the hint of a bow.

"Darian must look to the care of his men," Uwert continued. "There's much to organise. I'll escort you to your wagons and he'll speak with you later." His face broke into a grin as he turned to Ro. "It's good to see you again, Ro—no doubt you have a fine story to tell, not least how that idiot, Jubb, sent back all the geese at once."

Ro smiled. "Jubb's looking forward to seeing you too."

Thoughts of the fool seemed to lighten all their moods. Uwert and Ro supported Lar through the Amrad camp towards the wagons. They passed many men grimacing with weariness and pain, or wandering about with the blank looks of sleepwalkers.

Lar halted. "I should help the healers."

"Most of the men are just battle weary," Uwert assured her. "Talking it over with their comrades around the camp fires is all they need."

"It's more than that. They need to feel that they can trust the ground they walk on. To feel once more that all things are connected."

The look that passed between the Earth-hearer and the courtier showed Ro that Uwert felt what Lar spoke of. Ro had never experienced that connection. All things were connected to everything except her. She had always been excluded.

She spoke to prevent the bitterness welling up. "Rest first, Mother. You can't help anyone if you're exhausted."

"Your daughter's right." Uwert helped Ro move Lar on. "Perhaps Raimi can... " He caught Ro's swift shake of the head too late, but mention of her marriage-son did not upset Lar as Ro had expected.

"When he returns his ears will ring with the sound of my displeasure, so that he'll be incapable of hearing his own excuses." Anger added strength to Lar's steps and they progressed more swiftly. Maybe Lar would have felt it if Raimi had been hurt, but with so much death around them, who could be sure?

The sound of a squabble greeted them as they reached Edun's wagon. Mirri was giving Jubb a thorough scolding. He grinned when he saw them, and Chickens struggled out of his arms to come and dance around Ro's feet.

"So someone sees fit to come and let us know what's going on at last! We could all have been massacred for all anyone cares!"

Uwert gave her an exaggerated bow. "Forgive us, Mirri, but we've been rather busy fending off the enemy on the field. King Darian sends his good wishes."

Mention of the King seemed to mollify the wet-nurse a little. Her scowl was replaced by a fluttering girlishness as Edun approached with the onddikins swooping around him. When they saw Ro, Pirik and Quinik settled on her shoulders and crooned in her ears while Finik performed aerobatics over her. Ignoring them, Mirri grabbed Edun's arm, which produced a look of mild alarm.

"If it hadn't been for Edun's bravery we would all have been stabbed and killed!"

Edun smiled awkwardly, gently disengaging himself. "I caught a couple of Ortanians trying the back door, that's all."

Uwert looked impressed.

"He caught me too," Jubb added cheerfully. "One minute I was standing on the ground, then, whoosh! I was down a hole."

"Quite a trick," Uwert commented drily.

"Not as impressive as Lar's," Edun hurriedly turned the subject.

Uwert left so they could get Lar settled. Mirri's scolding set up again as Jubb tried to bring Chickens into the wagon.

"Flea-bitten, filthy mongrel! You needn't think you're letting it anywhere near my baby–and look at the state of you!"

Jubb bore it all with a cheerful grin. "It's good to be home," he said to Ro.

"Home? Call this rackety pile of firewood home? There's no proper beds, no... "

Ro giggled. "Yes, Jubb. Right now, I never want to leave it again."

She looked at Lalli sleeping contentedly in her cradle. Her own eyes were closing when Jubb spoke again.

"What did Uwert say when you told him about our 'prize'? I wish I'd been there to see his face."

Ro's eyes opened wide. "I forgot to tell him."

"Forgot to tell him what?" Edun asked.

Ro explained, with Jubb gesturing embellishments to the tale.

"Fah! King Channan indeed!" Mirri was scornful. "If it was I'll eat my apron!"

"That won't taste very good. Perhaps if you cut it up and cook it in gravy," Jubb suggested, and Ro had to hide her face so that Mirri would not see her laughter.

The wet-nurse tutted and turned her attention to Edun. "I wish you'd let me put some salve on those singes. It's the least I can do," she simpered.

"No, no. I'll go and make sure King Darian knows he has an important guest." He scrambled off the wagon.

Jubb called after him. "No need, he'll visit the wounded anyway."

But the magician must have been too preoccupied to hear. The sky had faded to a faint wash of pink along the horizon and the camp fires absorbed all other traces of light, burning the brighter while casting all else into deep shadow. King Darian and

Uwert were dressed in the uniforms of ordinary soldiers with cloaks cast about them, but if they had hoped to walk the encampment incognito Jubb's jubilant welcome soon disappointed them.

"Master!" he shouted, all but throwing himself off the wagon into Darian's arms.

"Friend," corrected the King, clasping the fool to him with a broad grin of pleasure, despite the excited yapping of Chickens darting about his feet.

Uwert's nose wrinkled. "Where did you get that foul ball of fur and fleas?"

Jubb scooped up the mongrel, which set about washing his face. "It's a long story."

"Well, that's what we've come for; to hear all about your adventures, and find out how Lar is. Amradoc owes her a debt it won't be easy to repay."

The Earth-hearer emerged from the wagon, steadying herself on its frame. "Lar is better for the sleep thank you, Highness, and for having her daughter by," she whispered as she put an arm about Ro's waist. "But it's as well you've come for stories and not songs." She gestured at her throat.

Darian nodded, his eyes travelling over the group.

"Edun went looking for you," Jubb explained his friend's absence.

"And Raimi?"

"He hasn't returned yet," Lar said.

"Hmph!" Mirri rocked Lalli so hard that the baby began to grizzle.

Darian took the child from her and settled himself with her in the crook of his arm. The lack of ceremony and Jubb's prompting helped Ro begin their tale. Lar held her hand and when Ro spoke of being trapped in Ayif's room and Torslin's murderous plans for Ersilla, gripped it harder. Ro blocked out the gasps and exclamations of her friends, concentrating instead on the intent face of Darian. When she reached the part where only Chickens's persistence had saved them from succumbing to Torslin's poison, Mirri burst out.

"Oh, you precious puppy! Mirri shall have to find you a nice bone–once she's given you a bath." She fended off the enthusiastic dog.

"So Princess Anni knows the truth. Do you think she'll be able to convince King Channan when he returns to the city?" Darian asked.

"There's more." Ro took a deep breath and narrated the last installment of their journey and of how they had found King Channan. "He's in Dovinna's care in the hospital tent," she said as Darian jerked out of his seat with an oath.

He handed the baby back to Mirri and strode off in the direction of the healers. Ro ran after him and Jubb ran after her. Chickens would have followed too had Uwert not grabbed him.

"I'm sorry, I should have told you earlier, but–oh, too late, I'm always too late."

"That's yet to be seen," Darian murmured. If the words were meant to console her, they failed.

Darian moved among the pallets in the healers' tent sharing a joke with those who were awake and eager for news, and murmuring encouragement to those too sick to register that it was their king speaking. Ro and Jubb trailed silently behind him. The healers and their helpers barely broke off from their efforts to salute. A makeshift surgery had been set up and the thick scent of blood vied with the astringent aroma of herbs. Then Ro detected another smell, fresh and full of promise. She inhaled deeply and felt she was drawing in vigour and hope. They followed the scent to its source. Behind one of the curtained areas where the most seriously injured gained some measure of peace and privacy, Dovinna was crushing herbs into a bowl of steaming water. Far from being cheered by the smell, tears ran down her cheeks. She brushed them away impatiently, with a laugh that was half sob.

"So much suffering," Darian said. "Who wouldn't weep for the waste of it all?"

"The one who started it," Dovinna nodded at her patient.

"Great Ondd!" Darian muttered, taking an automatic step forward as he recognised Channan.

"If he had loved me, truly loved me, than he never could have believed Torslin, he would never have gone to war."

"How badly is he injured?"

"Some broken ribs, a dislocated shoulder, cuts and bruising. The worst is the damage to his head. He may wake at any moment–or never."

"Tell no one who he is for now. If you can prevent others seeing him without arousing suspicion, do so, and let me know

246

straight away if there's any change in his condition. This could either be our greatest opportunity or our greatest danger."

Dovinna nodded, and the tears flooded her eyes again. Darian took her hands. "I'm sure he'll recover, if for no other reason than because he hears your voice."

As if he had heard Darian's words, Channan sighed and his fingers flexed gently.

"Channan? Channan!" Dovinna called him. "You might as well wake up, because I'm going to tell you what I think of you whether you do or not. You needn't think you can hide." She wrung a cloth in the herb infused water. As she raised her eyes she caught sight of Ro and Jubb hovering at Darian's shoulder. She stood up with a cry and Ro hugged her, the excitement of the news she had to tell dampened by the anguish in Dovinna's defeated demeanour.

"There wasn't time to tell you before, but Jubb and I got the proof we need. I tried to get it to King Channan in time–I failed."

Darian interrupted. "Everyone's so eager to take the blame for all this. What's important is what we do next."

"Go to bed, I should think. I could sleep for a week." Jubb yawned and stretched, flinging his arms wide so that Ro and Darian were sent darting to save toppled basins and pots.

"Not a bad idea." Darian slapped the fool on the shoulder. "First, I think Ro should tell Channan a bedtime story of treachery and murder in a royal palace. One designed to wake its listeners rather than send them to sleep. Come." Darian spread his arms to shoo Jubb out.

Ro and Dovinna found themselves alone beside Channan's bed. The Iyessi girl shivered remembering the last time they had watched and waited for a sleeping king to wake. Lamplight flickered on the walls of the healers' tent casting grotesque shadows echoing the patients' disturbed dreams. Healers and injured alike seemed too weary to talk above a murmur. Her tale took some while. The lamps burned lower and the sounds of movement outside ceased as she spoke. It was hard to tell whether the changes in Dovinna's expression were the result of her story, or the wavering light. Throughout it all, Channan lay still and quiet.

"I hope Princess Anni won't suffer for helping us. If Torslin finds out I wouldn't give that for her life." Ro snapped her fingers. "Murder seems to be his answer for every difficulty."

A small frown lodged between Channan's eyes as Ro went on to tell Dovinna about Natann. "Ondd knows how the poor man had thwarted Torslin, but he died believing that traitor was his friend, and almost took us with him. And in so doing, how many other lives were lost? If we'd reached the army even an hour sooner... " she let the sentence hang.

"So now we have proof of our innocence and no one to show it to," Dovinna said. Her tone puzzled Ro. "Channan wouldn't listen to our story from the start, and he's still not listening now." She gestured at the still form on the pallet.

"We haven't heard his either," Ro reasoned. "And maybe he is listening. Lar would be able to tell us if she wasn't too tired to stand herself, or Raimi." Her marriage-brother's name faltered on her lips.

Dovinna took a long shuddering breath. "I'll keep watch over Channan. Why don't you go back to the wagons? Raimi might be back by now."

Ro shook her head. While she remained there she could believe that Dovinna was right. So the two waited, sometimes talking quietly, sometimes watching the unconscious king in silence. In one of these thoughtful spells Dovinna's head finally dropped forward and she slept. Ro felt her own eyes closing. To keep herself awake, she began to inspect the contents of the curtained area. There was a small table bearing the lamp and Dovinna's medicines, beneath which was a neat pile of Channan's clothing. Ro could not resist looking through it. Mistress Hexem would have been appalled at the condition it was in, stained with blood and dirt, scuffed and ripped. Ro smoothed the tunic. There was a small hard lump beneath the right breast. Ro turned it over. Beneath the quilting was a pocket. She felt inside and gasped. Dovinna started awake.

"What? Is he waking?"

Ro held up the jewel, which caught the little light in the room and cast it back magnified into brilliance.

"My ring!"

"It was in his pocket—next to his heart," Ro whispered.

"Probably just to remind him that he once loved a power-hungry poisoner!"

"I can understand your bitterness... "

Dovinna cut her off with a contemptuous noise. "How can you!"

"All my life I've been blamed for things that weren't my fault." Ro's cheeks burned.

"That's hardly the same thing!" Dovinna held out her hand for the ring.

"No? How do you think it feels to have your whole family exiled because of you?"

"How do you think it feels to have your country go to war because your sweetheart's love has turned to hate? What would you know about love anyway?"

They stood on either side of Channan's pallet as if it was all that kept them from tearing at each other.

Ro was stung. "So why bother about your precious Channan? Why not let him die, if he's so pathetic?"

"How dare you!" Dovinna grabbed at the ring, but Ro snatched her hand away. The King's frown deepened and his fingers curled.

"If it wasn't for him believing anything that worm-trail Torslin tells him, I'd still have a sister!" Ro spat.

"It's not his fault! Torslin was a trusted adviser before Channan was even born."

"So why are you blaming him?" Ro tightened her fist around the ring so that the stone dug into her palm.

Dovinna stamped her foot. "Give it to me!"

"Take it then!" Ro flung it at her. Dovinna ducked. The ring glanced off the hand warding her face and rolled under the pallet.

"Ro!" Dovinna gasped, stopping in the act of bending to retrieve it. Channan's eyes were open. He was staring at them with detachment as if they were a puzzle to be solved. Dovinna dropped to her knees and grasped his hand, which lay passive in hers.

"Channan? Can you hear me?"

He turned blank eyes on her intent ones. She looked imploringly at Ro.

"Channan, my dear. It's me, Dovinna. You've been injured, but it's all right, you're among friends."

"I know who you are," Channan whispered. Suddenly his face twisted as if he suffered a violent pain. He wrenched his hand from Dovinna's. "And you are no friend." He struggled to rise, clutching his head at the movement.

Dovinna held him with ease. "Hush! You mustn't struggle, your wounds..."

He glared at her, then subsided.

"You're in King Darian's encampment. You were found injured and brought here to recover."

"To be a prisoner, a hostage."

Dovinna shook her head, unable to speak. Ro hardly dared to move, the bands of tension between them were so strong.

"I'll fetch Darian," she whispered.

Outside, the air seemed buoyant by comparison. Darian was still hearing reports from his patrols when Ro entered.

"He's awake."

As the King and Uwert accompanied her back to the healers' tent, Darian was silent. He nodded mechanically at the few men still awake who recognised him.

"The patrols have been bringing unexpected news that makes dealing with our reluctant guest rather more of a gamble."

As they approached Channan's pallet the Najarindian levered himself onto one elbow.

"I demand to see the king! Even you Amrads must have some notion of how to treat those with royal blood, though they are prisoners." The effort of speaking was too much and he had to lie back on the pallet.

"Indeed we do, King Channan. I am King Darian." He stepped into the lamplight as he spoke. "And whether you're a prisoner or not is your decision."

Channan considered him with eyes narrowed, summing up his easy authority. "Then exchange me for Amrad prisoners."

"That's rather difficult."

Channan's face pulled into a bitter smile. "Are you trying to tell me there are no Amrad prisoners?"

"We've yet to contact anyone in your army with authority to negotiate," Darian answered.

"Liar! Torslin would have made it his first priority," Channan broke in.

"Your army has abandoned its injured and dead to our care, it would appear. No embassies have been sent to us."

Dovinna interposed. "He's not fit enough for this."

"I agree," Darian nodded. "King Channan, there's nothing to be done before morning. Then you shall see all the evidence for yourself and make your choice." He turned.

"Wait!" Channan tried to rise. "I won't be nursed by this." He jerked his head at Dovinna. "How do I know I won't be murdered in my bed?"

"Because if Mistress Dovinna had harboured any such intention you wouldn't have woken up," Darian said coolly, but his eyes flashed.

"No, it's all right. Let one of the other healers care for him," Dovinna's voice shook as she strode out.

Ro followed.

"I'm sorry," Dovinna began.

"No need," Ro said simply. "We're both too tired."

There was still no word of Raimi when they reached the wagons. Only Edun was awake.

"I hope he gets back soon." He looked pointedly at Mirri, who was snoring gently next to Lalli's cot. "Being a hero has some rather unexpected hazards."

"You'll have to show her your vanishing act," Ro teased, all the while watching Dovinna as she curled up on a couch. There was more than weariness in the slump of the healer's shoulders.

Edun was talking again. "Lar would've waited up, but... "

"I know," Ro said. Darian's words returned to her. "There's nothing to be done until morning."

Her bed seemed the most welcoming place in the world and her sleep was sound. So sound that the wagons were empty and the camp was bustling all around her when she woke. She made herself presentable as swiftly as she could and went outside. Lar was standing letting the sun warm her upturned face. Her eyes were closed, but she smiled as Ro approached.

"You're feeling better now," the Earth-hearer said.

"Yes. Are you?"

For answer, Lar took Ro's arm. "I thought I'd offer my help to the healers. We can go together. Edun is trying to escape Mirri, Jubb and Chickens are somewhere about the place, and I believe Dovinna is conferring with Uwert and King Darian about Channan's condition." She halted and looked at Ro earnestly. "I'm afraid he still doesn't believe your innocence. He refused even to look at Ayif's book." They continued walking. "If only he had Iyessi sensitivity he'd need no other proof."

"But he hasn't heard everything. Perhaps I can convince him. There must be something, some detail that will put our innocence beyond doubt."

"Not if he refuses to listen." Lar patted her hand.

They entered the healers' tent and Lar stiffened. For a moment Ro thought she was distracted by the vibrations of suffering which must have emanated from the injured. Then she realised her mother was listening. Ro strained her ears, as she followed her towards Channan's pallet. She heard a man laughing.

"I thought no one was to have access to the King," she whispered. Lar placed a finger to her lips. They stood outside the curtain listening.

"It's good to see you awake. When that traitor's horse trampled you into the earth I thought I was probably trying to rescue a dead man."

"Describe him again," Channan's voice was a whisper.

"A stocky man. He was riding a black horse... " The voice went on to describe Torslin's armour and emblem.

"You're sure?"

Ro could hold back no longer. "Raimi!" She pulled aside the curtain. Her marriage-brother's face split into a wide grin as he gave her a hug that lifted her from her feet. As he set her down she thumped his chest. "Where have you been?"

"Helping on the field. Forgive me, Lar. I know I was needed here, but the song of revenge was too loud in my heart."

"Iyessi!" Channan exclaimed. "I almost believed you, but now I see this is just another plot."

"No, King Channan." Raimi sat on the end of the King's pallet. The book that was on it slid towards him. Ro recognised the cover as belonging to Ayif's journal. "I grant you I went on the field looking for a chance to kill the man who murdered Ussu. If I'd seen Pachand he'd no longer be breathing. I would even have put a sword through you given the chance, but when I saw Torslin butcher your horse and try to do the same to you, without the courage or honour to challenge you or give you a chance to defend yourself, I saw myself–what I was about to become. I found you a horse and would have brought you back, but for another dishonourable soldier with designs on your mount. I had to stay to persuade him otherwise." Raimi's face was grim.

"But Raimi," Ro blurted. "I know you've done nothing but train these last months, but you're useless with a sword."

"Ah, but I had two advantages." His face became mischievous. "One, we were on the edge of the marsh and two, when I began to sing it distracted him enough for me to manoeuvre him into it. It slowed him down enough for me to prevail. I don't think I killed him, I didn't wait to find out. Since then I've been helping the stretcher-bearers and healers on the field. Putting my true skills to some use calming the discord." The last was said with an apologetic look at Lar.

"So, you're yourself once more–almost worth nearly losing a battle for," she said.

"And now, Marriage-sister, let's give the King some peace and find a place where you can tell me your adventures."

"No," Ro took a deep breath. "I'll tell you everything, but King Channan must hear it too."

So she began once more. Channan stared at her as she spoke, lips pressed into a sneer. When she reached the part about Natann he started.

"Ondd knows how the poor man had thwarted Torslin." Channan interrupted. "I heard you say that before."

"Last night, I told Dovinna."

"Why bother lying when I was unconscious?" he said as if to himself.

"Why indeed?" Lar asked drily.

Ro waited unsure whether to continue.

"How do you know Natann's name?"

"Because he told us. He was heading home, away from the army."

"If he'd been in the encampment I would have heard about it." As Channan spoke his eyes caught on Ayif's book. "Leave me, I'm tired."

Raimi stood, picking up the book. Channan caught his wrist. "I'll take that."

Ro stepped back into the sunny morning. There was hope. If Raimi could return from the battlefield unscathed, then it was possible that Channan would recognise the truth. Before they had gone far there was a shriek that made Raimi and Lar wince and men reach for their swords. Suddenly, they were the centre of a maelstrom as Mirri hurtled towards Raimi raining blows and insults on him while Edun struggled to catch her arms. Jubb followed closely, hampered by holding Lalli and trying not to trip over Chickens, who had caught the general excitement.

"Call yourself a man–going off and leaving a poor woman to fend for herself? You don't care about me or Lalli!"

Other people joined the group attracted by the commotion. Raimi stood patiently under the tirade, until Mirri stood red-faced trying to catch her breath.

"What's going on here?" It was King Darian's voice. "Get about your duties, or I shall give you some more."

The crowd began to slink away, allowing the King, Uwert and Dovinna to press through. Dovinna anxiously looked from one to the other.

"Who's hurt? I expected to see blood everywhere–that awful noise."

"Mirri attacked Raimi," Jubb explained in an awestruck voice.

Edun's face had blanched. Mirri looked like an overheated red-fruit that was about to burst, but no one felt like laughing.

Raimi added: "It's Mirri who's hurt, and it's for me to mend. I'm sorry, Mirri, but if I hadn't been on the field, I would've been helping Lar. You and Lalli were as safe as you could be."

Mirri sniffed and smoothed her apron. "Well, you needn't trouble yourself with me any more. I've found someone else to protect me." She looked proprietorially at Edun.

The magician opened and closed his mouth a couple of times before anything came out. "Um... I think... " He was saved by one of the healers' assistants.

"Mistress Dovinna! Mistress Dovinna!" He ran breathlessly into the group. "Your patient–he's gone! I only slipped off for a minute... "

"How long ago?"

The assistant jumped at the sound of the King's voice. He bowed. "Only minutes, Sire." He turned to Dovinna. "One of the patients had opened his wound again. I had to see to him."

"So, he's chosen to see himself as a prisoner, after all," Uwert said. "He'll probably make for the horses."

Dovinna shook her head. "I doubt he'll get that far."

"Chickens'll find him." Jubb went dashing off after the dog.

Darian called after him with no effect. "Wait! Let's be methodical about this. If we set the whole camp in uproar, we'll get nowhere."

They split up to search the most likely places. Dovinna and King Darian returned together to Channan's pallet.

"His clothes have gone," Darian confirmed.

Dovinna lingered by the curtain. "If he returns to his army, Torslin will kill him, won't he?"

Darian looked grim. "Probably."

Dovinna closed her eyes.

"How could he have left without anyone noticing?" Darian's tone boded ill for anyone caught slacking.

"The healers are so busy... " Struck by a sudden thought, Dovinna looked behind the curtain. "My healer's apron's gone."

"And you say he wouldn't be able to get far."

Dovinna caught Darian's thought, she drew back the curtain and they surveyed the tent's occupants.

"How many healers are there?" Darian asked.

"No more than six would be on duty now."

"I count seven."

Dovinna touched Darian's arm and indicated the pallet in the shade of the door flap. A healer was rising wearily from it. He pulled the covers closer about the patient, supporting himself on the mattress. He straightened, holding his side, glanced round and headed for the opening. Darian strode quickly after him.

"Wait!"

Channan checked his step an instant, then quickened it. On the other side of the opening, Jubb's shambling figure appeared hot on the trail of Chickens.

"Naughty dog! Not in there!"

Channan tried to step around them but could not move quickly enough to avoid the waving tail and arms and all three hit the floor in a knot. Darian and Dovinna hurried to untangle them. The effort of walking had given Channan's brow a sheen of sweat but he smiled at Dovinna's anxious look.

"Are you quite mad?" she scolded.

"You must let me go," he whispered.

Darian helped him to his feet. "Is Amrad hospitality so bad that it can't wait until you can sit a horse without killing yourself?"

They set him down on the nearest pallet.

"Every minute I stay here gives that traitor a chance to tighten his grip on my kingdom. I have to get back."

"Or die in the attempt?" Dovinna snapped. Channan smiled. "What?"

"You still love me–after all my stupidity."

"I don't know what gives you that idea." Dovinna blushed.

"You're angry." He took her hand. "I have to go back and set things right."

She snatched her hand away. "But not today."

They both looked an appeal at Darian.

"King Channan's right, he does have to get back." He held up a hand against Dovinna's protest. "Somehow we must let Najarind know that he's still alive before Torslin can convince everyone otherwise. But you can't just go riding into Torslin's camp, King Channan. Right now, he believes you're dead. It'll keep you safe and buy us some time. No, we have to do something he won't expect."

"Well, Highness, whatever plan you may come up with won't be worth that," Dovinna snapped her fingers. "If Channan kills himself pretending he's not injured. Your first priority is to get well, and king or no king, that means following my commands!"

Jubb recounted the scolding Dovinna had given the kings with great glee when he returned to Edun's and Lar's wagons.

"You should have seen their faces. Like this... " He struck a pose with head lowered and a sulky expression. "It makes a change for it not to be me who's in the dog house."

"Or Chickens," Ro said.

"Yes," he agreed, then realising it was a joke, burst out laughing. The memory of the kings' discomfort still made him burst into giggles at intervals that evening when Uwert came to summon them.

Darian was sitting beside Channan's pallet as they entered. The Ortanian king was propped against his pillows with Dovinna tending him unobtrusively. The looks that passed between them were more wary than tender, but whenever their eyes met they lingered and could scarcely be dragged elsewhere. As Dovinna rearranged his covers there was a brilliant flash. She was wearing Channan's ring once more. She caught Ro's smile and blushed.

"Ro," Channan greeted her. "I owe you an apology and a debt I can scarcely repay."

Ro shuffled and murmured, unable to find a gracious reply.

"But a debt I fear I am about to add to."

Ro looked questioningly at Darian.

"We've been discussing the best way to get news of Channan's survival to those who are loyal to him in Najarind. It's not as easy as it seems. Of course, we'll send a conventional embassy ahead, while we follow with the army. After our victory, it would seem odd if we didn't, but we need some insurance should things go wrong. As you and Jubb are already known and trusted by Princess Anni... "

"...you want us to go," Ro finished for him. She did not know whether the giggle which formed a lump that threatened to choke her was mirth or despair.

Darian spoke gently. "It may not be necessary, if the embassy's successful, you won't have to go."

Ro shook her head. There was unfinished business for her in Najarind. The city still had not given up its secrets to cure Lalli and her of their 'deafnesses'. She thought of the serene tree-fringed pool in Iyessa where only the rustle of branches troubled the thoughts. Would she ever know its peace again?

# Chapter Twenty

The whispering stopped as Anni entered her chamber. For the past few days it had been happening all over the palace. Whenever Anni entered a room, the servants would spring apart as if caught conspiring to steal the silver. She waved permission for them to carry on making her bed as she sat by the window. She picked up her embroidery, but her thoughts were not on silks. There had been no news from Channan. Surely Ro must have reached him by now. She found herself staring at one of the maids. The girl looked about fifteen or sixteen and folded the sheets clumsily. Her eyes were red and swollen.

"You're new, aren't you?"

The girl dropped an awkward curtsy with eyes lowered. "Yes'm."

"Highness," prompted the other maid. Anni tried to place her.

"Is Mistress Hexem making things difficult for you? I see you've been crying."

The girl tried to smother a sob. Her companion comforted her.

"It's her sweetheart, Highness. He joined the army to earn enough so they could marry."

"I told him it didn't matter to me where we lived," the girl wailed.

"And now you're worried he won't come back," Anni put her arm around the new girl's shoulders. "We all have loved ones in the army, er..."

"Tillenne," offered the familiar maid. Tillenne; Ro's friend.

"We're all scared of losing them. We just have to trust in Ondd and hope." The triteness of her words made Anni wince.

"But, Highness," Tillenne said. "Haven't you heard? The whole city's full of the news."

"Rumours most likely. Why don't you tell me what you've heard?"

Anni tried to reassure them, but hurrying along the corridor in search of Ersilla a few minutes later she had to fight not to sink to the floor under the weight of what they had said. Her sister was not in her room, neither was she in the audience chamber. Anni ignored the heads turned hopefully in her direction and hurried out again. Where else would she be so early in the day? Anni shuddered, then set off towards the back stairs and the vaults. Ersilla was emerging from the guarded entrance as Anni arrived. Her bland expression wrinkled into a frown at sight of her.

"What are you doing here?" Ersilla demanded.

"I might ask you the same thing–checking my housekeeping?"

"I wouldn't dream of it, Anni. If there was ever a person who could be relied upon to dutifully attend to every boring detail, it's you, sister."

To her irritation, Anni felt her cheeks grow heated. "So why are you here?"

"Since when have I had to answer to you?" Ersilla said.

Anni changed her tone. "If you wanted something you only had to ask."

They headed back to Ersilla's apartments. "Don't sulk, Anni. It looks bad in front of the servants, especially at an uncertain time like this."

"Actually, it's the uncertainty I wanted to talk to you about."

"Oh?"

"In private."

When they reached Ersilla's sitting room, she dismissed her maid. "Well?"

"Have you heard the rumours that are everywhere in the city?"

"I don't make a habit of listening to gutter gossip." Ersilla picked up her mirror and began preening.

Anni ignored the implied insult. "They say there's been a disastrous battle–that we've been defeated."

"You know how the ordinary people love scaremongering."

"Then you've heard nothing?"

Ersilla busied herself with her cosmetics. "If I had, would I be sitting here so calmly?"

"You've heard nothing from the army at all?"

"Nothing of any moment."

Anni changed position so that she was standing in line with Ersilla's mirror and could see her sister's face rather than her reflection. "They say the army's scattered and Channan's dead on the battlefield."

"Extraordinary!" Ersilla put the mirror down and looked Anni in the eyes. "I assure you we haven't lost a brother or a battle. Rumours–nothing more. They'll be saying the earth erupted under them and the stars fell next." She turned away calmly.

Anni stared at her. The earth erupted under them. What was it Tillenne had said? That the earth sang and danced under their feet. It was too close to be a coincidence.

"I just wish we'd heard something, that's all."

"Be assured, as soon as I have news, I'll let you know." Ersilla's manner was dismissive. As Anni was about to let herself out there was a knock at the door. Ayif's face split into a greasy smile as she opened it.

"Is someone ill?" She blocked his entry.

Behind her Ersilla called. "Have you brought that lotion I asked for?"

Anni stood aside, allowing Ayif to parade into the chamber holding aloft an intricately decorated pot.

"The very finest quality skin dew, as you desired." He bowed as low as his double chins and stomach would allow.

"Wonderful." Ersilla's face came alive as she snatched the pot from him and smelled the contents.

Anni bit back a warning. "May I?" She too breathed in the aroma of blossoms watching the physician's reaction.

"Shall I make some for you too, Highness?"

"It's a little too heady for me." She set the pot down on the table. "I'll take my leave." She turned, knocked against the table and sent the pot crashing to the floor.

"Clumsy!" Ersilla almost choked on the unladylike abuse she was not able to direct at Anni in front of Ayif. Anni hid her enjoyment at the sight by scrambling to retrieve the pieces.

"Leave it." Ayif hurried to stop her.

"Yes, Anni, it's servant's work not a princess's."

"I'm so sorry," Anni said. "All your hard work for nothing."

"No matter." Ayif treated her to his most obsequious smile. I can soon make more."

Anni's feeling of triumph turned to nausea.

"Haven't you got something else to do, Anni?"

"Of course." Anni hurried out, desperate for fresh air.

No sooner had the door closed behind her than Ersilla slapped her hand on the table.

"Great Ondd! How can that graceless lump be my sister?"

"She hasn't your regal bearing, that's true."

"She's an embarrassment, Ayif."

"It can't be easy for her, Highness, being compared with you all the time, without your wit or elegance. It's no wonder she's jealous of you."

"Jealous?" Ersilla's face took on a satisfied smile.

"Why, yes. I've often noticed it in the way she looks at you, and am I not correct in thinking that she often opposes your wishes?"

"Well... "

"Why else would she spill your lotion, but that she's jealous of your beauty?"

"Don't patronise me, Ayif. I'm not a fool." She looked pleased nonetheless.

Ayif bowed. "I only speak the truth. We must pity her and make allowance for her little acts of mischief."

"You must, you mean. I don't see why I should have to. It's a shame you can't make up a lotion that would work on people and not just skin blemishes, then I could make everyone disagreeable disappear."

"Highness, you have only to say the word." The physician's expression was bland.

Ersilla's eyes narrowed. "I thought you were Torslin's creature."

"I serve the best interests of Ortann, as you do, Highness."

"Hmm.... and just what do you see as Ortann's best interests?"

There was another knock at the door.

"Am I to have no peace this morning? Yes? What is it?"

The head of her maid appeared around the door. "Excuse me, Highness." She bobbed a nervous curtsy. "Only Lord Fordel said to tell you straight away, he's had some news and needs to speak to you urgently."

"We'll have to continue our conversation later, Ayif."

The physician bowed himself out.

"Tell Fordel, this had better be important!"

A rider had returned from the nearest messenger post. Torslin and the army—what was left of it—were approaching the city and should arrive by nightfall. Ersilla stormed about the palace berating servants and courtiers who strayed into her path as she prepared to greet them. Meanwhile news seeped into every crevice of the city. Even an Iyessi hearer would have found Najarind quiet enough as the citizens prayed to Ondd and filed silently down to the city walls. They massed near the gates, straining for the first sound of hooves, the first glimpse of the weary faces, hoping that they would see the dear features of their loved ones. Torches were lit, gaining brilliance as the lights faded.

Captain Pachand formed his men in a guard of honour before the main gate. The army approached in good order. Some attempt had been made to clean the armour and put some heart into the march, but the ranks no longer stretched off into the distance. At their head rode Torslin, his bearing as confident and defiant as when he had ridden out. Pachand stepped forward to salute him even as the murmuring began behind them. Where was the king?

"Welcome home, Lord Torslin. I must speak to you."

Torslin nodded, then kicked his horse on past the gates to be escorted by Fordel and the royal guard to the palace. He seemed oblivious to the silent mass of people lining the streets. There were no enthusiastic cheers or strewing of sweet-smelling blossoms. Only the occasional unbelieving shout of recognition and a sigh that followed his passage like a ripple. The Lord's expression warned Fordel not to ask any questions as they rode to the citadel. Princess Ersilla waited at the top of the palace steps with Anni at her side. She stood with hands clasped calmly in front of her as the lords dismounted and approached her.

Torslin dropped to one knee. "Highness. Ortann's army returns victorious. Your brother, King Channan, led his men courageously against the Amrad's. He fought with great courage. If it had not been for the intervention of Iyessi witchery he would be standing before you now, covered in glory." Torslin bowed his head. "He fell to their spells and is now at rest with your honoured father."

Anni lit a glowstick. From the side chapel she could see people beginning to assemble. All over the temple of Ondd, Anni's action was being repeated by grief-stricken Najarindians. Their purple robes and pale faces contrasted with the gold and green walls hung for the thanksgiving ceremony with the banners of Ortann's regiments. The temple seemed like one vast jewel to Anni's tear-blurred eyes. Among the throng she saw Fordel, his face white as the moon. He nodded to her; too late for her to pretend she had not seen him. She took a place on the bench next to him, a hard lump of tears pressing on her chest making it impossible for her to do more than nod a greeting in return.

"What are we going to do now?" he murmured allowing his lazy gaze to travel over the congregation. The rich robes of courtiers brushed against the faded apparel of labourers and servants. People from every level of Najarind were there, but none had any apparent interest in the Lord and Princess.

Anni had to swallow before she could answer. "Channan's dead, what is there to do? Everything's finished, settled for good."

"No!" Fordel's vehemence made the nearest heads turn. "Not for good! I don't like any of this. If we won such a great victory, what's Torslin doing back here? He should be tightening our hold on Amradoc. And why is half the army missing? Where's Channan's body? It should have been brought home in state."

Anni heard the pain in his voice and touched his arm. "Ersilla says he was buried by falling rocks, that a monument will be raised for him where he fell."

Fordel waved one of the smoking glowsticks under his nose. "Why would she lie about it?"

"Anni, you mustn't let grief bury you with him."

There was a stir at the entrance and those nearest it fell silent.

Fordel whispered hurriedly. "The soldiers all tell the same story: the Amrad army was greatly outnumbered and had fallen back to make a last stand–then the earth began to split and heave. Soldiers were separated from comrades, officers lost contact with one another. By the time they regrouped, news of their victory was already widespread. No one saw Channan fall."

The words buzzed about Anni's head as the priests at the front of the procession preceded the Patriarch up the main aisle, carrying braziers of Ondd's breath. The spiced smoke fogged the brain, removing humdrum thoughts and helping the faithfuls' prayers to rise to Ondd. Anni struggled against it. Behind her she heard moans and sighs as the bereaved let their sorrow drift on the smoke.

The deep humming chant of the priests accompanied the progress of the Patriarch, Princess Ersilla and Torslin. The

Patriarch was almost buried by his gaudy vestments. To Anni's eyes he seemed smaller than before, as if suddenly shrunk with age. His lips moved in prayer and his eyes fixed on the altar. Ersilla paced after him, her unveiled head held high so that Anni could see the excited glitter in her eyes and the hot pink of her cheeks. She passed, accompanied by an undercurrent of murmurs and the rustling of cloth as the congregation bowed or curtsied. Instead of being draped from head to toe in purple, Ersilla blazed in the green and gold of Najarind. Behind her Torslin looked like a rough cliff-face next to polished marble.

"Children of Ondd." The Patriarch called all attention to himself. "Give praise! The followers of the worm are defeated and our loved ones have returned triumphant. Give praise to Ondd the Mighty, whose cause we serve and who breathes strength into our soldiers! Give praise to those who led them and who brought them safely home! Give praise to those who fell! They shall live forever in places of honour in the great dragon's eternal domain. Give praise to King Channan! Give praise indeed, for by his courage he set the example that led his men to glory, and now he leads them to the glory of Ondd's presence. Give praise!"

With each repetition of the exhortation, the congregation's response became more fervent. Anni struggled to focus. She found the smoke luring her to a place where she would give over her will to the Patriarch. She concentrated on the faces of the leading participants. The Patriarch's eyes strayed to Torslin with each demand for praise. The Lord nodded, as if counting them off. Ersilla's expression cleared a space in Anni's head. It was a look she had seen many times before when her sister had wheedled and thrown tantrums until their father had granted her some undeserved request.

The Patriarch cleared his throat, his eyes flicking to Torslin. "Give praise for the wisdom and mercy of Ondd, that although he has taken King Channan from us, he has provided us with a successor... "

Torslin's head came up sharply.

"... the fruit of the same seed. Give praise for Princess Ersilla, princess no longer, but Queen of Ortann. Give praise!"

The response was a bellow of agreement. Torslin's eyes narrowed as the sound reverberated around the dome.

"Step forward, Queen of Ortann, defender of Ondd's truth, scourge to its enemies, and receive Ondd's blessing."

Ersilla did as she was bid with a serene smile that Anni knew was holding back a malicious giggle. She knelt and the Patriarch held both his hands above her head.

"See, great Ondd, your daughter, and grant her your blessing that she... "

A whirring of mechanical wings drowned out the words as the automaton of Ondd swooped down from its eyrie, singing its Iyessi song. A sigh went through the congregation. Here was confirmation of the great dragon's approval. The Patriarch looked disconcerted and hesitated. The dragon circled the dome and caught the braid on one of the banners sending it crashing into a brazier exhaling Ondd's breath. The whole tumbled to the floor sending flames licking in all directions. With a final trill the dragon soared back into the secret heights of the dome. Pandemonium broke out as priests rushed to extinguish the blaze, spreading it on the hems of robes.

Torslin brushed past the transfixed Patriarch, picked up a ewer of blessed water used to purify supplicants, and tossed the contents over the flames. The hiss of steam rose on silence. Many of the faces in the congregation looked as if they had been slapped awake.

"I told Lar I always liked that toy," Fordel murmured. "And so, the best laid plans are wrecked."

"I don't think Torslin planned this."

Fordel followed Anni's gaze. Torslin had supplanted the Patriarch's position before the altar.

"Give praise that you are here to see this day," he commanded as if addressing his troops. "The day that sees an end to our somnolence. Ondd has given us a sign that we have been complacent and slothful—we must take its rule into all places—within the empire and without—that challenge Najarind and therefore, Ondd's supremacy. Go to your homes and be grateful that you were here to see the start of Najarind's rise to her former glory."

Ersilla had no alternative but to lead the way out. Torslin strode after her without waiting to see what impact his words had. Near the entrance Captain Pachand caught his eye. The Lord nodded and spoke briefly to him.

"I wonder what's going on there," Fordel said.

As the congregation closed in after them, Anni saw the yellow robes of the Gindullan physician trailing in Torslin's wake.

265

Her stomach cramped and she had to clench her fists and her teeth against the sobs that built up wave on wave, insisting on being let out. The throng parted to let her through.

"Anni, wait." Fordel hurried after her. "We can't just give up."

She shook her head and left.

Pacing about her chamber did nothing to ease the pressure, neither did telling herself that virtually everyone in the city had cause to grieve. Anni had tried checking the household accounts but the figures would not keep still. She pushed the papers away not caring that they fell to the floor. There had to be some relief from this unbearable ache. She stood abruptly, straightening her gown and smoothing her hair. She was lucky, she still had her routine tasks to attend to. People needed food and warmth and clean bedding no matter what catastrophe occurred.

She started out for the kitchen, intending to check on the next day's menus. Yet eating and drinking, carrying on the daily round seemed so pointless. All she really wanted was to sleep and forget. Suddenly, facing the bustle and heat of the kitchen was more than she could stand. Everyone expected her to put on a brave shell and constantly looked for cracks in it. There must be some place where no one would call on her to pretend everything was fine. A moment's hesitation was enough for her to reject the rose bower. Instead, she headed up the back stairs to the old nursery.

Laughter met her as she opened the door, yet no one else was there. For a moment she expected Channan to come running towards her with some new piece of mischief to impart.

"Look, Anni. Look what Fordel's done."

He had been the only one who had ever known where to look for her when she was sad.

"Don't cry, Anni. Daddy's very busy being king. He hasn't got time to see what you drew for him. But if he could he'd play with us all day."

They would huddle together in the window-seat, looking down on the servants and courtiers far below, and feel as if they were isolated from the whole world, from everyone and everything except each other.

Sobs wrenched her body, so that she had to steady herself against the wall to stand. Each breath was silent agony, but still there were no tears. She wanted to wail and tear her hair as she had seen some of the soldiers' women do, when their men had not returned. Nothing would come.

Ersilla's spiteful giggle seemed to mock her. Anni spun around. She was alone. Then she realised where the sound must have come from. She crossed to the fireplace. The giggle was cut off by Torslin's gruff voice.

"I see you've been busy while I was away."

"Of course, running a city, not to mention an empire, takes every waking moment. I'm quite fatigued." Anni heard her yawn.

"You know very well what I mean. Having yourself proclaimed queen."

"People need a leader and who else should it be? I'm next in line."

"Impatience will only arouse suspicions needlessly."

"It will get people used to the idea."

"And the fiasco with the dragon will arouse their superstitions."

Ersilla made a dismissive noise. "I think we should go ahead and plan the coronation. I've told the Patriarch he's to make ready for it."

"It would be better to wait."

"Why? Channan's dead, isn't he?"

There was a pause that made Anni catch her breath.

"He should be, but thanks to the Iyessi bitch's tricks, his body wasn't found."

There was the sound of glass shattering. "Wonderful! Do I have to do everything myself?" Anni heard the swish of her gown. "All the more reason to go ahead as swiftly as possible. And if any embarrassing stragglers return from the battlefield you'd better finish the job properly."

Torslin's voice grated. "Be sure, I have no intention of being 'embarrassed', by Channan or anyone else. Take no further action without consulting me. It's caused enough trouble as it is."

"Oh?"

"Thanks to you, I have Pachand to deal with. Somehow I have to distract him. Your tame priest told him enough to suspect a religious conspiracy at least."

"I don't think you need to worry about that."

Torslin spoke as if explaining to a child. "He'll want an investigation, a search of the abbey... "

"Let him search."

"I would rather not arrange an 'accident' for him. Pachand's a useful soldier, but when he finds the Patriarch's little friends... "

"Ah... but he won't." There was another swish of cloth and Ersilla's voice faded as she walked to the window.

"What have you done?"

Ersilla burst into giggles. "Your face! Don't worry, the Patriarch has them in a safe place. When Pachand finds nothing, I'm sure you'll be able to persuade him to blame someone else. I have it!" She clapped her hands as if struck by a new idea. "Blame the Iyessi; they killed my father, their spells killed Channan. It was even an Iyessi who helped make that damned machine that sabotaged my proclamation. Why not?"

There was a pause.

"Well?"

"I'll consider it, Princess."

"Queen."

"But you must exercise patience. No more impulsive actions without consulting me first."

"Oh, very well," she snapped. "All this arguing makes my head ache."

"Your pardon. I'll leave you to rest." There was the sound of a door closing quietly.

Anni bit her knuckle so that she would not cry out. Even Torslin could not be sure that Channan was dead. Somehow she had to find out. Her blood was pounding too loudly in her ears for her to think clearly. Torslin had counseled Ersilla not to act rashly, and the same advice held good for her. There was too much uncertainty and too much at stake. One thing did seem certain, however. Ersilla had moved something that Torslin wanted. If Fordel was right and her sister was nurturing monsters in the palace vaults, then she had to destroy them before Torslin found them.

The acolyte's face peered around the gate at them as if the dawn light was too bright for his eyes. Pachand pushed through followed by his men.

"I have orders to search the abbey. Fetch the Patriarch and then see to our horses."

"The Patriarch's not at the beck and call of every peasant or nosy soldier. Where's your authority?" The acolyte rubbed the sleep off his face.

Pachand's fingers twitched to connect with the acolyte's nose. His smile made the acolyte take a step back. "Oh no? I thought all you monks and priests took an oath of service and humility."

The acolyte stumbled over a protest. Another voice cut in.

"Indeed we do, Captain. How can I serve you?" It was the Patriarch.

"There are rumours of spies and traitors. I have orders to search–nowhere's to be left out."

The Patriarch's smile never wavered, but the sleepy monk was heard to mumble something about 'outrage'.

"You must make allowances, the brothers are not at their best at this early hour. See to the Captain's horse, and give his men whatever assistance they require. Perhaps I can offer you some refreshment while they carry out their task." He was already turning to lead the way.

"No, Patriarch, that won't be possible. You must accompany our search so that there can be no question of honesty–on either side."

"I see." The smile became more fixed. "Does Lord Torslin know of this?"

"I'm here at his command." Pachand handed over the relevant papers.

Some of the stiffness left the Patriarch's pose. "Why don't you start with my quarters? As you say–we must all be seen to be above suspicion."

The sun was at its highest before they had finished. Pachand's men were thorough. Every book in the library was shaken, even the hen coops were checked in case the roosts were lined with more than straw. They found nothing. As the search had continued the Patriarch's bonhomie had increased.

"A fruitless morning for you, I'm afraid."

"Don't be," Pachand said. "Only enemies of Ortann need be scared, and no search that reveals loyal subjects is fruitless. Queen Ersilla was certain we'd find nothing incriminating, but... "

"All must be seen to be fairly done. I do appreciate that." The Patriarch's smile made Pachand want to reach for his sword. He declined the invitation to join the priests at their midday meal.

There were some murmurs from the men as they started the ride back to Najarind.

"What are they grumbling about? That I didn't let them stuff their bellies with Ondd's finest?" he demanded of his lieutenant.

The man grinned. "Glad to be out of there, if you ask me. Give me a straightforward battle any day."

"You won't be taking vows then?"

The lieutenant spat. "All those smiles and mild words are too sickly for my taste. And it's all too clean, as if they scour the words and their personalities clean every day."

He had hit upon it. It had all been too clean and smooth for Pachand's liking too. The Patriarch had been warned.

At the moment Pachand's fingers itched to waken the acolyte, Torslin was riding hard for the nearest messenger post. A soldier stepped out of the shadows to challenge him as his horse slithered to a halt outside the squat building. He threw the soldier the reins and strode inside, catching the commanding officer before he had time to do more than half rise from his seat.

"Where is he?" the Lord demanded.

The officer jerked his head towards a door at the back of the room. "He's been allowed to talk to no one, as you commanded."

Torslin nodded, taking in the sparse furnishings of the room: two pallets, a table, two chairs and a campaign stove.

"Who else saw him arrive."

"Just the two sentries."

"Good." Torslin held out his hand for the bunch of keys the officer had at his waist. "I suggest you get some fresh air. Walking's good for the health."

The officer complied without comment. Torslin checked from the window that he had not given in to the temptation to listen at the door, then entered the cell. A man jumped to his feet.

"This is disgraceful!"

Torslin said nothing. The man was of middle years, but looked sinewy. No palace-bound courtier. His unornamented garb proclaimed him to be an Amrad.

"What else should we do with enemy spies?"

"I've told the officer, I'm on an embassy from King Darian to Najarind. I carry the banner of diplomacy, I carry no weapons."

"Anyone can wave a piece of cloth."

"Take me to Najarind and let your betters decide. I have sealed letters of command." He pulled two packets from the breast of his tunic. One bore the seal of Najarind. "I must be allowed to speak to the royal princesses and the Najarind council."

"Must, is it? We each have 'musts' to obey."

"Who are you?" The messenger looked anxiously at the door. Torslin had left it temptingly ajar.

"One of those betters you wanted to see." Torslin held out his hands for the packets. The messenger tucked them back in his tunic.

"My embassy is to Najarind." The messenger circled away from him.

"Let me guess, your king is playing host to a very special guest."

"Where's the other officer? Hey! Hey! In here!" he shouted.

A slow smile spread over Torslin's face. "They won't hear you. They've gone for a walk. There's just you and me."

"You'd do well to let me continue my embassy. Killing an ambassador is recognised throughout the world as one of the greatest crimes."

"But you're a spy."

"He'll send others."

"Any spy he sends will be dealt with the same way."

Their circling had brought the messenger close to the door.

"You can't hide the truth forever. King Darian will come himself–he'll have an army behind him."

"I don't need forever." Torslin took a step towards him.

The messenger glanced over his shoulder. "I suppose you'll tell the others I tried to escape!"

On the last word he feinted towards Torslin, dodged and slipped through the door, slamming it behind him. He made it past the table. Torslin calmly opened the door and drew the knife at his waist. The messenger was at the entrance. The force of the knife striking his back flung him through it. He crawled on another couple of paces. Torslin stood over him.

"Good guess. Not everyone dies knowing they were right." He braced his foot on the messenger's back and withdrew his knife, then turned the body over. He had just finished stowing the packets in his own tunic when the officer reappeared.

"As I thought," Torslin said. "Darian's taken to sending spies and assassins under banners of truce."

The officer shoved the body with a booted toe. "What do you want done with this one? Send him back as a warning?"

"Find somewhere out of the way and let the scavengers have him. I want you looking out for live spies not dead ones." He remounted his horse and set off at a leisurely pace for Najarind. As the soldiers were dragging the messenger's corpse away they heard him whistling a love song.

# Chapter Twenty-one

"It has to be now, Fordel." Anni wrung her hands, wishing Channan's friend would look up from his wine goblet. She paced the short width of the room.

"I can't leave, I'm in charge of the palace guard."

"I've thought of that. Tell Ersilla there are reports of another attack by these monsters near your family estates. She'll have to let you go."

"She must know there hasn't been one."

"But she can't admit it without incriminating herself. Besides, it means she'll be able to get you out of the way."

Fordel rocked back in his chair and looked her in the eye. "It means you'll be alone here."

"Someone has to find Channan. You can do that more easily than I, just as I can more easily find out what's happening here."

Fordel stared into his goblet again.

"There's no time to waste, Fordel. You have to be well on your way before Torslin gets back to challenge Ersilla's permission."

"There's no guarantee that she'll grant it."

"Then you'll go?"

Fordel drained his wine and set his chair right with a thud. "If I don't, I suppose I'll never hear the end of it. I can't stand being nagged."

Anni took his face in her hands and planted a kiss full on his lips.

"Now, if you'd tried that kind of persuasion in the first place... "

"Give me a chance to get to her sitting room first."

"But... "

Anni paused at the door. "Trust me."

Minutes later she entered Ersilla's sitting room carrying swatches of cloth and braid.

"I need your approval for the coronation decorations."

Ersilla's frown of irritation immediately disappeared. She pushed aside the papers she had been scanning, and the two were deep in discussions on the relative merits of velvets and brocades when a maid entered to announce that Fordel was begging an urgent audience.

"You always call at such inconvenient moments," she complained as he saluted her.

"Pardon, Highness, but I've had news that demands my immediate return to my estates."

"Impossible! How can you think of it with the coronation taking place?"

"There are reports of fal-worm attacks nearby. I have to... "

"Impossible!" Ersilla threw down the cloth she had been considering.

Anni had snatched a hand to her face in horror. "So there were others!"

"Impossible!" Ersilla insisted.

"But they're getting closer to the city," Anni blurted. "They can't be allowed to get here." She clutched Ersilla's hand in apparent panic, draping the fine silk she was holding over it. Ersilla was distracted. "Perhaps we should ask Lord Torslin... "

"I am queen!" Ersilla stiffened. "I don't have to consult anyone."

"I only thought... "

"Well, don't! You haven't even the wit to choose a gown befitting your station." Ersilla tossed the silk back at her. "Very well, go. I'm sure I shall be able to manage without you. Right now I have other things to attend to." She flicked her fingers at Fordel to indicate he was dismissed. He gave her a formal salute.

"Ondd's wings protect you, Highness." His eyes met Anni's and then he was gone. For a moment Anni found the fine weave of the cloth blurred.

Ersilla demanded her attention. "Are these all the samples you have?" She sorted through them, checking one against another.

"Do you want me to leave them here? Give you a chance to choose properly, only Mistress Hexem will be waiting and... "

"Yes, yes, go." Ersilla took some swatches to the window and was holding them to the light as Anni slipped out.

She reached the corridor overlooking the courtyard just in time to see Fordel's horse clatter through the gates. She craned her neck for a last glimpse. Passing servants seeing her there a few minutes later, shook their heads and whispered sympathetically. King Channan's youngest sister evidently grieved for him as keenly as they did for their own loved ones.

Ersilla's maid was white-faced apart from a spreading red blotch on one cheek. She stood inside Anni's door as if she would melt through it if she could.

"At this time of night?" Anni swung her legs out of bed and began hauling on her dressing-robe.

"I'm sorry, Highness, but she said straight away."

Screamed it, more like, thought Anni. "All right, tell her I'm coming."

"She said I was to bring you back."

Anni's fingers fumbled with her buttons. It was not the first time Ersilla had woken her in the middle of the night on a whim.

"What is it this time? Didn't the maid smooth her sheets properly?"

The maid shook her head. "He's there," she whispered, and Anni felt fear breathe on her neck.

Ersilla's voice could be heard as they approached her door. "I don't need to explain myself to anyone. I'm queen."

"Only if I back you, and your stupidity's making that increasingly difficult," Torslin growled.

"How dare you!"

"You let Channan's best friend leave the palace, when you must have known he was lying! Unless there's something you're not telling me. Where are the... "

The maid knocked and quickly stood aside for Anni. The argument broke off instantly, but as Ersilla and Torslin turned their attention to her she felt the force of their anger.

"You took your time," Ersilla snapped.

"What's the matter? We're not under attack, are we?" Anni allowed her apprehension to show as she looked from one to the other.

"No, Highness, which is just as well since I returned to find the commander of the palace guard absent." Torslin held a chair for her and stood behind her shoulder, his bulk intimidating.

"Didn't Fordel leave things in good order?"

"Fah! He never puts them in good order when he's here. I don't see what the fuss is about." Ersilla threw herself down on a chair by the fire, glowering at Torslin.

"It seems he was in such a hurry to leave, Princess Anni, that he took no one with him. If he should have the misfortune to come across an Amrad patrol... "

"Why should he do that? His estates lie in the opposite direction."

"Indeed, but the party I sent to escort him found no sign of him on the road."

"Perhaps he knows a shortcut."

"Perhaps." Torslin grasped the back of her chair and suddenly brought his mouth close to her ear. "Do you, Princess? Did Fordel tell you his route?"

"I don't think he mentioned it at all, did he, Ersilla? We were discussing fabrics for the coronation when he asked for leave, but I'm sure we'd have remembered." Anni looked at Ersilla for confirmation.

"And he didn't mention it to you before?"

"No, I was as surprised as Ersilla."

Torslin straightened. "Well, we shall just have to hope he doesn't meet with misfortune."

"Truly. It would be awful if the rumours were true." Anni rose. "I'll remember him in my prayers."

Torslin smiled and bowed as she left, but Anni had the uneasy feeling that he had understood her double meaning as easily as she had his. No sooner had the door closed behind her than she heard Ersilla's rage burst.

"You see? I told you... "

"Yes, yes... " Torslin's voice was tightly controlled.

A movement caught Anni's eye. Ersilla's maid was cowering in the shadows.

"I always liked Lord Fordel," she said.

Anni's face pulled into a smile: so many of the maids and courtiers' wives did.

"I hope he's careful," the maid continued.

"So do I, dear."

Anni headed quietly back to her bed. Torslin would not be convinced so easily that she knew nothing. She would have to take greater care herself.

At that moment the guard was changing at the messenger post.

"About time too! It's freezing out here–any spies or assassins'd have too much sense to be mucking about on a night like this." There was a spurt of flame as the soldier going off duty attempted to light his pipe. His comrade struck the igniter from his hand and stamped on it.

"Are you mad? Do you want to get us both killed? Tell the world where we are, why don't you?"

"You're jumpy tonight."

"With good cause, I reckon. If Amradoc can send one spy it can send a handful of warriors."

"He weren't no spy neither, and he weren't the type to make a break for it. Why'd he ride in here bold as you like, tell me that? Nah, it was his whole bearing–I reckon he was what he said he was."

"Well, he's dead now, so it don't really matter."

"Don't it though? Then why's the old man so tightlipped about it?"

"Don't know. Maybe the answer'll come to me once I've slept on... "

"Shh!"

They stood statue-like and listened.

"Nothing."

"Thought I heard a horse whinny."

"Probably one of ours."

They waited a moment more.

"I'm turning in, before you make me as jumpy as you."

From the darkness beyond the messenger post's corral Fordel stroked his horse's muzzle. He had intended leading the tired beast until they were beyond sight and earshot, but something was making the horse skittish. He waited to let the new sentry settle and relax. His journey so far had been a series of such detours and cautious waits. Although Torslin had travelled the road himself earlier in the day, his horse pounding past Fordel's hiding place on its way back to the city, that would not stop him sending out patrols to check on Fordel's tale. His horse tossed its head and shifted against him. Whatever was making it nervous would provoke another whinny before long. Fordel decided to risk moving.

He led the horse further down the slope away from the road. They had only gone a yard or two when the horse side-stepped and would have bolted but for Fordel's tight grip on the bridle. His foot met with something soft. Gingerly he felt around with one hand. A body: no doubt the Amrad spy the guards had mentioned, if that was what he was. Fordel patted the corpse, feeling for papers or some sort of identification. He traced the outline of a signet ring on the man's little finger. The body was stiff and the ring was not easy to remove, especially with the horse tugging at its reins, but he managed it. Once over the border, it might mean the difference between finding Channan and meeting the same fate as this poor soul–if he got that far.

Ro leaned over the maps in Darian's counsel tent. Uwert stood beside her pointing out features. The lamplight cast mischievous shadows and patterns from his hand to confuse her further.

"Here's where we are now, there's where we camped yesterday and there's Ondd's Basin. Over here is the border with Ortann."

Ro frowned. "I felt sure there'd be a connection, but it doesn't fit. I've tried linking the line of the melody on the stone to all sorts of features around it–there's nothing."

She straightened as Darian, Jubb and Lar entered.

"I'm sorry, I've wasted everyone's time." She blushed as she explained her theory, hardly daring to meet Lar's gaze.

Darian took a closer look at the map. "Yes, the lines of a song could be stylised river courses or roads." He gave Ro a smile. "It was a good theory."

"Except it doesn't work." Ro began to roll up the map, but Darian stopped her.

"Perhaps you missed something. What did you use as your starting point, the stone?" He began comparing the song with the map. "Maybe it begins elsewhere."

"Or maybe the scale's wrong," Jubb suggested. "Perhaps you need a map this big." He flung his arms wide making them all duck.

Lar joined the others in looking. "This only shows surface features, not the lines of power in the stone or the sweep of the vitae."

"Don't be disheartened," Darian reassured Ro. "Everything that might help is worth exploring."

Lar still looked closely at the map as she spoke. "But this map's wrong."

"It's extremely accurate. The most experienced charters in Amradoc drew it only two years ago." Uwert pushed out his chin.

"Yes, Uwert commissioned them himself." Jubb nodded.

"But the land changed a few days ago. There should now be ripples in Ondd's Basin and a kink in the road, and the course of the river has altered," Lar insisted.

"So, the songs might refer to a time past or a time in the future." Ro's frown cleared for an instant.

"Maybe you just chose the wrong song," Jubb teased.

"Whatever, it's hopeless. Even if there is a connection it would take years of studying to find it."

"Try this one, Ro." Jubb struck a pose. "There once was a handsome young courtier, whose wisdom brought glory and fame. Admired by the men and adored by the girls and Jubb was his name!"

Uwert sighed and shook his head. "Lar's right." He winced as Jubb's song almost obliterated his words. "I'll see these are amended." He strode out with Jubb capering after him.

Ro and Lar followed. As they neared their wagons, they heard the sound of a man's laughter and a gasp of pain.

"Channan!" Dovinna's whisper was anxious.

Ro would have headed for their voices. Lar's hand on her arm prevented her. The Earth-hearer shook her head.

"Sometimes, my dear, the help of a third person is not only unnecessary but quite undesirable." She walked on.

Ro's mouth formed an 'O'. She placed her hands over her ears so she could be sure not to overhear until she was safely in the wagon.

Dovinna and Channan continued walking slowly towards the healers' tent oblivious of any observation.

"I knew this was a bad idea, you'll open your wounds," Dovinna scolded.

"There's a limit to how much staring at four canvas walls a man can take." He grimaced as he straightened. "Anyway, it wasn't walking that made me wince, it was you making me laugh."

"That's right, blame me," Dovinna said lightly, but mention of 'blame' made Channan's smile vanish.

"Dovi, I... "

She put her fingers to his lips. "All the evidence was against me, I know."

"I never wanted to believe it. I couldn't believe it despite everything–that's what tore me apart. It was easier to go along with what everyone else wanted than to think. I've made a complete pig's breakfast of things. So many people have died because I let Torslin do as he pleased–and now I'm marching on my own city with a foreign army. It's no excuse, but I couldn't help thinking of all the times I'd wished father dead. It was as if you were being punished for my guilt."

"He wasn't the most affectionate father."

"Still... "

"Still, I've asked myself many times how I would've acted had I been in your position, and I truly don't know." They gazed silently at each other until Dovinna blushed. "What I do know is that you've tested your strength enough for one day. Come, you must return to your bed."

"I'd go more willingly if you came too." He cast her a sideways glance.

"If you weren't injured I'd give that suggestion the response it deserves!"

"Give it to me anyway."

Dovinna aimed a playful blow at his arm, but Channan staggered coughing. Alarmed, she rushed to support him. Instantly, he grabbed her close with both arms. She stopped struggling and they looked long into each other's eyes. Their lips slowly met. When Channan released her, Dovinna tottered trying to get her balance. Arm in arm they supported each other back to the healers' tent.

The slow-moving column was on its way once more. Darian kept the pace leisurely to give men and beasts a chance to recover from the battle and allow the ambassador time to return. Their progress from the Basin of Ondd had been slow from the start. The roads were ruptured by the earth-dance and they frequently came upon pockets of fleeing Ortanian soldiers. All were taken before Channan and given a choice whether to return to the city with him or discard their weapons and head for home. For many, Lar's song had shaken their bones as well as the earth's. The column passed a handful of demoralized soldiers as they started off again after one of these halts. Ro sat in Edun's wagon making a fuss of the onddikins.

"At least we'll have plenty of weapons to fight Torslin with," Edun commented.

Ro pushed the image away and concentrated on the onddikins. Edun had spent much of his time of late feeding, grooming and exercising them. He said they needed constant care and attention to make sure they remembered their parts in his act, but Ro had a feeling it was in some measure to avoid Mirri, who detested them almost as much as she did the unruly Chickens.

"Perhaps I should take them for their exercise this evening, give you and Mirri a chance to be together," she teased. Pirik, who was having its leathery neck stroked, made a chirring noise in its throat almost as if it was chuckling.

"I can always throw you off this wagon, you know."

"Or blast me onto the mystic plane."

"Don't tempt me. Hello, what's going on now?" Edun hauled on the reins.

"I'll go and see." Ro jumped down with Pirik flapping on her shoulder. She was not the only one curious to see what the hold-up was. Channan's stooped figure was being helped along by Dovinna.

The healer called to her. "Scouting party's come back with another rider. Perhaps it's the ambassador."

The three hurried on as fast as they could. The scene they came on made them cry out.

"Fordel!"

The Lord had his hands tied behind his back and was on his knees before King Darian, Uwert and Jubb, who was trying to restrain Chickens from licking him.

"Naughty dog!"

Fordel laughed. "No doubt I could do with a wash, especially after your officer's kind assistance from my horse." He looked at the dusting of earth over the front of his tunic.

"We caught him on the road coming from the border. He must've been hiding in the rushes." The officer in charge of the scouting party looked inclined to push him into the dirt again.

"On the contrary, I came in search of a friend–I see I've found him." He hitched round on his knees the better to face Channan. His laugh of delight made the faces of many around him break into grins. "You don't look too bad for a ghost. I've seen you look worse with a hangover."

"Fordel." Channan would have gone to him, but Darian interrupted.

"Who sent you?"

"You're an enemy, King Darian. Why should I tell you?"

The officer made to strike him, but Darian gestured a halt.

"Whether I'm your enemy or not depends on who sent you."

"Say rather an enemy of Ortann. You're holding my king and my friend prisoner."

"No, Fordel. I've learned the truth while I've been here. I'm no prisoner," Channan intervened.

"Save for the chains of a lady's soft arms, eh?" Fordel winked at Dovinna.

"I'll vouch for him, Darian. Fordel prefers carousing to intrigue. He's not one of Torslin's tools."

Uwert stepped forward. "Then why won't he say who sent him?"

"Perhaps he wants us to guess," Jubb said. "Look Pirik's whispering its guess to him."

The onddikin had left Ro's shoulder to settle on the ground beside Fordel where it sat with its head cocked as if weighing him up. The animal flittered to his shoulder and began sorting his hair with its beak.

"We've no time for games, Jubb," Uwert reproved.

"If it helps, Sire, we found this on him." The officer stepped forward and handed Darian something. The King held it up. It was a ring. There was a hiss of indrawn breath from Uwert.

"What happened to the owner of this?"

"I found him dead by the roadside."

"Liar!"

"I... " Ro interrupted, but Darian's frown silenced her.

Fordel saw her for the first time. "Well, well, my Iyessi friend. Remember what I told you all those double-weeks ago in Najarind? It takes a liar to spot a liar."

"I... " Ro began again.

Uwert interrupted. "This is not a matter for you to decide."

"I was only going to suggest that we should continue this somewhere where King Channan can sit down."

All eyes turned to Channan, whose face was drained to such an extent that even his lips were grey. Only Dovinna's support was keeping him upright. Ignoring his protests, a chair was brought for him and a canopy hastily erected a little apart from the main body of the army.

"So, Lord Fordel, what name did the onddikins whisper to you?" Darian asked drily.

"The Princess's–Anni's," Fordel said to Channan. "She couldn't accept that you were dead. I thought it improbable, but she was the one with the courage to act."

"What about Ersilla? What does she believe?"

Fordel shrugged. "Whatever suits her–and it suits her to believe you're dead. Your arrival at Najarind will be highly inconvenient for her, spoiling her plans for the coronation as it will."

"What? Without even a period of mourning?" Channan was open-mouthed.

"One fault your darling sister doesn't have is hypocrisy. Deceit isn't the same thing."

"What of our embassy to the city?" Uwert demanded. "They can't pretend they don't know King Channan's still living."

"They can if he never arrived. I took that ring from the hand of a man killed as a spy trying to escape. Any other such embassy will meet a similar fate. If you arrive at the city with King Darian's army behind you, they'll no doubt claim you're an impostor, and who'll question it?"

"So what are you proposing? That I retire to the country and allow those traitors to do what they want?"

"No, somehow you have to convince enough of the population of the truth. Once you're back in the city, no one will be able to deny who you are."

Channan nodded. "There are many Najarindian soldiers marching with us. We could send them back in the small groups we found them. They could spread the word."

Uwert agreed. "It would need to be carefully done, but it could work. Especially if we continue our march on the city and draw their attention our way."

"You'll still need a way into the city," Fordel cautioned. "I can't go back, and there's more." He told them of his suspicions regarding the fal-worms.

"Dear Ondd!" Channan's fists tightened. "They'd use such monsters? And you left Anni there with them!"

"Someone had to stay, and she wouldn't have come with me. They'd have missed her immediately, and we'd both have been caught."

"But what do they want the creatures for?" Dovinna clutched Channan's hand.

"An excuse to attack the Iyessi or a weapon to use against them. We don't know all. Anni hoped... she intends finding them and destroying them."

"Then I have no choice. I must lay siege to my own city." Channan's mouth formed a determined line.

"Unless you can get in another way." Ro's cheeks burned as all eyes turned on her. "I've already agreed to return to Najarind if need be. It seems that now's the time." She spoke with light confidence. If they had been Iyessi they would have felt immediately how much of an act it was.

# Chapter Twenty-two

The door was locked. Anni fumbled through the bunch of keys at her waist; keys to trunks, keys to store rooms. Many of the palace's locks were old and would submit to a different key. Hopefully, the door leading to the room above the under-cellar would too. A swift glance told her the guards had resumed their game of dice. She found a key that looked the right size and tried it. The guards would force the door if she commanded them to, but better that they should not notice where she had gone. She tried another key. The lock had been oiled recently. As she jiggled the key, she felt the lock give a little. She eased the key back and felt again, resisting the urge to force it. Her hand felt clammy. She wiped it on her skirt, and exhaling slowly eased the key into place. When it suddenly gave, Anni almost fell into the room on the other side. Checking the guards were still occupied, she drew the door to behind her.

The cellar was dark and she had to wait while her eyes adjusted. The sliver of light around the door showed her a lamp on a shelf. She lit it and held it up, bracing herself against what might be revealed. The room contained a few opened crates, otherwise it was empty. A trail in the dusty floor showed where Ersilla's gown had swept a path to a trapdoor. The lamp sent shivering shadows around the room. She hesitated. The smell of mildew and damp was stronger here, as if something long dead was oozing decay. Anni looked about her, trying not to hear the words of the messenger who had reported the fal-worm attack. The horror in his voice had left her with the sick feeling of inescapable nightmare. By one of the crates an iron rod had been left forgotten. Anni hefted it in her hand, set the lamp down, and prised the trapdoor open as quietly as she could. There were sounds of something dragging.

With the lamp in one hand and the iron rod in the other, Anni started down the narrow dogleg steps. She turned the corner and almost dropped her makeshift weapon as the stench assaulted her. She retched. Ahead of her in the gloom was a row of heavy metal cages. Beyond was a metal grille through which a draught drove the stink towards her. There was a dappling pattern of light on the curved ceiling. The under-cellar must lead to the palace waste channels, but the smell was closer to her. Anni forced herself down the remaining steps. The dragging sound was now accompanied by a moist crunching. The cages drew her.

The nearest writhed with the bulbous pallid bodies of fal-worms the size of large dogs. The mandibles worked methodically champing through something which looked like one of their number. Anni did not care to think what else it might be. She lowered the rod. There was no way she could get near enough to strike an effective blow with such a weapon, and if she did manage to despatch one, the others would rend her to shreds. She walked on. The five cages at the end were bigger reaching almost as high as herself.

"Great Ondd! Ersilla, what have you done?" She fell to her knees. The world swung crazily.

At the centre of the cage was an immense monster with a slavering maw, whose sole desire in life was to devour all that came in its path. It shifted its bulk, perhaps hearing her terrified whisper and sensing the nearness of warm blood, and thudded against the bars. The metal had bubbled into sores of corrosion, slick with saliva. Eventually, in days perhaps, the bars would weaken and disintegrate under the monster's weight and it would be free. There were four more cages.

"This is worse, far worse... " Anni choked on the smell, feeling herself sinking under it.

Gripping the iron rod so tightly that the edges bit into her hand, Anni anchored herself. She pushed to her feet and forced herself to walk calmly back along the row of cages. At the foot of the steps, she turned to face them again. The lamplight caught on the looming shapes. She drew her hand back as if to throw the lamp, then stopped. Whatever she did, she had to be sure that it would kill all the beasts, without accidentally freeing any of them. She headed up the steps. As she rounded the dogleg, a figure emerged from the deepest shadow at the far end of the cages. The reflected light from the waste channel made his bald head appear polished, and gleamed on his teeth as Ayif smiled.

"So, little princess–neither so innocent nor so stupid as you want us to believe."

He bowed extravagantly before each of the cages. "Mighty Lethir, I worship you in the form of your lesser creatures. Witness my devotion!"

He nicked his arm with his surgeon's knife, draining the trickle of blood into a shallow cup. When there was enough to flow around the base, he flung the contents over the largest fal-worm. It writhed trying to reach each spatter of warm liquid, its saliva frothing around its gape. The Gindullan bowed before the beast once more, then stepped up to the grille between the under-cellar and the waste channel.

It slid back easily and silently. There was a ledge on either side of the channel, which was joined by lesser runnels, before flowing out to join the river beyond the city walls. At intervals metal ladders climbed to the surface where they emerged from the ground as chimney-like structures. They had been constructed at the same time as the waste channels to provide access for maintenance and were generally avoided due to the smell. Ayif had claimed the ground around the base of one in which to grow herbs for his medicines. It had allowed him access to many areas of the palace where he would otherwise have been unwelcome. The Gindullan hurried along the ledge until he reached the ladder he wanted. He emerged into the fresh air without appearing to appreciate the change, picked a bundle of herbs and re-entered the palace.

The courtiers he passed drew away from him. One snatched a handkerchief to his nose, muttering "foreigners!". The smell of the under-cellar clung to him, but he did not pause even to wipe the sweat from his bald crown. He tried several chambers before he found the one he wanted. Lord Torslin was brooding by the fire in what had been King Berinn's bedchamber.

"What do you want?" Ignoring the Lord's frown of annoyance, Ayif adopted a carnivorous smile and began his tale.

Anni could not get warm. She stared into the flames of the fire she had ordered set in her sitting chamber, wishing they could burn away the memory of what she had seen. On leaving the under-cellar she had headed for Ersilla's chamber, but had discarded the idea of trying to reason with her sister before she had gone three steps. Her sister had never listened to her before, and now... no one sane would have kept the monsters in the first place. An appeal to Ersilla's reason was bound to fail. No, she had to rid Najarind of the pestilence Ersilla had brought into it, even if it meant destroying the palace in the process. She had to go back down there. She shuddered and put another log on the fire. Flames caught a trickle of sap, spurting into a fizz of heat. Quick-fire! She would have to use quick-fire. Fordel would have known the best way, but she had sent him away.

"If only Channan was here," she sighed.

"We all grieve for him, Highness."

Anni started. She had forgotten the maids were still there.

The younger girl blushed and bobbed a curtsy. "I wanted to say–thank you, Miss."

"Highness," Tillenne corrected.

"Thank you, Highness. You were right. My man arrived back last night, just before curfew. He got lost after the battle and he's been dodging Amrad soldiers since. I just wish there'd been a happy ending for you too." She stumbled over the words.

"Thank you. Are many soldiers still returning?" Anni felt reluctant to let them go. She wanted to talk away the nightmare.

"Quite a few, Highness." Tillenne curtsied. "We'd better be getting on, Highness."

"Of course."

They took their bundle of clean linen through to the bedchamber. The new maid did not quite fasten the door, and Anni could hear Tillenne's hushed voice giving her instructions. Her gaze drifted back to the fire. There was a tap at the door.

"Come."

Anni suppressed a shudder as Ayif entered.

"Highness. Queen Ersilla–please, you must come straight away."

The Princess's heart leapt higher than the rest of her body. "What's happened? Is she ill? Why aren't you with her? Where's her maid?" She was halfway across the room before the triumph in Ayif's smile halted her.

"Please, I'll answer your questions on the way."

As Anni hesitated, Ayif grasped her elbow and steered her towards the door. She wrested it free swinging round in the process. There was a glimpse of a worried face through the open crack of her bedroom door, then Ayif bundled her out.

"There's no time to waste."

"I insist on knowing where we're going."

"Don't you know your own palace?"

She did indeed. They were heading towards the military apartments and beyond them lay the jail cells. Anni gave up verbal protestations, casting about for witnesses instead. The corridors and guard chambers were empty.

"Lord Torslin has commanded a full drill of the royal guard. He fears they're growing sloppy."

Anni composed herself as best she could. So, this was Torslin's work; at least he was open to reason where his best interests were concerned. Her suspicion was confirmed as Ayif halted before an isolated cell door. Torslin was waiting for them. The physician pushed her into the middle of the cell, remaining in front of the door to bar her exit.

"Well, well, Anni," Torslin began, his tone and look that of a disappointed father. "How long have we known each other? Since you were a babe. Yet it seems I haven't known you at all." He nodded at her to sit on the cell's lone stool. She remained standing.

"I fear we've both been mistaken in many things," she replied.

"But harbouring monsters in the palace... "

Anni heard Ayif move behind her. Torslin threw him a warning look. She hesitated; he could be testing her.

"We both know I didn't put them there."

"Then why didn't you report them to me?" Torslin reproved gently.

"My sister is queen. Surely she should be the first to know of such things."

"Shall I tell you what I think?" Torslin began pacing around her. "I think you want the crown for yourself and would use these creatures to hold us all to ransom."

"And I think Ersilla will take it as a personal affront to her status when she hears how you've treated me."

"She won't know," Ayif blurted.

Torslin rounded on him. "Silence!"

"But, Lord. Why go to all this trouble?"

"Because we need to know who's involved with her." Torslin's face was full of disgust. "Now, tell us all, and maybe you can go back to your duties."

"Don't you think I'll be missed?" Anni's one hope was to keep them guessing.

Torslin smiled. "Of course, my dear. The servants will miss you ordering them about, and Ersilla will eventually realise that she has one less person to bully, but you've always been such a plain little mouse–it's bound to take them some while. Anything can happen in the meanwhile."

"That's very true, Lord Torslin. Who knows who might come looking for me?"

Torslin threw back his head in over-hearty laughter. "Fordel, you mean? I'm sorry, Anni, but that Lord's had and discarded some of the prettiest women in Najarind. Do you honestly think he'd jeopardise his comfort, let alone his life, to rescue you?" He thrust his face close to hers. "Why don't we leave you to think about it for a while? Don't take too long though, eh? These cells are such damp unhealthy places, and it's anyone's guess what infection the last occupant may have had. We wouldn't want you to fall sick, would we?"

Anni returned his stare coolly. When the door clanged shut behind him, she seated herself calmly on the stool. She was a daughter of the royal house. Whatever Torslin might say, she would be missed. She would not show fear.

Ro found herself in the uniform of a Najarindian soldier again. At first she had been inclined to be offended at Edun complimenting her on how well the role of a gangling youth suited her, but now she and Jubb were approaching the walls of the city, she was relieved. Even the homecoming soldiers they travelled with tended to forget and call her "boy". Unfortunately, the role of a soldier did not sit so well on Jubb. Even his attempts to march were marred by irrepressible skips and hops. The city walls seemed to lean over them. Jubb hung his head.

"Come on, Jubb. Look relieved at least. This is meant to be a joyous homecoming," Ro urged.

"I wish Chickens was here."

Ro sighed. It had taken all Darian's persuasion to convince Jubb to leave the dog behind.

"You'd never have smuggled him into the palace. Besides, he'll protect Darian while we're away."

The fool nodded.

"And irritate Uwert," Ro added and was rewarded with an impish chuckle.

"Did you see his face when... " he broke off as their small band halted.

The officer in charge, who was a burly middle-aged man born to be a sergeant, walked along the line.

"This is it then, lads. You all know your stories, but don't volunteer anything. Unless you're asked something, leave the talking to me."

He called them to attention and they marched smartly up to the main gate, where the sentries halted them. Ro's breath came out in a hiss as she recognised Pachand standing to one side surveying the proceedings. As his eyes travelled over them, she hastily looked away, staring to the front as if on parade. She was aware of Jubb shifting from one foot to the other. Then she saw the sergeant salute. He called them to attention and the sentries stood aside. Out of the corner of her eye Ro saw Pachand move away from the wall and say something to one of the sentries. Cold fingers of panic gripped the base of her neck.

"Wait!" The sentry strode into their lines and stopped in front of Jubb. "This is no soldier."

The men around them grinned, and the sergeant laughed as he too scrutinised Jubb.

"You can say that again. Reckon his wits have been scrambled by one blow too many. Not much use to anyone in a battle, but the men think he brings 'em luck–sort of a mascot."

Ro held her breath as Jubb's face began to contort and his hand jerked towards the place where he had stowed his Words of Power. The sentry looked at Pachand. The Captain nodded.

"Very well, report to the barracks."

Pachand watched them march through the gates. When they turned the corner, Ro risked a glance back. He was standing in the gateway looking after them. For an instant their gaze met. The Captain's pose did not alter. At the entrance to the barracks the press of people still waiting in hope of finding missing loved ones, forced them to break formation. Ro struggled forward, ignoring the grasping hands and pleas for news. Another glance over her shoulder showed a familiar figure following.

The sergeant had his arm about a woman caught between laughter and sobs. "Best get off while you can, lad." He winked at Ro. "We'll make sure you're not followed."

The woman looked about to scold, but he kissed the words from her lips.

"Come on." Ro grabbed Jubb and dragged the reluctant fool away from the celebrating soldiers, who formed an unruly barrier across the road. "Quick march!"

"Where to?"

"Here!" Ro yanked Jubb behind a building. She peeped around the edge. Someone was pushing through the news-thirsty crowd. Behind them there was the easy clop of hooves.

"Starlight!" Jubb cried.

Ro turned to see him throwing his arms about the neck of a horse led by the head ostler.

"Back again then," he said, eyeing their uniforms. "I suppose you'll be wanting some dinner and your old place back."

Jubb let go of the horse and threw his arms about the ostler instead. Keeping the horse between them and sight of the main thoroughfare they walked back to the stables. Surrounded by the comforting smells of hay and the warm earthiness of horses, Ro felt safer. The ostler's unflappable manner reassured her as well as it did his charges.

"You'll be wanting to see your laundry-maid friends then, young lady."

Ro nodded excitedly.

"You'd better not go like that. Mistress Hexem'll take you for a good-for-nothing trying to tumble her girls." He chuckled quietly pleased with his joke.

He was right, she would have to find something else to wear.

The ostler did not notice her discomfort. "Why don't we all go and celebrate your safe return at the Flighty Mare? The ale's good and we might be able to squeeze an old gown out of the landlady." He gave Jubb a knowing wink.

"Hah! That's a good one. 'Squeeze' it out of her!" Jubb jogged the ostler with his elbow. He stood up smacking his lips. "Lead us to it."

Ro shook her head violently.

"I dare say you're right," the ostler said. "Inns are no place for polite young ladies. Come on, Jubb m'lad."

He linked arms with the fool, who waved to Ro over his shoulder as he allowed himself to be led away. She threw up her hands exasperated by the need to resume her mute role. Still, the phlegmatic ostler should keep Jubb from drawing too much attention to himself, and it was she Pachand had recognised. But she could not afford to sit there and wait for them to return with or without a gown. King Channan and the Amrad army had not been far behind them, and they would be relying on her to secure them safe entry to the city.

She peeped through the stable doors, checking the figures milling about for the purposeful form of Pachand. Another glance in the direction of the laundry-yard showed no one familiar. She took a deep breath and strode towards the flapping washing lines with a swagger as she had seen other young soldiers do. Once among the maze of wet laundry she crouched to check for feet waiting hidden behind the shirts and tablecloths. Keeping well away from the laundry doors, she skirted the rows of bedlinen. When she found a line with clothes on it she straightened and walked confidently, her heart pounding, towards the nearest gown. Without stopping to check whether it was dry or the right size, she unpegged it, rolled it into an indeterminate bundle and swaggered back to the stable. She had almost regained its safety when the martial chimes of the city and citadel gates made her stumble. The gates were being closed, but curfew was still hours away. As she hurried back to the stall, she knew it could mean only one thing– Darian's army must be in sight.

When she put on the stolen clothes, Ro realised her mistake. This was not the plain garb of a servant but the flamboyant dress of a lady. The feel of the smooth fabric would have given her pleasure in other circumstances, but no one belonging in such fancy clothes would haunt the servants' passages. She tidied her hair as best she could and unclipped the scarf draped over the gown's breast, drawing it over her head veil-like instead. There was no alternative but to be bold.

News of the approaching army must have spread fast. Soldiers tramped away from the citadel in the direction of the outer gates, while men and women struggled to find vantage points from where they could see the road to Amradoc. Many finely dressed ladies scooped up their trailing gowns and headed for the upper floors of the palace. Ro joined them, grateful that all eyes were turned outside the city. She threaded her way through the jostling courtiers, each competing to be the most affected or courageous. Only once, as she patiently made her way towards Anni's apartments, did she catch a view through one of the windows. The front ranks of Darian's army were already outside the city beyond catapult shot, and the long tail of soldiers flowed around them forming an encircling moat of men.

Nearer the royal apartments there were fewer people. Ro's progress here was swifter, but more dangerous. She darted back into a doorway as Ersilla swept out of a chamber, demanding that Torslin should attend her immediately in the audience chamber. As soon as the way was clear Ro continued.

The more deserted the corridors became, the more jumpy she grew. She kept thinking she could hear footsteps behind her, but when she turned, ostensibly to check the hem of her gown, no one was there. She was so pre-occupied with listening that she had already taken several steps along the corridor leading to Anni's chambers before she saw the guard outside her door. She managed to keep going without changing pace, until she rounded the next bend. There she allowed herself to lean against the wall while she tried to calm her breathing. Without Anni what hope had she of opening the gates? At the end of the corridor was a tapestry, behind which Ro knew there was a door to the servants' stairs. It was tempting to slip down them and flee the palace. But then what? The gates were closed: she and Jubb were trapped in the city.

There was a sudden hush, as the chatter of excited courtiers in the public wings stilled. Something must be happening. In the silence, Ro suddenly heard the unmistakable sound of quick footsteps, but from ahead of her, not behind. Ro forced herself to walk on with the arrogant nonchalance of a courtier, not deigning to notice others. The maid coming the other way almost collided with her.

"Tch... Really!" Ro adopted a nasal tone.

"Sorry, Mistress." The maid bobbed a curtsy. As she rose her eyes widened with recognition.

Ro put a finger to her lips. "Tillenne," she whispered. "If I could've wished to meet anyone, it would be you!"

"How did you get here? You can talk!" The maid glanced about nervously.

"I need to see Princess Anni."

The name made Tillenne start.

"And you? If you were meant to be here you wouldn't be so nervous."

"The same as you. I need to see Princess Anni. Listen." She knocked at the nearest door and pulled Ro behind her into the room. She threw open the casement allowing the voices outside to float clearly up to them. Darian's army was now virtually in place blocking all exits from the city. In the space between them were two riders, one bearing a parley banner and the dragon banner of the royal house. Gold glinted on the helmet of the other rider.

"He says he's King Channan and that Princess Ersilla's to let him in. Can it be possible?"

Ro nodded. The figures were so far away they looked unreal. Torslin's harsh voice cut across the awestruck silence.

"Lies! I saw King Channan fall. Do you think if there was any hope of his survival I would've left the field without him? This is an Amrad trick. Darian seeks to fool us into admitting an impostor!"

The words were echoed by heralds relaying the message to the figures on the field. "Impostor! Impostor!" hung on the air.

Ro strained to hear Channan's response before it was overlaid with the voice of the messenger. She knew what it would be.

"Send Princess Anni, if she will, with an escort to verify my claim."

"Why Anni? I am queen. I am Ersilla, King Channan's dearest sister, and I say you lie!" Her voice was raw spite, stripped of its regal grace.

The pause while the words were relayed was maddening. Eventually the reply came back.

"Why not, Anni? Her honesty and good-nature are well known."

There were murmurs at this. Torslin's voice quelled them.

"All the palace knows Princess Anni is sick in her chamber and may not be moved. Prayers have been said for her recovery in Ondd's temple. No doubt word has reached this 'pretender' and he seeks to gain from our beloved princess's illness. Look at him, citizens of Najarind, he doesn't even look like King Channan. There's no nobility in his bearing. And what king threatens his people with a foreign army? There's no more to be said until he sends the Amrad invaders back across our borders."

Ro saw the tiny figures of Channan and the banner-rider turn back to the Amrad lines.

"But it's not true," Tillenne whispered.

"What isn't?" Ro felt her throat tighten as she saw the tears well in the maid's eyes.

"Yes, what isn't true?"

The man's voice almost made Ro jump through the window. She had been so engrossed in the drama outside that she had forgotten to be wary.

"You've led me a pretty dance, Iyessi. Halfway across the empire! And now I find you right here, where we started. If it hadn't been for finding your idiot friend carousing with the ostler I might have lost you again. Spies should know how to hold their liquor."

Ro weighed up her chances of reaching the door. "What have you done with him?" As she spoke she aimed a kick at his groin and tried to dart past. Pachand dodged easily and twisted her arm behind her.

"Run!" she urged Tillenne, but the maid remained fixed to the spot.

"She has more sense. There's nowhere she could go."

"But what they said wasn't true," Tillenne repeated. "They took her away." She clasped Pachand's arm imploringly. "Princess Anni isn't sick. I saw Ayif drag her away."

"Ayif? He's a physician, girl. Does that tell you nothing?"

Ro chose her words carefully. "Perhaps Princess Anni found out something they didn't want her to know–that Channan's alive, or that they've brought an abomination into the palace."

Pachand's expression didn't alter, but his grip on her arm tightened.

"There's one way to be sure; pay her sick room a visit."

"Her condition is contagious. No one may visit her. And I wouldn't disturb her rest; I've seen the consequences of allowing you in a sick room."

Ro thought desperately. It was Tillenne who spoke.

"But I've seen Ayif come and go freely."

"What's more important to you, Pachand? The safety of Najarind or your own health?"

Pachand wrenched Ro around to face the door. He gestured at Tillenne. "You go first, and no stupid tricks."

A moment later they were heading back down the corridor towards Anni's chambers.

# Chapter Twenty-three

"King Darian, please tell him he mustn't!" Dovinna turned anxiously to the King. They were all seated around a table outside Darian's counsel tent, where they had been planning their next move.

While Fordel had described the city's defences and weaknesses, and Lar and Raimi discussed water channels and vibrations from the stone, Channan had remained silent, gazing at the walls of Najarind. The gleaming dome of the temple of Ondd and the banners snapping in the brisk breeze above the palace were barely visible. Since they had sat down the sun had vanished behind them, hidden by purplish heads of clouds that seemed to erupt like smoke from behind the city.

"With all respect to King Darian, it doesn't matter what he says. I won't besiege my own city. Torslin was right in that: how can I make war on my own people?"

"You might not need to. Ro and Jubb might manage to open the gates, and the soldiers you sent back will support you," Uwert advised.

"If you're right, then the more I can occupy Torslin's attention the better. It might just buy them the time they need."

"You can barely sit your horse, let alone fight!" Dovinna protested. "Lar, you'll back me up. Channan's not strong enough to challenge Torslin to single combat."

"Why not wait another day?" Lar obliged.

"And while we're waiting, who knows what they're doing to Anni?"

Uwert interrupted. "She might already be dead. Forgive me, but if all I've heard about them is true, neither Torslin nor Ersilla would hesitate."

Fordel stood up. "Very well. I'll challenge Torslin as Channan's champion. At the very least it'll create a diversion, and who knows? I might stick the traitor!"

Channan shook his head. "If I can send a champion, so can he. No, it's got to be me."

Darian spoke at last. "Channan's right. He must challenge Torslin."

Dovinna rose from the table impatiently.

Channan smiled at her. "It's settled then. If you'll consent to be my squire, Fordel, and help me prepare–we'll try how much of a gambler Torslin really is."

The three headed for Channan's quarters.

Edun frowned as they left. "Is that wise? If Torslin kills him... "

Darian smiled. "You think he'll take the challenge?" He let the doubt hang in the air. "Come, Uwert, we must prepare in case Torslin decides to come out with an army behind him."

The Amrad army stood in silent respect as Channan rode into the no-man's land between it and the city, with Fordel as his second. Beside the Lord he looked slight, more suited to dancing than swordplay. He sweated under the weight of the armour, but his mouth was pressed shut on his pain.

"Fordel, if I don't survive this, promise me you'll care for Dovi. She's not as strong as she thinks."

The healer had turned away from the farewell kiss he would have given her.

"She's angry with me now, but... "

"Of course, I promise, but there's no need."

The pair halted. Channan swallowed and took a deep breath. There must be no faltering now, no weakness in his voice or hesitation in his speech.

"Torslin!" he roared. "Lord Torslin, traitor, I, King Channan of Ortann challenge you to single combat to answer for your treason!"

The words were tossed about by the strengthening wind. He repeated the challenge and heard it relayed within the city. Watching on the walls of the citadel, Ersilla's face wore a malicious grin.

"Well?" she taunted Torslin.

The Lord gestured contempt. "Let him shout. He knows the city can withstand a siege for months. All we have to do is wait and he'll run out of supplies."

Ersilla shook her head. "You should have finished the job properly in Amradoc. I seem to remember you saying that Channan was dead and Darian's army defeated."

"And I seem to remember telling you to be patient."

"Well, I think you should go out there and finish the job now. We wouldn't want the men to think you're afraid."

Torslin grinned at her and shouted back to the waiting king. "What assurance have I that I won't be attacked by Darian's army?"

As the reply was relayed, Torslin turned to Ersilla. "That should convince them."

"It doesn't convince me," Ersilla said. "I think my brother's injured and he was never much of a swordsman to begin with. Even I could beat him."

"Be my guest."

"It's you he's asking for."

"My dear, I may not trust the Amrad army, but I trust you even less. How do I know that once I'm outside the gates you'll let me in again?"

"Now, there's a thought. Unfortunately, I still need you to command the military, the men respect you. For how much longer though?" She looked pointedly at the streets below them where people had begun to gather. Faces were turned expectantly up at them: soldiers, stallholders, housewives, craftspeople, all were waiting, as Channan waited, for Torslin to act. One uniformed figure spat deliberately on the ground.

Torslin spoke loud enough for them to hear. "I command the army and I say we wait." He strode back into the palace. Ersilla amused herself staring down at the people for a further minute or two, then followed.

Outside the city, Channan turned his horse.

"Dovinna will be relieved," Fordel said, sounding not a little relieved himself.

"We'll try again in an hour," Channan answered. "And the hour after, and every other daylight hour until the coward comes out." He kicked his horse and the pair cantered towards the Amrad lines.

Keeping a firm grip on Ro, Pachand marched her and Tillenne to the cells. A guard sprang to attention at their approach. Ro could not repress a shudder remembering the finality of the door closing behind her and Dovinna, and the smell of confinement.

Pachand returned the guard's salute. "Where's the other guard?"

"Gone to see what all the excitement's about. Sorry, Captain, we don't get the news down here." His manner was a mixture of deference and sulky defiance.

"I've got another two customers for you–caught thieving."

The guard's face broke into a smile that made Ro want to scratch it off. "Going to teach 'em a lesson, Captain?"

"I suggest you take yourself off to see what's happening in the city."

The guard looked inclined to protest.

"If anyone questions you, I'll take responsibility."

"As you say, Captain." The guard licked his lips as he backed out of the guard room. "Enjoy your lessons."

Pachand's face twisted with disgust. Immediately the guard had gone, he released Ro and locked the door behind him.

"Follow me." He led the way past the main cells, down a short flight of steps to a series of narrower doors without observation grilles.

"Princess? Princess Anni?" Ro began calling as Pachand searched for the appropriate keys.

"Who's there?"

"Let me out!"

"Have mercy."

Voices responded from behind every door.

"There! That was her, I'm sure of it." Ro turned her head trying to catch which direction it came from. "It's Ro. Keep talking, Princess."

"Ro! How could it be? This is another of your tricks, Torslin."

"Here!" Ro beckoned Pachand over. He found the key and the door swung back.

Anni stood in the middle of the room, pale but erect, her face composed and her hands folded in front of her. An untouched tray of food lay at her feet. When she recognised Ro she sank to the stool.

"Have we won? How long have I been in here? I tried to keep track, but... "

"There's no time now," Ro explained. "We must open the gates."

Anni nodded. "There's a master control in the gate tower on the citadel wall. I don't know how it works. It will override the individual gate mechanisms. I'll show you." She rose and swayed.

"You're ill." Pachand caught her.

"No, just hungry. I daredn't touch anything they left." She looked up as if recognising Pachand for the first time. "Ah, Captain. I'd hoped we could rely on you."

Pachand gave Anni his arm as she regained her balance. "I've only ever sought to serve Najarind." He looked at Ro as he spoke.

"Later, Pachand. Find somewhere safe for your princess. Jubb and I'll manage the gates."

"Wait." Anni stopped her. "You should know how mad my sister's become."

They listened while Anni recounted what she had found in the under-cellar. Her words were unadorned, but they carried force.

"We must destroy them before she has a chance to use them. I think quick-fire would work."

"Quick-fire?" Ro had never heard of it.

"I know how to use it, Highness, if you're strong enough to show me the way."

"You'd feel better... " Tillenne hesitated. "I know where you can get something to eat and drink."

"But... "

"Do it," Pachand ordered. "I need to know you won't faint on me."

Anni drew herself up stiffly, but Ro could see the effort it cost her. Her vision misted with tears.

"Ondd protect," she hugged the Princess. "Pachand, bring her safely through this."

He nodded and she hurried out without daring to take another look. Anni's "Ondd protect" followed her. As she reached the stableyard, Torslin's rough voice made her start. She almost ducked for cover before she realised it was coming from a distance.

"I'll not sully my blade in single combat with a low impostor!"

He was answered by a rising swell of murmurs from outside the citadel walls. Ro heard cries of "Shame!". Jubb and the ostler emerged from the stables as Ro arrived. Jubb's face was pale.

"Channan's challenged Lord Torslin to single combat," he whispered. "He doesn't stand a chance, unless his horse has got more sense than he has and runs away."

"That's a true king. Always put the good of their people above their own safety," the ostler said. "I'm not the only one who'll know it either."

"Surely Torslin won't go." Ro strained to hear over the crowd. There was a sudden hush.

"Very well, boy!" Torslin shouted angrily. "The people of Najarind want your blood. Prepare to meet your end!"

"Come on, Jubb. They'll have to open the gates for him. Perhaps we can see how they work." She caught hold of Jubb's sleeve and began pulling him towards the walls.

Reaching the foot of the gate tower without attracting attention would have been easy enough, had the crowd that camouflaged them not also trapped them in the press to see Torslin depart. All they could do was watch as he and his second rode towards the citadel gates. Torslin's horse was as bulky as its rider in his armour, both as dull and stormy as if they were born of the threatening sky. Torslin nodded to the gatekeeper. The chimes sounded and the gates swung open.

"Never quite the same twice," Ro muttered. For all she could see of how they worked, they could have been magic.

"Perhaps we should have brought Edun." Jubb unconsciously tapped his tunic, reassured by the feel of his hidden Words of Power.

The riders passed sedately through the gates as if going for a stroll in a hay meadow. The chimes sounded even louder in the expectant silence as the gates closed behind them. The process was repeated as Torslin reached the outer gates. The chimes played a different tune, but one that also changed subtly with each repetition. Ro tried to hold the tunes in her head, but the sound of the formal challenges outside vied for her attention. The crowds began to drift towards better vantage points, leaving Ro and Jubb uncomfortably exposed to the gatekeepers.

"Smash it, I say!" Ersilla's voice screeched through the air from above. "Why must everyone argue?"

People began stepping back from the wall to get a better view of what was happening above. Jubb almost followed, his face a picture of curiosity, but Ro pulled him back. The keepers had left a gap between them and the gate tower entrance. They slipped behind them and a moment later were hidden in the shadows behind the door. Ro willed her pulse into a calmer rhythm. She had only set foot on the first stair, when the squeal of metal being torn from metal and a nerve-jangling rush of tumbling chimes stopped her.

"But, Highness," came a dismayed voice. "We won't be able to open them again."

"Would you rather I had a headache? If Fordel had got rid of that noise weeks ago as I asked... but no, I have to do everything myself."

"But, Highness. Lord Torslin won't be able to get back in."

"Let me explain." There was a sharp sound of flesh hitting flesh. "If he loses, he won't need to get back in, and if he wins there's no hurry. Is there?"

"No, Highness."

"No, Highness," she mimicked. "Now get out of my way so I can watch the fight."

"Yes, Highness."

Ro heard a scramble as of someone tangling with furniture in their hurry to be gone. She waited until all had been quiet for ten heartbeats. Using all her years' experience of trying to avoid discord in Iyessa, she started quietly up the stairs. The room at the top looked as if it was full of flotsam deposited by an angry tide. Ro put her hand to her lips. She felt sick.

"Whew!" Jubb came up behind her. Ro gestured for quiet and he looked sheepish. "Never mind," he whispered. "You're good at tidying up, you'll soon work out where everything goes."

She gazed hopelessly at the mess. Not all of the mechanism had submitted to Ersilla's fury. The framework was still standing, and although scattered, the chimes were unbroken. She mouthed to Jubb "Keep watch" and gestured for him to tiptoe. He crossed the small room to the open doorway. Ro would have to hope that his attention remained this side of the wall and he would not be distracted by the struggle going on outside. She ignored the sounds that gusted and faded on the wind, and pushed away the fear that brought a bitter taste to her mouth. All that mattered was the puzzle in front of her.

A few yards away, Ersilla had commanded a chair to be set and a table with sweetmeats. Ayif stood beside it handing her dishes. She nibbled at the delicacies as she watched the preparations for combat.

"Are the formalities going to go on all day? It'll be dark at this rate before they get started." She pouted.

"Everything has to be seen to be fair, Highness. Ondd has to be invoked... "

"I don't see why. Care to have a bet on the winner, Ayif?"

"If you wish, Highness."

She put down the sweet in her hand with a look of distaste. "There is such a thing as too much sugar, you know."

Ayif bowed and smiled his shark's grin.

"You'd do anything to be on the winning side, wouldn't you?"

"Highness."

"Don't deny it. I have a way that will ensure that whoever kills whom out there, we shall be the winners."

"Highness?"

"You like my little pets, don't you? If Torslin appears to be losing, you have my permission to set them free." She clapped her hands gleefully. "Isn't it delicious? I get rid of them all–Torslin, Channan–the whole army and no one will ever know it was me. Although, of course, once they've all gone it won't matter who knows, because I'll have all the power. Do you like my little scheme?" She turned suddenly on Ayif. The physician fell to his knees and kissed her hand. She wiped it on her gown.

"Highness, you are truly great."

"Mmm... Ah, look–they're starting."

"So you'd kill your old friend, would you?" Torslin and Channan faced each other at the centre of the marked ground.

"No friend of mine, no friend of Ortann."

"No, I'll not have that. I was always true to the empire. It was me who was the vigilant one, keeping watch for trouble on the borders, squashing trouble before it could get a hold. Your father went soft. We had plans, and he betrayed them. Ran home to his comfortable wife and a life of ease. I might have known he'd raise weaklings, afraid to take what they want, what Ortann wants. Only Ersilla ran true to the line."

"You disgust me. Keep your excuses for Ondd, I'm not going to listen to them."

"Not excuses, sense. It's still not too late for us to work together."

For answer Channan turned his horse and headed for the far end of the ground.

Watching from the still lines of Darian's men, the exiles saw the seconds dip their banners. The ground shuddered as the horses gathered momentum and passed with a crash of metal. Dovinna gripped Lar's hand tighter. The combatants turned for another run. There was another crash and the squeal of a horse in agony.

"Low! Not an honourable blow!" Uwert exclaimed.

Channan's horse slumped to its knees with Torslin's spear in its flank. A sigh went up from the watching Amrads as Channan scrambled clear.

"Honour!" Mirri peeped around Edun's shoulder to watch the proceedings. "Only men could think there's any honour in killing each other. It's certainly not the sort of thing a baby should be exposed to." She jogged Lalli for emphasis.

Raimi turned on her. "Put her to bed then."

"Hm!" The wet-nurse retreated in the direction of the wagons, but no one spared her a glance.

Torslin was battering at Channan with his sword from horseback. Channan caught the blows on his shield, but was sinking under their violence.

Dovinna let go of Lar's hand and covered her face. "He can't survive much more."

But Torslin had leaned too far. His horse lunged forward. As he struggled to regain his balance, Channan took the chance to grab his sword-arm and pull him from the horse. The Lord landed heavily and was slow rising. Channan struck him around the head with his shield while he tried to untangle his sword from its scabbard.

"That's more like it!" Uwert urged.

A gush of wind snapped the banners taut with a crack. Lar's head jerked up. Her eyes narrowed on the city.

"Do you feel that, Raimi?"

But Raimi was intent on the combat. Torslin had rolled away from Channan's sword, which struck harmlessly in the ground. It was enough to unbalance the weakened king. He grabbed at his ribs. Seeping around the edge of his armour, blood made the leather straps slick. Torslin saw it and struck at Channan again. The King used his shield to slide the sword away and the point of his own blade found a weak point in Torslin's armour, under the arm. Torslin hissed and drew back. He looked incredulously at the wound, while Channan struggled to breathe against the pain in his chest.

"Now, you die."

For a heavyset man, Torslin was still quick on his feet. Dovinna had to turn away.

Anni's hands trembled on the inventory lists. "It should be down here."

Pachand hefted down the crate Anni pointed out. "Yes, that's everything: black powder, gum paste and wax wire." He began moulding the ingredients into patties.

"Can I help?" Anni could not resist looking back at the door as he worked, despite the fact that Pachand had used his rank to dismiss the guards. She had sent Tillenne to persuade as many people as she could to leave that side of the palace. Thankfully, most were watching the combat outside.

"It'll be quicker if I do it, Highness," Pachand answered without looking up. "In fact, once they're ready, I want you to lock the door to the under-cellar behind me and find somewhere safe. No need for you to take more risk."

"No, Pachand. Two of us will have twice the chance of destroying the creatures. Besides, there is no safe place for me."

Pachand gathered up the quick-fire cakes. "All right, let's get on with it."

Anni led the way. She raised the trapdoor. If anything, the reek was worse than she remembered. Pachand started down the steps. Weakened by lack of food and the fumes from the fal-worms, Anni felt she was walking down a staircase in a nightmare. She tried to hold the lamp steady as Pachand set about putting the quick-fire cakes in place. The work required care. To be sure of doing the most damage they had to be attached to the cages, and although the fal-worms' bodies were unwieldy, their awful heads could dart and strike swiftly enough. Stinging saliva spattered the front of Pachand's uniform and face. He took a gasp of fresher air through the waste channel grille.

"Start trailing the wax wire back to the turn in the steps, if you will, Highness, while I finish this."

Anni nodded. Something about the scene niggled at her. She shook her head to clear it. No time now to worry over what might prove to be no more than imagination. She had reached the dogleg before she realised what bothered her. The grille was open. She turned. Sure enough, there was a gap wide enough to slide an arm through, as if someone had left in too great a hurry to close it properly—or had been caught entering.

"Pachand!"

He looked up as she started down the steps. Behind the end cage a shadow slipped away from the wall.

"There!" She pointed, but instead of attacking the soldier, who swung round at Anni's warning, there was a screech of metal against metal as the figure drew back a cage bolt.

"That's enough, Physician," Pachand mouthed the title like an insult. "Step away from the cages."

Ayif moved into the lamplight. His sweating skin was as yellow as his robes. He was still smiling although his eyes kept flicking to the side.

"It's the Queen's command. You wouldn't disobey your queen."

Pachand snarled and made a grab for the Gindullan. Anni expected him to dodge, but instead he stepped into Pachand's embrace. The Captain's grip slackened. As the physician stepped away, Anni saw a dark stain spreading across Pachand's tunic. She began running down the stairs, tripped and slid to the bottom. Clutching his chest, Pachand stepped menacingly towards Ayif. The smile of anticipatory pleasure on his face made the Princess step back.

"Light the wire, Princess."

"But... "

"Do it."

Anni retreated a few steps up the stairs. Ayif had succeeded in loosening the first bolt and was working on the second. As he dodged Pachand's hold, Anni heard the second bolt draw back. The fal-worm in the first cage, shifted its weight and the door opened a crack. Sensing freedom and the nearness of food it thrust its head out, seeming to sniff the air. Anni stumbled back up the steps. At the dogleg she turned. Pachand was behind Ayif with his arm around the physician's throat. Ayif threw his weight back, his bald head connecting with Pachand's jaw as the Captain was hurled against the wall. The physician lunged for the next cage before Pachand could shake his head clear, and another bolt slid back. By now, the first fal-worm was out of its cage and hissing malevolence at the fighting figures, which were beyond its clumsy reach behind the other cages. Its efforts to snatch at them rocked one of the smaller cages sending it crashing on its side. Only the bulk of the fal-worms in the confined space of the under-cellar had saved the men from their maws so far.

Anni began desperately clicking the igniter. Her hands trembled so violently that each flame was shaken out before it could catch on the wax wire. She closed her eyes an instant, trying to forget the chaos below and imagine she was lighting a lamp in her chamber. She tried again, passing the flame unhurriedly from the igniter to the wax wire. Instantly, it fizzed into life. She watched the fire wriggle down the steps towards the cages.

Ayif aimed a kick at Pachand. He drew his knife and sawed at the wax wire. Weakened now, the Captain struggled to stand. He fell against the physician, knocking him away from the cage. The knife was still in Ayif's hand. Pachand saw the slash at his face and caught Ayif's wrist. He allowed himself to drop heavily to his knees on the physician's chest and Anni heard a graunch of breaking bone. The physician cried out. Instantly, Pachand twisted the physician's wrist, and plunged the knife into his chest. Ayif seemed to sigh. His eyes fluttered upwards and his features slowly formed his shark's grin, the gleaming teeth now marred by bubbles of red. Anni followed his gaze: the fizzing flame had gone out. The struggle had taken the pair into the open space and the confused movements of the fal-worms now became focused by the smell of blood.

"The igniter," Pachand gasped.

Anni threw it to him. He reached for it, but his hand was raked by claws, pinning it to the ground. Anni screamed as the dripping mouth plunged towards Pachand's back.

"Save yourself, Princess!"

She wanted to cover her eyes and ears, wipe away the sight of the fal-worm's head rising with Pachand's flesh trailing from its mouth, blot out the shriek of agony as the beast struck and the bubbling moan that still escaped Pachand's lips. She picked up the lamp. Her aim had better be good. Some of the beasts lumbered towards the grille. Another raised its head scenting warm flesh and turned her way. Steady. She threw. There was a shower of sparks and the nearest beasts drew back. Anni waited long enough to be sure the fire had taken proper hold and ran; up the stairs, tearing her gown, skinning her knuckles on the trapdoor as she threw it shut behind her, across the under-cellar, through the door–slam it! Lock it! She ran from the beasts and the nightmare, from the death and the fire, from the scream that had risen from her stomach and now filled her head and would come out. The door shuddered behind her and she felt the roaring and tumbling of stone blown out of the space it had occupied for centuries. A crack ran up the wall opposite her and met the ceiling. For a moment she thought the floor would shake into crumbs and deposit her back into the waiting mouths of the monsters. They must be dead, crushed or blown to bits. They must be. She could do no more. Slowly, Anni slid to the floor.

The wet-nurse hurried away from the scene of combat with Lalli. Someone was going to die again, and it was probably the wrong one.

"Men, Lalli. Sometimes I think all they know how to do is kill each other."

The mess in Edun's wagon made her sigh. The onddikins were whistling and agitated, scattering bedding and food morsels from their cage.

"If I had my way, they'd go." She tried to settle Lalli on the bed, but the baby was fretful. "Be a good girl, now." Mirri jigged her on her knee, but the baby struggled to be out of her grasp, reaching for the onddikins.

"Oh, very well." Mirri set the baby on the floor next to their cage. Perhaps you'll quiet each other down."

She rested her head against the pillows. A boom that seemed to come from the core of the earth made her eyes fly open. A stunned listening silence was destroyed by a scream of triumph and pain.

"Great Ondd, what was that?" Mirri whispered.

From the battlefield, a moan arose that made the hairs rise on Mirri's arms, and the onddikins began to shriek. In the distance, the first scream was joined by another and another in a mindless chorus.

"Have mercy."

Mirri grabbed the pillow and scrambled under the bed. Lalli was oblivious to the noise, but she frowned at the onddikins' agitation. Her chubby fist reached for the cage. The onddikins huddled watching and crooning. A moment later the door swung open.

"Now, you die." Torslin feinted towards the King's right, skipped out of the way of Channan's sword thrust and aimed a heavy blow at the back of his head with his sword pommel as Channan's momentum carried him past. Channan recovered his balance and reversed his sword, dropping to one knee as he did so. The suddenness of the move made Torslin stumble backwards to keep from falling on the blade. A sound of thunder underground made the earth shudder beneath them. Torslin spat.

"So, your Iyessi hirelings have set the earth shaking while we fight. Where's your honour now? Single combat?" He spat again, and raised his sword. Before he could bring it down a scream that burned through the bones erupted from the direction of the city. He swung round in the direction of Channan's disbelieving gaze as a moan went up from the watching armies on both sides of the city walls.

Released from the constrictions of the under-cellar and waste channels, fal-worms burst onto the hillside. The last one was on fire and snarled and snapped at the flames spreading them further. Its companions rose on the gathering wind, screeching their triumph before plunging on the watching soldiers.

"Treason!" Torslin roared his fury. He yelled to his second, who cantered over with his horse.

"Yes, Torslin, yours." Channan struck one last blow at the Lord, before Torslin mounted and spurred the horse back towards the city gates.

They did not open. As Fordel raced to Channan's aid, he saw the traitor lord urging his horse towards the next entrance to the city. A fal-worm dropped out of the sky and swooped up again with his screaming second in its talons. Then he too was occupied in fending off the attentions of the fal-worms. The one that was in flames tried to struggle into the air, dripping fire onto those beneath. The stench of burning flesh and the beast's screams of fury and pain were too much for the horses. They reared and bolted scattering riders and trampling the unwary. Many of those who were thrown found themselves raked by the vicious talons of the fal-worms. The insatiable beasts trailed saliva, which burrowed through armour and burned into exposed flesh.

King Darian struggled forwards to Channan's position, his men forming a shell of shields above and around them, against the fal-worm attacks. His face was grim.

"This was an enemy we hadn't bargained for. No one can get close enough to harm them."

As they retreated, the voices of Lar and Raimi seemed to rise and greet them. Dovinna darted out to inspect Channan's wounds almost before he reached the dubious safety of the shield wall.

"Can Lar and Raimi stop them? Call the winds to crush them... something?"

Dovinna shook her head. "All they can try to do is dispel the fear," she whispered. "After the battle, the men believe in their powers."

"It's not enough," Channan groaned watching the havoc as the fal-worms swooped and screeched over them, tearing men and beasts at random. Anyone who broke the cover of the shield shell was instantly seized. Their screams did not last long.

Uwert hurried over with Edun at his elbow. "The magician has something that might help."

"This time I'll get thrown out of the secret order of magicians for sure," Edun added, but for once there was no mischief in his eyes. He held out his hand. It held several pellets about the size of onddikin droppings. "Flash pellets. They're what allow me to vanish in a cloud of smoke on stage. If we can make enough and mix them with something that'll stick... "

"... we can use slings to get them onto the fal-worms and when they go off–with Ondd's grace–they'll flash into bonfires," Uwert finished.

Darian nodded. "Do it."

Edun turned, then stopped and looked up at the sky. Quinik, Finik and Pirik streaked above him whistling a challenge to the fal-worms. Uwert followed his gaze.

"Oh, no."

Ro held her breath. Despite her care, she could not avoid the chimes giving off ghostly echoes as she reassembled them in what she hoped was the correct order. The mechanism was a huge instrument operated by air pressure provided by a bellows pumping air into a sac of cured skins. When the handle was turned, air was forced from the sac into the pipes, whose different pitches opened levers at corresponding points like keys turning in locks. She began pumping the bellows slowly. She hesitated at its first wheezy protests, but not even Jubb appeared to notice. When the sac was as full as she dared make it in its injured state, she stood and surveyed her handiwork. The tune the chimes played was never quite the same twice running. At first Ro had thought it was an arbitrary change, but now she realised that it must obey extremely precise rules, to coincide with the lock mechanism on the lower gates. She tried to blot out all external sounds and hear again in her head the last few renditions when the gates had closed. Her mind flew back to Lalli's naming day and the round song of the gathered women. Each one had added her own embellishments, often no more than a simple transposition of two notes. Her pulse quickened. She touched Jubb's arm, hoping he would not start and knock something over.

"Get ready," she whispered.

She set the stops to play the chosen tune and grasped the handle. The crack and roar of stone splitting shook the wall, making Ro fall against the sac. It expelled its air in a sad sigh and the chimes resonated, but nothing else happened. Before she had a chance to do more than throw a startled glance at Jubb, the screams began. Jubb clapped his hands over his ears and crumpled into a foetal ball on the floor. Ro knew immediately what he had seen. The fal-worms were free. Anni! The Princess's face had been pale but her jaw was stubbornly set when she and Ro had parted, clamped into a determined line. Something had gone wrong. So, only the fool and the freak were left. Ro set to work once more.

Shrill laughter broke into her thoughts. Ersilla clapped her hands and leaned over the battlements, pointing out the destruction to the nearest sentries. They gazed on the scene transfixed. Their fear made Ersilla laugh all the harder, so that she had to sit back in her chair. Jubb raised his eyes to Ro. Tears streaked his face, but for once he seemed to have control of his limbs. He resumed his post. Ro began to adjust the instrument. There was a split in the connection to the sac. She stripped off her gauzy scarf and bandaged the wound. With greater haste she pumped the bellows, relying on the horror outside to occupy the Princess and those with her. Wiping her hands on her costly skirts, Ro grasped the handle and turned it steadily. The chimes sang out, delicate and unreal against the screams and blasts outside.

"What's that? Guards! Quickly, someone's trying to open the gates!"

A glance told Ro she was unsuccessful and worse. Ersilla, white-lipped with fury, caught hold of the nearest sentry and pushed him towards the gate tower. He regained his balance and looked warily from her to his fellows.

"Do as I say, or I'll have you thrown to the beasts."

Ro itched to grab Jubb and run down the stairs.

"Try again," Jubb told her. "You've got to open the gates. I'll hold them off."

What with? Ro wanted to ask. Neither of them had thought to arm themselves. Why had the gates not opened? She tried to ignore Ersilla's hissed threats to the sentry and replayed the tune in her head. Perhaps the modification had been wrong.

"Here he comes," Jubb's voice distracted her.

The guard moved reluctantly towards the doorway. At the threshold he paused, and Jubb tensed to attack. The sentry darted inside, too quickly for Jubb, who closed his arms on empty air as he hurtled down the stairs. Ro released her breath. Suddenly she heard the tune as clearly as if she was sitting calmly by her pool in the forest back home.

"Come out, you cowards!" Ersilla's voice commanded.

Ro pumped the bellows desperately. "Just a few more seconds."

"Don't worry." Jubb grinned and slipped outside.

Ro cried out, but it was too late. Ersilla stood with her fists on her hips and a sneer on her face.

"And what exactly are you?"

"You can't stop us, Miss." He felt in his tunic for Edun's Words of Power.

"Oh no?"

"No. We're protected by Words of Power, you see. You can't harm us. Now, why don't you let us open the gates. I'm sure my master won't hurt you, poor mad thing."

Ersilla's face twisted into an expression that was barely human. Ro felt for the handle and turned. The instrument wheezed and began the first notes. She spun back in time to see Ersilla snatch Jubb's Words of Power from his hand. She quickly scanned the contents.

"Fool!" She laughed unpleasantly holding up the paper and shredding it in front of his eyes. "Words of Power? Hah!"

The chimes continued playing, valves clicked and whirred. The tune was playing in reverse, forming a counterpoint to the drawn out ring of Ersilla taking the sword from the remaining sentry's scabbard. As she raised it above her head, she seemed caught for a moment by the beauty of the sinking sunlight glancing off the blade. Then she was engulfed in shadow. The draft of wings almost knocked Jubb over as a fal-worm plunged its talons into Ersilla, landing heavily on her. It screeched is pleasure as it tore at her flesh. Ro pulled Jubb back into the gate tower.

"She didn't even have time to scream," he said.

"More than she deserved." Ro saw again the face of Anni. Who knew how many more of those she cared for would be dead before the sun finally sank beneath the horizon?

A ragged cheer brought her back to herself. Soldiers were streaming out of the gates to join the Amrads fighting off the beasts.

"What now?" Jubb asked her.

She listened to the sickening sounds from outside. The other sentry had taken his chance to run while the fal-worm gorged itself on his erstwhile mistress. It would not be long before it was ready to hunt a second course.

"Get out of here while we can."

They hurried down the steps. As they emerged at the bottom, the fal-worm launched itself into the air once more and people scattered in all directions. The way back to the gate tower was blocked by panicking Najarindians seeking a hiding place. Expecting to feel the sharp agony of claws in her back at any moment, Ro looked up. The fal-worm was circling higher, snapping and hissing at three tiny creatures which dived and circled about it. Ro caught her bottom lip in her teeth, certain that the snapping jaws would fasten on one of them at any moment. But the fal-worm had a full belly and the pickings were easier elsewhere. The onddikins fluted their triumph as the fal-worm allowed the strengthening wind to speed it from the city. Suddenly she found herself sitting in the courtyard crying. When there were no more tears left, still she sat there unable to summon the will to move.

# Chapter Twenty-four

Ro was sitting there with her hands over her face when she became aware of something cold and wet pressed against her hand. She parted her fingers slightly and received a warm lick across her face. Only a faint trace of light was left in the sky, but there was no mistaking the enthusiastic greeting.

"Chickens!"

The mongrel let out a joyous series of barks.

"Here she is!" It was Jubb.

A moment later she found herself hauled to her feet by the fool and Edun.

"You've singed your eyebrows again," she said.

He grinned. "We thought we'd lost you. I sent Pirik, Quinik and Finik to find you, but they're exhausted and flying in the dark's dangerous."

"The onddikins–they saved us." She closed her eyes caught between giggling and sobbing. "I'm glad they're alive."

Jubb took her hand. "I didn't mean to leave you, Ro. I got caught in the people pushing to get out."

She smiled at him. "No need to apologise–you're a hero."

Jubb blushed with pleasure.

"Did he tell you he rushed out to meet Ersilla with nothing to protect himself?"

"I had the Words of Power," he corrected.

Ro and Edun exchanged a look.

"Ersilla mocked them and she... she... " he broke off.

"Well," Edun looked uncomfortable. "I'll give you some new Words of Power–tomorrow." He yawned.

"Where are the others?"

"Darian and Uwert are putting the camp in order and setting watch for any monsters that survived, should they choose to return. Darian won't enter the city before Channan's back on his throne and invites him," Edun said.

"Mirri's still in Edun's wagon," Jubb interrupted.

"Mm... I'm surprised she let you out of her sight," Ro teased the magician.

"She's trying to keep out of Raimi's way."

"Oh?"

Edun became serious. "When Raimi returned to the wagon she was hiding under the bed and Lalli was in the onddikins' cage."

They looked at each other for a moment, then Ro burst out laughing. Soon all three were helpless with mirth, provoking head-shaking and sympathetic murmurs from others nearby. Chickens bounded around them barking.

"Come on, we told Lar and Raimi we'd meet them in Channan's rooms. Princess Anni's having supper prepared for us there."

"Anni?" Ro felt her knees give.

"Whoa there!" Edun put his arm under hers to steady her.

"I thought... "

"She's knocked about by the blast, but Fordel says she never could stand a mess. While there's clearing up to do she'll be all right."

It hardly seemed possible. She looked up at the bulk of the palace ahead. Lights flared from the windows as if the occupants were expecting guests to a party. One wing seemed to sag like an old door and exhaled wisps of smoke, reflecting the gold of the torches. In the corridor leading to the royal apartments they were greeted by Tillenne.

"Mistress Hexem's going to go wild at all this extra washing, and they emptied all the tubs to stop the fire spreading."

"Poor Tillenne. You won't get a moment's rest," Ro sympathised.

"Not me. Princess Anni's asked me to help her organise things. Says another cool head's always needed." The girl grinned. "And the first thing she asked me to organise is this." She threw open a door. "Your apartments. There's freshly drawn hot water for a bath, clean sheets, new clothes. When supper's ready I'm to come and fetch you."

Ro was speechless. She put her arms around the maid and hugged her. Jubb and Chickens would have followed her into the room, but Tillenne shooed them out.

"Plenty of time for news later."

When she tapped at Ro's door again, the Iyessi girl was ready. The bath was enough to ease her physical tiredness, but the horrors of the day would not release her. She longed to be with the others. There was an expectant air about the place. Instead of leading Ro to Channan's chambers, Tillenne took her to the steps at the main entrance. The road ahead was lined with flaring torches and row upon row of silent people. There at the top of the steps were those she held most dear: Lar and Raimi with Lalli, Edun and Jubb and Anni. Ro made her a formal salute, but Anni hugged her.

"For a while I thought... " the Princess began.

"Me too," Ro confessed.

Then they fell silent as a great cheer began from the outer gate of the city. It travelled closer and closer, until Ro felt it swell in her own lungs, as the solitary mounted figure of King Channan rode into view. She heard Anni's breath catch and saw tears well in her eyes.

"Doesn't he look grand? A great king down to the last hair on his head."

At a short distance there followed Lord Fordel with Dovinna riding beside him. Her face was so pale it was almost translucent, as if she had come from another world, but it was full of love and pride. Behind them came the Najarindian soldiers. They flowed up to the base of the steps as Channan dismounted. Anni met him halfway. As she turned, the change in her expression made Ro's smile falter. Channan held himself upright, but his knuckles grasping Anni's hand were white. The walk up the steps was not without cost. At the top he kissed Anni's cheek and turned to face his people, retaining her hand all the while.

"People of Najarind–Ortanians, we have been betrayed and suffered greatly. Much blame for this is to be laid at my feet. But I promise you this: henceforward I will be your king in deed as well as name. I shall strive with you to put right the wrongs inflicted on you and bring peace to the land. Tomorrow, we shall begin to build Najarind anew, but tonight you must know: King Berinn was slain by followers of Torslin and my poor mad sister, Ersilla. They have paid for their evil. If it was not for our Iyessi friends, the wisdom and honour of King Darian of Amradoc and most of all, the unfailing love of Mistress Dovinna, our land would still be under their hold. All honour to them!"

Fordel led the cheers that made Lar wince.

"Now, friends, go to your homes. Tomorrow we have work to do."

The people began to disperse, and the welcoming party followed Channan into the palace. As soon as they reached his private chambers, Channan slumped. Dovinna and Fordel rushed forward.

"You must let me tend your wounds. You must rest," Dovinna scolded.

He allowed himself to be virtually carried through to his bedchamber. Anni followed to tend him, leaving the others to look at a feast none now felt like eating.

Over the next few days things settled into a routine. Channan was still weak and continued to provoke worried looks between Anni, Dovinna and Fordel, but slowly he improved.

"You do too much. Those wounds won't heal if you never sit still for more than a minute," Dovinna chided once again as he prepared to inspect the repairs to the city.

"There's too much to do, love. None of us can rest until we can be sure Torslin and those creatures of Lethir are destroyed. The city needs repairs at least and the people outside are behind sowing their crops. There are traitors to seek out–oh, and there's a wedding to arrange."

"A wedding?" Dovinna asked.

"Yes, dear. Ours." He mounted his horse, leaving her open-mouthed, and knowing grins on the faces of the others.

Despite the search there was no sign of Torslin, nor of the fal-worms which had escaped. Each time riders approached the city, Ro expected they would bring news of a fresh attack. Watching at the gates one morning, she feared the worst as a lone rider slumped on a sorry-looking mule ambled up to the city. She hurried to get a closer look. Nearer to, the mule appeared bad-tempered rather than exhausted. The rider was swathed in a nut-brown cloak. It suddenly straightened on a snorted intake of breath.

"Varda!" Ro exclaimed.

"So? I fell asleep, what of it? It's a long ride from Kabonn."

"But what're you doing here?"

"A fine welcome, Miss Dragon-waker. I might ask the same thing of you. Why aren't you about your business?"

Before Ro had time to frame an answer the old healer continued. "If you must know, I'm here because I took it into my head that some of you might have need of me. I suppose Dovinna's at the palace."

Ro nodded and led the way. Dovinna all but fell into her teacher's arms.

"Now, now, I'm pleased to see you too." The wrinkled face creased into a broad grin. "Let's take a look at the patient then."

"He's out surveying damage to the walls."

"He, girl?"

"Yes, Channan. You have come to help him?"

Varda's face grew serious. "I came to attend to this." She patted Dovinna's stomach, making her blush. "I see there's more work for me here than I thought."

The pair withdrew, leaving Ro stammering half-formed questions. When Channan returned he was immediately hustled into his chamber to submit to Varda's ministrations.

"But... " he protested. "Explain, Dovi."

Since the catastrophic departure of Torslin, Amrads and Ortanians had freely mixed, working together to restore the city, and with it the harmony between their two people, but King Darian had yet to be officially welcomed into Najarind. Today was the day, and all was bustle.

Varda would not be put off. All three emerged from his chambers paler, although in Channan's case his ears were pink too. As they waited at the head of the palace steps for King Darian's entry with his closest advisers, Fordel looked amused.

"It seems our king has had a good telling off."

Ro agreed. "I know what that feels like."

They watched as Darian and his entourage were greeted with all the pageantry Najarind could muster. Channan winced as he and Darian embraced as brothers.

"Everything will be all right now, won't it?" Ro asked the Lord.

"I don't see why not."

"Ondd's still asleep."

"But the evil's gone."

"Gone, not defeated."

Later that evening when the celebratory feast was being digested in contented stomachs, Channan and Dovinna approached

Ro where she sat with Lar and Raimi, rocking Lalli in time with the baby's soft breathing.

"We wanted to ask. What do you intend doing now?" Channan said. His face was flushed.

Lar looked at Ro.

"He means we'd like you to stay here. You never did get a proper chance to look for a cure," Dovinna interrupted.

Uwert sauntered up. "Would the Iyessi let you return now?"

It was Ro's turn to look at Lar. The Earth-hearer shook her head. "Now, less than ever, and I don't think we should try. Who knows what danger we might bring down on them?"

Ro's heart sank. "I think we should go, at least I should."

"Where?" Edun had overheard the conversation.

"I don't know, but somewhere."

"That's settled then," Jubb joined in. "You'll be going somewhere, but not until after the wedding. Darian says I'm to have a new suit and you can sing something special." He looked hopefully at Lar and Raimi.

Ro laughed. "All right, not until after the wedding.

The sunshine was brilliant. It made the golden dome of Ondd's temple burn like a lesser star, and glanced off the mosaics of coloured glass inside it as if the sky was strewn with jewels. The ceremony had taken longer to plan than Channan had hoped due to the disappearance of the Patriarch with much of the temple's treasure. The late spring sunshine made up for its loss.

"What a day for a wedding!" Mirri was seated next to one of Darian's army cooks on the bench behind the one Ro shared with the others. She had recovered from her shame on the day of the combat, but had moved her belongings to her new beau's wagon.

"I hope it's a good omen," she said.

Ro found herself fervently praying to Ondd that it was too. She looked at the others. They seemed to have no more on their minds than the day's celebrations, but worn cheeks and thin hands testified to the trials they had endured. Only Lalli appeared unscathed. She looked about her gurgling with delight and trying to grab the colours in her pudgy fist. Yes, it was a great day. A day for joy and celebration. A cheer went up outside, announcing the arrival of King Channan and his bride. As they set foot in the temple the mechanical dragon fluttered down from its eyrie high in the dome and greeted them with its strange mischievous song.

# The End

# ABOUT THE AUTHOR

K. S. Dearsley began writing stories and plays as a child (often inspired by Dr Who), and has been writing ever since. She is now a prizewinning playwright, poet and author of short stories and flash fiction with work appearing in numerous publications on both sides of the Atlantic. Discover more about the author and where her work can be read at http://www.ksdearsley.com.

# Connect with K. S. Dearsley

I hope you enjoyed reading Discord's Child. You can stay in touch with me and my work at the following coordinates:

Follow me on Twitter: http://twitter.com/ksdearsley
Favourite my Smashwords author page:
https://www.smashwords.com/profile/view/ksdearsley
Become a fan on Goodreads:
http://www.goodreads.com/author/show/6576334.K_S_Dear
sley
Visit my website: http://www.ksdearsley.com

K. S. Dearsley

# BY THE SAME AUTHOR

## Discord's Apprentice: The Exiles of Ondd Book Two

The followers of Lethir have been defeated and King Channan controls Najarind once more. Ro thinks that she and her fellow exiles can rest, but as guests from all over the empire gather to celebrate the naming of the heir, she makes a disturbing discovery. The forces that would plunge the world into chaos are regrouping, and a storm is gathering about her. The only way she can keep those she loves safe is to find the Dragon and wake it.

## Discord's Shadow: The Exiles of Ondd Book Three

To wake the Dragon, first Ro has to find it.

So far, her travels have taken her exiled family into danger, but no closer to the answers she needs. Now, in Najarind people are falling into unending sleep. With danger behind them and unknown perils waiting ahead, the exiles are forced to set out again. The one thing Ro knows for sure is–time is running out.

## Artists & Liars

Clumsy cleaners, bashful models, self-centred divas, disciples and devotees–the short stories, flash fiction and poetry in Artists & Liars look at the art world from every angle.

As Pablo Picasso said: "Art is a lie that reveals the truth."

Art and artists show us who we are and what the world could be. Whether you love visiting galleries or think conceptual art is something to do with birth control–whether you are conscious of it or not, art influences all our lives. Artists, models, dealers, collectors, voyeurs, where would be without them?

Printed in Great Britain
by Amazon

41967890R00185